MMORPG

How a computer game becomes deadly serious...

Emile van Veen

This is a work of fiction. All characters and events in this book are fictitious and any resemblance to real persons, living or dead, flesh and blood or digital, is purely coincidental.

World of Warcraft and Blizzard Entertainment® are registered trademarks of Blizzard Entertainment, Inc. World of Warcraft, the world of Azeroth, all its permanent inhabitants and the lore on which the game is based are the sole property of Blizzard Entertainment®.

In no way did the author of MMORPG expand on any property of Blizzard Entertainment®. This story is not about World of Warcraft, but about how terrorists could potentially make use of an online platform like the one created by Blizzard Entertainment®.

All information in this book pertaining to World of Warcraft or other MMORPGs is also available in the public domain through open sources like Internet, YouTube, or other media like newspapers and magazines. This includes the occasional mention of locations, NPC's, mobs and game mechanics. The author adhered to the "fair use policy". The interaction of this book's main characters with the game in the broadest sense are based on the author's interpretation or simply sprang from the author's fantasy. Any opinions or observations by the author are his alone, and do not necessarily reflect the opinions of Blizzard Entertainment, Inc.

Any mistakes or inaccuracies are the author's and must be subscribed to the fact that the author used only his own fantasy in creating this book.

Visit the author's website on www.emilevanveen.com

ISBN-10: 145631808X
ISBN-13: 9781456318086

Cover concept and design by Alwine van Winsen, www.vrij-werk.nl

My name is printed on the cover of this book, identifying me as the author. In truth, MMORPG is as much a creation of Adrienne, my beloved wife. Adrienne worked with me every step of the way. It was truly a joint effort. Especially in the final process, wrestling with the comments of Michael Garrett the editor (not the bat handler), she made the difference. At some point I couldn't even distinguish the passages that were written by her from my own text anymore. Her patience and perseverance made the difference in the end. I am eternally grateful to her for her support and for being the best mother imaginable to Nikki and Annaïs.

Other people deserve recognition as well. First of all, Paul and "Riet", the parents of Adrienne. If not for them, MMORPG would never have been completed, not to mention a lot of other things. They're our fiercest supporters and set the standard for the kind of parent I aspire to be to my own kids one day. Maarten van Luyn, not only for introducing me to online gaming in the first place; Maarten and Rachelle came to our aid when we really needed it, and proved by doing so how rare true friendship is. Also Robert-Jan van Aken and Janice Lachman for enduring our late night sessions about MMORPG. Katja Meertens warned us of the final pitfalls and forced us to go over the manuscript one more time. The book is better because of her insightful comments.

On February 15, 2008, the office of the Director of National Intelligence provided Congress with the *Data Mining Report*. In this report the existence of the so-called Reynard Project was disclosed. The aim of the Reynard Project is described as follows:

> *Reynard is a seedling effort to study the emerging phenomenon of social (particular terrorist) dynamics in virtual worlds and large-scale online games and their implications for the Intelligence Community.*
>
> *The cultural and behavioral norms of virtual worlds and gaming are generally unstudied. Therefore, Reynard will seek to identify the emerging social, behavioral and cultural norms in virtual worlds and gaming environments. The project would then apply the lessons learned to determine the feasibility of automatically detecting suspicious behavior and actions in the virtual World. If it shows early promise, this small seedling effort may increase its scope to a full project.*

Several months later Dwight Toavs, a senior CIA analyst and a Professor at the National Defense University, spoke on the Director of Intelligence's *Open Source Conference*, which was held in the Ronald Reagan Building on September 11-12, 2008.

In his presentation he showed the audience an imaginary cyber-conversation which supposedly took place inside the virtual world of World of Warcraft. He demonstrated convincingly how easy it would be for terrorists to communicate the details of a nuclear attack on the White House through an online game.

AUTHOR'S NOTE

Those of you, dear readers, who play the Massively Multiplayer Online Role Playing Game (MMORPG) called World of Warcraft will notice flaws in my descriptions of that game. I ask you to realize that I never meant to recreate Azeroth, but merely used the general mechanics of that marvellous virtual world as part of the setting of my book.

At many times I used shortcuts or simplified often complex issues. At other times I deliberately left things out, like most of the massive changes that were introduced in anticipation of Cataclysm. It was never my intention to give a minute and detailed representation of the game.

I did try to convey the general working and the look and feel of a game like this. Many people never played a MMORPG in their lives. This book reaches out to them as well. Robert Barnes, one of my main characters, is a complete novice to gaming and his introduction to the virtual world serves to gently guide non-gamers into the virtual realm.

I sincerely hope you'll enjoy the story, gamers and non-gamers alike.

It's a chilling thought that evil lurks in the virtual world as well.

PROLOGUE

Dusk was slowly turning into evening, making the heavy grey clouds stand out more prominently against a background of changing colors. With the fading daylight the land changed as well. By day, the relentless sun beat down on never-ending stretches of yellowish prairie. Just enough grass managed to cling desperately to some kind of shrivelled life, to prevent this place from being called a desert. At many places, though, the soil was nothing more than hard rock and caked sand. Now, in the twilight, the sparse grass had taken on an improbable, but magnificent hue of green, softening the harsh colors of the day.

The road ran from east to west through this vast land. It was paved with rocks from the nearby mountains, though at places the persistent vegetation threatened to overrun the pavement. Travellers were warned not to stray too far from the road. Many predators had found a way to survive here.

Only one rider was travelling the road. When he reached the point where it veered slightly northward, he held in for a moment. A huge lion had wandered close to the road, and he eyed it warily. Even though he judged he was out of the range that would make the animal attack him, he nudged his horse just off the other side of the pavement. Giving the lion a wide berth, he continued his journey.

Eventually he approached the mountains that had been looming on the horizon for quite some time. The mountain range ran along the entire coastline, from the north, where a great river spilled into the ocean, to the far south, where the marshes began. The road ran through the only pass in the mountains.

The man followed the road downward into the ravine. It was like a wide gully that cut all the way through the mountains, steeply descending to sea level on the other side. It wasn't long before he encountered signs of habitation. The first thing he spotted were fences, belonging to the farms just outside the little town that was his destination. Soon after, he passed the communal graveyard. The road made a sharp turn to the left, followed by another turn to the right, then he finally saw the roofs of the town below him. In the far distance he could see the surface of the ocean glimmering in the light of the moon.

The road led into the centre of the town and ended at the large pier of the harbour. This modest settlement was one of the major ports of the continent, handling a fair amount of the traffic to and from the continent on the other side of the ocean.

Instead of following the road all the way downtown, the traveller turned right and entered a street that was actually a ledge on the mountainside. Some houses were built on the right side of the street. On the left side, a sturdy wooden fence protected the reckless from a fall onto the roofs of the buildings below. This was no superfluous precaution. At the end of the street, just past the general goods store, a tavern was to be found.

This was where the traveller was headed. He dismounted in front of the inn and ducked inside. Many places like this were gloomy and depressing, but this particular tavern was airy and open. The taproom was empty save the innkeeper and one customer.

The customer was sitting at a table in the left corner. When their eyes met, the man winked. The traveller walked up to him and sat with his back to the room.

"You're late," the man said.

The traveller nodded. "It took longer to get here than I thought. I'm sorry."

It remained silent for nearly a full minute. Finally, the man reached into his bag and traded a document to the other.

"These are your new personal orders. Read them carefully. Memorize them."

The traveller didn't read the document immediately, but stored it away for later. He stood, as did the man he'd come to meet.

"Yes, sir."

The man nodded. "Good. I expect you to."

With these words, he turned and walked out of the tavern into the night. The traveller watched how he mounted his horse and rode down the ledge to the main road. For a moment he disappeared behind a building, then he saw him again, descending to the docks. His eyes followed him all the way along the pier, where he boarded a large ship anchored there. A few moments later, the ship slowly started to move. It turned sharply and sailed out of the bay.

Only then did the traveller open the document he just received and start to read.

In hotel rooms some three thousand miles apart, two men disconnected their laptop computers. Both had paid for the use of the hotel network in cash at the reception. One of them started to pack. It didn't take long, as he always travelled light. Fifteen minutes after the rendez-vous he was in a taxi on his way to the nearest train station.

CHAPTER I

It was only much later that he was able to look back on that crucial moment and admit that chance really had nothing to do with it. True, they arrived at the house on the same day, Khalid only minutes before him. And yes, their rooms were directly opposite each other, with only a narrow corridor separating them. That could be put down to chance, coincidence, or fate, or whatever one wished to call it. From there on, it was Robert himself who was partial to the events to follow.

He had been kept waiting in the main hall for about ten minutes while the building attendant took Khalid through the registration process and issued him a key. When it was Robert's turn and they passed each other in the doorway, they'd exchanged a glance and a cordial nod. One freshly arrived resident to another.

Of course, he didn't *need* to make the effort to introduce himself to his next door neighbour, did he? Especially not at that specific moment, right after he had unpacked. In fact, wasn't it a little rude of him to force himself upon someone who so obviously didn't relish his company?

And certainly nobody *told* him to nearly strain his neck, so he could read those fateful messages on that computer screen. At that moment of course, those meant nothing to him. That came only later, when the great Robert Barnes, foreign exchange student from England freshly arrived in the Netherlands, decided to stick his nose in places where it didn't belong.

After his first knock had gone unanswered, Robert had been about to turn away, should have turned away. But his overzealous ears had detected a faint noise from inside. So he stooped, pressing his ear against the wood of the door. Now he heard it again, clearer this time: the sound of keyboard strokes. So the young man he saw earlier that day was in. Maybe he just hadn't heard him knocking?

To make sure, he knocked again, really hard now. This time he was rewarded by some undistinguishable noise from inside, definitely a reaction to his knocking. Robert decided to turn the knob and open the door.

His step positioned him directly in the middle of the room. It was identical to his own room, though set up in mirror image.

He guessed this place must have a view of the picturesque square around the medieval church. They were on the third floor, and his own small window looked out on a dreary blistering concrete wall that had probably been white once. Or gray. Or yellow. There was no telling. It belonged to the adjacent building that obviously didn't share the same long history. The rooms were small, maybe ten by fifteen feet, but offered everything a student needed. A bed, a small couch, and two sturdy chairs at a narrow table bolted to the wall. And, of course, a comfortable desk for studying.

The big difference with his own place was that the curtains were drawn, shutting out most of the daylight. The only illumination came from the screen of a laptop computer on the desk. The young man was sitting behind the computer. He was half turned toward him, his attention divided between his screen and Robert. He looked annoyed at being disturbed.

"Hello, I'm Robert Barnes," Robert began, realizing he wasn't exactly welcome. "I live in the room across from yours. Arrived just today, same as you, I believe?"

"Excuse me?" his neighbour answered, clearly not understanding what he was saying. It was only now that Robert noticed that he was wearing earphones.

He raised his voice. "Sorry to disturb you. I arrived today. I thought I should say hello. I live in the room directly opposite yours."

Clearly torn between his computer and basic civility, the young Arab-looking man cast a glance at his computer screen, then at his visitor. After a few seconds, he came to a decision and grudgingly pulled off his earphones.

"Hello, my name is Khalid."

Robert extended his hand, which was taken after half a second of consideration.

"My name is Robert. I arrived today. I believe you're new as well?"

"Yes."

Robert suddenly was at a loss about how to continue this conversation. He considered asking where Khalid came from, but decided to go for what obviously occupied the other so much. Judging by the computer screen, he guessed the man called Khalid had been playing some computer game. At the centre of the screen he saw some weird character floating over a mysterious landscape of snow-capped mountains, perched on a flying dragon or something like that. The dragon was patiently flapping its wings while it hovered stationary. In a box to the lower left of the screen text was scrolling by in a blue color.

Robert took a step closer to examine the screen better. For a split second he thought that Khalid was going to stop him, but that would be ridiculous, wouldn't it? It was just a computer game!

"What are you playing? It looks awesome!" Robert tried to make conversation.

For a few seconds it remained silent. "World of Warcraft," Khalid answered shortly.

Robert had never heard of it. "Really?" He smiled at Khalid. "What's that?"

Khalid turned to the screen and Robert saw him cast a quick glance at the text box. "It's a multi-player game. Millions of people play it at the same time. You can play it alone, but also team up with others. Like I do at the moment," he hinted not so subtly, without looking up at Robert.

"That's impressive! What do you have to do?"

This question was answered by a half shrug of Khalid's shoulders. "Nothing, really. You can do whatever you want."

Even though Robert clearly felt that the man wanted him out of his room, he didn't want to give up yet. He was here now, and he wanted to achieve at least some connection with his new neighbour. He was about to ask another question, when he noticed that he'd lost Khalid's attention. He was looking intently at the text box. Robert stooped to see what had drawn his attention.

In the box with the blue text, the same message was repeated four times, on four different lines:

[Party] [Pharad]: drimm, are you there?

Khalid stole a glance at Robert, seemed about to say something, but didn't. Instead, he quickly hit the Enter key. Immediately, an extra text box appeared on the underside of the screen. He hunched over his keyboard and quickly typed a few words. Robert saw them appear on the screen:

[Party] [Drimm]: yes was afk for a few sec.

Khalid turned back to Robert, rolling his chair a bit to the left as if to block Robert's view of the computer screen. He wasn't successful, because Robert could still see and read everything. He gave something that even approached a smile.

"I apologize, but I'm playing with some people. Would you mind coming back another time?"

"No, of course not!" Robert replied. "Sorry to disturb you. I just wanted to say hello."

At that moment a new message appeared in the box. Khalid didn't see it, as he had his back to his computer. But Robert did. It was in capitals, so he could read it easily:

[Party] [Pharad]: WE MEET AGAIN IN TEN DAYS AND THEN WE STRIKE! THE WORLD WILL TREMBLE FOR THE HAMMER OF RIGHTEOUS JUSTICE!

Robert read the message twice and decided that this was a strange game indeed. He focussed on Khalid again.

"You know, I live right across from your room. Drop by whenever you want. How about that?"

Khalid nodded. "Yes, we'll see each other again. Now I have to go back to my game. See you later!"

CHAPTER II

The bomb at The Hague Station Hollands Spoor went off exactly at the moment that the doors of the Intercity to Amsterdam hissed closed. The people who had just disembarked were hurrying down escalators and stairs to the tunnels below the tracks, eager to be home after a long day at work.

There was no immediate fire, or smoke. People later said that it was just a loud noise like heavy thunder. What people did feel, was a sudden wall of hot air, that came rushing out of nowhere and that threw hordes of unsuspecting people around in the traversing tunnel under the train station. The blast was followed by a thick cloak of grey smoke trying to find its way up to the tracks above.

In the first moments after the explosion, maybe even minutes, everybody was in blind panic. People were frantically trying to get out of the tunnel, out of the station, away from the source of the destruction. Even though the tunnels and exits were quite wide they quickly became jammed.

Now a different kind of fright settled over the writhing mass of people. Having survived the explosion, it seemed as if the most basic survival instincts took over. People started clawing at each other, fighting, tearing and pushing to get outside. Some inevitably fell and were in danger of being trampled to death.

Suddenly the resistance gave. Like a cork plopping out of a bottle, people poured out of the station. The people who had fallen down clambered to their feet and followed. Some were injured and had to drag themselves outside.

It was only after the initial shock was over that people started to notice the dead in the middle of the tunnel, between the stairs that led up to tracks five and six. There were twelve of them lying haphazardly on the ground, all in a heap against the base of the same wall. Later, the official investigation would reveal that they didn't die from the bomb blast itself, but from the force with which they were slammed against the concrete wall. They died from head injuries and massive internal bleedings, even though the official report also stated that most victims suffered extreme suffocation as well. The blast had sucked away nearly all oxygen from the tunnel.

Within ten minutes of the blast, five ambulances were at the scene. Another five minutes later that number had grown to fifteen. Teams of medical personnel were attending to the wounded, taking them gently away to a secluded emergency pavilion that had been erected.

The first police officers on the scene were the two pairs who had been patrolling the train station. They had been relatively far away from the explosion. The first patrol was down in the main hall, talking to a backpacking tourist from Australia who had just been relieved of his wallet by a pickpocket. The second team was on the ramp of track three when it happened. They saw the smoke billowing out of the stairway right after the explosion and radioed for assistance only twenty seconds after the blast.

It was a credit to the police of The Hague that they had so many police officers on the scene so quickly. Only fifteen minutes after the disaster happened, they had cordoned off the area and had cleared a corridor for the ambulances and the fire brigade. Hastily erected fences forced the crowd of sensation-seeking onlookers back from the scene. Every twenty feet a police officer stood guard in front of the fence to make sure that nobody tried to climb over.

Suddenly, a young man at the front of the crowd noticed a large oblong parcel leaning against a traffic sign. It was wrapped in dark gray plastic, resembling a garbage bag. Frightened, he alerted a nearby police officer. Maybe it was another explosive? It looked suspicious.

The authorities weren't taking any risks. They immediately cleared the area around the parcel. Most spectators hastily left the scene, not wanting to witness another explosion. After that, a bomb squad moved in.

When two men wearing protective suits finally opened the parcel, after what seemed to have taken hours, they didn't find a bomb, but a painting fixed to an easel. It depicted the magnificent historic train station from exactly the point of view where the painting was found. It was as if an artist had been standing there to paint the station and had forgotten to take his painting home. The only difference was that the artist had painted the station engulfed in flames. They were leaping out of the huge glass domes that shrouded the tracks. Thick smoke was rolling out of the entrance.

At the bottom of the painting was a signature. In neat calligraphed letters it said: *The world will tremble for the Hammer of Righteous Justice.*

CHAPTER III

Robert drew a thick line under the last scribbling in his note-book. He stood and made ready to leave the class room.

"Are you coming for a drink with us?"

He turned around and saw Andy, one of the first students he'd made contact with. Andy was twenty-one and Dutch, although he usually looked like a Hawaiian surf boy. His full name was Andries van Eck van den Berghe. Such a distinguished name didn't fit his image at all. Today he was dressed in a flowery shirt of an incredibly bright hue of orange.

Robert had liked him from the moment Andy had come up to him on his first day at the university. Andy had seated himself next to Robert in class, and they had fallen into easy conversation. After hearing that Robert was English and a fresh arrival, Andy had made it a point to introduce him to some of the people around, which was a great help in getting established. Andy seemed to know everybody, and even more people seemed to know him.

"Sure. No, great! Where are we going?"

Andy shrugged, as if to apologize. "They want to go to Barrera."

Of course, Robert had never even heard of the place. But he was simply glad to be invited. "Fine with me. Who's coming?"

"Just some friends. They study law, so they probably need a few drinks to flush away the boredom of today."

Talking, they exited the building and started to walk down a narrow street toward the canal. Suddenly Robert realized that he did know where Barrera was. It was close to his house, actually right around the corner of the Rapenburg.

For a history student like Robert, Leiden was a marvellous city to stay. If it weren't for the cars parked nearly everywhere, large parts of the inner city were almost completely unchanged from the Golden Age. The Rapenburg, running through the city centre, was still the same majestic *gracht* as hundreds of years ago, with stately and costly houses of successful merchants dating from the sixteenth and seventeenth century lining the canal. Today, many of the priceless antique buildings were converted to expensive offices or were, curiously enough, inhabited by penniless students.

"Damn, we have to sit inside," said Andy as they approached the bridge near the café. He pointed at the small sunny terrace completely packed with people. Some people were standing, making the terrace overflow onto the narrow street. There was absolutely no chance of them getting seats outside.

As they came near, someone called out to Andy and engaged him in conversation. They were talking in Dutch, so Robert took a moment to look around. It was a fantastic day for late September, and most people were walking around in short sleeves. Several boats were floating idly on the canal, most filled with students drinking beer and shouting at each other. There was a bright and careless atmosphere in the air. He inhaled deeply and leaned against the railing of the bridge. Closing his eyes for a moment, he simply savoured the moment.

He felt a tug at his elbow. It was Andy. "Are you coming?"

They entered the café and walked up to the bar.

"Mag ik twee bier?" Andy asked of one of the girls behind the counter.

She drew the beers and handed them over. "Five Euros please," she answered in English.

Robert looked up. "Hey, where are you from?"

She looked at him and smiled. "From Scotland, Englishman."

Robert grinned back. "I hope that doesn't offend you too much. Are you studying here?"

She threw the towel she had been using to clean the bar over her shoulder and leaned against the woodwork. "I was. I finished last semester, but I could stay on working here during the summer. I have to go back now and finish my thesis, so in ten days it's over. I booked my ticket today, so this is a sad day indeed!"

Smiling, he raised his glass to her. "I just got here two weeks ago. Maybe you can tell me some of the things I need to know to survive in Holland as a foreigner?"

She was about to respond when a small group of people came running inside shouting and yelling in Dutch. There was some heated discussion with a man whom Robert perceived to be the owner of the café, then the large TV screen in the corner was switched on. More and more people ran in to watch, talking agitatedly. Many were using their phones to access Internet at the same time. Robert noted a lot of upset expressions.

"My God, there's been a terrorist attack in The Hague!", Andy shouted. He turned around and pushed his way through the growing crowd toward the screen, on which Robert could now see a scene with a lot of police cars and ambulances.

"Go!" the girl said. "We'll see each other again. I work here, remember?"

"Right, I will remember!" said Robert.

He joined Andy at the agitated crowd around the television at the moment that the law students they were to meet arrived. Andy made short introductions, briefing the others at the same time about what was happening on the television.

Soon, Robert found himself standing alone at the back of the crowd. People were watching and listening intently, discussing with each other in Dutch. He didn't understand a word of what was being said. Judging from what he could see on the screen, there had been a serious terrorist attack. There were images of a historic train station with a lot of smoke, a lot of people and a lot of police. Some anchorwoman was on the scene, talking all the time.

He felt a vibration in his pocket and checked his phone; his parents' number. He answered, walking outside to escape the loud noise. It was his mother.

"Robert, you should turn on the telly. There's been a terrorist attack in Holland!"

"Yes, mum, I just heard. The thing is, I don't understand a word of what everyone is saying."

Robert smiled, as his anxious mother started to tell him exactly what he expected her to say. "Will you be careful? You never know what can happen. Why don't you come back home? I don't like it a bit that you're there when bombs are going off. Will you stay out of buses and trains?"

Assuring her that he would do all of those things, he started to walk home. She was still giving him advice when he opened the front door and stepped into the shady hall.

"Mum, I'm home now, and I'm going to watch the tube. I'll call you back tomorrow. Will that be fine?"

Trying to end the conversation, he started to walk upstairs. Just as he reached his door, his mother finally hung up. He heard a noise behind him and turned around. It was Khalid. He hadn't seen him for a few days, not that they talked regularly. When they met, their conversation was limited to the exchange of greetings.

"Hi. Have you heard about the bombs?"

Khalid made an undistinguishable sound and started to put his key in the lock. He was wearing a large backpack, so Robert had to step aside to avoid being squashed against the wall.

"Well, see you later!" Robert said to the backpack, as Khalid disappeared into his room.

"Yes, see you later," came the answer, and the door was shut. Robert heard the key turn. All efforts on this man were wasted.

Once inside, he turned on the small television and switched to BBC World. Some expert was talking about the likelihood of the Netherlands as the target of a terrorist attack, assuming that it was done by Muslim extremists. He was expanding broadly on the Dutch support for the US invasion of Iraq, and their troops in Afghanistan.

He continued to watch for a while until he got bored. Leaving the television on with the sound muted, he moved to his computer and started to work on his notes of the day.

Twenty minutes later, he was totally engrossed in his work.

He was interrupted by a knock on his door. He shook his head to clear the cobwebs away.

"Come in!" he yelled.

The door opened and admitted Andy carrying a bottle of red wine.

"I've heard enough depressing news for one day. Are you ready for another drink?"

Robert smiled and pushed his work aside. In answer, he swivelled his desk chair around and wheeled it to the tiny cupboard that held 'two of everything'. He took out two wine glasses and rummaged for the corkscrew. Finding it, he tossed it to Andy.

"I already had enough of it over an hour ago. Any interesting development I missed?"

Andy grunted while he wrestled with the cork. With a loud plop it finally came free. Robert held out the glasses, and Andy filled them to the brim.

"Not really, just confirmation of what everybody already thought. It was the work of some Muslim group."

"Really?" Robert sniffed the wine, which made Andy laugh. It wasn't good, but it would certainly do.

"And mister connoisseur, where do you think this fine wine comes from?"

Robert started to laugh too as he realised how snobbish his sniffing probably looked. "Chateau soix-cente neuf du Pape," he replied smiling. More seriously he continued: "And how do they know the attack was the work of a Muslim group?"

"Because the bastards left a fucking painting on the scene, with the burning station on it. Proof enough for me that they did it!"

"Okay, but how do they know that they're Muslim fanatics?"

"I don't know. The breaking news right before I left was that they found a painting, which showed the station in flames. Somehow that told them it was some Muslim group."

Robert glanced at the silent television screen. It showed three people talking, but judging by the images, they were discussing the abysmal prospects of the American car industry. He took another slug of the cheap red wine and held out his glass. Bad wine tended to improve with the amount you drank of it, so he'd better get on with it.

They sat chatting for a while, each asking questions of the other. After an hour Robert opened one of his own bottles of wine. At his home in England, the art of drinking wine was taken seriously. His father was the general manager of one of the better restaurants in Leeds and a professional connoisseur. On the spare nights he was home for dinner, the food was chosen to suit the wine, instead of the other way around. Endless knowledge and trivia about grapes, suitable soils, and humidity in ageing cellars had been absorbed by Robert and his younger brother while they grew up.

One of the first things Robert had done upon arriving in Leiden was to search out a good wine shop. He'd bought a selection of promising bottles, always on the lookout for bargains of less known Chateaux that should offer quality above price.

Even though Andy obviously didn't share this finer passion for wines, Robert was pleased to see that the Dutchman did take notice of the improved quality of the drink in his glass. They toasted again and resumed their conversation. When Andy finally stood to leave and they shook hands, Robert had the pleasant feeling that he was making a real friend. He liked Andy a lot. He was unpretending and uncomplicated, but also intelligent with a sense of humour as sharp as a Swiss kitchen knife.

Alone again, Robert fruitlessly tried to finish his notes. He simply wasn't up to it after drinking so much wine. His watch told him it was almost nine o'clock. He decided to go out for something to eat.

Close to his house was a huge self-service restaurant for students called the Mensa that offered fast, edible food for ridiculously low prices.

He arrived at a closed door. He looked at the week menu stuck to the window to discover that the restaurant closed at seven o'clock. No haddock or vegetarian cheeseburger with carrots for him tonight.

Walking back, he passed Barrera. Through the window he saw the nice Scottish girl in the black polo shirt behind the bar. The place that had been so busy in the afternoon was nearly empty now. On an impulse, he went inside.

He walked up to the bar and sat on one of the high stools. The girl smiled, recognizing him.

"Hi. I walked by and decided to come in for a drink."

"Good idea, because I'm being bored to death by polishing these glasses." She held a wine glass up to the light, inspecting it. Satisfied, she put it away in the rack over her head. "What kind of drink did you have in mind?"

"Do you have any decent red wine?"

She walked over to the other side of the bar and returned with a bottle. It was half full. She handed it over to him for inspection. He studied the label for a few seconds and smiled.

"This is better than some of the wine I had earlier today."

With a rueful smile, she retrieved the glass she'd just cleaned from the rack and filled it. It gave Robert a chance to study her for a few seconds. She wasn't so much beautiful, as attractive in a spontaneous way, he decided. She had long jet black hair that hung down on both sides of her face in careless curls. This wasn't the kind of girl who spent half an hour in front of the mirror each morning. She wasn't even wearing any make-up.

He saluted her with his glass of wine. "I'm Robert," he introduced himself.

"Hello, Robert from England. I'm Rebecca."

He searched for something to say and came up with the obvious. "That was quite something, don't you think, terrorist attack?"

Rebecca finished another glass, stretching to put it away overhead. "Yes, reminds me of my time in London. These poor Dutchies are totally unprepared for this kind of thing. I mean, did you know that they actually have a minister in the government who goes to

15

work each day on his bicycle? And do you believe that I saw one of the princes walking all by himself in a busy street last week? I could have shot him on the spot, if I wanted to!"

"You must be kidding!"

"No, really, one of the sons of the Queen, no less. Just by himself. I didn't even see a guard or anything."

Robert was about to remark that this could actually mean that the prince's security was so good that it was virtually invisible, but decided to drop the subject. "Well, let's hope that these Al Qaida types don't get the same idea."

She sighed. "I don't understand why people have to kill each other over their stupid religion. It wasn't Al Qaida, by the way. It was some other group. A new group. Hammer of Righteous Justice or something. It was on the news just now."

Robert furrowed his eyebrows. "That's not a new group, is it? I've heard that name before."

She made a dismissive gesture. "No, they said on television that this was a first appearance. They also said that it looked like the work of a professional organization, so who knows. I mean, you don't get experienced and professional in anything without practice, do you?"

Robert handed his empty glass over. "Still, I have the feeling that I heard that name before. Maybe it'll come to me if you give me some more wine."

She took the glass, refilled it, and handed it back. "So, which need-to-knows do you want me to share with you before I vanish in ten days?"

Taking an appreciative sip of the wine, Robert smiled. "Anything you can tell me. I've been here for nearly two weeks now, and I still have the feeling that everything is new and foreign to me."

"Isn't that exactly why you decided to live in a foreign country? Living here is easy. Nearly all Dutchies speak English. As well as German and French, by the way. They all like to show off their skills in foreign languages, so you'll never be short of people to talk to. The second thing you need to know is that drugs are legal here, so you can blow your mind as often as you like."

"Sorry but I'm too dull to use drugs. I try to make up for it by drinking too much."

Rebecca laughed. "Good for you. I only smoke a joint now and then when I'm doing long and hard raids on WoW." Seeing his uncomprehending look, she exclaimed, "That you don't use drugs is one thing, but how can you fail to know what WoW is! I mean, which planet have you been living on?"

Apologetic, Robert raised his hands. "I'm really sorry. Clearly not in your Milky Way. Now tell me what I've been missing."

She took a quick look around to check for other customers. They were alone, save for two elderly women at a table in the corner. They were progressing so slowly through their drinks that it was going to take at least another fifteen minutes before they hit the bottom of their glasses. Satisfied, she sat on her side of the bar, making herself comfortable. "WoW stands for World of Warcraft. It's a **MMORPG**, which means Massively Multiplayer Online Role Playing Game. World of Warcraft is not just a game; it's the mother of all online games that ever were, or ever will be. It's played by more than twelve million people around the world, and that number is growing each day. For many people, this is not a game; it's their life. No, not just their life; it's their life and their religion in one!"

Robert was a little taken aback by this fierce speech. "Okay, maybe I'm not so stupid. Actually, I heard about it a few days ago. I even saw something of it. One of the people at my house was playing it."

She gave him a triumphant smile. "You see, everybody knows about it. Even you!" Then, seeing his pensive expression, she asked, "What's the matter? You seem a light year away suddenly."

Looking back up at her, he shook his head. For a second he was unsure whether he should share his thought or not.

"I suddenly remember where I heard that name of the Hammer of Righteous Justice before. I saw it on your World of Warcraft."

"What do you mean?"

"Okay, listen. The day I arrived, I went into the room of someone who lives at my house. He's in the room right across from mine. I wanted to introduce myself. This guy was sitting behind his computer with headphones on. Saying that he wasn't happy to be disturbed is putting it mildly. Still, he had the decency to tell me that he was playing World of Warcraft and that I should come back another time.

We talked for maybe a minute and I could read some messages in a text box. First, it seemed as if someone was calling him, sending messages. He didn't see them, because he was talking to me. Suddenly he noticed, and he quickly typed something. I don't remember what. Some abbreviation. Right after that, a text in capitals appeared and I'm absolutely sure that it read THE WORLD WILL TREMBLE FOR THE HAMMER OF RIGHTEOUS JUSTICE."

Rebecca stared at him for a few seconds. "That doesn't mean anything. I mean, it doesn't *have* to mean anything."

"I know. I don't know. I mean, I'm thinking. There was more; it's just that I can't remember what exactly. You see, we were talking, and he seemed to try to block the screen from me. The text was scrolling in a box in the bottom left corner."

"What was the color of the text?"

He thought for a second. "Blue."

"Blue means Party Chat."

He nodded. "Yes, because it also said 'Party' at the beginning of each line. What does that mean?"

"It means that they were having a private conversation. When several players join together, that's called a Party. Those players can communicate in a Party channel, which is private and invisible to all the other players."

"So if you're not in a Party, everybody can hear what you're saying? That must be confusing."

With a theatrical sigh she shook her head. "Of course not. That would mean chaos. You have to know the game to understand. The basics are the same as in real life. If you say something in WoW, only the people who are close to you will hear you. If you yell, a little more people will hear it. And there are certain channels where a lot of people will hear you. But that's what those channels are for."

"So, is what I saw suspicious or not?"

Rebecca made a dismissive gesture. "No, not at all. Most people are in private channels. Parties, guilds, raids; there are several kinds. Even if it had been an open conversation, nobody would have given it a second thought." She brushed a hand through her hair, pushing some curls behind her ear. "I mean, in WoW people are constantly talking about killing and attacking things. A lot of people use bombs to do that, by the way. If you were looking for people who say suspicious or even violent things, you could arrest nearly everyone."

Robert thought for a second. "You're right. For a while I used to play Hitman on the X-Box with a friend. If people overheard us talking about it, killing people with all kinds of weapons and such, they'd have called the police and we would've been arrested on the spot."

"That's what I mean. Now, would you like another glass of wine?"

Robert smiled. "Yes, I would." He shrugged the conversation about Khalid and World of Warcraft off. He wasn't living next to a terrorist, was he? Of course he wasn't. He would do better to get some useful information about life in Holland out of this girl; this nice and attractive girl.

"So, what have you been studying here?" he asked.

CHAPTER IV

R obert woke up with a sharp headache that wouldn't go away. He stayed in bed for nearly an hour, but that didn't improve things. In the end, he dragged himself to the small bathroom at the end of the corridor to take a shower. Even that didn't help.

Cursing himself for drinking so much wine, especially mediocre wine, he went downstairs in search for food.

The student house had a large communal room on the ground floor furnished with large sofas that looked as if they were the cast offs of a shelter for the homeless. Apart from the stains, they were actually quite comfortable. There also was a large dinner table surrounded by battered but sturdy wooden chairs. At the far end of the room was a door that gave access to the kitchen. On it was a large paper that held the rotation roster for the cleaning duties. Robert knew he was due in two days.

Michael, an American of about his own age, was sprawled on one of the sofas. He was assigned to this house during his sojourn at Webster University, an international business school. Although Michael was only in his second year, he'd adopted the role of 'nestor'. This exalted status granted all kinds of privileges, one of which was exemption from the duty roster.

He was reading a newspaper and greeted him with a wave and a grunt. "If you pass the coffee machine, could you get some for me?"

"Sure. I need some myself."

The kitchen was dominated by three enormous American refrigerators. One was completely dedicated to Heineken beer. Next to it was a whiteboard with the names of all residents on it. When taking a beer, all you had to do was to put a scratch behind your name. At the end of the week, it was pay-time for personal consumption. Judging from the list, there were some heavy drinkers around. Michael was one of them.

The other two refrigerators were filled with everyone's food. The rules were simple: everything with your name on it was yours. If it didn't have a name on it, it was free booty.

Robert retrieved his milk and, leaning against the sink, he finished the entire pack. Finally, he began to feel a little better. He turned to the coffee machine and poured two coffees. Also taking his bread, butter, and *hagelslag*, some delicious kind of tiny crisp chocolate crumbs the Dutch put on their bread, he returned to the living room.

"Here you are," he said, handing a cup to Michael. He noticed the American was reading the *Herald Tribune*. "Could I have a piece of your paper?"

"Sure. Take the front section, I just finished it. It's about yesterday's bombing."

Robert spread the paper on the table and started to scan the front page while he prepared a sandwich. Finished, he turned to the full article on the bombing, eating at the same time.

Halfway through, he suddenly froze. His brain came to a full stop for a second, then started to run on full speed. He almost felt a physical click when several things came together in his mind. Not bothering to clean up, he moved to the door.

"Hey, where the hell are you going?" Michael had half risen from the couch and was staring at him curiously. "Are you all right?"

Robert gave him a wave to indicate that he was fine and ran upstairs, taking two steps at a time. At the top floor he nearly collided with Khalid, who was about to go downstairs. Robert stared at him. For a moment he hesitated, inclined to say something about what was bothering him. Instead, he simply said "Hi!" and moved on.

In his room, he grabbed his mobile phone. Last night, Rebecca had given him her cell phone number. Before calling her, he opened the diary function and looked up some dates. Satisfied, he called her number. She answered on the first ring.

"Rebecca, it's Robert. I need to talk to you. Now. Where can we meet?"

She came to his place wearing jeans and her black Barrera polo shirt, since she had to be at work an hour later anyway. When she arrived, Robert waved her to one of the tiny chairs. He'd searched his memory several times and put his findings to paper.

"I'm so glad you could come, I must talk to someone about this. It may mean nothing, but there are too many coincidences. I need your opinion."

She looked around and folded herself carefully on the indicated seat. A smile was on her lips, but she also looked serious. Robert was glad she seemed to take his sudden summoning so well.

"Is this about what you told me yesterday? About that guy and World of Warcraft?"

He nodded, holding a finger in the air. "Yes, but yesterday I didn't remember everything. And I hadn't read today's paper."

She held his gaze. "So what did you remember exactly? And what's in the paper?"

"Yesterday, you told me that the bombing was supposedly done by some terrorist group that called itself the Hammer of Righteous Justice, right? And that they had written their name on a painting?"

"Yes. At least, that's what I heard on the news."

"Okay, but that's not all!" He held up the front page of the *Herald Tribune*. "An hour ago, I was reading this newspaper. And in this paper is one thing that wasn't on the news, at least you didn't hear it. Or maybe it wasn't released yesterday. Listen to what the paper says, I'll only read the important part:

> *The attack is claimed by an unknown organization called The Hammer of Righteous Justice. The official spokeswoman of the Department of Justice confirmed that they are certain that the painting was meant to claim responsibility for the attack. She also confirmed*

that it was signed with the text 'The world will tremble for the Hammer of Righteous Justice'.

Rebecca shook her head. "I'm sorry, but I still don't see what you're getting at."

"That's because I haven't told you the rest yet." Robert started to pace the room, not saying anything for a few seconds. Rebecca started to open her mouth, but he motioned her to silence. "I'm just trying to explain this to you in the clearest way possible. Look, I told you that I saw the name Hammer of Righteous Justice on the computer screen of Khalid, who lives right across from my room, by the way. What I didn't remember until I read the paper this morning, is that there was more. I don't know why it took me so long to remember, because it was all in capitals! Now listen to me, I wrote it down."

He stopped his pacing and turned to face her. Standing right in the middle of the room, he read directly from his notebook:

We meet again in ten days and then we strike! The world will tremble for the Hammer of Righteous Justice!

She stared at him. "So what you're saying is-"

"Exactly!" he interrupted. "It's not just the name; it's the entire sentence. The world will tremble for the Hammer of Righteous Justice. Exactly the same words as in the terrorist painting. Coincidence? Who knows. But that's not all. Listen again:

We meet together in ten days and then we strike!"

"When was this? When did you see this?"

"Aha!" He looked at her in triumph. "Today." He held up the paper as proof, pointing at the date. "Is September twenty-one. So yesterday, the day of the attack, it was the twentieth. The day I first met Khalid, and saw what I saw, was on my first day here. And I arrived on Friday September ten. In other words, exactly ten days before the attack took place."

Rebecca was listening intently, doing the math in her head. Now she also stood and walked to the tiny window. She answered with her back to him. "You read the text 'We meet again in ten days and then we strike! The world will tremble for the Hammer of Righteous Justice!' ten days before a terrorist attack occurs which is claimed by a painting on the scene that bears exactly the same message."

She shivered. "This is serious. I mean, we don't know anything for sure, but it's strange. At least it's a lot of coincidence. What do you think we should do? Should we go to the police?"

"I don't know. I was thinking the same thing. But is it proof? And are they going to arrest the guy who lives next to me?"

"Maybe we should confront him with it."

Robert laughed. "I ran into him earlier today. For a second I wanted to do that, but I chickened out."

Suddenly, Rebecca leaned forward, an intent look in her eyes. "Can you tell me what you saw? On the screen, in World of Warcraft? All of it. Try to remember and tell me."

"All right." He sat on his desk, closing his eyes. "I saw a man in weird clothing. He was flying. Not by himself; he was sitting on the back of some flying animal that looked like some kind of dragon. They weren't moving. They were just stationary in the air. The dragon was flapping its wings to keep aloft."

"Good," she said encouragingly. "What else can you remember?"

"Well, they were floating over something that looked like a mountain ridge. Really high. And there were all kinds of buttons to the side of the screen."

"Okay. Now we go back to the flying animal. What color was it? And would you describe it as a huge bird or as a flying dragon? A lion with wings perhaps?"

He flicked his fingers. "It was brownish. And I'd say it wasn't a bird, but a dragon. It might have been a lion with wings, but not a bird. Why is that important?"

"Never mind. I'll tell you later. Now, what exactly can you remember of the text you saw? Were there any names?"

Robert concentrated hard, going back in his mind to that afternoon. After a few seconds it came to him. "I think someone was calling him, waiting for a response. Repeating his name, several times. It was Drimm, or Grimm, or something similar."

"You mean 'Grimm' like the author of the fairy tales?"

"Yes, exactly. It was with a double m at the end, I'm sure about that. And I think it was Drimm, not Grimm."

"That gives us something to work with. Do you have a computer with Internet here?"

"Of course!" He jumped off the desk and turned around to open his laptop. It was on standby, so it quickly whirred to life. He logged on and pushed it over to her. She seated herself in his desk chair and opened the Internet browser.

"We're going to see if we can find him." She typed in a web address and whistled as a website came up immediately. "This is impressive. You have a fast Internet connection. At my place, the Armory is always slow."

Robert was studying the page. It was rather dark, with a World of Warcraft logo on top. "What is this?" he asked curiously.

"This is the European section of The Armory. It's an online database with all the characters that exist in WoW. If you reckon that over twelve million people play the game, this is a gigantic database. Most people have several characters, so it probably contains over fifty million profiles. Look, I'll show you."

She typed in 'Drimm' and hit enter. After a second, a list about thirty long came up. Robert surmised that these were all the characters with the name Drimm.

"It looks like this is a fairly common name in WoW. Myself, I've never heard of it. Now let's have a look at what we've got."

She studied the list for a few seconds and smiled. "This is easy," she said.

Robert didn't understand a thing of what she was looking for. "Could you please explain what you're doing? What does it mean?"

"Right, I'll try to explain it. First of all, you told me the character you saw was flying. That means that it has to be at least level sixty."

"Why?"

Because only at level sixty can a character obtain the flying skill. You said that the character you saw was riding a dragon. Well, those can only be acquired by characters who are at the maximum level of eighty. Ergo: the Drimm we're looking for is level eighty."

This was easy. Robert nodded his understanding. She continued, as if she was educating him. "Now, you can see that only four characters on the list are level eighty, so our target is one of them. Two are Alliance and two are Horde."

Seeing his incomprehension, she explained, "Every character in WoW is a member of either one of two different factions. They're called the Alliance and the Horde. They're opposed to each other.

She suddenly pointed at the screen. "We don't need to guess anymore. The giveaway is in the guild name. Look at that!"

Robert bent over to see what she was pointing at. "The Hammer of Grimstone," he read aloud. "That's different!"

"Sure, but it's a hammer. Don't forget, out of a possible fifty million characters, we've pinpointed it to only four remaining possibilities. I put my money on the one with the hammer in the guild name."

"You may be right. Besides, I know nothing about this game!"

Absentmindedly, she patted his hand. "No worries, I know enough. Now let's see if we can find out a bit more."

She typed a new web address and another website came up. "This is Wowhead," she explained. "It's one of the few Internet sites that contains all the information on WoW you might ever need. It's my personal favorite, I use it all the time. You can look up anything you can think of."

"And what are we looking for?"

"We're checking the significance of the word Grimstone," she answered, typing the word in a box at the same time and hitting Enter. After a few seconds, a new page came up in response to her query. There was only one result. Robert sucked in his breath when he read it.

"My God," he stammered, "No more coincidence!"

Rebecca clicked on the search result and a new window sprang open. "High Justice Grimstone," she read out loud.

"What does it mean? What is it?"

"High Justice Grimstone is a NPC. In other words: a Non Playing Character. That means that it's one of the computer controlled characters in the world. I think it's Grimstone's title that's the issue here."

"The Hammer of Grimstone, The Hammer of High Justice," Robert said aloud.

"Right. I think we've just found the character of your neighbour. With that guild name, there can be no doubt about it."

He was getting so much information that he suddenly felt overloaded. "What's a guild name? I mean, I'm a history student, and I certainly know what a guild is, but what is it in WoW?"

"A guild is like a club of people. You have to be invited to become a member of one. Every guild has a leader and there are different ranks. From officers down to initiates. The purpose of a guild is to create a kind of family within the virtual world. The world is big, and you need a lot of help to be successful. Or even to survive. You need advice, all kinds of stuff, and often also simply some strong friends to defeat your enemies. That's where your guild kicks in. Guild members are supposed to help each other."

"And what do we know about this guild?"

She gave him a broad smile. "That's what we're going to find out now!" She hit the Back button twice, and they were back at the page with all the Drimms. She clicked on their target, and the screen was filled with a colorful diagram. There were several bars and a lot of boxes. Rebecca studied some additional information. Robert deduced it was about the gear that Drimm was wearing.

"This is impressive," Rebecca said. "We have ourselves a serious player here. This is not your average recreational player."

"How do you know?"

"Because he's wearing high end stuff that you only get by raiding the most difficult instances in the game."

She accessed another tab and browsed something called Achievements. She whistled. "Yes, it's as I thought. Your Khalid spends a lot of time behind his computer. I expect that he's also good at it."

She hit another tab and started studying the results, scrolling down slowly. Robert saw it was called Reputation.

"He's a real WoW veteran. I suspect he's been playing the game for at least five years, even before the first expansion came out." She pointed at the screen. "While playing and exploring the world, a player encounters all kinds of different peoples and tribes. Most are hostile, some are not. Some of those even allow you to raise your reputation with them by performing tasks or simply by killing huge numbers of their enemies for them. Gaining the highest reputation level with a certain group takes many weeks of hard and dull work. Now, our friend here has achieved exalted reputation with all the ancient factions in the game."

Robert tried to digest this information. "Why does that mean he's a veteran player?"

With a half smile that expressed her effort to simplify a complex matter, she explained, "Because nobody bothers with those antique factions anymore. For new players there's absolutely no point in wasting countless days to gain exalted reputation with them. The rewards that were once fantastic and sought after are totally worthless and meaningless today. It would be like working your ass off washing dishes in some restaurant for months, then use the money to buy a fifteen year old desktop computer, while you could have had the newest and fastest laptop available for the same money."

"So this means that he did all that while it still meant something?

Rebecca nodded. "Before 2007 I would say." She hit another tab, and now a list of the members of the guild called The Hammer of Grimstone appeared. There were ten different characters. Rebecca opened a few of them, quickly scanning the results.

"He's not the only one. They're all more or less the same. Top notch players. This is a guild that can take on nearly anything by itself."

She pushed herself away from the desk and looked at her watch. "I have to hurry. What are you going to do with this?"

He thought for a moment and shook his head. "I have no idea. Maybe we should think about it until tomorrow. Maybe you're the one who should think really hard. After all, I know absolutely nothing about this game."

She nodded. "I will."

"Can you come back tomorrow morning? Then we can decide what to do. I have no classes until three o'clock."

He walked her downstairs and let her out of the door. When she was gone, he slowly went back to his room, deep in thought. He was not only thinking about bombs, about Khalid and about World of Warcraft, but also about the pleasing prospect of seeing Rebecca again the next day.

CHAPTER V

" I've not only been thinking, but I've been doing some research as well," Rebecca announced when she entered, wearing her black Barerra shirt again. With some disappointment Robert noticed she would have to go to work again.

"Could you get me a cup of tea?"

Robert closed the door behind her. "Sure. What have you been thinking? And doing?"

She grinned at him. "Patience, patience. I need some tea first!"

While Robert boiled water in the electrical heater, she toured his tiny room. She examined the photo of his parents on his desk and flipped through some of his books. When the tea was finished, Robert handed her his favorite mug. Sitting, he looked expectantly at her.

"Last night, after work, I searched the Internet. And I found some interesting things." She opened the bag at her feet and retrieved a sheaf of paper. "I even printed some of it."

Robert held out his hand, but she didn't hand it over. Instead, she browsed the prints and pulled several out, scanning them.

"Right, let's start here. On February fifteen of 2008, the CIA published a report about the dangers of MMORPG's as a hideout for terrorists. I have it right here. I actually found the original report on the web and downloaded it."

She held up a stack of paper. *UNCLASSIFIED, Office of the Director of National Intelligence, Data Mining Report,* the title page read. She handed it over, and Robert quickly flipped through it.

He smiled broadly. "So I'm not stupid after all!" Checking the last page, he saw that the report was fifteen pages long. "Do I have to read this first?"

"No, you can do that later. Most of it is terribly boring anyway."

She swirled the tea in her cup before continuing. "The report caught the attention of the press, and within a few days there were reactions and discussions on numerous websites and forums. Look, I'll show you some."

She gave Robert a printout of a website. The header read *U.S. Spies Want to Find Terrorists in World of Warcraft*. He started to read out loud:

> *"Be careful who you frag. Having eliminated all terrorism in the real world, the U.S. intelligence community is working to develop software that will detect violent extremists infiltrating World of Warcraft and other massive multiplayer games, according to a data-mining report from the Director of National Intelligence. The Reynard project will begin by profiling online gaming behavior, then potentially move on to its ultimate goal of 'automatically detecting suspicious behavior and actions in the virtual world."*

"So we really may be onto something," he said. "Even the CIA is taking it seriously.'

She shrugged. "How seriously it's being taken remains to be seen. Now please finish the article."

"Yes, boss!" he said, before continuing.

> *"The cultural and behavioral norms of virtual worlds and gaming are generally unstudied. Therefore, Reynard will seek to identify the emerging social, behavioral and cultural norms in virtual worlds and gaming environments. The project would then apply the lessons learned to determine the feasibility of automatically detecting suspicious behavior and actions in the virtual World. If it shows early promise, this small seedling effort may increase its scope to a full project."*

"Reynard will conduct unclassified research in a public virtual World environment. The research will use publicly available data and will begin with observational studies to establish baseline normative behaviors."

He was silent for a moment, digesting the information. "From what I read, it's still going to take some time before something is really happening," he finally said.

"Yes, that's what I thought too," she answered. "According to the gamers, there's nothing to worry about. Thousands of people have commented on various forums and ninety-nine percent thinks it's plain stupidity. A lot of flack about the waste of taxpayers' money and how the virtual world has nothing to do with the real world. The same goes for the 'official' comments on gaming sites. They all say that it's an unnecessary nuisance."

She half raised from her chair to reach for the tea pot.

"And what do you think?" Robert asked.

"I think it's really stupid to ignore the possibilities. Have you ever read an article or something about the surveillance that the intelligence community is supposed to impose on us?"

He nodded. "Yes, I have. Only last week, it was a big deal. It said that nearly all telephone calls in the world are automatically screened and that if you say something suspicious like 'nuclear bomb' on the phone, the call is recorded and checked by a human operator later on. The same goes for email. Specialized search engines scan all email, looking for suspicious word combinations. The newspaper was rather worried about privacy issues."

"Big brother is watching you. He's eavesdropping as well."

He smiled at that. "So if a game like World of Warcraft isn't under surveillance, it would be the perfect medium to exchange information. The perfect hideout."

Enthusiastically, she sat forward, eyes glittering. "Exactly. That's what I told myself last night. Regardless of whether it's true or not, nearly everyone has been scared into believing that telephone and email are not secure. So what better way to communicate safely than through WoW?"

"But how easy is it to communicate in WoW? You both have to be online, haven't you?"

"No, not at all!" She shook her head vigorously. "That's the beauty of it. World of Warcraft has every communication facility you could possibly desire. For instance, you can send in-game emails that will wait in a mailbox for thirty days to be picked up. You can even send notes that you can store for later reference. Of course, when you're both online, you can chat in secure channels, but you can also actually talk to each other. There are several options like Teamspeak that allow you to have a VOIP conversation much like a conference call."

"So why are the reactions so negative on the Internet, do you think? Why do the gamers think it's nonsense?"

"That's exactly what surprised me so much. If you're into this game, you simply *must* recognize the potential opportunities it offers for clandestine communication. It's perfect. The accounts are anonymous. You can access it from any place on earth, it's completely secure, and it's untraceable on top of all that. What more could a criminal wish for?"

"So do you think that we should go to the police?"

She shrugged. "I don't know."

Robert came to a decision. "After all we've been discussing, do you actually think we can stop here? No, I think it's our duty to report what we've found. Even if it all means nothing, I think I'll feel better for having reported it."

***

"I still feel a bit uncomfortable about this," Andy said as they approached the police station. "There's an Arab looking guy living opposite your room who's playing an online computer game. People spam all kinds of idiocy in computer games. That doesn't make them terrorists, you know!"

Last night, Robert had told his friend at length about what was bothering him. He had taken him step by step through everything he had seen and learned. Andy had been hesitant about believing that a terrorist might live right under his friend's nose. He also admitted there were a lot of coincidences and, above all, that the decision wasn't theirs to make, so he volunteered to go to the police with Robert.

This morning, he had made an appointment by telephone. He had explained shortly that they possibly had some information about the recent terrorist attack. At that, he was asked to come to the station in an hour. Even though they were right on time, they were told to wait by a rather grumpy receptionist.

After twenty minutes, they were approached by a female officer with broad shoulders and short hair. They followed her to a small chamber, where they were asked to sit on cheap plastic chairs. This time, they only had to wait a few minutes. A woman in civilian clothes entered the room and reached out her hand to them. Robert's eyes were drawn to her nails that were painted the brightest color red he had ever seen. She was followed by an older man, who was wearing Nike Airs under his jeans and navy sports jacket.

"You're English?" inquired the female officer, who had introduced herself as Astrid van der Bosch. "And you're here to translate, is that right?" She nodded in the direction of Andy, who was wearing a remarkably presentable pullover for the occasion. She seemed to be insulted by the arrangement.

"Not exactly," Robert interceded before Andy could respond. "Of course I realize that you speak English well. It's just that I've been here for a short time, and I'm still unfamiliar with many things. So I asked Andy to help me."

"Hm," she said, somewhat mollified. "Maybe that's a good idea. So who's going to give me the information?"

Her colleague leaned back in his plastic chair, studying them. Robert hadn't quite caught his name when the introductions were made. He was older than Astrid van der Bosch, maybe in his late fifties, early sixties. The man was looking at him with unblinking blue eyes, which made him feel a bit uncomfortable. He quickly looked back at Andy, who was just embarking on his narrative. He explained about Robert being an exchange student, how he'd met with his neighbour called Khalid, and how several things he'd observed had come together with what they had learned about the attack through the media.

They let him talk for more than five minutes. Only once did the female officer interrupt, to let him repeat and clarify something. Robert couldn't understand what he was saying, but he got the feeling that Andy wasn't impressing them. When Andy had finished, it remained silent for a few seconds. She scrawled something in her notebook.

Suddenly she looked at Robert and addressed him in English. "Do you play World of Warcraft yourself? I mean, do you know the game?"

"No," he answered truthfully, taken aback by the direct question. "Nevertheless, I don't need to play the game to be able to recognize suspicious coincidences."

"My son plays World of Warcraft. In fact, he's addicted to it. I have no choice but to take an interest in what he's doing at the computer for so many hours each day." She stopped there, looking at them one at a time. They simply looked back at her, not knowing what to say.

She shook her head. "If I took everything that he's doing and saying online seriously, I'd have had to arrest my own son many times over. Not only him, but also all the people he's playing with. I happen to know that his guild is called the Hammer of Thrall. Does that make him an accomplice in a terrorist bombing?"

"No, but this is different," Robert exclaimed. "I saw an Arab guy, a Muslim presumably, who came to the Netherlands just before a terrorist attack, who's receiving WoW messages that happen to coincide precisely with a message that's left at the bombing scene, exactly on the date mentioned! We're talking about some weird coincidences here, if they're coincidences at all! And don't you think that exactly *because* the whole game is about killing, there's no better place for a terrorist to do his business unobserved?"

"Maybe." She closed her notebook.

Andy, who had been listening to the exchange silently, as if ashamed of having come up with the theory, suddenly spoke up. "Wasn't there an attack by a student from Leiden a couple of years back?"

"Yes, there was," Astrid van der Bosch replied curtly. She rose from the table. Her colleague did the same.

"We'll take your information under consideration. If we have any further questions, we'll contact you."

Robert and Andy exchanged a quick look and moved to the door. The interview was clearly over. They shook hands with the two officials. The man, who still hadn't said a word, escorted them back to the lobby. Unexpectedly, he addressed Robert. "It was good of you to come to us with this information. We're investigating many leads at the moment, and we'll also look into what you told us."

A little surprised, Robert nodded. "Thank you," was all he could think of.

The man nodded back. He reached into his jacket and retrieved two business cards. He gave one to each of them. "Keep an eye on this Khalid. If you really think something is going on, give me a call."

CHAPTER VI

Rebecca had been fiercely angry when he'd told her of the reaction of the police to their information.

"How can they be so stupid and so ignorant?" she'd exclaimed, going off on a rant about stuffy public servants who still lived in the twentieth century. She made it sound like the Stone Age. "Just because that lady has a son who plays World of Warcraft, she's not an expert all of a sudden. The CIA recognises the dangers of World of Warcraft, but some stupid Dutch lady thinks she knows better. If she understood what we're talking about only a little, she wouldn't dismiss the opportunities an online multi player game presents!"

"Why are you suddenly so sure that all this really has something to do with the terrorists?" he had asked.

"I'm not sure. I never said that! It's just that we can't be sure that it isn't either. What they should have done is thank you on their knees for coming to them, and investigate it to the bottom. They should follow any lead! Because they don't understand it, they'll just let it go."

"The elder policeman did ask us to keep an eye on Khalid and contact him if we found out something else."

She had nodded and looked him in the eye. "And that's exactly what we're going to do. But we're going to do more than just keep an eye out. We're going to start our own investigation."

"And how are we going to accomplish that? I can't break into his room or follow him around all day!"

She smiled broadly and gave him a hard poke in the shoulder. "Sure we can! Just not here, in broad daylight! No, Robert, we're going to do our sneaking in the place where we think they meet each other: World of Warcraft!"

Now, Robert was about to embark on his first journey into World of Warcraft.

"We're going to do this together," she'd told him, "even when I'm back in Scotland next week. That means that you'll have to work hard to become an adequate player. I'm going to help you, but you have a lot of work to do!"

As promised, he called her when the installation was complete and he'd established an account. That part was easy. He just followed the steps, which ended by giving in his credit card details.

"Great, now you're ready to enter the world of Azeroth!"

"Sorry, but explain that to me. I thought it was called World of Warcraft?"

She laughed over the phone. "Yes indeed, but the imaginary world is called Azeroth, like our planet is called Earth."

"I see. And what do I do now?"

"Now you're going to create a character. First you have to select the right realm. You have to select Sylvanas."

Robert was browsing through a list of different realms. "What does a realm mean? And why do I have to choose that one?"

"You don't really think that twelve million people are at the same place at the same time, do you?"

He didn't answer, not understanding what she meant.

"No virtual world can be big enough to accommodate that many people. Besides, no server in the world would have the capacity to facilitate that. Therefore, WoW is divided into a number of different servers. Each server has several hundred thousand people on it."

"Hmmm," Robert grumbled. He wasn't sure he understood.

Rebecca was a patient teacher. "You can compare it to a tennis club. Everybody is a member of the same club and plays exactly the same game, by the same rules. It's just that they don't all play on the same court at the same time. It's the same in WoW. Every server, which is called a realm, is a different court. Every tennis court is exactly the same."

Robert laughed and complimented her on the way she explained it to him. "This is WoW for Dummies, but it works for me. So why do I have to select the Sylvanas realm?"

"Do you remember how we looked up Drimm on the Internet? On the Armory? One of the things I learned is that Drimm and his guild are on the Sylvanas server. So if we're going to investigate them, we have to be on their server. It's no use to watch court number seven while our subjects are playing on court number twelve."

He nodded, unaware that she couldn't see him over the phone. The next screen asked him to create a character. "What do I do now?"

"I think it's best to create a character who's exactly similar to Drimm. That means you're going to create a Tauren hunter."

After some searching, Robert saw what he had to do. "Yak, he's ugly!" he laughed. Then he noticed that he could alter the appearance, and started fiddling with the skin color and hairstyle. It didn't improve the looks of his character much. The Tauren race resembled huge bulls that had somehow learned to walk upright on their hind legs, and had grown fingers on their front hooves.

"Yes, the Horde side doesn't give you the prettiest characters. You'll get used to it. Now, are you ready?"

He saw that he still had to choose a name for his Tauren hunter. He thought briefly and decided. Then he hit 'Enter World' and was rewarded by an introduction movie. It showed friendly plains of grasslands with smooth hills. He was floating in the air over the prairie. Robert leaned back in his chair, amazed by how friendly the virtual world looked.

A voice was telling him about the race of the Tauren, but Robert wasn't really taking in what it was saying. Now he was floating through a city of tents, perched high in the altitude of some huge cliffs that rose steeply from the rolling plains. Next he was accelerating over more grasslands, seeing many kinds of animals below. Then he was descending toward a small village, circling some figures who were standing together at the centre of the village. Only when the movie finished did he realize that he was one of those figures.

He was standing right in front of another Tauren. Above its head stood the name 'Grull Hawkwind'. Also above its head was a large yellow exclamation mark. He had no idea what he should do now.

"Are you still there?" he asked.

Rebecca chuckled. "Yes, I am. Are you ready?"

"I think so. I'm in some kind of village. There's a guy with an exclamation mark over his head."

"Don't panic, I'm going to help you. Is your character called Gunslinger?"

"Yes, it is. How do you know that?"

In answer, his phone gave the tiny beep that told him the call had ended. He checked the display. Indeed, the connection was broken. At the same moment he heard a sound from his computer. He turned his attention back to the screen. In purple, a text had appeared on the bottom of his screen:

[Killermage] whispers: because I am standing right next to you.

He looked closely at his screen, but saw no one else but the Tauren he'd seen earlier.

[Killermage] whispers: you can move with the arrow keys. turn left.

Turning he saw Rebecca. Or at least, he saw someone on a huge horse with the name Killermage above his head. Or her head, in this case. Like his own bull-like appearance, the looks of Killermage were definitely lacking charm. She had a human form, but apart from that, there was nothing ordinary about her. She looked like a half-decayed corpse that had somehow risen from its grave. Hints of a ghastly skeletal body protruded through her clothing, that would have been of shining magnificence, if it didn't appear so frayed at most places.

The text *Killermage waves at you* appeared, and indeed she was waving at him. He smiled. This was a lot more fun than he'd expected. He decided to try something. He hit Enter and was rewarded by an empty textbox at the bottom of the screen. He typed a message and hit Enter again. Immediately, it appeared in a text balloon above his head, just like in a comic book: 'Hello to you too!'

[Killermage] whispers: that message could be seen by everyone in this village. If you type R of Reply you can send a message to me alone. That is called a whisper.

After some minutes of chatting back and forth, he was getting used to it. "What are we going to do next?" he asked.

"Now you're going to accept your first quest. Talk to that guy with the exclamation mark. If you see an exclamation mark over someone's head, it means he has a quest for you."

He selected Grull Hawkwind. A box opened with a lot of text. He was welcomed to the tribe and was asked to prove his worth by adding to the supplies of the village. More specifically, he'd have to prove his worth to Chief Hawkwind, who was the father of Grull. He was to kill Plainstriders to collect seven Plainstrider feathers and seven Plainstrider Meat. He pressed the button with 'Accept' and was rewarded by a sound and the confirmation 'Quest Accepted' in his screen.

Although Rebecca probably understood, Robert happily typed "I accepted the quest. I must kill some animals called Plainstriders to collect feathers and meat."

"You must always kill something, and you must always collect something. Follow me!" The huge horse of Killermage reared on its hind legs and turned whinnying around. She galloped away from him. Robert used the arrow keys to start moving as well. After some trial and error he got the hang of it. Still, it took some time to catch up. He started to develop some sense of the distances in this digital world.

"I need a horse too. How do I get one?"

Killermage rolls on the floor laughing at you appeared on his screen. At the same time, he heard a laughing voice. "You need to be level twenty to learn how to ride a mount. It used to be level forty, but they changed that. Lucky you. At level forty you can get a much faster mount. If you have enough gold."

Robert saw an animal walk up to him. He moved his mouse over it and saw that it was a 'Plainstrider'. It looked like a terribly over-sized turkey. Now it was walking away again.

"How do I kill that Plainstrider over there?"

"Do you see those buttons under the text box?"

"Yes." Robert moused over them. They were numbered one to ten. Numbers one to four had a symbol in them. The rest was empty.

"Is there one that says 'Autoshot'?"

"Yes, number three." Robert decided to get on with it. Suddenly, his character had a gun in his hands, and a loud shot sounded. A puff of smoke swirled upward from the gun. Although the bird was hit, it didn't drop down dead. On the contrary, it charged right at him.

Just before it reached him, Robert's character fired off another shot. Robert started wondering if he'd hit some firing button, but before he could look on his keyboard the animal was on him. Its huge head reared back and it started pecking at him with its vicious beak. At the same time, it made aggressive sounds and Robert heard the blows landing on him. Well, on Gunslinger, but somehow it felt close and personal. He had no idea what to do. He was fruitlessly pounc-ing his keyboard. It somehow didn't react. Just when he thought the animal was going to kill the poor Gunslinger, his character suddenly swung a kind of primitive axe. And again. It appeared that Robert didn't have to do anything, it went completely automatic. Gunslin-ger took a few more hits from the bird, but on the next swing of his axe, the Plainstrider gave a piercing death shriek. It swayed on its legs for a long moment before collapsing on the ground. Its head came up one more time, then flopped powerless back on the ground. Robert found that his hands were clammy. The fight had been more realistic then he'd ever believed possible.

"Gratz with your first kill," said Rebecca.

"Huh? Gratz as in congrats?"

"Exactly. Most people in WoW just say Gratz or even GZ."

"Well, thanks. How do I get the feathers and the meat?"

"If you move your cursor over the corpse, you'll see the icon of a little bag. That means that you can loot the corpse."

Robert did as he was told. It was incredibly easy. He looted one feather and one meat from the dead Plainstrider. He also got a cracked egg shell. He still had six more feathers and meat to go.

He saw another Plainstrider. Again, he clicked Autoshot. He hit the animal and it turned to attack him. This time however, the fight took a lot longer.

"You must shoot from as far away as possible," Rebecca said. "When the Plainstrider comes too close, your gun is useless and your character switches to hand combat. So when you start shooting from as far away as possible, you get off a few extra shots, and it's almost dead before it reaches you."

"How do I know it's almost dead?"

"Every creature has a health bar. It's the green bar you see when you click on it with your mouse. You have one yourself. Look at your own icon at the top of your screen. Your health is down to about fifty percent at the moment."

Robert checked and saw she was right. His health was at forty-five of ninety-four. He also saw it was regenerating slowly.

"Why is the maximum ninety-four instead of a hundred?" Robert wondered.

"It's not a percentage but a number, called hitpoints. Look at me, I have over twenty thousand hitpoints."

"My hitpoints are increasing," Robert noted.

"You heal slowly when you're out of combat. By eating food, by drinking a health potion, or by bandaging yourself you heal faster. Or another player can heal you." At that moment he saw little red crosses emanating from his own character and his health bar suddenly shot up to maximum. "I bandaged you just now."

"Thank you!" He looted the corpse of the slain Plainstrider and got only one feather.

"Somehow I don't get the meat out of this chicken," he complained.

Killermage laughs at you appeared in the screen. She replied. "It's not that easy. Sometimes you get what you want, sometimes luck isn't on your side."

After maybe five minutes, he had collected all the feathers and meat he required. He had also found more cracked egg shells, as well as a pair of Flimsy Chain Pants, a Battered Buckler and a Frayed Belt. There were more than ten Plainstriders lying dead on the grassy plain. Just for fun, he shot at the one remaining bird in sight. As the others had done, it charged him after being hit, but died after a few blows of his axe. Right at that moment, a circle of golden beams came from above and surrounded his character. A message appeared on his screen that congratulated him on reaching level two. It also informed him that he'd gained hit points and mana, and that his agility, stamina, intellect and spirit each had increased by one.

"GZ!" Rebecca said. "Only seventy-eight more levels to go!"

Robert moved his mouse over Killermage and saw that she was level eighty. He calculated. He hadn't even been playing for ten minutes, so he should be able to reach level eighty in a few days. When he told her so, he was rewarded by a lot of laughter.

"Look at the thin bar with all the small brackets that's right on top of the numbered icons at the bottom of your screen."

"Yes?" Robert moved his mouse over it. "It reads XP 32/900."

"XP stands for Experience Points. For killing, completing quests or discovering new areas, you receive experience points. When the bar is full, you reach a new level. In your case, you go to level three when you collect nine hundred points. Every time you progress to a higher level, the required amount to reach the next level is raised."

"How many of those points is it from level seventy nine to level eighty?"

"I don't remember exactly, but I think it's something like one point seven million. The upside is that you receive more points per kill when you get higher. Still, the average player takes about six months to reach level eighty."

Now that he was done with the quest, he had to return to the village, but he was unsure where it was exactly. He had drifted away while seeking out the birds and killing them. Not wanting to show Rebecca he was lost, he set off in the direction in which he thought the village was. After walking for a few minutes, he knew he wasn't going in the right direction. The land was now gently sloping upward and he saw a few vicious looking predators called Mountain Cougars.

"Shouldn't you go back to village?"

"I would, if I knew where it was."

Killermage was laughing loudly at him. "Why don't you ask me then?"

Robert was a bit irritated. His sense of directions wasn't his strongest point to begin with, and in real life he always made sure to remember landmarks. "Well?" he asked.

"If you press the M key, you get a map. You can see where you are."

He did as she said. His screen was replaced by a map called Mulgore. Most of the map was blank. Only a small portion was filled in green. He saw Camp Narache, which he remembered was the name of the village. His own position was marked by a tiny arrow, which showed that he was indeed walking away from the village. He closed the map and turned Gunslinger around. A few minutes later, he arrived back at the safety of Camp Narache. Killermage was lying on the ground at the feet of Grull Hawkwind, fast asleep. Little 'Z's' were floating over her face.

"Very funny!" Gunslinger said.

"Finally, there you are," Killermage said, standing up. "Now, turn in your quest!"

Robert saw that the Tauren he'd got the quest from now had a yellow question mark over his head. He approached him and completed the quest. He got a belt as a reward. Grull Hawkwind wasn't finished with him yet. He had a new quest for him called The Hunt Continues, which required him to kill Mountain Cougars and collect ten of their pelts. At least he knew where to find them. He also had a message for him.

"I just got a note. How do I read it?" he asked of Rebecca.

She rode up to him and dismounted. "Click on your backpack. It's in the right hand corner at the bottom."

Inside the leather bag were all the things he had looted, and also the note. When he clicked on the note, it opened in a large window. It was written on some kind of parchment and detailed how important hunters were to the tribe. The sender was Lanka Farshot, who offered to train him in the ways of the hunter.

"I have to go to the hunter trainer," he said. "Where's that?"

"Where does it say it is?"

"Here in Camp Narache."

Killermage sat on the ground, right in front of him. "I'm supposed to introduce you to WoW, but that doesn't mean I have to tell you exactly what to do all the time. One of the challenges of this game is that you have to find out where you have to go. If the message says she's in Camp Narache, you'll just have to look around. Good luck!"

Robert felt a bit rebuked by her. On the other hand, wasn't it fun to find it out for himself? He left her behind and walked the short distance to the main building, which was in fact the largest tent. When he entered the large tent, he saw another Tauren with an exclamation mark. Rebecca explained to him that you could be on more than one quest at the same time. The Tauren was Grull's father, Chief Hawkwing. Also in the tent, he found Lanka Farshot. After some introduction text, she offered to train him. For nine Copper she would teach him something called Track Beasts. He had no money at all. This time, Rebecca didn't make fun of him.

"Money is incredibly important in this game. Without Gold, you miss out on a lot of things. You can make your first money now by selling the other things you collected while killing those Plainstriders. Come!"

He followed her out of the tent and she led him to Kawnee Softbreeze, a General Goods Vendor, according to her tag.

"You can sell your stuff to her."

Robert sold everything in his bags for a total sum of fifty-six Copper. With the money, he returned to Lanka Farshot and was taught a skill called Track Beasts. Apparently, this skill allowed him to see the location of all animals around him on the mini map in the upper right corner. Handy indeed.

"Now let's spend the rest of your money," Rebecca said. "Hunters must always have enough ammunition!" She motioned him back to the General Goods Vendor. "Fill your ammunition bag with Light Shot. She sells it."

He did as she told him. The cost was nine Copper for two hundred Light Shot. He now had more than a thousand bullets.

Suddenly, with a thud, a new window opened on his screen, accompanied by the text *Killermage wants to trade with you*. He studied the new window for a moment and saw that she wanted to give him one hundred Gold.

"Press 'Trade' now," she said.

After receiving the money, he asked how much it was worth.

"There are one hundred Copper in one Silver, and there are one hundred Silver in one Gold. So I just gave you a present of one million Copper."

"Wow, that's a lot. Do I need that much?"

"No, not at all. There are many players who don't have that much money until they reach level fifty. You're now officially the richest newcomer on the whole Realm!"

"Thanks." He didn't know what to say.

Killermage clapped him on the shoulder. "No worries. I have to go now. Keep on playing. I'll drop by your place at about eight o'clock tonight. Is that all right?"

Before he could answer, she disappeared, as if she had dissolved into thin air right before his eyes.

CHAPTER VII

By the time it was eight o'clock, Robert had reached level six. He had finished all the quests in and around Camp Narache, which included going into a hostile village at the far east of the area. A hard challenge, which taught him what happened when you died in World of Warcraft. Although dying wasn't the right word. His character was transported to a graveyard. Well, actually it wasn't the corpse but the spirit of his character that appeared at the cemetery. This spirit turned out to be alive: it appeared as a ghost. This ghost had to run all the way back to the corpse to resurrect. Then the difficulties arose. Back to life again, you were at half health, at approximately the same location where you had died. This meant that the enemy who killed you in the first place was all over you again in a few seconds, while you were only half as strong.

He was jolted by a knock on his door. He had been playing so intently that he had forgotten the time. It was Rebecca.

"Well done, level six!" she congratulated him after a glance at the screen. "Now let's start doing some real work. Could you log off now?"

When he got back to the opening screen, she gently pushed him out of the desk chair. Robert pulled another chair close and sat next to her at the computer. Rebecca poked his arm, laughingly accusing him of being a WoW addict already. He smiled in return. It was fun, he had to admit. He suddenly noticed his stomach grumbling. An addict indeed; already he was neglecting the needs of his body. He opened a can of Pringles, Bolognese flavor, his favorite.

"Now let's take a look at what our friends are doing," Rebecca said. She pulled a paper out of her pocket and unfolded it. It was a print of the website of the Armory, listing the members of the guild called The Hammer of Grimstone. "I'm going to put them all on your friends list now."

"My friends list?"

"Amazing, isn't it?" She opened a tab under 'Social' and a window appeared. She started with Drimm, typing his name and hitting Enter. *Drimm added to friends* came the confirmation.

"Can he see this?" Robert asked.

She shook her head. "No, that's the beauty of it. When you add someone to your friends list, he doesn't get a notification or something like that. Once a person is on your list, you automatically get a notification when he comes online and also when he goes offline. What's even better, when he's online, you can see where he is." She pointed at the friends list, which only showed Drimm. His status was listed as 'unknown' Quickly, she added the rest of the names. Done, she logged off and entered the virtual world again using her own account. She opened the same tab to show him how she'd already added the Hammer of Grimstone to Killermage's contacts.

"When one of them comes online, this tab will show us in which zone he is."

"What's a zone, exactly?"

"A zone is much like a province. Or maybe a state of the United States." She opened the map. "Look. We're now in a zone called Mulgore."

Robert peered at the map, noticing that the map of Killermage showed all of Mulgore, whereas his own map only showed about one third of the area. The rest was grey. He'd already noticed that new areas were revealed on the map when you discovered them, simply by going there. The map of Killermage showed him that Mulgore was a huge piece of territory.

"You may think that Mulgore is big, but in fact it's one of the smaller zones." She clicked on a button that read 'Zoom Out' and now the map showed a large continent called Kalimdor surrounded by oceans on all sides. By moving her mouse over the different zones, their names came up. She clicked on one to the north called Winterspring, and he could see in detail all the different areas, roads and villages. She opened a few others at random to give him an impression.

"Holy shit, it's huge!" he exclaimed. "Have you been everywhere?"

She smiled wickedly. "Yes I have, but you haven't seen anything yet!" She zoomed out again and now he saw a world map showing three large continents. Two were parallel to each other, stretching all the way from the south nearly to the north. They were separated by an ocean. Near the northern polar cap, another large continent lay between the two others. The western continent was called Kalimdor, the opposite one was called Eastern Kingdoms, and the landmass to the north was called Northrend. She zoomed out again. This time a fourth continent called Outland appeared that looked nearly as big as Kalimdor and Eastern Kingdoms combined.

"What's that?"

"Outland, which came with the first large addition to the game. It's the Burning Crusade package you installed." She held up the box still lying on his desk. "A new continent was added, and the level cap was raised from sixty to seventy. Outland is restricted to players of level fifty-eight and higher and you must access it from a portal situated somewhere in the deserts in Eastern Kingdoms. She clicked on it, and Robert could see that it consisted of only ten different zones, each of extraordinary size. She opened one called Terokkar Forest, and he could see that there were two major cities, two smaller ones, and about eight villages.

"Now let's finish the list and get some proper food," she said, closing the map. She quickly entered the names of all the guild members of The Hammer of Grimstone. Only one was online, a character called Pharad. According to the displayed information, he was in a place called Dalaran. "Dalaran is the capital city of Northrend," Rebecca explained. "No use trying to find him. There are too many players crawling around like ants over there." She exited the game and turned around. "Now, what's for dinner?"

They went to a small Italian restaurant, which was only a five minute walk from where he lived. The pizzas were so large that Robert was truly amazed that he actually finished his Pizza Vulcano, his favorite *pizza picante*. His appetite was caused by a combination of feeling famished by an afternoon of playing World of Warcraft, the skill of the Italian cook, and the company of Rebecca. They didn't talk about the game at all.

She told him an endless parade of hilarious stories about her childhood in a small village in northern Scotland. She was a gifted storyteller who could turn the most mundane happenings into glorious events. Her undertone of sarcasm had him laughing all the time. It was nearly eleven o'clock when Robert poured the last drops of their second bottle of Barolo into her empty glass. He paid the bill and, without any discussion, they walked back to his place together. He felt a quickening of his heartbeat when she followed him upstairs to his room. Inside, she tossed her coat on his bed and sat behind his desk.

While Robert searched the small wine cabinet for a suitable successor to the Barolo, she brought the computer back to life. A few seconds later, he heard the distinctive music of World of Warcraft.

"Robert, come here, look at this!" She sounded truly distressed.

In the restaurant, the thought of a romantic turn of the evening had crossed his mind several times, and he felt a momentary pang of disappointment. It was going to end in playing a computer game together.

He crossed the room and looked over her shoulder. She had her friends list open and was pointing at it. He could see that most of The Hammer of Grimstone were online now.

"This isn't making any sense!"

He didn't understand what was bothering her. "What's not making sense?"

She tapped the screen with the point of her index finger. "Do you see that? They're all in Ashenvale. That doesn't make any sense at all!"

"Why? What's the problem with Ashenvale? Is it a zone?"

"Yes, it is. The problem is that there's no reason at all for ten level eighties to be in Ashenvale. No reason at all!"

"Why not?"

She took a deep breath, calming herself. "Because Ashenvale is a level twenty-five to level thirty zone. That means that the enemies, called 'mobs' by the way, are all between those levels. Players of those levels find worthy opposition and quests there. That doesn't mean that you'll never find a level eighty there, as there are always people helping a guild mate with a difficult quest or something."

To show her that he was paying attention, he said, "Just like your Killermage is in Mulgore to help my Gunslinger."

"Exactly, and Mulgore is a level one to ten zone!"

"So what does this mean?"

She held her hands up in the air to show her incomprehension. "I don't know. But we're going to see what they're doing!"

She clicked on one of the many icons surrounding the screen and Killermage started to cast a spell: *Teleport: Ogrimmar*. Bolts of light appeared at her fingertips.

A few seconds later she materialized at another location, on top of some wooden platform. Killermage summoned her mount and jumped off the platform onto the path below. She galloped down the path. Suddenly she veered to the right and jumped right on top of the roof of a house built on the ledge below the path. This was definitely not the official way down. They hopped to another roof and again to another. One final jump brought them on the ground.

There were a lot of other players around, Robert guessed there must be hundreds. Rebecca charged right through them on her horse and rode straight into a building. Briefly, Robert glimpsed the sign on the outside of the building, which read *Bank of Ogrimmar*. Inside, she dismounted and walked up to one of the men standing there. She clicked on him, and a window opened. It held a lot of slots, and to the bottom was a row of purple bags. She opened a few of them, searching for something. After a few tries she found what she was looking for, some bottle. She took it before Robert could read what it was.

She ran outside and mounted again, turning sharply around. In a gallop they skirted around the huge bank building, following a road that veered rather steeply upward. She charged into another building consisting solely of a spiral staircase. Halfway up, she dismounted, apparently automatically. A few seconds later they arrived at the top. Robert saw they were on a tower, higher than all the other buildings around. Killermage headed straight for the character standing on the edge of the platform. His tag read *Doras, Wind Rider Master*. A new window opened, showing a spider web of flight routes and destinations. Without hesitation, Rebecca selected one, a puff of dust appeared, and a split second later they were on the back of a huge winged animal carrying them upward and away at incredible speed.

Robert was watching all this in awe. "Wow, this is amazing!" They had now left the city behind and were floating down a river. "Where are we going?"

"Splintertree Post," she answered, opening the Friends Window again. They saw that all the members of The Hammer of Grimstone were still listed as being in Ashenvale. "Splintertree Post is the central flight path in Ashenvale."

"Will it be easy to find them?"

She shook her head emphatically. "No, not at all. Ashenvale is, in fact, a huge forest, with all kinds of secluded areas that are way off the roads. I can't think of many zones that are worse for trying to find someone."

Now they were descending toward a small settlement. When they landed, Rebecca opened her bag and clicked on the bottle she had retrieved from the bank earlier. Next she summoned her horse and they charged out of Splintertree Post.

"I just drank an Elixir of Detect Undead," she explained. "Because it's so hard to find someone out here, we need another way to scan the woods for them. Two of their members are Undead, so they're going to show up on the tracking screen."

"Is this like the Track Beasts ability my hunter has?" Robert asked.

She gave him a wide smile. "Good, you're learning fast! Yes, it is, but hunters are the only class with the ability to track all kinds of races. Other classes have to rely on elixirs, but there are only elixirs for tracking a few races. Hunters can learn to track literarily everything."

***

They had been at it for over two hours today, for the fifth day in a row. Drimm thought it was enough. He'd been thinking that for at least forty minutes, but he knew better than to say anything about it. Pharad was the leader, and they wouldn't stop before he was completely satisfied.

"We do it one more time," said Pharad. They were standing in the woods outside the gate at the backside of Raynewood Retreat. "Last time was almost perfect. Now we do it one more time to make sure that nobody will forget what he has to do."

"I think we'll have to clear the building again first," said Gilead, who stood next to Drimm.

Pharad turned around and peered at the structure of Raynewood Retreat that loomed over them. The entrance to the building was over a kind of terrace-like bridge, and Drimm could see that a Cenarion Defender had appeared in the doorway and was looking out at the back garden. That meant that there would be others inside the building as well. Gilead was right. The lower floors had to be cleared first. Again.

"Yes," said Pharad, and he pointed at Gilead. "You do it, but be quick about it."

Without another word, Gilead took a few steps forward and raised his gun. The shot boomed through the forest and Drimm could see that the Cenarion Defender was critically hit. He went down immediately. Gilead went inside and they could hear him shooting. The sounds diminished, then vanished altogether as he moved deeper into the building and went up the stairs. It was no easy task that Gilead had been given. His assignment was to leave an exact number of enemies alive in the building and kill the rest.

Pharad turned back to the little group. "Okay, we wait until Gilead has finished, then we do it one more time." He made a rude gesture to one of them. "And you, Jakky, will not try to loot again. You leave the bodies where they are and just try to control yourself. Besides, what do you expect to find? Some epic item dropping here?"

"Yes, Commander," Jakky said, and Drimm wished he could see the expression on his face. Drimm himself had suppressed the urge to search the bodies they left behind because he knew how much Pharad hated their greed.

Shortly after that, Gilead returned. "It's ready, we can start," he said.

"Okay, let's take up the positions. If we get it right again, this was the last rehearsal."

Immediately everybody moved into position. Drimm had the farthest to go. He moved all the way around the building and halfway down the path that led to the road. He scanned left and right. Nobody in sight.

"Team X in position. All clear," he reported in.

"Acknowledged, X. Everyone is now ready and in position. Wait for my sign to commence."

After that followed maybe twenty seconds of silence. Drimm kept looking left and right. The road remained empty.

"Go, go, go!"

Raynewood Retreat was built along a rarely travelled road in the Nightsong Woods, which covered most of the province of Ashenvale. The retreat was separated from Splintertree Post, the nearest village, by the Falfarren River and some steep hills. From the road Raynewood Retreat was nothing more than some dim building on a hill. What was happening up there couldn't be seen from the road, as the entrance was in the back garden.

Drimm had an important job, because he was to ensure that nobody would know what was happening. He was to raise the alarm if anyone was actually approaching, or maybe even to prevent that from happening.

In his mind Drimm saw the carefully rehearsed plan enfolding. Team Y was approaching the main entrance from the left, Team Z came running in from the right. At the same time, Team Q had taken up position at the back entrance to cut off any possible intruders.

Y and Z entered the building. Team Z immediately went for the stairs, while team Y secured the ground floor. After doing that, one of Y guarded the door. The other member covered the stairs.

The two people from Team Z, Pharad being one of them, secured the first floor, silently and swiftly killing the two guards stationed there.

"Phase one concluded. Execute two. Go, go, go!"

On cue, one of the members of Team Q left his station at the gate and moved up to the entrance. Like a relay race, the one guarding the door moved up to the position of the other member of Y, who ran up the stairs to secure that floor.

"Phase two ready."

"Execute three, go, go, go!"

The two of Team Z sprinted up the second stairs and exploded onto the floor above. An incredible burst of violence killed the two guardians there in a matter of seconds. Next, onto the main target, total surprise and again an explosion of extreme violence.

"Phase three concluded. Execute four, go, go, go!"

Now, Drimm came into action. His responsibility was to make sure that they had a clean getaway. He ran up the path and stopped next to the building. He drew his gun and started to sweep the area with his eyes. No enemies moving. Only a few moments later, he was passed by team Q, then team Y and after maybe twenty seconds, team Z.

When he was sure that everybody was clear and that there was no pursuit, Drimm, too, ran to the road below and to safety.

***

Rebecca had swept the areas close to the main road that ran from east to west twice now. They were standing near their starting point again. She had opened the zone map and they were discussing where they should go next. Robert suggested they follow the main road to the north that ran just to the west of Splintertree Post, whereas Rebecca thought they should go to the coast all the way to the west.

"We're now close to where I want to go," he pointed out. To stress his point, he tapped the screen with his finger.

"True, but we can fly to the Zoram Strand. While we do that, we have another sweep from above." She sighed. "Your guess is as good as mine. Let's try your suggestion first."

She turned Killermage around and veered to the north when they reached a junction. Robert was studying the mini map.

"There!" he shouted. "I saw a golden dot on the map, but it's gone now!"

Rebecca turned the horse around and trotted back the way they had come. Close to a place marked 'Raynewood Retreat' on the map, two golden dots appeared on the mini map. Rebecca moved her mouse over the dots.

"Bingo!" She checked the names against the printed list again, just to make sure. "Yes, here we have Frakk and Caliburr close together. I think we can assume that the others are there as well."

Robert cheered and put a hand on her shoulder. "Well done!"

"We still don't know what they're doing here. They're at Raynewood Retreat, but what the hell are they up to? I can barely remember the place, I believe there's only one insignificant quest that involves it."

"Can we get closer?"

She waited a moment before answering. "Yes, we can, but they will see us as well. And we're just as much out of place as they are. If we assume that they're doing something in secret, they'll be alerted by the sudden appearance of a level eighty mage. There can be only so much coincidence, and we might want to save an accidental meeting for another time."

Robert felt like a balloon suddenly deflated. "So we came here for nothing?"

"In a way." Her response made Robert feel even worse. Tired he stared at the screen.

Suddenly she hit her hand on the table. "No! I disagree. We saw that they are behaving strangely. For nearly five years I have been playing this game, and I have never seen a bunch of level eighties crowding around a level twenty-six building before."

***

They were all standing just outside the back garden again. An Elder Shadowhorn Stag had wandered into the grounds, but everybody ignored the huge beautiful deer. They were all focused on Pharad.

"Well done. We had it down to four minutes, forty-one seconds in and out."

One of the members of team Q cheered.

Pharad continued as if he heard nothing. "Remember, we still have to do this one more time, and we'll have to do it even better. We've rehearsed this operation so many times, that everybody should know what he has to do. Are there any questions?"

It remained silent.

"All right, we'll meet again in six days time. Make sure that you're well equipped for the Raid. We will not fail. THE WORLD WILL TREMBLE FOR THE HAMMER OF RIGHTEOUS JUSTICE!"

***

"There is one thing that we can do, but it's going to take some time. Ten minutes at least."

Robert looked hopefully at her. It didn't feel right to have come all this way, and not be able to actually observe what was going on.

"I could get m-" She broke off in midsentence. "SHIT!"

Robert turned to see what she was looking at. On the screen, the two dots had disappeared. Rebecca immediately opened the friends window. There they were, all of them still online, but not in Ashenvale anymore. Three were in Dalaran, two in Ogrimmar, and the rest in different other locations.

"Damn, they used their hearthstones to move out. All at the same time. We're too late!"

"What-" He started to ask what she meant, but seeing the expression on her face, he thought better of it. Instead, he watched as Killermage rode her horse right through the bushes and trees into the grounds of Raynewood Retreat. He saw a large gloomy building in a big dark clearing. Killermage dismounted right in front of the entrance and they stared down at the corpse of the Cenarion Defender that lay sprawled in the doorway.

"Now we'll never know what they were doing!" Rebecca said bitterly.

CHAPTER VIII

The next day, Robert actually had a conversation with Khalid. Until then, their encounters had been brief, no more than a greeting when they accidentally met in the corridor. He'd casually asked several fellow students in the house about their opinion of the man, but most people just shrugged. Khalid obviously kept to himself, not engaging in the many social events of the student house. Only Lisa Duchamps, the good looking girl from France, had really talked with him on two occasions. According to her, he was from Egypt and was in Leiden to follow a course on the faculty of Art History. She thought he didn't mingle well because he drank no alcohol, being a Muslim. Considering that drinking alcohol was one of the favorite pastimes of students anywhere in the world, the community in Leiden being no exception, this seemed a plausible explanation. That was, if you didn't know anything else.

It happened when Robert was returning from the kitchen. The front door opened and Khalid stepped out of the pouring rain. He was wearing jeans and a dark blue wind breaker, dripping great rivulets of water onto the floor. He shook his head vigorously, sending small droplets of water flying. Robert decided to seize the moment.

"Hello, Khalid. You're brave to go outside in this weather!"

The subject obviously didn't feel heroic, but he managed a smile. "You mean stupid," he answered. He spoke English with a slight accent.

Robert smiled back. "I'm from England, the weather is even worse where I come from. For you it must be terrible. You're from Egypt, aren't you?"

Khalid narrowed his eyes and nodded. "Yes, Cairo. Hot and dry. We never have rain like this."

With these words he started up the stairs. Robert walked right behind him. He kept the conversation going.

"So how do you like it here?"

"It's okay. The classes are good."

"Really? What are you studying?"

Khalid halted and turned half around to look at him. He seemed a bit surprised to be talking to him. He answered nonetheless pleasantly and without noticeable hesitation, "I study Art History. I follow the courses Highlights of Dutch Art and Highlights of Dutch Architecture. Rembrandt, Vermeer, Van Gogh, and many more. I like it."

Robert gave him another smile. "So do I. I study History myself, specializing in the Dutch Golden Age. Rembrandt van Rijn pops up now and then."

When they reached the landing, Robert changed the subject. "Do you still play that computer game? World of War or something?"

"Yes, I do," he answered, reaching with some effort into the tight pocket of his soaked jeans for his key. "World of War*craft*."

"Right, that's what I mean. Someone else told me about it yesterday. He said that I'd like it. Do you think I should buy the game?"

Khalid laughed. "That depends on how much spare time you have. It can be addictive. You wouldn't be the first student who failed because he spent all his time playing WoW!"

Robert laughed back. "Will you help me a bit if I buy it?"

The Egyptian shrugged. "Sure, just ask me."

With these words he turned the key and opened the door. He gave a last nod and disappeared inside. Robert stood looking at the closed door for a few moments. He had to admit there seemed to be nothing wrong nor suspicious with Khalid's behavior. Suddenly doubts about what they were doing assailed him. Were they judging someone prematurely? Was it all a waste of time?

***

"Of course not!" Rebecca answered when he expressed his doubts. "I think we have good reason to be worried. Besides, you're playing WoW now and I suspect you're having fun. So we're not really wasting time anyway."

She was right on the mark. Robert was surprised by how quickly he'd become involved in the game. It was the combination of the magnificent fairy tale world, the thrill of taking on and killing the creatures and also the multiplayer aspect that made it so compelling. Robert had played other computer games before, but none gave that special feeling of being human in an entire living and breathing world.

"What are we going to do now? More quests?" They were talking by typing messages to each other.

Killermage sat on the ground. "No. You must do that by yourself. When it gets too hard for you, you can ask me for help. It would be too easy if I were going to help you all the time."

"Why?"

She sighed. "Because it would take away all the fun for you. Do you have any idea how powerful I am?"

"Ehhh. No."

"Do you see that Prairie Wolf there?" She pointed. At least, there was a red message in the text log that read: *Killermage points at Prairie Wolf.*

"Yes."

One moment later, there was a brief flash of light. The Prairie Wolf gave a surprised yelp and tumbled to the ground. Apparently, it had died instantly. Robert was impressed. Those wolves were tough animals. It took him several shots with his gun, followed by a fight with his axe, to kill one.

"If I killed everything for you, it would be boring. No fun at all, because you wouldn't achieve anything yourself. More important: you wouldn't learn anything. The whole point is that, by discovering things for yourself, you gradually start to understand how things work here."

"Okay," he answered. "Is it going to take long to reach level eighty?"

"I already told you that. The answer is yes. It will become easier and more fun when you progress. I'll explain it all to you later."

Robert saw a chance for a new date. "How about tonight? We can go out for a beer and you can tell me all about it."

Killermage's horse reared on its hind legs, whinnying loudly. "All right, but now back to work!" she agreed.

The next moment, Killermage started to cast a spell. It took some seconds, then suddenly a portal appeared right in front of him. When Robert moved his cursor over it, he saw it was a portal to a place called Undercity.

"This is one of the advantages of being a mage," Rebecca explained. "Mages are the only ones who never have to worry about travel. We can teleport ourselves to every major city on any continent. Travelling and distances are the greatest nuisance of WoW. The world is so large that going from one place to another often takes a lot of time. Fortunately, mages can also provide portals for other players to use. Like this one. Step through, please!"

He clicked on the portal. A few seconds later, Gunslinger found himself at a new location.

He was standing on some plateau in a big gloomy cavern. At least, that's what it seemed to be, judging by the arching ceiling of rough masonry high above his head. The surroundings gave off an indefinable purple glow. Immediately to his right was a kind of waterfall of a sickly bright green color. More of the same unhealthy green substance was cascading down from outlets in the wall that were sculpted to resemble human skulls. After the friendly and sunny grasslands of Mulgore, this was quite a transition.

As if reading his mind, Killermage poked him. "Hey, cheer up, it's not real!"

"It's depressing. Where are we?"

"This is Undercity, home city of the Undead the race Killermage belongs to and the capital of the Horde on the continent of The Eastern Kingdoms. As a fellow member of the Horde, you're welcome here!"

Killermage started to descend some stairs, turned left and walked to a bridge. Following, Robert noticed that the bridge spanned a whole river of the green fluid. Huge guards, fat and bulging like sumo wrestlers, were standing near the bridge armed with enormous cleavers that looked bigger than Gunslinger himself.

Suddenly it came to him: "Are we in some kind of sewers?"

"Yes, we're in the catacombs of the Ruins of Lordearon, a once magnificent city that stood on the shores of a large lake. The city has been sacked and destroyed. Only some ruins remain. Or so the story tells us. The Undead have taken over the extensive underground catacombs, including the sewers, and made it their home. That's why it's called the Undercity. It's not as bad as you think, by the way. This city isn't nearly as depressing as it seems."

His screen told him they had entered the Trade Quarter.

"Where are we going?"

"We're not doing the sightseeing tour. We're just here to pick up your flight path. Patience!"

Killermage ascended some stairs and they came onto a small platform. In the centre were windows that looked to be barred, like at a bank. Robert moved his cursor. It was as he thought. The man behind the window was labelled Mortimer Montague, banker.

"How do the banks work? Do I have to put my money there?"

"No, the banks are there to store your stuff. You're going to accumulate many things that you don't want to throw away. But you can't carry it all with you because your bags simply don't have enough room. So you put them in a bank. You can access your bank account at any bank around the world, no matter where you are."

Killermage had already passed the bank and was halfway a stone ramp that led farther upward, when she suddenly stopped. She turned around and went back to the bank. Robert couldn't see what she was doing. The next thing that happened was that Rebecca opened a trade window with him. She was giving him three bags.

"I suddenly realized that you have no good bags yet. Bags are important, and expensive. I just gave you the second best bags in the entire game. Many players can't afford them."

He grinned and typed another thank you. He fitted the bags in the empty slots on the bottom of his screen.

"Are you ready?" Without waiting for an answer, Killermage walked away again. Robert followed her up the ramp, which brought them onto a broad ledge. Now he could see that they were inside a huge cavern that appeared to be the city centre. The ledge they were on circled the entire space, like a gigantic balcony. On the outer side were many smaller caves that accommodated all kinds of different shops. They were right in front of a shop that sold trade supplies. Out of curiosity, he clicked on Felicia Doan, the shop keeper. Browsing her wares, he saw all kinds of thread, a fishing pole, skinning knives, and many colors of dye.

"Are you coming?"

He looked up and saw that Killermage was waiting for him. She was standing next to a rather shabby looking man. He had a green exclamation mark above his head. His tag read *Michael Garret, Bat Handler*.

"Can you click on him, please?" she asked.

He walked up to them and did as she asked. Immediately, he got a message on his screen: *New flight path discovered*.

"What does this mean? Can I fly now?"

"No, because you don't know any flight paths that are connected to this one. It's an important flight path though, because this is the major city on the continent of the Eastern Kingdoms."

"Will I be coming back here?"

"Certainly. Sooner or later your quests will lead you here."

"How do I get more flight paths?"

"By discovering them. Flying is the fastest way to travel. The only problem is, you have to discover each destination first. In other words, you have to take the walk before you can take the flight. So pay attention while you're discovering the world. Check every village or town for a flight master. They're not in every village, but there are many."

"So I have to look for green exclamation marks?"

Killermage nodded. "Now, Undercity is one of the most confusing cities there is, unless you understand its system. On the lower level, there are four quarters. The Magic Quarter, the War Quarter, the Rogues Quarter, and the Apothecarium. They're on the outer circle. The city is set up like an onion, with different layers. If you go one layer inward, you find shops that are directly connected to the quarters. One layer more inside, you find the auction house. The nucleus is the bank. From there you can take stairs to go a level up, where you find more shops. That's where we're now."

In Robert's opinion it sounded like an enormous shopping mall. Comparable to the one they once went to in Florida. Ashamed, Robert's thoughts flashed back to the trip his family had taken for his parents' twentieth wedding anniversary. He and his brother had wanted to do some shopping as the prices in the United States were ridiculously low. They decided to all go their own way for two hours in a huge shopping mall. After two hours Robert couldn't find the rendez-vous point. When the police finally brought him back to his panicked parents, he had to admit once and for all that his sense of direction was way below average. In the real world he avoided complex places, now he had to face them again in the virtual world.

"Follow me. Please don't stop. I'd hate to go back and search for you."

She ran away and Robert followed her through a maze of corridors. They passed a kind of shrine where candles burned at a sarcophagus. After taking more turns, they emerged into a courtyard. Even though everything was virtual, Robert felt glad to be in the open air again. Killermage didn't stop until they were outside the gates of the Ruins of Lordearon. A broad and perfectly maintained road led away from the city. A message on his screen told him that they were now in a zone called Tirisfall Glades.

It looked friendly enough. He saw a lot of trees and grass. It wasn't as sunny and bright as Mulgore had been, but it was certainly not unpleasant.

"Now it's time we start you off with your first profession," Killermage told him.

She started to move away again, followed by a confused Robert. When they came upon some tents set up on the side of the road, Killermage stopped.

"Here lives the skinning trainer. You can learn your first trade skill now."

Indeed, one of the men at the tented camp was a skinning trainer. They were all Undead, with the same bony look as Rebecca's Killermage. Robert selected the trainer and for a few copper he became an Apprentice Skinner.

"What can I do with this?" he asked.

"Nothing, because you still need a skinning knife. They don't sell it here. The skill allows you to skin dead animals. You can sell the leather and start making your own money from now on."

Robert had no idea how this worked. "Can you show me?"

"No, I can't because I have other professions. I'll explain some things about the WoW economy tonight. Now, let's move and take the zep."

"The zep?"

Killermage laughed in that sinister way again. "The Zeppelin. I told you how important going from A to B is. Several kinds of public transport help getting around. There are ships, zeppelins, and even a subway. The Horde has five zeppelin connections. You can use them for free, by the way."

With these words, they arrived at some platform where a huge floating ship docked. They stepped on board.

"Where are we going?"

"We're going to Ogrimmar, on Kalimdor, the other continent."

To Robert, who didn't have a map in his head, all these different names were confusing. He decided to study the world map as soon as they finished.

The ship was made of wood, just like a trading ship out of the Golden Age he was studying. The only differences were the large balloon above their heads held in place by ropes, and the propeller at the rear. Suddenly they began to move. He saw tree tops floating by beneath them, and he glimpsed two players walking through a clearing in the forest below. Shortly after, the view was replaced by a world map that showed their position and destination. This feature was the same as in an airplane. Their progress was marked by a dotted line. It started in the north of the Eastern Kingdoms, crossed the ocean, and ended with a red cross in a place somewhere on the continent of Kalimdor. The map disappeared again, and he was back on the ship. They were flying toward a tower where the zeppelin docked at another platform. Looking around, he saw that he was in a landscape that could only be described as a rocky desert.

"The zeppelin to Undercity has just arrived. All board for Tirisfal Glades!" someone yelled.

"Get off, before you're back on the way to Undercity again," Rebecca warned.

He disembarked quickly and followed Killermage down a winding staircase. When they had left the tower, Gunslinger followed her past a farm with pigs in an enclosure. They went through a monstrous gate in a huge defensive wall and emerged in the same rocky valley where they had been briefly before, en route to Raynewood Retreat.

"Ogrimmar is larger than Undercity. It consists of four valleys. We're now in the Valley of Strength. The others are the Valleys of Spirits, Wisdom, and Honor. There's also a quarter with lots of shops called The Drag."

"I'll try to remember!"

"Never mind. Come on, I'll show you the auction house."

They went into a large building where it was extremely busy. A continuous flow of people was entering and leaving through the large entrance. Robert saw that the newcomers all went to one of the clusters of people who were deeper inside. He moved closer, and exactly at that moment, by chance, a small space appeared in the crowd. This gave him a view of a burly man standing behind a low stone barricade that separated him from the crowd. It was Auctioneer Wabang, according to his tag.

"What is there to sell?" Robert asked.

"More than you could possibly imagine. The economy of WoW is almost as complex as the economy in the real world. Players need all kinds of things, from food and drink to clothing and weapons. Like in the real world there are professions, so players can learn how to craft things."

"And then they sell them here?"

"Exactly. You can set a price and the duration of the auction, and when the time is up, the item goes to the highest bidder. Most people also set a 'buy out' price. If someone pays that price, they win the auction at once."

Robert started to understand how it worked. "So if I skin some leather and put it up for auction, who would buy it from me?"

"Most likely it would be a leatherworker."

"I see. And how many professions are there?"

"Ten. Every character can only learn two different professions. Generally speaking, there are three kinds of professions. You have gathering and crafting professions. Gathering means that you collect raw materials in the world and bring them to town to be sold, like Skinning, Mining and Herbalism. These materials are used by engineers, blacksmiths, tailors, alchemists, jewel crafters and leatherworkers. Those are the Crafters. The third profession is a bit different. If you're an Enchanter, you collect your own materials."

"What's an Enchanter? Is it like a mage, someone who does magic?"

Killermage laughed. "Not exactly. Enchanting means that you magically enhance the properties of items. Every item has certain base statistics. For instance, suppose a pair of gloves has an armor value of a hundred, which gives a certain protection level. It also gives an extra twelve stamina and eight intellect. This means that the wearer gets more hit points from the bonus stamina, which grants extra health and makes him harder to kill. He also gains mana thanks to the extra intellect. Enchanters can put extra properties on an item. Extra health, extra damage, extra skill, you name it."

"All right, I understand the concept. What is mana?"

"Look at your own character icon on top of your screen. You have a green bar that indicates your health and a blue bar that indicates your amount of mana. Mana is used for all the magic you do. Your hunter will learn many magical shots, stings, traps and other abilities that consume a certain amount of mana each time you use them."

Robert checked and saw she was right.

Killermage walked out of the building. "Come on, we don't have all day. We have more things to do."

Robert followed her up the same platform where they had taken a flight that one time they had been here before. The wind rider master had a green exclamation mark. He clicked on it and learned another flight path.

"Now click again. You'll see that you have one destination you can fly to."

"To Thunder Bluff? How can that be? I've never been there. Where is it?"

"In Mulgore. As a Tauren you got that flight path because Thunder Bluff is the hometown of your race. Come on, let's fly!"

One click later, and forty-five Copper poorer, Gunslinger was on a flying animal, taking him swiftly away from the tower. He found out that he could do nothing to control the creature. He was in a taxi. Robert sat back to enjoy the flight. It took him over a river, then through a dry landscape called the Barrens. It wasn't exactly a desert, but looked more like a land that could be fertile if it rained only a little more often. A kind of oasis looked lush and happy in these surroundings. There was a lot of wildlife. He saw multitudes of giraffes, zebras called zehvras, prehistoric-looking raptors, lions, and hyenas. A herd of gazelles ran by right underneath him, so close that he felt he could almost touch them.

After maybe two minutes, his mount began to climb, and they crossed a mountain ridge. On the other side the landscape was a lot greener. A message told him they were now in Mulgore, the zone he'd started in. Shortly after, they ascended again and climbed toward a huge town built on cliffs that he recognized from the introduction movie he saw when he first launched his Tauren character Gunslinger. He landed in some kind of tower that could best be described as a hundred fifty feet high totem pole.

"Welcome to Thunder Bluff," Rebecca said. "Follow me!"

Going down, he saw two exits, through which he glimpsed parts of the town. All the houses were made of wood and canvas. When they reached the bottom, Killermage led him onto a plateau ringed with tents. In the middle was a small lake. They turned to the right.

"This will be your home town for the next few days. Remember, here's the auction house of Thunder Bluff." She pointed. "There's an auction house in each major city. They work together, so if you put something up for sale in Thunder Bluff, a player in Undercity can buy it on the auction house there." Before he could say something, she started off again.

"This is the bank, right here is the mailbox. Watch it for messages from me. I'll be sending you new gear to wear as you progress. So check your mail!"

"Yes, boss!" he answered, unsure if he was ever going to find his way back here again.

As if reading his mind, she said, "If you get lost in a big city, you can always ask one of the guards for directions. Remember that, at least."

She walked into a different building that wasn't so much a tent as a real building.

"This is the Inn of Thunder Bluff. Click on the Innkeeper and make this your home."

Robert did as she told him. A shower of rays descended on him.

"What does this mean?"

"Look inside your backpack. Do you see the hearthstone in there?"

71

He checked and saw it. He moved his cursor and saw that it would take him back to Thunder Bluff with a cooldown of half an hour.

"You can use that twice every hour to transport yourself back to your home. You can set it at any inn you like. It can be a way to get yourself out of trouble, but it's also a way to win precious travelling time."

She showed him how to enter and leave the city. Because it was built high on some isolated cliffs connected to each other by bridges, there was an elevator to the plains below. She continued to show him where to buy ammunition and where to go for training.

After that, Robert had had enough. There was only so much one could absorb. He told Rebecca so, and she agreed. He used his hearthstone to return to Thunder Bluff. Seeing that Killermage was still online, he sent her a message just before logging off: "See you tonight!"

CHAPTER IX

She was early. Robert arrived exactly at nine o'clock to find her already sitting at a table at the window. She had a large beer in front of her that was half finished. In her oversized denim shirt she looked very much at ease. The place was moderately full of people, hanging around a huge copper plated bar.

"Did you ever wonder why there are so many Irish pubs all over the world, and no English or Scottish pubs at all?" she asked by way of greeting.

"Eh, no, not really," he answered. "Do you know why?"

She shook her head. "It's not as if the Irish make the best beer in the world. Far from it. And they're certainly not the most cheerful people of our sunny island. I can't see why there are Irish pubs all over the place."

Laughing, Robert sat opposite her. The bartender came over and he ordered a large Jupiler beer. "It's even more mysterious that they serve Belgian beer," he remarked. "I'm not sure I can handle so many mysteries at the same time."

She leaned forward, bringing their heads closer together. In a slightly softer tone, just audible over the music, she said, "Right after you logged off, your neighbour came online."

He looked around. Nobody was paying attention to them. "What happened?"

She shrugged. "Not much. There were five of them, all from The Hammer of Grimstone. They met in Shattrath City, which could be called a little unusual. It used to be the hotspot and meeting point once, but was replaced as such by Dalaran two years ago. They went

73

to the Forge of Souls. They did the whole sequence, so also the Pit of Saron and the Halls of Reflection."

He held up his hands. "You lost me. What are you telling me?"

"Apart from the ordinary world, there are places called instances. The typical thing about an instance is that a player or group has it entirely to themselves. Also, they are many times more difficult."

Robert didn't understand a word. "Please clarify. I still don't get it."

For the first time, he got the feeling that she was getting irritated. The moment passed quickly, however. She brushed some curls behind her ears and answered patiently, "When you go anywhere in the regular world, any other player can be there as well. You would see each other, and he could pick the thing you came for, from right under your nose. If the player was from the other faction, say from the Alliance while you're Horde, he could attack you as well, of course. Instances are different. When you enter an instance, it's created especially for you or your group. Other players can't enter and can't interfere. If another player enters an instance at exactly the same moment as you, all that would happen is that the game would generate two separate instances."

"So it's like a parallel universe?"

She smiled warmly at him. "Very good! That's exactly how it works."

He smiled back, proud of her praise. "So you couldn't follow them?"

"No. I waited for them to finish, just out of curiosity. I must admit, they did very well. They finished in under an hour, which is fast for that set of instances. Quite an accomplishment."

Robert thought for a minute, looking out of the window at the rain. "At least that means that they weren't doing anything they shouldn't. And what happened after they finished?"

"Nothing, really. They broke up. Drimm went to Ogrimmar and bummed around the auction house for some time. He logged off after half an hour."

"So what are we going to do now?"

"We'll keep our eyes open. We must find out whether they're terrorists who are using WoW as their secret place, or if they're just innocent players with an unfortunate guild name and some strange behavior."

He looked at her, softly tapping on the table with one of the peanuts that came together with the beer in a miserable little plastic container. "This means we'll have to maintain around the clock surveillance. That's quite something. There's just the two of us!"

She looked unflinchingly back at him, holding his brown eyes for a second too long. "Yes, I realize that. You forgot to mention that I'm leaving for Edinburgh before long. This means that you're going to have all the fun, because he's your neighbour. We have to follow them in WoW, but also in the real world."

That thought had occurred to him as well, but he hadn't followed up on it until now. "Do you really think that's necessary?" He heard the denial in his own voice and answered his own question. "You're right. This is going to have consequences for my study, though. I mean, we're talking about 24/7 surveillance, in and out of the real world."

Suddenly he felt Rebecca's hand on his own. He looked up. Her eyes were on his, carrying a serious look. "In a few days we'll know whether our suspicion is correct or not. We saw them at Raynewood Retreat. We know something strange was going on there. This isn't going to take months."

He moved his head slightly to indicate his agreement. "I hope so. If what they were doing has any impact on reality, we'll know soon enough. I'll try to follow Khalid when he goes outside. Maybe we'll learn more that way."

"Just promise that you'll be careful. If these are the people who blew up an entire train station, killing twenty people just to make a point, they'll not hesitate to kill one more."

At that moment the bartender approached. Rebecca hastily removed her hand and smiled at him. He was carrying Robert's beer and also one more for Rebecca. Robert was quite sure that she hadn't ordered another drink. He felt a flicker of jealousy and arched an eyebrow at her.

"Yeah, I know, I come here too often. Let's just say that they anticipate my wishes."

He laughed and raised his glass to her. "Here's to anticipation and to wishes!"

Rebecca touched his glass with hers. "To anticipation and wishes!"

She drank deeply, draining the glass for one third. "I always get thirsty when I play WoW. Did I tell you that I joined a guild today?"

"Weren't you in a guild yet?" he asked surprised.

This time, Rebecca really laughed out loud. People at the bar looked up trying to find out what was so funny. She wasn't mocking him: it was just pure mirth finding its way out. She actually shook with it. When she had calmed down a little, she steadied herself with more beer.

"Did you really think that I just 'happened' to be on this server? Out of all those realms out there, I just happened to be on the same one as our friends?"

"I don't know. I hadn't thought about it."

"Well, let me tell you then. No, I wasn't on the Sylvanas realm before. It's possible to transfer to another realm, if you pay for it. That's what I did. I moved two characters from my own server to the Sylvanas server."

"Two? I thought you only had Killermage."

She waved her finger at him, as if he were a naughty child. "Never underestimate a girl! No, Sir, I have ten different characters!"

With a deferential bow, he picked up her empty glass and walked to the bar. The bartender made eye contact with him and nodded when Robert raised two fingers at him. He sat again opposite Rebecca. "Why ten?" he resumed.

"Because there are ten different classes. I wanted to have one of each class."

He thought back to the game for a few seconds, but couldn't come up with so many. She saw him racking his brains.

"The available classes are priest, mage, warlock, shaman, hunter, rogue, druid, paladin, warrior and deathknight."

He was impressed. "Maybe you'd better tell me a little more about it. But I mean a little more. My brain can't hold much more information after today."

"Okay, I'll keep it short. The only important thing to remember is that every class has its strengths and weaknesses. A mage for example, can do a lot of damage in a short time. That damage can also be done from a distance. The drawback is that mages can only wear armor made of cloth, which makes them extremely vulnerable. The armor value of cloth is almost zero. That's why mages are often called glass cannons. If the enemy gets too close the mage is as good as dead. On the other side of the spectrum you have the warrior, who wears heavy plate armor and can take quite a beating without dying. In between you have classes that wear leather, like rogues, and classes that wear mail, which gives even more protection."

"And does heavy plate protect against magical spells?"

"Good question, and the answer is, no, it doesn't. Resistance to magic is something else entirely, but let's not go there. I'm trying to keep it simple." Robert felt his head tumbling with all this information, but he nodded at her, not to disappoint her.

"In general, the classes are divided into three categories, according to the roles they fulfil when operating in a group. First you have the DPS'ers, which means Damage Per Second. They dish it out to the enemy. Second you have the Tanks. They are the people who close with the enemy, making them focus their attention and aggression on them. It's their job to make sure that the enemy doesn't go after the DPS guys who are actually killing him. The last category are the healers. They keep up the health of the rest of the group by casting healing spells."

"I see. And what exactly is my hunter, Gunslinger?"

"A hunter is a damage dealer, no doubt about it. So they're DPS. Hunters are strong versus cloth wearers, but pretty useless against plate wearers. Those bullets don't worry someone wearing an inch of plate."

He nodded, starting to see the logic of it.

After a big gulp Rebecca continued, "I also transferred my rogue. Rogues can make themselves invisible, which might come in handy. My rogue is Alliance by the way, so on the opposite side of the fence from your point of view. That makes it easier to sneak around. If she had been Horde, those guys from the Hammer of Grimstone could see her even when in stealth mode. No use hiding from friends, you see."

She kept up his education for over an hour and two more large beers. Robert started to become confused over the different races and classes. In his head he repeated: "Gunslinger is a hunter, belonging to the race of the Tauren, like Drimm. Killermage is a mage, belonging to the race of the Undead. There are many different races and classes, but not every combination is allowed. Undead can't become hunters, so if you want to play a hunter, you should choose from races like Tauren or ...."

After so much information about WoW Robert wanted to talk about other things with this nice girl sitting opposite. He also started to wonder why he had to know all this. When he asked her, she became dead serious again.

"I think you need the ultimate WoW crash course, because if those guys are who we think they are, you need to become an experienced player quickly. I can't do it all by myself."

"What do you mean, why are my skills so important?"

She fixed him with a penetrating stare. "First, because there are many areas where you can't follow them if you're not high enough level."

She fell silent, looking out at a wanderer and his four-legged friend resisting the rain. He watched her in turn, a little unsure. When she remained silent, he started to fidget in his chair. Finally, she seemed to notice. Without looking away, she continued, this time speaking so softly that he could barely hear her.

"Second, because I think there will come a time when we'll have to infiltrate their guild. In other words, we're going to hijack an account. Khalid's account. We're going to pretend to be him, while doing things with The Hammer of Grimstone."

He took another sip of his beer, letting it sink in. "So when I'll be playing with the character named Drimm-"

"You really have to know what you're doing," Rebecca finished for him. "If you fumble and fail, especially in a complex raid, they'll see through the subterfuge immediately. So that's why I'm trying to teach you as much as I can."

Suddenly, a thought came to him. "When exactly are you leaving?"

"In three days. As of Monday, you're on your own."

CHAPTER X

Robert didn't see or even speak to Rebecca for the next two days. She was out of town on a surprise farewell weekend organized by her colleagues from Barrera, the bar where she had worked for several months. He was amazed at how easy she had mingled with the locals, how popular she was. Although thinking about her, he wasn't really that amazed. She was simply a very nice and spontaneous person. He decided to start working on his own social contacts himself soon.

While she was gone, he threw himself at World of Warcraft, becoming addicted like he never had thought possible. He played for more than sixteen hours a day, barely taking time to eat and sleep. When he did sleep, his dreams were filled with the game. When he went out to the supermarket, he realized that his thoughts were constantly returning to the quests he was doing. In all his enthusiasm, he realized this was scary. But he had a job to do, and incidentally this job was to become an adequate WoW player. So he pressed on.

He reached level ten after a little more than four hours of playtime on Saturday. He learned how to make use of the different skills the trainer taught him along the way. He developed a kind of killing routine which didn't require him to fight prolonged close combat battles with his targets. He skinned all the animals he killed, and other dead animals as well. He quickly got the hang of the auctioning process, and soon he was making his first gold.

At level ten, he got a quest from the Hunter trainer that required him to tame and bring back an Adult Plainstrider by using some rod. What it came down to was that he had to stand motionless while the enraged animal tore into him, waiting for the taming spell to take effect. After two failed efforts because he defended himself, thereby killing it, he got it right. After that, he had to tame a ferocious wolf, which was followed by the task of taming a Swoop, one of the dangerous birds of prey.

When he'd finished these tasks, he was officially taught the skill of taming animals out of the wild to become his pet. The last thing the trainer did was send him on his way to Thunder Bluff, to seek out the trainer there. On his way to the big city, he tamed a Prairie Stalker, which nearly killed him in the process. After nursing himself back to full health, he amused himself by killing everything that came too close. This was a lot easier with the help of the sharp fangs and claws of the gray wolf that now walked by his side.

All this time, none of the members of The Hammer of Grimstone came online. When he went out at lunchtime to buy bread, he quickly put his ear to the door of his neighbour. The only thing to be heard was absolute silence. After looking right and left, he pulled a hair out of his head. He wetted it with his tongue and stuck it to the door at the point where it met the framework. If the door was opened, he would know. If it wasn't, he would know as well.

With fresh cheese and tomato sandwiches next to the keyboard, he continued his adventures in Thunder Bluff. He picked up several more quests in town, some of which required him to seek out other people in Thunder Bluff. He started to appreciate the time Rebecca had taken to give him a brief sightseeing tour. Many of the things she'd told him now started to make sense. When he began to run out of work, he was sent to a place called the Crossroads. He realised that the sandwiches were still lying untouched in the same place next to his keyboard. At once he felt hungry and devoured the food.

The instruction was to follow the road to the east, then to the north. The walk took so long that he started to wonder if he'd taken a wrong turn somewhere. But he pressed on and eventually crossed a pass that took him out of Mulgore and into a new zone called the

Barrens. The biggest difference was the level of the animals that wandered around. The wildlife in the Barrens was of a much higher level than that of Mulgore, so Robert kept Gunslinger precisely in the middle of the road with his wolf at his side. Still, he drew the attention of a level fifteen Savannah Prowler. The huge lion seemed to smell him from a distance and charged, roaring loudly. Even with the help of his pet, he didn't have a chance. It was over before he could even hurt the animal. Cursing, he walked his spirit all the way from the graveyard back to his corpse.

Even more cautious he continued his journey. After a while, another traveller appeared around a bend in the road. Robert halted him and asked if he was on the right road to the Crossroads. The level eighteen Blood Elf confirmed that he was, and that he was almost there. Relieved, he continued. He arrived at the tented town soon after. Following Rebecca's instructions, the first thing he did was to search for a flight path. No way that he was going to walk that stretch again! He found it close to the inn. Considering the multitude of quest givers around, he guessed he would be in this place for awhile. He set his hearthstone at the inn, feeling proud of himself.

He was right. There were so many quests in The Barrens that he remained there until he was level eighteen: in other words, until four o'clock that night. When he finally logged off, he'd been playing nonstop for nearly twenty hours. During that time he was invited to join a guild. This happened when he came to the aid of another player, who was beset by four lions about to chew him to pieces. Robert happened to be in the same remote place and together they fought the animals off, both of them surviving the encounter by a hair. The player was an officer of a rather large guild and Robert entered the guild at the rank of initiate.

Although Robert was sometimes called a loner in real life, in the virtual world he appreciated being a member of a guild. Three guild members were also active in the Barrens, with whom he formed a team to tackle challenges together. In a group Robert didn't receive as many experience points for his kills, but that was made up for by the advantage of rapid progression and quest completion.

On top of this his new friends taught him how to care for his pet, feeding it and training it. He became the object of much admiration and jealousy as he pulled one after another piece of equipment out of his mailbox. Rebecca had sent him a pile of leather clothing and also several guns. This meant that he could put on new gear when he reached higher levels, constantly improving his character statistics. Others told him that he was wearing the best gear imaginable. Especially the enchants that Rebecca had added seemed to be quite outrageous. Some people asked him for money, thinking he must be extremely rich to be able to afford such gear with expensive enchants on such a low character.

Finally, when he felt that he had seen every nook and cranny of the dreary zone called the Barrens, he was sent on a mission to another zone, called Stonetalon Mountains. Even though his eyes burned from the many hours of staring at a computer screen, he didn't want to go to sleep before he'd reached his new destination. Another long and hazardous journey eventually brought him to a place called Sun Rock Retreat. He acquired the flight path and took Gunslinger to the inn for some well deserved rest. For the last time he checked the whereabouts of the Hammer of Grimstone. Still there was not a single member online.

He opened the door and sneaked into the corridor, quickly checking the door of his neighbour. The hair was still there.

He awoke early, feeling stiff and tired. After playing for so many hours in a row the game had haunted his dreams. It was as if it had taken over his head. While he walked to the shower he stretched, trying to remove the most bothersome kinks in this body. Only after he'd brewed a large coffee and stretched himself out on the derelict couch in the communal room did he begin to feel a little better. There was no one around yet. It wasn't even nine o'clock on Sunday morning, so it would remain quiet in the large house a little longer. He felt something hard poking in his back and, fumbling behind him, pulled out a remote control device. Sitting back, he used it to turn on the television, tuning to BBC World.

The news was the same as ever. His thoughts wandered back to his eighteenth birthday, when his mother had presented him with the newspaper of the day he was born. They had studied it together and compared it to the paper of that present day. It had been appalling to see how little had changed over the years. People were still getting killed in more or less the same wars and for the same reasons, and the scandals in politics were interchangeable.

His interest waned, and he idly started to browse a women's magazine that had been left on the sofa. His awareness slipped away until he was almost dozing when he suddenly registered the words 'The Hammer of Righteous Justice'. It took a millisecond for these words to sink in, after which he bolted upright, pressing the remote control like a maniac to turn up the volume.

A female reporter was standing in front of an obviously expensive home. The camera panned to the right and he saw that it was situated quite secluded, like in the middle of a forest. Something seemed to be wrong with the sound. He finally noticed that he was pressing the wrong button on the remote control and corrected this. The sound came up again.

> "...from the police. So that's all we know for now, Richard."
> "Thank you, Kathleen. Please wait for us to come back to you. That was Kathleen Jones, our reporter on the scene in Jezus Eik, Belgium, where the body of Israeli top banker Benjamin Natale was found this morning. There were six body guards in the house with Natale, who have all been killed as well. The police found a painting on the scene that links the brutal murders to the same terrorist organization that bombed a train station in The Netherlands eleven days ago. Let's go back to the brief press conference that the Belgian Police gave half an hour ago."

There were images of a bald man behind a table, talking into several microphones. The sound was muted.

"Kathleen, you were at the press conference. What did the police say exactly?"

"Not much Richard. It happened only hours ago. At 2 a.m. to be exact, according to one of the neighbours who heard the sounds of shooting."

"Benjamin Natale had six armed body guards in the house, who were all killed by the attackers. What does that tell us, Kathleen?"

"That's exactly what worries the police so much, Richard. These weren't just some hired body guards, all of them were suspected former protection officers of the Mossad, the Israeli secret service. They're considered the best in the world."

"So what does that tells us?"

"That this was probably a military operation, most likely executed by special forces. There's no doubt that this operation has been prepared and trained for well."

"Kathleen, who was Mr. Natale exactly? What do you think made him a target?"

"Well, Richard, nothing is certain yet, of course. Some sources think it must be connected to the work of Mr. Benjamin Natale. He wasn't just a banker, but he was generally seen as a man behind the scenes who financed all kinds of clandestine operations against Arab interests. I just heard a rumour that insiders even connect him to a failed assassination attempt against the president of Iran."

"What can you tell us about the organization that claims responsibility?"

"They're called The Hammer of Righteous Justice and are believed to be an extreme right wing Muslim terrorist group. They claimed responsibility for the bombing of a train station in Holland not even two weeks ago. On that occasion, they left a painting on the scene with their signature on it, just like today. The police have not yet revealed more about the painting, just that they found it."

"Thank you, Kathleen. We'll be hearing more from you when there are new developments. Now we go over to Norway, where scientists claim to have found proof that the climate is warming up even faster than we thought."

Robert muted the sound again and sat looking at the screen with unseeing eyes. When he finally got up, he noticed that his coffee had gone cold. He threw it into the sink without bothering to make a new one.

He left the door of his room slightly ajar so he would hear Khalid if he returned. He called Rebecca's cell phone, but got her voicemail. He left a message and sent her a text message as well.

Not knowing anything better to do, he switched on his computer, first browsing some news sites. When they didn't tell him anything new, he logged on to World of Warcraft. The first thing he checked was the status of The Hammer of Grimstone. They were still offline, all of them.

He checked his phone several times for a reply of Rebecca. Should he call her again? He decided not to, not wanting to give the impression he was stalking her.

The members of his guild were probably still in bed, so he started doing quests by himself. There were a lot of quests available in Sun Rock Retreat, so there was plenty of work to be done.

Around noon he hit level twenty. He let out a loud whoop, slamming his fist on the table. Finally, his walking days were over! As expected, he found a message in his mailbox from some Kar Stormsinger. It invited him to come back to Bloodhoof Village in Mulgore to learn the riding skill. He went immediately, and afterward bought a mount. The Kodo was a monstrous animal. It was huge and bulky and moved with a peculiar rolling gait. Nevertheless, it took him around a lot faster and that improved life considerably.

Now that he was so much more mobile, he wanted to make use of this. He discussed his options with some members of the guild. Again, he was finding how helpful it was to be in a guild. All those people together formed an enormous pool of knowledge, and yesterday a level sixty-six warrior had even come over to help them out of an impossible fix. All in all, it made virtual life a lot easier.

There seemed to be a number of options to choose from. Several zones accommodated players levelling from twenty to twenty-five.

In the end, he decided on going to the Hillsbrad Foothills, simply because it was on the other continent and he was eager to explore a little more of the world.

So he took the zeppelin to Undercity. On the Internet he had found a website that contained an incredible amount of information about the game, including interactive maps. These helped him to his destination. Once there, he followed the main road to the village of Tarren Mill and was killed three times on the way. A level twenty-one player had to keep far away from a level twenty-five creature around here. The most stunning lesson, however, was that from now on he had to be aware of other players as well. The place was crawling with members of the Alliance, who seemed to attack every Horde player they came across. Still, he reached his destination in the end, adding Tarren Mill to his flight paths. Looking at the map, he saw that he now had one connection in the Eastern Kingdoms, from the flight point at Tarren Mill to the one he had acquired in the Undercity, when he was there with Rebecca briefly. For now, it would do.

CHAPTER XI

It was much harder than before. He was taking a lot more time to progress to the next level. He watched his experience bar all the time, getting frustrated by how slowly it was progressing. After he made it to level twenty-four, he tried to call Rebecca again. Still no answer: it just rang without being picked up. He left another message on her voicemail.

Annoyed he tried to call Andy, who happened to be at his parents' for the weekend and promised to drop by the next day. Feeling a little down, he stood to go to the toilet. Just when he was about to open the door of his room, he heard stumbling noises in the corridor. His heartbeat went up with a hundred beats a minute. Stealthily, he moved his eye to the tiny slit he had left by not closing the door entirely. It was Khalid, carrying a small sports bag in one hand and a plastic sack of some weekend store in the other hand.

Robert sprinted back to his computer and checked the friends window. He felt excited and scared at the same time. None of the Grimstones was online. He sat back in his chair, eyes fixed on the screen. He didn't have to wait longer than three minutes before he got the message *Drimm has come online*. He checked the window again and saw that Drimm was in Dalaran. A few seconds later, that changed to Ogrimmar. Another ten seconds later, Gunslinger was airborne, on his way to the zeppelin station at Undercity. He suppressed the urge that had him going to the bathroom earlier.

In his hurry, he lost his way three times in the maze called Undercity. He became so desperate that he asked a random player for the way out. When he declined, claiming he was too busy, he paid him an outrageous twenty gold just to show him to the zeppelin.

To make things worse, the zeppelin departed right before his nose. He had to wait a long time for the vehicle to make the entire return trip. When it finally berthed again, Pharad had come online also. He was in some place called Borean Tundra. Robert stepped on board, keeping the screen with the members of The Hammer of Grimstone open. Finally, the zeppelin began to move again, taking him to Durotar, the zone where Ogrimmar was situated.

Robert didn't wait for the airship to stop, but jumped Gunslinger onto the platform as soon as it came alongside. He rushed down the stairs of the zeppelin station and speeded to the city. When he went through the gates of the city, the location of Pharad changed to Ogrimmar as well. He smiled.

It was busier than it had been at his earlier visits to Ogrimmar. No doubt this was because it was Sunday, and many people had time to play. He despaired how he was ever going to find two specific players in these crowds. In the end, it was easier than he thought.

While looking at the mass of players, his eye was drawn by a movement that stood out from the rest in some way. Looking more closely, he saw it was Pharad. He also noticed what made him stand out. Most players had their name and guild designation in dark blue and some in bright green. Pharad was the only one who had a light blue text above his head. He deduced that this must be because he was in Gunslinger's friends list. To test the concept, he selected a random other player and added him to his friends list. Sure enough, his tag color immediately changed to light blue.

Meanwhile, Pharad was standing in front of the bank some distance from the mailbox. Watching the scene, Robert suddenly noticed some people on the roof of the bank building. That would make a perfect spot for him as well, because it would allow him to keep the entire square between the auction house and the bank under surveillance. He ascended the road around the bank building, discovering that on the backside of the building the roof met with the steeply rising rock bottom. He jumped onto the roof.

He sat there for nearly half an hour. All that time, nothing happened. Pharad went into the auction house once and collected some things from the mailbox afterward. Otherwise, he just stood there. According to his friends window Drimm was still in Ogrimmar, but he was nowhere to be seen. Robert didn't dare leave his post, afraid that he'd lose Pharad. Besides, the city was so big, there was no guarantee that he would actually find Drimm. He could be anywhere.

Drimm did show up in the end. Robert didn't notice him until he walked up to Pharad. He had no idea where he came from. The two moved slightly away from the crowd and stood motionless for a few more minutes. Then a mage joined them, and started to cast a spell, creating a portal. Robert moved his cursor and saw that it was to Dalaran. Drimm and Pharad stepped through and disappeared. In his window their location changed as well.

Undecided Robert hung around for a little longer, annoyed that Rebecca wasn't there to help him. He was so close, he didn't want to lose them. He supposed he could follow them to the capital city of the continent of Northrend by bribing a mage. He also knew that a level twenty-four hunter walking around in Dalaran would stick out like a Honda Civic on the grid of a Formula One race. In the end he decided to clear up those last few quests in the Barrens, that had been too hard before. Now that he was some levels higher, he should be able to complete them easily.

He flew to Ratchet and went to work on the large ridge situated to the north of the small town. After bagging the required kills, he rode back into town, straight into Drimm.

At first he didn't realize what was happening. Only when he noticed Pharad standing nearby did his brain process the information. His first reaction was one of shock. Had they somehow followed him here? Now he even experienced a moment of fear. How had they found out about him?

There was nothing to worry about. The Grimstones completely ignored the low level hunter hovering nearby. They mounted their horses and rode down to the pier. He deduced that they had just arrived at the flight path. Although it was a major coincidence, he was going to grab the opportunity with both hands.

Excited he followed them to the harbour, keeping some distance between them. Robert had seen a ship depart from there once, but had no idea where it went. It seemed that he was going to find out now. Soon, a large wooden ship sailed into the bay. It moored at the end of the pier. Several players disembarked. They were Alliance, and for a moment Robert feared they were going to kill him just for the fun of it. When they left him in peace, he realized that this was because of the proximity of Drimm and Pharad. Those Alliance cowards were probably afraid for possible retaliation of the obviously superior pair of Hordes. With clammy hands he smiled at the irony of being protected by Drimm and Pharad.

He saw them disappear into the cabin. A little hesitant, he also boarded the ship. He looked at the doorway where he'd seen them enter, but saw nobody. To remain as inconspicuous as possible, he climbed the stairs to what appeared to be another deck. Now he saw that he could climb to an even higher deck, which he did. There he sat behind one of the massive mast poles, making himself completely invisible from anybody else on the ship.

The ship started to move slowly, accelerating when it gained open water. Nervously he watched the coast fall away. He wasn't afraid, he told himself, was he? The worst that could happen to him was being killed in the virtual world. He sent Rebecca another text message for help.

The ship docked at a pier like the one at Ratchet. His screen told him he was at a place called Booty Bay. Drimm and Pharad appeared out of the cabin and left the ship. Gunslinger also stepped onto the pier. Before him was a town built on wooden poles, right against a steep rock wall.

The two of The Hammer of Grimstone didn't go into the town as he expected. Instead, they jumped right off the pier and into the water. Robert was taken completely by surprise. The last thing he expected them to do was to jump into the water. He wasn't sure what to do now. When they started to swim away and threatened to disappear, he jumped into the water as well. Wondering where this was going to lead him, he started to follow.

The swim took at least a few minutes. After that time, sandy beaches had replaced the forbidding steep rocky cliffs. He saw the two men climb out of the water at some deserted beach and start to walk along it. He was aware that he was only level twenty-four and that there were many creatures around that could easily kill him. After some thinking, he decided to follow them while remaining more or less safely in the water. Unfortunately, he couldn't swim as fast as they could walk, which meant he was losing ground to them. In the end, he took the gamble of stepping onto the beach as well. Soon after, he spotted them standing at the waterline in the distance looking at some ships that lay anchored in the shallow water just off the coast.

Suddenly, he was attacked from behind. Turning around, he saw a Human mob called a Bloodsail buccaneer swinging a curved scimitar at him. Already, he had lost nearly half his health. He popped a health potion, wondering where the hell Wolfie was. Only then did he realize that his pet had disappeared, which happened now and then. He blew the summoning whistle, and there his wolf was, immediately tearing into the pirate.

The enemy transferred his attention to the animal, giving Gunslinger some respite. He started to run away, all the while keeping an eye on the health bar of his pet. It was definitely losing the fight. Fast. As soon as the poor animal had died, the Bloodsail buccaneer started to chase Gunslinger again.

Unexpectedly, he heard gunshots. At the same moment, the pirate who had been pursuing him tumbled into the sand. Robert quit running.

"You shouldn't be here," Drimm said.

Robert scanned around and saw the level eighty hunter standing no more than ten feet away. He did some quick thinking. Should he answer? He decided to act as normal as possible. "I know. Thank you for saving me," he replied.

"This is no place for a level twenty-four. Better get out of here and return when you're stronger."

"I didn't know what was here. I saw some people swimming and wanted to see what was around the cape."

"Be careful then," Drimm said, and he turned away. Pharad had been watching this exchange silently from a few feet away. Now they both walked into the surf and started to swim away from the beach. Robert waited long enough to confirm that they were going to the ships.

Half an hour later, Rebecca finally called back. She was at Schiphol airport, about to board a plane to Edinburgh. Her grandmother had died yesterday, and she was going home a day early. And yes, she had seen the news.

Robert quickly brought her up to speed on everything that he'd seen and done. "I think they're planning something," he concluded.

"You're probably right," she agreed. "And considering the short time between the last two attacks, we'd better get onto it as soon as possible."

"I need your help," Robert pleaded. "Gunslinger is not strong enough to do anything there."

"I know. Listen, the funeral is on Wednesday. Tomorrow I'm at my parents', but in the evening I'll have all the time. Tuesday we have all day."

He felt relieved that he wasn't going to have to do this all by himself anymore. He felt sorry for her for losing her grandmother, but he also felt sorry for himself for not seeing her the next day. He had looked forward to spending another day with her and had planned a little farewell surprise himself. He pushed these selfish thoughts away.

"When will we meet?" he asked, consoling himself with the thought that he had at least the digital Rebecca to rendez-vous with.

"Tomorrow at 8 p.m. in Booty Bay," she replied. "We'll set up a webcam and a VOIP connection first. I'll email you the information. Be there!"

CHAPTER XII

Robert waited for her at the jetty at Booty Bay, a proud level twenty-seven hunter. The extra day had given him the opportunity to grab another three levels. He was getting the hang of the game.

Rebecca had been right again. *They were scouting locations. I bet we'll see them go back there very soon* she had emailed him. Indeed, a whole bunch of the Hammer of Grimstone had converged on this zone today.

Because Rebecca's rogue was an Alliance character, they couldn't talk to each other using the regular chat channel. Setting up a VOIP connection had been quite easy, so now they were talking with headsets.

Booty Bay looked exactly like a pirate town out of a cartoon. Rival ships of a faction called the Bloodsail buccaneers were anchored just around the cape, waiting to invade Booty Bay if the opportunity presented itself. They had also set up camps and minor settlements on beachfronts in the immediate vicinity of the town to disrupt trade or simply to harass the occasional traveler.

Finally, the boat arrived carrying several passengers. An impressive looking Night Elf lithely jumped off and appeared to be Rebecca's rogue. Compared to the Horde mage he was used to, the Alliance rogue looked quite different. She was tall and athletic, walking with a smooth gracefulness that was completely lacking in the mage's Undead skeleton. She was dressed in dark clothing. By her sides hung two swords, each glowing with a bright white light. She exuded danger.

"Hi, are you ready?" Robert heard over the earphones.

"Yes, how's your character called?"

"Magekiller. Let's try the webcam first." Robert laughed quietly at the pun. It was typical for Rebecca to call her Horde mage 'Killer-mage' and her Alliance rogue 'Magekiller'.

Still smiling he replied: "Okay, one moment. I've already set up Andy's laptop, and it should be ready!"

Robert opened the video chat website they were going to use to communicate and to share each other's view on the digital world. He let World of Warcraft run in the background. After a few seconds he got a notification that Rebecca had logged on, immediately followed by a shaky video feed. Then the focus steadied, and Robert saw the smiling face of Rebecca. She was just as attractive as he remembered.

"Just wanted to say hello!" she said into the camera before turning it around again. After some minor adjustments, she got it exactly right. It was focused directly on her computer screen, giving Robert a view as if he was seeing the action on Rebecca's computer almost as if it was happening on his own screen. Satisfied, Robert switched back to World of Warcraft.

"Shall we go?" he asked.

"Yes, but check if they're still here first."

Robert opened the window, and saw eight members of The Hammer of Grimstone still listed in Stranglethorn Vale, the zone Booty Bay was in. "They are," he confirmed.

"Right, you go first. It's been such a long time since I've been in this remote corner. Show me the way!"

Robert walked to the edge of the pier and jumped into the water. He started to swim southward toward the cliffs of Cape Stranglethorn. He rounded the cape close to the cliffs that loomed high over them. After a few minutes he struck out in easterly direction, letting the shoreline fall away from him. After crossing the open sea for a short while, a sand bank loomed up before him. Soon, the water became shallow, and he walked up to the sand bank. He stopped when the water reached only to his knees. He heard splashing sounds behind him. When he turned, he saw Magekiller coming out of the water as well.

"I'll clear the way for you," Rebecca assured him over the headphones.

The sand bank was populated by quite a lot of the so-called Bloodsail buccaneers. Some pirates were patrolling the coastline, others were just hanging around a few shabby tents that seemed to be erected from discarded sails and driftwood. They were all around level forty, which meant that it would be an impossible challenge for Robert, at level twenty-seven, to fight his way past one of them, let alone a number of enemies.

He heard the characteristic 'whooz' which he'd learned to recognize as someone entering stealth mode. At the same moment, he saw Magekiller disappear from sight. A few seconds later, she reappeared some distance away, right in the midst of a cluster of four buccaneers. A knife glittered, weapons clashed, and a few heartbeats later the four pirates were down. Without hesitation, Magekiller stormed the next two targets, transforming them to corpses just as swiftly and efficiently.

Robert started to follow her, carefully using her path, staying out of 'aggro range' of the surviving buccaneers. He safely reached the other side of the bank, where Magekiller stood waiting for him.

"I think the Grimstones are at the farthest ship," Rebecca said.

Robert looked at the silhouettes of the three pirate ships that could be seen in the distance. The one Rebecca meant was barely visible from where they were standing.

"Maybe we should check the others out as well, just to be sure."

In answer, Rebecca started to swim toward the nearest ship. It was anchored at a tiny island, that sported a fairly large palm tree. As they came closer, Robert could see that another pirate ship was anchored at the same island as well, just on the other side. Both ships had their gangways down close to each other. Several Bloodsail buccaneers were patrolling the island.

"You hide behind the palm tree, near that rowing boat," Rebecca instructed him. Obediently, Robert steered Gunslinger toward the south side of the island, moving behind the tree and out of sight of the ships. When Robert had finished positioning Gunslinger, he switched his view over to Rebecca's screen. She was on the ship already.

"We'll have it checked out in a minute." With these words, Magekiller became invisible and walked right past two level forty-two Bloodsail deckhands standing on the deck. She entered the superstructure through an open door and descended some stairs. Swiftly she walked through the ship, obviously knowing her way around. There was nobody to be seen, apart from the crew of Bloodsail personnel. In a separate room she came on Captain Keelhaul. Rebecca moved behind him and suddenly stabbed him in the back. He went down immediately.

"No reason to leave the bugger alive, wouldn't you say?"

Robert swallowed. "No, not really. Do we check the other ship now?"

At the other ship Rebecca found more or less the same. She moved stealthily past the pirates, only killing Fleetmaster Firallon when she encountered him. Rebecca jumped off the ship and walked over to Gunslinger.

"Let's go. They must be at the third ship."

Robert switched back to his own screen and followed Magekiller into the water. Now they were closer, he could see that the third ship was anchored at a little island as well. They set out for the southern tip of the island.

Soon, Robert saw that they had found their quarries. A group of players huddled together at the base of the ship's gangway. He moved his curser over the group, getting the confirmation. These were members of The Hammer of Grimstone, Drimm among them.

"It's them!"

"Yes, I saw. Now we have to be careful. You're going to the other side of this tiny island. Stay well clear of the coast. Hurry up!'

Robert did as she told him, positioning Gunslinger some thirty yards south of the beach, treading water. After that, he switched back to the video link with Rebecca's computer screen. She was

97

already in stealth mode, standing no more than fifteen yards away from the Grimstones. Two of them were turned in her direction, looking straight through the invisible rogue.

"Are we going in?" he asked her.

"Let's observe them from a distance first. Just to get some idea of what they're up to."

Right at that moment something happened. The group of eight split up, four players moving to the stern of the ship, the other four positioning themselves directly opposite the gangway. When they passed her, Rebecca moved backward a little, so she was standing ankle deep in the water.

"What do you think they're doing?" Speaking the words, Robert noticed that he was whispering involuntarily.

"I don't know," Rebecca replied, also in a hushed tone. "It looks like they're preparing for something."

Abruptly, they all started to move. The group of four that was closest to them rushed the gangway and disappeared from view as they boarded the ship. There was a short burst of gunfire. It took little imagination to guess the fate of the crew on the deck. Two Grimstones briefly appeared at the railing as they mounted the stairs to the elevated upper deck. Again, gunfire told the story.

Meanwhile, the other group had split up again. Two were now guarding the lower side of the gangway resting in the sand, while the other two were standing guard at the railing above.

After maybe four minutes in which nothing happened, the four who had boarded the ship first came running down the gangway. They turned right as soon as their feet hit the sand and ran away in the direction of the opposite side of the little island. The others ran in the other direction, coming close to the hidden Magekiller. Drimm was one of them, and Robert could see every detail of his clothing. He was wearing a magnificently colored cloak that billowed behind him as he ran. His shoulder armor looked most impressive, bulging like the protection of an American Football player with some electrical looking spark that pulsed on and off. On his back he wore a huge war axe glowing with a bright white light.

"I definitely think they're practicing for something," Rebecca said, reminding Robert of why they were here.

He nodded. "Yes, but for what?"

"Isn't it obvious? They're practicing how to attack a ship. The question is, why?"

At that moment, the Grimstones all returned to the spot where they had been standing when they first saw them. They stood close together about fifteen yards from Magekiller. Apparently, some conversation was taking place. Suddenly, Rebecca started to move Magekiller forward, right in the direction of the group.

"What are you doing?"

"I think they're going to do it again. We're going to sneak on board and watch the action from close by."

Robert held his breath as she walked slowly by the small crowd of Grimstones, passing them at a range of no more than five feet. It seemed she was going to successfully sneak on board. All of a sudden, when she was halfway up the gangway, something happened.

It was Drimm who suddenly shot some kind of flare into the sky, almost immediately followed by another flare fired by someone else. At the same time, the group dispersed, fanning out as if a poisonous snake had dropped out of the air right in their midst.

Rebecca reacted with lightning reflexes. Robert saw her click on a button, which increased her speed significantly. A second later she exploded onto the deck. Somehow the stealth of Magekiller was broken, because the Bloodsail Deckhand standing in her path immediately swung a sword at her. Without breaking stride, Rebecca pressed another button, making Magekiller disappear again. A few more steps brought her at the other side of the ship. With a huge jump Magekiller cleared the railing, hanging suspended between heaven and earth for a moment, before plummeting down into the water below. The fall took her several feet under the surface.

"Phew, that was a close call!" Rebecca exclaimed.

"Do you think they saw us?"

"I don't know. Sometimes players are alerted to the presence of a stealthed enemy by a sound. I think that's what happened. Call it bad luck."

"What do you think, did they spot us?"

"My guess is that they didn't, even though it was a close call. The most significant proof for that is that nobody shot at us or cast a spell on us. That means that none of them managed to actually target us."

"Right," Robert said unconvinced.

"Did you see the flares? Those are why hunters are so dangerous to rogues. When a hunter fires off a flare, all invisible enemies in a short range become exposed. Hunters also have the ability Track Hidden, which gives them an improved chance of detecting enemies in stealth mode."

Robert thought back to what had just happened. "So your reaction was probably quick enough?"

She laughed. "They're good, really good. Did you see how fast they reacted as a team? That was incredible teamwork and shows that they've fought many times together. But I'm at least as good as any of them. Never forget that on my own server, I am one of the three most successful Arena fighters. I think that I used Vanish just in time. That ability allows the rogue to disappear for a short time in the deepest stealth, even in the middle of a fight."

"But they do know that *someone* was there."

"Yes. That shouldn't bother us too much though. They don't know who, and they don't know why. There are a lot of Alliance players around."

She continued to swim away from the ship, only breaking the surface at a safe distance. They looked back at the ship for some time, not seeing any movement.

"You go back to Gunslinger and walk up to the ship. You're not too suspicious here, a level twenty-seven hunter doing a quest. You're low level, but it's not entirely impossible. Tell me what you see."

Robert activated World of Warcraft again and was back at the view of the still water treading Gunslinger. He swam toward the beach, hesitating a few seconds before actually leaving the safe water.

"What do you see?" Rebecca sounded impatient.

"One moment, I'm almost there!"

He walked up the beach toward the ship. All the Bloodsail buccaneers were dead.

"I see nothing, just a lot of dead pirates. They're gone."

"We're being stupid. Check your social tab!"

Cursing for not thinking of that himself, he opened the Friends window. Sure enough, all the members of The Hammer of Grimstone were listed in other locations. Only one was still in Stranglethorn Vale. It was Caliburr, an Undead rogue. He told Rebecca so.

"Damn! Let me think for a moment."

She remained silent for over a minute. When she spoke again, she sounded unsure for the first time. "Do you think we should send them a message? Or at least piss them off a bit?"

"What do you have in mind?"

"It's no coincidence that they left a rogue behind. I bet he's lying in ambush, to see if the invisible enemy returns. But what if we ambushed the ambusher? It might give away that we're here, but it'll also worry them. Maybe it'll worry them enough to postpone executing their little rehearsal in real life."

"Can we do that?"

"Sure, we have an advantage. You. Because you're Horde as well, he isn't invisible to you. You can enter the ship, pretend you're just a player on a quest, and tell me where he's hidden. He won't see me coming, but I'll know exactly where he is.

Robert thought about it. "I still think it's better to remain anonymous to them. Let them guess whether there was someone here or not. And what it meant. If we kill Caliburr now, we'll alert them to the fact that someone is actually taking an interest in them. We don't want them to become even more paranoid. It's hard enough as it is.

Rebecca let his words sink in. "I guess you're right. Sometimes I'm too enthusiastic. But I still think you should go in and check what Caliburr is doing."

"That's right. I'll do it now!"

Robert walked up the gangway and onto the deck. He saw nothing but more corpses. Cautiously, aware that any surviving Bloodsail buccaneer attacking him would pose serious problems, he entered the superstructure. The two guards were dead. He descended the stairs, coming into the hull of the ship. Large cannons were positioned at the gun ports. Crates were everywhere, as were the bodies of dead buccaneers. Robert saw at least six corpses scattered on the floor. One more was in a strange position, more or less hanging over a cross beam. He tried to remember the layout of the two other ships they had been in earlier, and turned right toward the captain's quarters.

He saw him in the hut adjacent to the captain's. Caliburr was in stealth mode, just standing there, a dead Bloodsail buccaneer at his feet. Through the other door, he could see the corpse of Captain Stillwater on the floor. On an impulse, he addressed the level eighty rogue. "Hi, could you help me with killing the Captain when he spawns again? I failed twice yesterday."

It took a few moments before Caliburr reacted. He wasn't subtle. "Piss off," was all he had to say. Immediately, Robert regretted holding Rebecca back from killing him.

"Thanks a lot," he replied, giving him a wave and a cheer. He walked into the next cabin, turning sharply to the right to stand immediately around the corner and out of sight of Caliburr. He started to use his hearthstone to return home.

"Rebecca, next time you may kill the bastard. Slowly and painfully!"

CHAPTER XIII

Afterward, Robert and Rebecca spoke on the phone for nearly two hours. She was adamant about her interpretation of what they had seen.

"There can be no doubt about it," she repeated again. "They're preparing for an attack on a boat."

Robert wasn't really arguing with her. He had to admit that, until today, he hadn't even considered the possibility of the Grimstones using WoW as a practice ground. Now the idea was taking root in his head. It wasn't unlikely that the terrorists were using the virtual world not only for communications, but for training and preparation as well. At the least, it was a scenario that had to be considered.

He just didn't jump to firm conclusions as fast as she did. On the other hand, there was no denying the facts. The question remained what they were going to do about it. Even if the Grimstones were preparing for an attack on some boat in the real world, what were they going to do about it? How were they going to stop them?

They discussed the question at length. Rebecca thought that Robert should return to the police with what they had discovered so far. Robert didn't see the point.

"We have no hard or conclusive evidence whatsoever," he repeated again. "I have nothing new to show them!"

He heard her yawn over the phone. He was getting tired as well. "Maybe we should sleep on it," he suggested. "Tomorrow is another day!"

"Yes, maybe we should. Hey, Robert-" She stalled.

"Yes?"

"I think we're a great team. Speak to you tomorrow. Sleep well!"
He smiled. "Sleep well!"

He sat thinking in his chair for a minute. A sudden sound drew his attention to his computer screen. *Drimm has gone offline* he read. On an impulse, he opened his Friends window again. Three of the members of The Hammer of Grimstone were still online in some place called Onyxia's Lair.

He debated what to do. Should he play on for awhile? Try to reach level twenty-eight tonight? He looked at his watch. It was two o'clock in the night.

"Just one more quest!" he promised himself.

The next morning he cursed his lack of discipline. He had played on for nearly three hours, telling himself time after time he would stop after *this* quest, and then, after the next. In the end, he played on until he reached level twenty-nine.

When the alarm clock woke him, he felt dead tired, just as if he had drank too much the night before. Even the headache felt the same. He shuffled to the shower and dressed in bright clothes afterward, adopting Andy's tactic for the day after a heavy drinking party. Feeling slightly better, he went downstairs in search of breakfast and coffee. After collecting all of this on a plate, he took one of the *Herald Tribunes* off the rickety narrow table in the hall and went back to his room.

The *Herald* had devoted a whole spread, two pages, to the assassination of the Israeli banker in Belgium. The article provided a detailed reconstruction drawing of the shooting, together with several photos of the house and the grounds. The movements and actions of the attackers had been marked with arrows. It was an informative article that showed exactly what had transpired on that night. Robert scanned the article and emailed it to Rebecca. He sent her a text message telling her to check her mail. Having done all that, he finally had breakfast.

She called him half an hour later. "Let's go back to Raynewood Retreat. I have a hunch. Let's compare the layout of that place to the pictures in the paper. Let's get confirmation."

He coughed. "Good morning to you, too!"

"Yes, yes, we don't have much time. I have to go in an hour. What level are you now?"

"Twenty-nine!" he answered proudly.

Robert wasn't getting the praise he was looking for. "You're not going fast enough. But it's more than enough to go to Ashenvale. Do you know where it is?"

"Eh, yes. It's to the north of The Barrens, isn't it?"

"Correct. You fly to Crossroads and take the northern road out of town. Follow it all the way to the border with Ashenvale. Don't stray. Ignore quest givers. Run from beasts that attack you. When you're in Ashenvale, keep following the road. When you get to a T-crossing, take the right fork. Follow the road signs to a place called Splinter-tree Post. I'll meet you there in fifteen minutes."

He started to answer, but before he could open his mouth, she had already finished the call. He looked at his phone for a few seconds, stunned by her brusque behavior.

She found him near to Splintertree Post, riding up to him as he reached the crossing. She motioned him to follow, which he did dutifully. A short while later, they were standing in front of the towering building of Raynewood Retreat again.

"What do you think?" she asked.

He moved backward to the sloping path that gave access to the retreat from the road below, taking in all of the relative positions. He compared them to the map from the newspaper once more.

"It's remarkably similar," he said. "Even the placing of the entrance at the back of the building is more or less similar."

"I feel the same. It looks as if they're indeed using WoW as their training ground. This can't be a coincidence." Killermage walked the short distance to the back yard, totally ignoring the Cenarion Defenders patrolling the area. She made a complete turn, studying the building, gardens, paths and access road.

Robert watched in fascination how she drew the aggression of no less than three Defenders, who rushed to attack her. Within seconds, they had her surrounded and were swinging and slashing swords at her, grunting with the effort. She made no move to defend herself. Suddenly, the body of Killermage was surrounded by a transparent nimbus of energy that seemed to absorb all the blows of the weapons. Robert clicked on her health bar and got confirmation that it was indeed still at one hundred percent. So they weren't even scratching her. If they had attacked Gunslinger instead of Killermage, he would have been dead on the ground.

"Impressive. They're not even touching you!"

"What? Oh, the mobs. Yes, irritating."

With that, Killermage raised her arms to the air and started channeling a spell. A terrible hailstorm descended from the clear sky, pummeling her assailants with the largest shards of ice Robert had ever seen. One by one they fell to the ground, killed by that sudden, local blizzard. When they were all dead, the weather returned to normal. The mage stood with three corpses at her feet and started to laugh. It sounded eerie in the silence of the gloomy forest.

"Maybe I should have chosen to become a mage after all," Robert said admiringly. "That was a nice trick!"

She winked at him. "The best protection is simply the ability to kill your opponent sooner than he can kill you. Mages are extremely good at that."

"I can see that. Are we done here?"

"I've seen enough. As far as I'm concerned, there's no doubt left. This is the place where they prepared for their attack on Benjamin Natale."

Although Robert had been playing WoW intensively the last days, Rebecca was unsatisfied with his progress. That evening, on the phone, she told him again that he wasn't going fast enough. "Besides, when we're going to infiltrate their guild at some point you need to be ready and capable for that," she repeated.

"How am I going to speed it up? I'm already playing nearly day and night!" Robert felt irritated. He had come to the Netherlands to study and to have a good time, not to hunt terrorists and be bullied to level up faster by some Scottish girl. Even if it was such a nice Scottish girl. Then he realized that without all this, he wouldn't know her at all. Robert sighed.

"I know, but you're not efficient. You're completely ignorant and you're running around like a headless chicken."

This remark stung. He was getting better and better and able to handle most situations. He had faced and killed many foes and overcome some daunting challenges. And wasn't he leveling a lot faster than the other people in his guild? No one had made such a jump in levels as he had. "What should I do better then?" he asked gruffly.

She remained silent for a few seconds. "Are you using any add-ons?"

"No. What are those?"

She cursed. "Little programs you can download and add to your WoW interface. They're designed to make life easier. The first one you should have is Quest Helper. And something like Map Coords."

"What do they do?" he asked curiously.

"My guess is that you're losing a lot of time by wandering around, trying to find the enemies or items that you need for your quests, am I right?"

This was true, and he said so. Only yesterday he'd spent nearly twenty minutes trying to locate some cave before he abandoned the quest in despair and frustration.

"Quest Helper will show you on the map where you have to go. Also, it'll tell you exactly which enemies to kill to get what you need. Besides it'll show you the most efficient order to complete the quests in your quest log, so you won't spend ten minutes getting to some place to do a quest, only to discover later that you had another objective in the area."

Robert smiled ruefully. "That happened more than a few times!" he admitted, although he wondered why she hadn't told him this before.

"That's what I thought. The other add-on will show you coordinates on the map of each zone. That helps when you look something up on the Internet. Many players use coordinates and will generally explain things by using those. For instance, they'll write that you must follow the road until 47.66, then head due west until you reach the entrance to the hidden path at exactly 49.55. Such advice is useless if you don't have an add-on that generates those coordinates for you."

She told him to open his Internet browser and guided him to an Internet site where he downloaded the add-ons. After that, she made sure that he installed them the right way.

"Sorry about this. I should have thought of this ages ago. Now you get some sleep. I'll take over your character tonight and make up some of the time lost."

He hesitated. "Does that mean I can't play?"

Laughter cascaded over the telephone line. "You're becoming addicted, aren't you? It's only for one night. Now get offline and to bed!" With these words she signed off, leaving Robert with no alternative than to obey her orders. Just before drifting off to sleep, he sent her a text message wishing her good luck.

***

He slept late. The last few nights his dreams had been filled with the game, but this night he slept peacefully and easy. When he finally woke up, it was nearly ten o'clock in the morning, and he felt refreshed and happy. Back from the shower, he dressed in sportswear and went outside for some exercise.

The weather was remarkably soft for the end of October, and Robert inhaled deeply while he strolled to the Witte Singel on his leisure. The Witte Singel was a minor slow river that ran just outside the city center, bedded between broad banks of gently sloping grass. He crossed a bridge and, when he reached the outer bank, he started running.

After twenty minutes his mobile phone rang. It was his mother. He settled on a public bench and spoke with home for nearly half an hour. He felt a little guilty about neglecting his study duties, especially as his parents were so interested in his progress. When he finished the call, he saw that he'd received a text message from Rebecca. It was sent ten minutes before, saying that she was finished with Gunslinger and that she was going to grab some quick sleep and would be out until the evening.

Have you been playing until now? he sent back, astonished.

The answer came immediately: *Yes, let me sleep now. Will explain later.*

Her 'later' proved to be hardly an hour in the future, when Robert had showered for the second time and was waiting for his computer to boot. He was sitting at his desk, accompanied by a container of milk and a plate of sandwiches.

"I thought you were sleeping," he said accusingly when he answered her call.

He heard her yawn. "Yes, but I couldn't sleep. And I have to go out in an hour anyway, so I decided it was no use."

The computer was ready, and Robert started World of Warcraft. A few seconds later he was looking at Gunslinger. He saw immediately that he was in another place. He also noted that his wolf had been replaced by a pig.

"Now tell me, what have you done?"

She laughed. "Congratulations! You're the proud owner of the ultimate level thirty-two character. I gained three levels and even dipped in battlegrounds to get you some extra gear."

"Battlegrounds?"

"Yes, those are places where players of the Alliance and the Horde meet each other in open combat. You receive special points and tokens for participating and winning in battlegrounds. With these, you can buy special items and gear that are significantly better than what you can get in normal play. At this level anyway."

Robert opened his character window and moved his cursor over all the new items that were equipped on his character. Then he checked his statistics.

"My God, I have double the health and power!"

The smugness oozed out of the phone's receiver. "Nice, isn't it? You may thank me now!"

Laughing, but still incredulous, he thanked her. "How did you do it?"

"First of all, I did the battlegrounds. You always play against opponents that are roughly your own level. This means that, at level twenty-nine, Gunslinger could still play in the bracket from level twenty to level twenty-nine. At twenty-nine you're strong, but at thirty, you're at the bottom of the bracket thirty to thirty-nine."

"I see."

"Next, I crafted some items myself and bought more at the auction house. The next few levels you'll especially appreciate the Raptor Hunter Tunic and the Master Hunter's Rifle. That gun is vastly superior to anything that's normally obtainable at your level. The same goes for the chest piece."

"The enchants are pretty special, too," he remarked.

"That's the bonus. The plus fifteen agility enchants on your two swords were pretty expensive, by the way."

"They look good!" he complimented her, noting the green magical glow coming off his swords. He was silent for awhile, studying his new equipment again.

"So what am I going to do now?"

"I've positioned Gunslinger in the Arathi Highlands. I want you to stay there until you're level thirty-three. After that, you go to Stranglethorn Vale and do the quests involving the trolls. Ignore everything else. Then you go on to Tanaris and right after, the Hinterlands. I already sent you an email with the details and the quests you have to do. Just follow the instructions and you'll be all right."

"Okay. One last question. Why the pig?"

Rebecca chuckled. "Don't be fooled by appearances. True, a pig doesn't look as slick or dangerous as a tiger or a wolf. But at this level, it's definitely superior. It has a capability called Charge, which means that it charges at the enemy really fast, knocking it senseless and stunning it for a moment. Charge also interrupts any spell casting an enemy is doing at that moment. Apart from that, a pig is a little sturdier than a cat. It may not do all the damage, but it can take a lot more damage before it dies."

It went like a breeze. Now, he was so strong that he was able to complete quests that were several levels above him. Many quests also rewarded pieces of equipment, but until he hit level forty, which was only one day later, nothing he found or won was better than what Rebecca had given him. He zipped through the grassy Arathi Highlands, the coastal area of the jungles of Stranglethorn Vale, the deserts of Tanaris and the woodlands of The Hinterlands.

At level forty Rebecca joined him with Killermage and together they ran through several instances, earning him another heap of experience points. Rebecca again provided him with a new set of gear and equipment, which was superior in another way.

"Hunters have to wear leather until they reach level forty," she explained. "After that, they can wear mail, which gives a lot more protection."

They played together for the next several days, becoming more and more attuned to each other's playing style. Robert enjoyed the time they spent together, although it was only in the virtual world. Rebecca gave him many useful tips and guidance, and at the end of the week he reached level fifty-eight, the minimum level required to go through the Dark Portal to Outland. For all of this time, none of the members of the Grimstones came online. Khalid hadn't been home for three full days. They worried many times about what they might be doing or where they were. They were both convinced that soon they would learn about a new attack, most certainly on a boat. Just like Rebecca, Robert felt powerless and frustrated about not being able to do anything to stop it. So the celebration at reaching the important milestone of level fifty-eight was muted and dull. He'd been working hard to reach it, but felt a little deflated now the moment was finally there.

They were standing in front of the Dark Portal in a zone called The Blasted Lands. It was one of the most depressing surroundings

Robert had encountered so far. He wondered for a moment about the people who had given names to the different zones. It seemed that the drearier the zone was, the better the name reflected the look and feel of the place. Like The Badlands, The Barrens, and now The Blasted Lands. Maybe it was to warn people who preferred nicer surroundings.

The Dark Portal was the only connection between Azeroth and Outland, that was added to the game as an expansion. Rebecca had explained how the two continents of Kalimdor and the Eastern Kingdoms had been the entire game until early 2007. The highest level a player could achieve back then had been level sixty. On January fifteen, 2007 the makers of World of Warcraft, Blizzard Entertainment, had added a whole new world. It was situated somewhere else in the Universe and could only be accessed by passing through the Dark Portal, which appeared right there in the Blasted Lands. Outland not only offered many new zones, challenges, and adventures, but also the possibility to progress to level seventy. Nearly two years later, Northrend was added, raising the level cap to eighty.

In only five weeks Blizzard would be releasing a new expansion again, this time not only adding new territories, but redesigning all of the original areas as well. The level cap would be raised to eighty-five. Rebecca had explained to him that the original game had become technologically outdated over the years and needed a complete makeover. This surprised him, as he'd been playing in exactly those areas until now and hadn't found them lacking in anything.

She was determined that Robert should be level eighty when the new expansion was released. She'd explained to him how important it would be to start exploring the new zones together with the members of the Hammer of Grimstone.

For now, he put all those thoughts aside and focused on his first steps outside Azeroth.

He stood staring at the enormous portal, which resembled a gigantic open doorway, with bolts and strobes of blue energy skittering and flashing on its circular surface. Stairs led to the entrance. Near the foot of the stairs was a quest giver. He approached the quest giver and received, surprise surprise, orders to go through to the other side.

"Say goodbye to Azeroth!" Killermage yelled. She guided her warhorse up the staircase and made it jump right at the moment she reached the portal. Floating a few feet above the ground, she disappeared as soon as she made contact with the surging energies.

Gunslinger walked up the stairs and hesitated for a moment. After a few seconds he took two more steps and vanished into the Dark Portal as well.

CHAPTER XIV

Dawn was still far away, and it was as silent as it would ever be. It's often said that sleep is the deepest around five o'clock in the morning. True or not, the stealthy movements in the darkness were so silent that they wouldn't even have woken the lightest of sleeper.

There were several yachts moored at the long wooden dock that jutted out into the lake, running parallel to a similar slippery boardwalk alongside the quay. Three of the ships were more or less permanently inhabited. The last ship at the dock had a few electrical lights burning at the railing and several more at various places on the deck. The faint humming of the heating system could be heard. It was, after all, early November.

The illumination on the luxurious yacht spilled over onto the dock, creating grotesque figures of light on the otherwise dark black wooden beams. The moving figures were careful to avoid those pools of light. They glided soundlessly in the edges of the darkness toward their positions. Only the faintest shuffle of rubber soles on solid wood could be heard.

When they stopped moving altogether, the silence deepened even more. It remained that way for at least three minutes.

Suddenly, at a signal that no observer could have seen, they came in motion again. Four shadows detached themselves from the utter darkness of the side of a small electricity divider positioned near the edge of the pier. They moved swiftly to the gangway and crossed it, diving left and right for the cover of dark patches as soon as they were on board. A voice whispered, issuing instructions only audible on the earpieces each of the men was wearing.

Right at the moment that the dark shapes had raised themselves, a door swung open. Bright light spilled out of the cabin, chasing away the shadows and revealing the four men on the deck.

The leader of the assault team immediately recognized the danger they were in. If the man raised the alarm, success would hinge on the outcome of the fire fight that was certain to erupt. He didn't doubt they would win, by numbers and the element of surprise on their side. He also realized that the law would descend on the scene swiftly, making their escape much harder.

He seized the instant during which the surprise of the man in the doorway was even greater than that of the intruders. He acted while all the others were still staring at each other in confusion or trying to look away from the bright light that was blinding them.

Training had taught him to focus on the darkest spot near the light. Experience had taught him that the oblong tool the man was carrying was a gun. Instinct had taught him how to act to survive. Before anyone understood what was happening, he had raised his hand and pulled the trigger. Twice. The muted plopping sounds hardly disturbed the silence of the night, but the clinking of shells on the metal deck did.

Hit in the chest, the man started to sway. It appeared as if he was undecided about whether to fall down or not. It didn't matter, because the one who had shot him reached him in three fast strides and grabbed him by his oversized coat. He jerked the man roughly out of the light and pushed him against the side of the superstructure, putting a hand over his mouth at the same time. Ignoring the muffled gurgling sounds that tried to escape, he put his gun against the underside of the man's chin and pulled the trigger again. This time, the tension left the body, and he let it slump to the ground.

"Hé, wat is dat? Waar is Bart? Wie ben jij?"

These challenges, voiced in loud Dutch, came from another man, who was standing in the doorway, backlit by the bright light inside. He was squinting in an effort to make some sense of what was happening. It would take his eyes at least thirty seconds to adjust to the darkness outside. That would never happen.

The other three infiltrators shook off their paralysis at the appearance of another target. And what a target it was! He was just standing there, completely blinded, in a halo of helpful light from inside.

A quick look was exchanged between them. A decision was made. One of the men in the dark clothes aimed his silenced gun and fired twice. Both shots hit the target right in his heart, killing him instantly.

The corpse didn't even hit the ground. Having put the first body neatly out of the way, the killer of the first victim was ready to collect the second one. One second after the two bullets had ended his life, exactly at the moment that the muscles in the legs had gotten the final orders to collapse, the dead man was taken under the armpits and held upright. Shuffling backward, his caretaker laid him next to his former friend in a dark spot on the deck.

The leader signaled with two fingers in the air and pointed at the open door. One of the men stayed on deck, while the other three entered. They closed the door behind them, plunging the deck in near darkness again.

Once inside, they split up. Two went down into the hull, the third made a quick sweep of the small upper cabin. Having established that there was no one hiding there, he took up his post at the upper side of the stairs.

Meanwhile, the team below had located another guard keeping watch in the kitchen area. They could see him sitting at a small table. A television with the sound turned on loud was showing replays of a boxing match. The man had his back to them. It appeared that he was eating a sandwich. On the left side of the table was a gun.

They were concealed behind a blue curtain meant to keep the warmth from escaping the lower cabins. From their position they had a good view of the kitchen area. The leader signaled something with his fingers and the other one nodded. He went into a crouch and shuffled slowly toward the man at the table, careful to keep below the level of the cupboards. When he was no more than two feet away, he looked back and got a nod in confirmation.

Two heartbeats later, he stood and approached the man from behind. He must have made a sound, because the man started to turn around. There was no alarm in his movement, probably because he just expected the return of his companions. He had no chance at all.

The attacker looped a thin cord around his neck and pulled hard. This was done in such a practiced manner that it was almost like a show by an illusionist. The man made no sound at all, having his windpipe closed so suddenly. With the same smooth fluid movement, the attacker conjured a knife from somewhere and moved it upward and sideways just below the ribcage of his victim. He held the man like that for a few seconds before he slowly and carefully lowered the body to the ground. There had been no struggle and no sound. The boat remained totally silent. Brief eye contact and a nod finished this stage. The knife was wiped clean on the clothing of the corpse on the ground and disappeared as magically as it had appeared.

The two men went down a small corridor. There was a door to the right and one in front of them. They ignored the first and focused on the latter. Again, the leader put up his hand, this time showing three outstretched fingers.

Silently, the leader opened the door. He moved it just so much that a small crack appeared. From inside, they could hear the sound of heavy breathing and faint intermittent snoring. The soft light from the bulb in the corridor showed some of the inside of the cabin. Without a sound, the door was opened further. The leader raised his gun and aimed at the immobile lump on the bed, covered by white sheets. He pulled the trigger six times.

Blossoms of bright scarlet appeared on the silken sheets. After the third shot there was a short convulsive movement from the shape on the bed, which lasted only until it was hit by the next shot.

While the leader walked purposefully to a small bench on the opposite site of the room, the other drew away the bed covers. He revealed a man with a short beard of perhaps forty years old. He checked for a pulse. Finding none, he grunted with satisfaction.

He turned upon hearing a click. The leader had revealed a safe hidden under the bench. He must have known the combination to open it so quickly.

The safe was quite large. Inside were several plastic bags with a powdery substance, which the leader threw carelessly aside. He was more interested in what lay underneath. Thick packets of paper money were stacked neatly side by side on the bottom of the safe. He took one out and held it up to the dim light. It was about two inches of hundred Euro bills. Quickly he removed the small bag from his back and started to put the stacks of money inside. When he was finished, the two men climbed back up again and met their partner in the small upper cabin. Together, they went out onto the deck and, taking the fourth one with them, they left the ship.

On the dock they were joined by two more dark clad men who had been keeping watch there. Forty yards away, another two men saw the group emerge, and they, too, left their positions silently. Only minutes later, three separate cars moved away from the small harbor. The small Dutch town on the edge of the IJsselmeer slumbered on, unaware of the horrible discovery that would be made in only a few hours.

CHAPTER XV

"He's back," Robert said as soon as he was out of possible earshot. He was bounding down the stairs while talking on his mobile. "No doubt about it. I heard him in the corridor, and the hair I fixed at the door is gone."

"When do you think he returned?"

"I don't know. Anytime last night or early this morning."

Rebecca calculated. "So he was gone for four days."

"That's right."

"I wonder what these absences mean," she answered. "The last time he was out for a couple of days, an Israeli banker died."

Robert grunted as he fixed the phone between his ear and his shoulder because he needed two hands to force open the heavy front door against the strong wind sweeping through the street.

They talked while he hurried to his class. Again, Rebecca stressed that he contacted the police again. Robert was still hesitant.

"Let's wait and see if anything happens. Only if there was indeed an attack involving a boat, I think we have something conclusive to tell them."

When class was finished, Robert hurried out of the classroom. He was almost through the main exit of the building when he felt a hand on his shoulder. Turning around, he saw it was Andy.

"Oh, man, you're busy these days! I almost feared you had returned to England without saying goodbye!"

Robert grinned. "Sorry. Yes, I've been busy."

Andy looked at him curiously. "You're not still on the terrorist thing, are you?"

Looking around at the throng of people pressing against them, trying to get out as soon as possible, Robert took his friend by the arm. He gently led him outside.

"Yes, I am. Rebecca, too. It seems we were right on the mark from the beginning."

Together, they started to walk toward Robert's house. Andy was incredulous. "Do you have proof? We should go to the police again!"

Robert made a helpless gesture. "What is proof? What is evidence? There's a lot of circumstantial evidence. To me, it's enough. But how do we prove that something that happened in the real world was prepared for in the virtual world?"

"I don't know. By showing those coincidences and circumstantial evidence to the right people? The question is, how do you know any violence or any attack is connected to your suspects? So many terrible things happen these days. I mean, why shouldn't yesterday's attack on that ship be connected?"

Andy walked on for two seconds until he realized that Robert had stopped. He looked back and saw his friend looking at him with wild eyes. "What? What's the matter?"

Robert shook his head and shoulders several times, as if he wanted to shake off some physical restraint. "What exactly did you say just now?" he asked urgently.

"No. No. No way!" Andy was waving a finger at him, looking a little frightened. "You're not going to tell me that it's connected are you? Are you?"

Robert didn't answer at first. He just looked at his Dutch friend, then finally repeated his question. "Andy, what did you mean by that? Please tell me!"

Hesitantly, speaking slowly and carefully, Andy said. "I said that it seems difficult to know which violence is connected to your terrorist. Because there are so many murders and terrible things in the papers these days. And then I mentioned yesterday's attack on that ship. As an example of an unrelated thing, nothing more!"

"What attack? What ship? Come on, tell me, Andy!"

"Well, you know." The Dutchman halted, looking for the right words. "I was referring to the attack on a rich man's yacht at some village at the IJsselmeer. Some people were killed. You know, this was all on the news?"

"I don't know what you're talking about. I don't read the Dutch papers. The *Herald*, *BBC* and *CNN* didn't say anything about it. Did they leave a painting this time as well?"

"No, they didn't. No doubt because it's not connected to your terrorists." Andy smiled, trying to put an end to the subject. Seeing that Robert wouldn't let it go, he continued: "The news said it was just a reckoning within the criminal circuit. A local thing. The victims were just a bunch of drug dealers. It had nothing to do with terrorists."

"Just tell me what happened. Please?"

"Shall we have a drink first?" Suddenly Robert realized it wasn't wise to discuss things like this in the open air. They went into Barerra and ordered two beers. After they seated themselves in a quiet corner, Andy started talking again.

"Well, as far as I know, two nights ago, a big boat in a small harbor was attacked. It belonged to some drugs king. I guess this guy must have been important because he'd several armed guards on board. It didn't help him, though. Four stiffs were found in the morning. A bloody affair, as far as I understood. Like I said, it was at some place at the IJsselmeer, if I remember correctly."

Robert looked at him for several seconds. "What's the IJsselmeer?"

The question seemed to take Andy aback for a second. "A big lake in the north of the country. It used to be open sea, but they built a twenty miles long dike, and now it's a lake."

"So it's in the Netherlands?"

"Yes."

Robert took Andy by the upper arm and squeezed hard. "This must be it!" he whispered urgently. "You know, we knew they were preparing for an attack on a water vessel. We saw them rehearsing it.

Then, suddenly, Khalid disappeared and the others were all offline for a few days. So most likely it went down during that period."

"Wait a second." Andy gently unwrapped Robert's fingers. "I thought your guys were terrorists, am I right? Are they drug dealers now?"

"Hell, do I know what they want? All I know is that we saw them preparing for a raid on a ship. We suspected it must have gone down in the last few days, and now you tell me that there actually was such an attack!"

Seeing the frustration and anger in his friend's eyes, Andy put a calming hand on his shoulder. "Come, let's have another beer. Then you can tell me exactly what you witnessed and what's going on."

Andy asked a lot of questions, forcing Robert to tell his story slowly and in a logical way. Several times he had to go back a few steps to explain things more elaborately. Robert found that he'd become such a veteran of the WoW game, that he was taking things for granted that non-players wouldn't understand.

When he was finished, they went to Roberts place as Andy wanted to show him some news articles on the Internet. Robert found himself quite upset by the news. Apart from the fact that the attack on a major drug dealer seemed uncharacteristic, it fitted the puzzle all too well.

After Robert made some notes, Andy insisted on seeing the locations in WoW himself. Robert logged on and showed him Raynewood Retreat and how it matched with the map of the grounds where Benjamin Natale was killed. He pointed the similarities out one by one. He was talking softly as he wasn't sure if Khalid was around.

Next, they went all the way to see the pirate ship. Robert wasn't above showing off a little, casually killing mobs that were far below his current level of sixty-two. He also enjoyed the compliments for Casper, his pet. At level fifty-five he'd tamed a Frostsaber Huntress in Winterspring, a magnificent cat that served him extremely well.

After Robert told his friend exactly what they had seen there and what had happened, Andy still wasn't satisfied.

"Now show me how you keep track of these Grimstone guys."

Obediently, Robert opened the social window. He explained how he'd added the members of The Hammer of Grimstone to his friends list and how this window showed their approximate location when they were online. At that moment, two of them actually were online. Gilead was in Ogrimmar and Pharad was in a place called Netherstorm. While they were watching, the name of Drimm became highlighted. This was accompanied by a text message and the characteristic sound alert that told him that one of his friends or guild mates had come online. Drimm's location was shown as Shattrath City.

"That's your neighbor, isn't it?" Andy asked.

Robert nodded. "Behind his computer right across the corridor."

Andy was silent for a few moments. "I'd like to talk to him," he suddenly said. "Just to get a feeling for him."

"Let's not do something rash," Robert answered. "Rebecca and I are trying to keep a low profile. Even then, there have been two unwanted encounters in the virtual world already. They don't know that we're stalking them, so let's keep as far away as possible."

The grunt he got in reply told Robert the other was brooding on something. Then he was distracted by more alerts, as nearly all the members of The Hammer of Grimstone came online in quick succession. Within two minutes, nine of them were online.

"What are they doing?" Andy asked, eyes glittering with excitement.

With a shrug, Robert answered. "No idea. It may mean nothing. I've seen many of them online at the same time quite often. They could be here to do an instance together."

This got him a gentle push in response. "Come on, you're the one who just told me that you don't believe in too many coincidences! There must be a reason. They're all logging on at more or less the same moment!"

"They're all coming to Shattrath," Robert announced. He pointed at the screen where they could see that seven were now listed in the capital city of Outland. "I bet that these two are flying to Shattrath as well." He pointed at the screen, where the location of Pharad and

Jakky had just changed. Jakky was in Terokkar Forest, and Pharad was listed in Blade's Edge Mountain. He opened his map and zoomed out until the overview map of Outland was shown. He pointed out the location of Netherstorm. "You see? Pharad's route takes him from Netherstorm to the zone of Blade's Edge Mountain. Next we'll probably see that he moves to the next zone on the itinerary, which is Zangarmarsh."

"Can we go to this Shattrath City as well?"

Robert nodded, holding his breath while he kept staring at the screen. As soon as Pharad's location did indeed change to Zangarmarsh, he sat up.

"Let's go!" With these words, he activated his hearthstone. Ten seconds later he was back in a place called Falcon's Watch in Hellfire Peninsula. He sprinted out of the inn and rushed to the flight master. Shattrath was relatively close to Falcon's Watch, so the flight didn't take long.

They got there before Pharad did.

Robert positioned Gunslinger ten yards away from the flight's arrival point, blending into a small knot of other players standing there. A little later the guild leader of The Hammer of Grimstone arrived. The huge Orc warrior looked awesome in his epic gear. A monstrous two-handed sword was slung over his back. As he walked past them, they could see that a bright magical glow surrounded the weapon, moving and twisting like a living thing.

"After him!" Andy urged.

"I am!" Robert replied with a grin. He followed Pharad, trailing a short distance behind, into the main building of the city. It wasn't so much a building as an immense hall, where A'dal, the ruler of the city, kept his eternal watch on the center pedestal. Pharad moved over to one of several coves, where portals to the major cities on the other continents were to be found. At the portal to Ogrimmar, the other members of The Hammer were assembled.

Pharad moved right through the group and went through the portal. The others followed, disappearing one by one. In a few seconds they were all gone.

"Are we going as well?"

In answer, Robert stepped up to the portal and went through. They had to wait a few seconds for the new location to load. Robert drummed his fingers on the desk impatiently. Finally, Ogrimmar appeared. They were just in time to see Gilead, one of the Grimstones, jump off the platform of the small building that all people who travelled by portal arrived in. He was mounted on a war raptor.

Gunslinger mounted as well and jumped down onto the path below. He thundered after the others, just in time to see how they were aiming for the flight master. One by one they took wing. They could see them flying in a tight curve through the valley, following the programmed departure path.

"Damn, we don't know where they're going!" he cursed.

Andy exhaled. "What can we do?"

"I don't know." Robert thought for a minute. "Yes, I do know. We can wait until they arrive. Soon, they'll all be in a certain zone and stay there. Then we could go there as well and see if we can find them again."

They didn't have to wait for long. Right after they left Durotar, where Ogrimmar was situated, the Grimstones entered a zone called Aszhara and remained there. Robert opened the map and discovered it was directly to the north.

"Do we go there as well?" Andy was eager.

Robert uttered a few profanities and shook his head. "I've never been there. That means that I don't have the flightpath that they've taken. God knows how to get there and how long it's going to take us."

He activated the website of Wowhead and started to scan the information about 'Aszhara'.

"Look, it's connected to Durotar!" Andy exclaimed. "That's where we are now, isn't it?"

Robert looked where Andy was pointing. "You're right. From the map, it's not clear how to get there."

He pointed at the mountain range that ran all the way along the border between the two zones. "No clear road is leading to Aszhara from here. According to the Internet there should be a connection. This probably means that there's a pass somewhere, but it could take an hour to find it. Besides, it looks quite impossible to get into those mountains from Ogrimmar."

"Maybe we should follow that river?" Andy put his finger on the Southfury River that ran from north to south and passed the city. "Is it possible to swim?"

"Swimming up that river? I don't know. I tried it once with another river, because it seemed a likely connection between two places. In the end I got stuck in the basin of some waterfall. There was simply no way to climb up. I had to go back all the way."

He opened another file that showed an overview atlas of the continent of Kalimdor. He studied it for a moment and started to laugh. "I found the way. Again, it takes us to Ashenvale. It's funny; there are nineteen zones on this continent, but my pursuit of these guys takes me back to Ashenvale all the times!"

He showed Andy where a road ran to the eastern border of Ashenvale, crossing into the neighboring zone of Aszhara. "When we get to Aszhara, we must look out for a place called Valormok. That's where the flightpath is."

With these words he clicked on the wind rider master and selected Splintertree Post. Again.

After a reckless ride through the Nightsong Woods they came upon a bridge spanning the Southfury River. They crossed and got the message: 'Discovered: Aszhara'.

"We're there. Now let's move!"

The road led them into a different landscape. The density of the trees faded out, allowing gradually more daylight to filter through the tree tops. The colors changed as well, giving the impression that they were riding out of late summer into early autumn.

Andy whistled. "This game is really, really neat!" Admiration and excitement were glowing on his face. "Is it dangerous here?"

"I don't know," Robert answered. "I'm level sixty-two, which means that, in theory, I should be able to handle anything we encounter. This continent was originally designed with level sixty as the highest possible level. Every zone has enemies of a certain level range. I believe this zone is fifty to fifty-five, which is pretty high. But if several level fifty-fives attack me at the same time, we might be in trouble."

There was nothing to fear. Without any trouble or incident they arrived at a place called Valormok. It wasn't exactly a village. All they saw was a campsite with two well made shelters covered by thatched roofs. The largest had hammocks tied between the supporting wooden poles. There was also something that looked like a large abandoned wagon. A campfire was burning at one of the shelters, but there were also some big smoldering braziers burning throughout the camp. Several computer controlled Horde characters were standing around. One of those was a flight master, and Robert acquired the flight path out of habit. There was nobody else to be seen, certainly none of the Grimstones. Robert checked and ascertained that they were, indeed, still in the zone. All of them.

"Now what?" Andy asked.

Robert hesitated. Suddenly he realized that, until now, he had always relied on Rebecca to make all of the important decisions. She always knew exactly what to do and her knowledge of World of Warcraft seemed endless. All of a sudden, he was cast in the role of tutor to Andy and decision-maker for both of them.

"Honestly, I don't know," he said. "We could try to find them, I guess.'

He started to move Gunslinger again, exiting Valormok on the other side and veering back into the direction of the road. They had gone no more than maybe a hundred yards when they were attacked for the first time. A Spitelash warrior, which looked like some mermaid out of a bad nightmare, attacked Gunslinger from behind. The hunter was knocked out of the saddle.

Robert cursed and frantically pressed keys to turn around to face the monster. It was level fifty-three and already having a bad time with Casper. The white animal was tearing into the Spitelash warrior with a vengeance. Robert started shooting with his gun, and after only two shots it lay dead on the ground.

"Let's try to avoid these guys," Andy said, while Robert remounted and continued their search. "Such sudden attacks are bad for my heart!"

They reached the road without any further incidents. They were closer to the temples now, and Robert noticed many more Spitelash warriors and also Spitelash sirens, which he suspected of having magical abilities. A message told him that he'd just discovered the Ruins of Elderath. He continued cautiously, wary of drawing any aggression. He realized fully that he could easily die here and have a hard time escaping this trap afterward. When there was a mob too close to the road that they couldn't avoid, Gunslinger would dismount and engage it from a safe distance. In this way they managed to clear a path into a city of ruined temples.

"It looks like the ruins of ancient Athens," Andy remarked. "These temples and pillars are definitely of Greek origin."

Robert nodded. They had reached a square with a defunct fountain in the middle. On the other side lay a magnificent temple that had somehow escaped the decay and demolition of all the other buildings. One more step forward revealed the name of this place: Temple of Zin-Malor.

"Are we going in?"

"We came this far, so I suppose we should."

There were three Spitelash sirens between them and the main temple, and Robert sent Casper to attack the first. After that one was killed, they took care of the rest. Cautiously they approached the doorway of the temple. Step by step Gunslinger sidled to the entrance until they were just able to cast a look inside.

"Damn!" Andy exclaimed. "Where the hell are they?"

"Again, I don't know," Robert said. Once more, he clicked the map open and asked Andy to study it. "Do you see how large this zone is? We've seen only a small part of it. They could be anywhere!"

He was about to suggest they give up the search when a message appeared at the bottom of the screen: *Frazier has come online*.

Robert stared at the message for a few seconds, then opened his Friends window for confirmation.

"We may be in luck," he said slowly. "This is another of the Grimstones. As far as we've been able to determine there are ten of them, total. So now they're all online. Maybe he's late for the appointment, and this could be our chance to locate them. He's already in Ogrimmar, so we must hurry!"

He summoned his Kodo and thundered out of the square, completely unmindful of the Spitelash monsters rushing to intercept him. Several hit him, and he lost quite some health, however none was able to unhorse Gunslinger. When they were clear of the Ruins of Elderath, the pursuit ceased, and they continued their way unhindered.

They arrived at Valormok two heartbeats before Frazier was brought there by his flying taxi. Frazier was a Blood Elf mage, dressed in magnificent clothing. Robert clicked on him and selected the option 'Inspect'. He nodded. "He's wearing all purple gear. He can kill me in a few seconds."

Andy threw an uncomprehending glance at him. "Shouldn't we hide?"

"No. Why should we? We're just another player who happens to be here. He won't think anything of our presence."

Frazier started to cast a spell. A moment later he was mounted on a colorful bird that resembled an oversized ostrich. He left in a gallop.

"One, two, three, four, five," Robert counted. He didn't dare to give more of a lead. They started to follow in northeastern direction.

"Hunters have an ability that allows them to track others," he explained to Andy. "I've set it to track humanoids, because that's what a Blood Elf is." He pointed at the mini map where Frazier was shown as a green dot. "If I concentrate on the terrain and avoiding enemies, will you keep an eye on the dot and make sure we don't lose him?"

Andy nodded his approval and sat forward, his eyes glued to the screen.

Frazier didn't go to the road. Instead, he kept to the north, following a route that ran parallel to the road. They followed him from a safe distance, now and then swerving to give a wide berth to dangerous spiders and flying monsters called Hippogryphs.

Shortly, they came upon a camp filled with Timbermaw warriors, who were patrolling the perimeter of the camp. Robert cursed himself for being lazy and abandoning the quests that would have given him a good reputation with this faction, because they let Frazier pass unhindered, but rushed to attack Gunslinger when he approached. He turned sharply to the left, trying to avoid as many of the Timbermaws as possible.

Riding around the campsite cost them precious time. Frazier was now at the extreme edge of the mini map. Any other distraction or detour would mean they lost him.

"Concentrate on the map," Robert admonished, quite unnecessary. "I'll try to follow a straight line from now on. It's a gamble. If some mob knocks us out of the saddle, we're done!"

They thundered on through the deserted lands of Aszhara. They saw no other players, just yellowed grass, sparse trees, and an occasional monster. They were lucky no mob pursued them for long. They even gained back some ground on Frazier when they came upon a place called the Legashi Encampment. The powerful mage went too close to the camp, resulting in several guards bolting after him.

Robert saw his chance and aimed his Kodo straight ahead, right behind the backs of the Legashi warriors who had left their posts to run after Frazier.

They passed a place called The Bitter Reaches, and the land started to slope gently downward. There was a change of colors ahead, which Robert deduced must be the beach. Indeed, not much later a message told him they had arrived at the Shattered Strand. Still, Frazier kept moving.

"Is he riding into the sea?" Andy wondered.

"Could be." Robert stretched his back, removing some of the knots in his muscles. "According to the map there's quite a lot of beach here." He opened the map again and pointed. "You see? There are two land tongues that encircle the Sea of Storms, creating a huge bay. We're at the northern tip, which is the largest."

Suddenly the grass under the Kodo's hooves gave way to sand. For a second Robert was distracted, but when he looked up again, he halted immediately.

"We found them!" he cried. He stomped Andy in the chest. "Hey, weren't you responsible for watching the mini map? Look!"

The mini map showed a cluster of humanoids at the extreme edge of the land tongue. They were standing in front of a gloomy deserted tower built at the place where the land ended. Maybe it served as a lighthouse once.

'Discovered: Tower of Eldara' his screen announced.

Gunslinger edged forward and to the left, trying to keep as much distance as possible while gaining a better and unobstructed view.

"There," Andy said. He pointed at some huge boulders between them and the tower. "If we're behind those, they won't notice us."

"You could be right." Robert studied the situation for a moment. Suddenly the prospect of getting so close was frightening. "Let's do it. Otherwise we went through all this trouble for nothing."

He approached the hiding place from the opposite side, which meant he tracked all the way to the north before turning toward the beach again. Twice he had to change direction to avoid huge monstrous crablike animals. It took several minutes to reach the dubious safety of the rocks. Once there, he shuffled sideways to get a view of the Grimstones.

"My God, what the hell are they doing?"

Robert didn't answer at first. He looked again and checked once more to make sure he wasn't dreaming. "They're *dancing*," he finally concluded.

"Dancing?"

"Yes, don't ask me why."

They watched the weird spectacle in silence. After several minutes, it suddenly ended in a spectacular way. All the members of The Hammer of Grimstone jumped into the air, which was followed by loud cheers. The sound carried all the way to their hiding place.

Suddenly Pharad yelled, "Enough! Thank you!"

The dancing, jumping, and cheering subsided. Robert and Andy exchanged a glance. Robert raised his eyebrows, which made Andy giggle nervously.

"What do you think they're doing?" the latter asked, just to break the tension.

"What do you think? Isn't it obvious? They're celebrating. And I fear we both know what they might be celebrating. Four dead men on a boat!"

Andy nodded. "I believe you're right."

They concentrated again on what was happening on the beach.

Below them, the Grimstones had lined up at the foot of the tower. Pharad was standing in front of them, like a general inspecting his troops. With Andy and Robert as silent spectators, he slowly moved from one to the other, taking a few moments with each of them.

Suddenly, it dawned on Robert. "He's giving them something!"

"What do you mean, giving them something?"

Breathless, Robert explained to Andy: "Players can exchange anything. Items, gold, you name it. This is done through a trade window. Somehow, I think we're witnessing such transactions."

Drimm didn't bother to read the orders immediately. That would come later. He was close to their leader, and he knew how Pharad feared that someday WoW would come under the scrutiny of the international intelligence community.

Pharad wasn't a man who took risks. He didn't mind using the regular secure channels like Party or Guild chat for the issuing of operational orders during training, because such messages were nearly undistinguishable from ordinary Party chat during a raid.

Orders that really meant something were kept as secure as possible. When real places, dates, time, or names were communicated, this was done by physical though digital letter.

He opened his bag to ascertain that he had the orders with him. Again, he resisted the impulse to read them now. He would know soon enough. Waving farewell to the others, he started to activate his hearthstone.

Right before he was whisked away to his home in Dalaran, his eyes froze a moment on the screen. He hadn't been paying attention to his surroundings, knowing they were absolutely secure at the most remote place thinkable in the entire game. Only now, just before he vanished, he looked up and took in the whole screen.

It didn't even last a second, but Drimm's experienced eye was immediately drawn to the dot on his mini map, slightly to the northeast of their group. Drimm was a hunter, and he, too, had the ability to track all kinds of adversaries. It was a *friendly* dot drawing his attention. There were no friendly mobs around here, therefore it must have been a player. A Horde player. He would have sworn to it.

Just before his view on the Shattered Strand disappeared, he looked at the place where the dot should be, according to the mini map. All he saw were some huge boulders that prohibited him from seeing anything. Had someone been hiding there? Observing them? Or was he mistaken? Should he warn Pharad?

He decided to let it rest for today. It was probably nothing, just some player stupid enough to think there was some fun in Aszhara. Four long days he'd been away from his temporary home, and he had slept little. He was dead tired. He yawned and promised himself he would tell Pharad anyway. Tomorrow.

CHAPTER XVI

There seemed to be no end to the pipe. It was filled with water. At some places clouds of tiny little air bubbles floated through the water, obscuring the view even more. From the point where they dived underwater, it had been a long swim all the way down to the opening of the center tube of Coilfang Reservoir. It seemed as if he would never get out of the pipe.

Gunslinger was holding his breath: the remaining oxygen in his lungs was depicted by a bar on the top of his screen. It was running out fast. He let himself be distracted by the oxygen bar and immediately the hunter became stuck. Cursing, he steered down a little to keep following the downward sloping pipe. What if he ran out of oxygen? He tried to swim faster. Finally, there was light coming from above. He swam upward and broke the surface. He involuntarily gasped, as the bar with his remaining breath was replenished again.

He was in a kind of cavern, with moss growing at places on the metal everywhere around them. Killermage was in front of him. She was already out of the water and stood next to a quest giver. Robert waded out of the water as well and collected the quest, which required him to search for some missing members of an expedition inside the instance.

"We'll look for them in the Underbog first," Rebecca said. "The Slave Pens come right after."

Robert made Gunslinger nod. He gave her a wave as well. It netted him a smile in return. On an impulse, he decided to use Gunslinger as an indicator for Rebecca's feelings for him and typed '/hug' while selecting Killermage as target.

Gunslinger hugs Killermage, the screen read. He held his breath.

Killermage chuckled. Two heartbeats later, he read, *Killermage blows Gunslinger a kiss.*

Feeling happy, even a little elated, he stepped up to the swirling entrance of the instance.

"Are you coming?" he asked bravely. Without waiting for her, he stepped through and into the Underbog.

Once inside, they turned to business again.

All enemies in the Underbog were Elites, which meant that they were a lot harder to kill and did a lot more damage than those of similar level found in the regular world. On top of that the mobs were linked. This meant that if one enemy was attacked, two or even three others joined the fight immediately. If the attacker wasn't careful, he could be swarmed by many more.

Instead of in the normal WoW world, the mobs always attacked the player who was hurting them most, which in this case was Magekiller. This so-called threat was especially difficult to manage as they were playing in a team of only two. A normal team consisted of five players, amongst whom a 'tank'. With a lot of armor and hit-points, the tank should be able to endure a severe beating. Robert and Rebecca made Casper play the role of tank in these encounters, while Gunslinger and Killermage did the damage from a distance. They had worked out several tactics together, and they both knew exactly what they should do.

Today, there was something different about Rebecca. Usually she played carefully, planning and executing her moves like a chess player. She was always mindful of her fragility as a cloth-wearing mage, with a lot less protective armor and hit points than most other classes. She was a 'glass cannon', as she liked to put it herself, and always made sure that her enemies couldn't lay a finger on her. She was the master of crowd control and long-range killing.

This time, in the Underbog, she was almost reckless, pulling mobs early and letting them near her, almost as if she relished the beatings she was taking. Not that she was in real danger, because she was so superior with her epic gear and vast experience. The difference was that the corpses now fell at her feet instead of in the distance, just as if she wanted to actually feel the blood she was spilling.

Suddenly, without warning, she walked right into a large group of enemies, who all had the word 'bog' in their names after the area they were in. Without a pause she continued into the next group, deliberately pulling no less than twelve of the elite mobs at the same time. Robert was stunned. This was completely contrary to any of their usual tactics. Not only that, it was suicidal. He didn't know what to do.

"What are you doing?"

"Let me!"

Among the mobs that were furiously attacking her were two Bog Giants, who were even harder to kill than the normal elite mobs. She froze them in a Frost Nova and proceeded to hit them with Arcane Explosions that radiated from her in angry purple circles. When the Bog Giants were on low health, she called down a huge pillar of fire that consumed all of the lesser Bog Lurkers. The two Bog Giants were still alive, pounding on her with a vengeance. She cast another Frost Nova, but didn't move away. She remained where she was, taking the beating, while summoning one of her devastating Blizzards. This killed one of the two Bog Giants.

The other Bog Giant was standing remarkably unscathed. Now she concentrated on her last opponent, dealing out massive burst damage with a Cone of Cold which looked like a whirlpool blast of frozen air. This was followed by a fiery Fire Blast. A few more Arcane Explosions, and it was over. The Bog Giant let out a loud bellow and started to sway. Then it tumbled spectacularly to the ground. She was left standing in the middle of a heap of corpses, her mana drained completely and with less than a quarter of her health left.

"Are you sure you're all right?" Robert asked.

Killermage sat on the ground, right in the middle of her slain enemies. She started to eat and drink to regain health and mana.

"Robert, we need to talk."

It was a completely surrealistic setting. They were in a large cavern with dead bodies strewn all over the ground. To make things worse, the cavern was several hundred feet under the surface of a huge lake. The place appeared to be constructed of living tissue, the floor and walls seemed to be made of vines, covered with moss and grossly inflated mushrooms. The entire place gave off a disgusting greenish glow.

"Could you sit down please? I hate talking to someone who's standing over me."

Robert shook his head in disbelief. They were in a digital world, controlling computer-generated avatars, yet she was insisting on real life courtesies. Still, he did as she asked and sat next to the mage.

"What do you want to talk about?"

"Everything," she replied. "I have a bad feeling about what's going on and how we're handling it."

"What's the problem? I think we're definitely making progress. I'm nearly level seventy!"

He heard his phone buzz and to his surprise he saw it was Rebecca. He picked it up and Rebecca started talking immediately, seamlessly continuing the conversation they had been having by typing messages to each other.

"That's not the issue. I'm worried and frustrated about the fact that we're back to square one. There's just the two of us, maybe three if we count your friend Andy, and we haven't got a clue how to handle things. We have no proof. We have no plan. We have no support. All we have are a lot of dead people. Now the attack on a ship has already happened, we don't even know what their next target will be. Even if we did, we'd be powerless to do anything about it. Just ask the four dead people on that boat. They may have been drug dealers, but their death could have been prevented."

"I agree. But I don't see what we could have done!"

"Neither do I. That's why we need a change of tactics. If we go on like this, we'll keep trailing behind, mourning the dead. We need to take some action."

"How?"

She remained silent for a minute. "You need to become friendly with Khalid. Not only that, we also have to follow him in real life, not just in the virtual world. And we need to find a way to know exactly what they're up to. You told me that you think that Pharad was giving something to each member of the Hammer of Grimstone. We need to know what that something was."

"I've been thinking about that. The only things that can be traded are gold or WoW items. How can that be significant? I just don't see it!"

Rebecca laughed. "That's what I thought as well. I've been wondering about that for the last days. An item is an item, so what could be important about it? Last night I finally figured it out. Look at your screen again!"

With these words, she opened a trade window with Gunslinger. Robert saw that she wanted to give him a piece of paper. He accepted and received the item. When he opened his bag, he saw it was called 'Plain Letter, written by Killermage <Right Click to Read>'. He did so, and a new window opened. The letter contained a message:

25/11/10 1700 EDI-AMS U26923

From,
Killermage

He read it twice, not understanding what it meant. He asked her to clarify.

"What it means is that it's possible to physically trade information or instructions between two players."

"I see. Why would they give instructions in this way?"

"Two reasons. The most practical could be that certain information is so valuable or important that the receiver should keep it for later reference. In case he forgot it for instance."

"Yes, that could be. And the other reason?"

"The second reason could be security. Suppose you were leading a terrorist organization. You're using World of Warcraft as your communication channel because you need something secure and unmonitored. You also know that, sooner or later, someone will get smart and start tapping the information in WoW, just like they're monitoring your phone calls and email."

"And this would be the answer?"

She walked up to him, standing so close their virtual characters were almost touching. "At least it would minimize the risk. If some agency was monitoring online computer games, it would concentrate on the chat channels first, don't you agree? Or the team speak channels. Who would suspect items traded between characters? Consider, we didn't even think of it!"

Robert thought it over and had to admit she was right. "What's the meaning of the message you just gave me?"

She smiled at him. "Oh, that? That's my flight information. I'm coming over to you. I arrive Thursday at 17:00 hours at Amsterdam airport. Will you pick me up?"

His heart jumped. "Sure! I'll be there. Where will you stay?"

"At your place, of course. Where else?"

CHAPTER XVII

Robert put a hand to his chest to feel the pounding of his heart. He tried to steady himself by taking some deep, slow breaths. It didn't help. He felt beads of perspiration forming on the nape of his neck. Telling himself to stop dithering, he finally knocked on the door. For a split second he felt the urge to run away, but he suppressed that thought with force.

His knock resulted in the sound of a chair scraping on the floor. Footsteps approached, then the door was opened.

"Yes?" Khalid looked impassively at him.

Robert forced a smile. "Hi! How are you!"

"Fine. Can I help you?"

This wasn't going as he had expected and rehearsed in his head several times. But there was no turning back now. He plunged ahead. "Well, you offered to help me a little with World of Warcraft, remember? I bought the game a few weeks ago, but it's confusing. I'm a little stuck."

A spark of interest gleamed in Khalid's eyes. Rebecca had predicted this. She claimed that nobody as involved in the game as Khalid would be able to turn down such a request.

We're all addicted and we all like to show off how great and fantastic we are, and we all like to flaunt our superior knowledge around. Her words resounded in his head.

As they had been hoping, his neighbor nodded. "Sure. What's the problem?"

Robert noticed the beginning stubbles of a beard. His mind conjured up images of bearded Mujahedeen fighters, but he pushed them away.

"Well, I'm at level eighteen now. I must do a quest in some place called Wailing Caverns or something. Suddenly, I get killed all the time. I don't understand it. I was doing all right but it won't work anymore."

Rebecca and Robert had prepared all of this beforehand. Rebecca had opened a new separate WoW account and leveled a Tauren hunter up to level eighteen yesterday and last night. No small feat. She'd explained to him how Khalid would never believe that he was already at level sixty-five, so he needed another low level character for the charade. If their ruse worked, Khalid would probably come to Robert's room at some point, to show him things. It wouldn't work if there was another high level character on Robert's account. So he needed a new account as well.

"Do you mean that you're actually inside the Wailing Caverns?"

Robert nodded. "Yes, I finally found the entrance at the end of some large cave. Another player pointed it out to me. Since I went through some strange gate, the game doesn't work correctly anymore. I just get killed over and over!"

For the first time, he saw Khalid actually laugh. For a second, he feared he'd overdone his story, but that fear was groundless. There was no suspicion in the man's response.

"Sorry, I didn't mean to make fun of you. Your game isn't broken: it's just that you entered an instance. A dungeon. Those are many times more difficult than regular play."

"Why did I suddenly enter an instance? I didn't mean to."

"No, there's just much to learn about World of Warcraft."

Robert smiled back at him. "Could you help me a little? Explain some things to me? Please?"

Khalid looked at his watch. He nodded. "Of course. Show me what you're doing."

Still with a pounding heart, but jubilant about his successful performance, Robert led the way to his room and his computer. He drew a chair near for Khalid to sit on and pointed at his computer. "That's me!"

On the screen, the hastily created hunter was visible. It was at the far end of a huge cavern system that sprawled underneath a minor mountain range just to the southeast of Crossroads. The entrance to the caverns was hidden in the lush vegetation of a deceptively tranquil-looking oasis in one of the drier parts of the Barrens. Hunterino, as the new character was called, was standing in front of the entrance of the hidden instance called Wailing Caverns.

Khalid reached over Robert's shoulder and gently took the mouse from him. He clicked open the Character window, staring at the various items equipped on Hunterino. They were nowhere near as good as what had been equipped on Gunslinger at that level. The gear Hunterino was wearing was exactly what was to be expected from a novice player at level eighteen: complete crap.

"I can give you some advice, but I can't help you," Khalid said. "For that, we need to be on the same server."

Robert managed a blank expression. "I don't understand. What's a server?"

With a sigh, the other sat down. "There are millions of people playing this game. They can't be all in the same world because it would be far too crowded. Therefore, they created many different Realms that function on different servers. The worlds are all exactly the same: it's just that people are not in the same place, so to say."

Robert nodded slowly, as if he had trouble comprehending. "And how do you know that we're on different servers?"

"Well, the chance that we're on the same is small. You should have chosen my realm out of a long list."

"How do I know on which server I am?"

"Don't you remember?"

He shook his head, trying to look as stupid as possible. "No. I selected a random one out of the list. I don't remember which one. I didn't understand what I was doing: I just wanted to get started."

Khalid rose again and took the mouse for the second time. He logged Hunterino off, not quitting the game, but going one step back to the screen where the character you wanted to play with was selected. He studied it for a second, then turned to look Robert sharply in the eyes. He held his gaze for several seconds.

"Well, this is a major coincidence," he said slowly. "You're on Sylvanas, the same server as I'm on."

Careful not to break eye contact and disguising his sudden fear, Robert managed a happy expression. "Wow, fancy that! I didn't even know what I was doing, and I took the right one! That's great! So that means that you can help me a little, right?"

Khalid broke eye contact and switched his attention back to the screen. He clicked and Hunterino was loaded again.

"Yes, I can help you a little. I'll take you through the Wailing Caverns. Give me five minutes."

Before Robert could say anything, the Egyptian turned around and walked out of the room.

[Drimm] whispers: Are you there?

Robert looked at his watch. It had been three minutes, not five. *So you're eager to show off!* he thought.

"Yes, he replied. I'm still in the same place."

"Good. Stay there. I'm on my way, but it'll take some time."

Immediately after these words, Robert received an invitation to join Drimm in a Party. He accepted.

This time it did take five minutes. Finally, Drimm walked up to him accompanied by a big bear. The two were followed on the heels by a host of raptors and lizards that were frantically attacking him.

"Sorry, I didn't want to take the time to kill them one by one," Drimm said. "I'll take care of it now."

With these words he shot a Volley, making it rain tiny arrows out of the air that killed all the mobs in short order. Robert knew that the damage of Volley was nowhere near as devastating as a mage's Blizzard, but that it was more than sufficient to deal with a bunch of low level mobs.

"Wow, that's impressive!"

"It's a long way to level eighty, but well worth it," Drimm replied. "Now let's go."

Drimm knew his way around the Wailing Caverns. The idea of this instance was to kill a number of Lords in a certain order. The demise of each lord was rewarded with special gear.

Drimm went about it in an efficient way. He killed everything they encountered from long range, leaving an endless supply of corpses for Hunterino to loot. The big difference was that Drimm didn't waste time on idle chatter, as Rebecca and Robert used to do. He gave short orders, like "Stay behind me here" or "Keep your pet away" but otherwise there was silence on the Party channel. They moved through the Caverns swiftly, arriving at Lady Anacondra shortly. Lady Anacondra was the first 'Boss' in the Wailing Caverns, an extra strong Elite opponent, with extra special loot, meaning priceless 'blue' items for a level eighteen. Drimm killed her in short order and Gunslinger bent over to loot the dead Lady. He got two blue items, Footpads of the Fang and Venomstrike, a blue bow.

Unexpectedly, Drimm cheered. "Gratz!" he said. "That's a good bow you got there. You're lucky!"

Robert thanked him profusely. "I can't use it yet, because I have no arrows with me," he mourned. "I'll try it out right after we finish here!"

Suddenly, the ice was broken. Drimm started to comment on how he was playing and gave him advice on various matters. Robert in turn asked him some innocent questions, like how often he played.

In this way they got to know each other a little, while they swept through the Wailing Caverns. They killed Cobrahn, Pythas and Serpentis, the three Lords that ruled the place, in quick succession, which rewarded Hunterino with a pair of Leggings of the Fang.

"Now you only need the Belt of the Fang," Khalid said. "The other items of the Embrace of the Viper are useless to a hunter."

"Well, you can't have it all," Robert replied. "I'm happy with what I got so far. And I finished my quest!"

"If you want, we can do it again. Try for the belt?"

Robert hesitated for a moment. "Sure. If you don't mind."

Right at that moment he received a text message on his cell phone. *How is it going?*

He abandoned the game for a second to reply: *Better than dreamed. Doing WC with Drimm ATM. Second run.*

Rebecca's reply came only seconds later: *Well done. Call me when ready.*

The second run went even faster than the first. They blasted through the instance, but the Belt of the Fang didn't drop. Drimm wasn't going to give up. He reset the instance, and they entered again. This time, they were lucky. The sought after item dropped off the Lady. Robert equipped it on his hunter, and they exited the instance.

"Now we go to DM," Drimm told him when they were standing outside in the sunshine again.

"DM. What's that?"

"Dead Mines. An instance in Westfall. It gives a lot of good blue stuff, weapons too."

Robert was clueless. He'd been in many places by now, but even the name Westfall was unfamiliar to him. Once again he realized how immense World of Warcraft was. Khalid didn't wait for his consent and started to walk back to Crossroads. Hunterino hurried after him.

"Where's this place?" he asked.

"In the south of Eastern Kingdoms. It's Alliance territory, but we're not afraid, are we? We take a bird to Ogrimmar. There you can buy arrows for your new bow, and I'll craft a good quiver for you. From there we take the zeppelin to Grom'Gol Basecamp. After that, we walk northward through the Vale. Just follow me."

They followed the route Khalid had described, traveling in silence. When they arrived at the fort at Grom'Gol, Khalid spoke again.

"Follow me. Always stay behind me. You'll get killed in seconds if you stray. If I stop, you stop. When I walk, you walk. When I fight, you stay behind me. If someone or something attacks you, tell me immediately. Understood?"

Hunterino nodded his understanding. He followed Drimm to the northern exit of the camp that was protected from the outlying jungle by a palisade of sharp tipped wooden beams. They went through and entered the dangerous wilderness full of raptors, tigers, gorillas and pumas. Because Drimm cleared the way like an ultra efficient mine sweeper, they crossed through the zone nearly as fast as if there was nothing to fear at all.

When they reached the most northern area, they entered territory where Robert hadn't been with Gunslinger. Drimm obviously knew the way and led him on, all the way to another zone. They followed a road for what seemed like an eternity until they finally reached the bank of a river.

"Stop!" Drimm said. They had been running for so long that it took a moment for Robert to register the command. He stopped, but he'd already passed Drimm. The other pointed ahead at some medieval fortified bridge guarded by several soldiers in blue livery.

"Alliance guards. We'll cross the river somewhere else. No use alerting every Alliance player in the neighborhood by killing those guards."

Drimm left the road and moved through some green fields until they reached the river again, out of sight of the bridge. They were in a pleasantly shaded area, with just enough trees to give them some privacy while they waded into the river. As soon as they reached the other bank, Robert got another automated notice: Discovered: Westfall.

Drimm immediately struck out westward again until they came upon a mountainous area called the Dagger Hills, where Drimm skirted the edge of the hills, maintaining roughly the same direction as before. Finally, they arrived at a small town called Moonbrook. From a distance, it looked nice and inviting. A cobblestone road led into the town that consisted of a church and numerous wooden buildings. In the distance the shimmering surface of the sea could be seen through a slight haze.

When they drew closer, Robert could see that the town was deserted and in disrepair, now inhabited by humanoid mobs that all seemed to be part of a group called the Defias. He asked Drimm what they were.

"The Defias Brotherhood is a large community of thieves, bandits and pirates. They've taken over Westfall. We're here to kill their boss, Edwin van Cleef. He's on a ship at the other end of the Dead Mines. First, we have to get to the entrance of the mines. It's right here in the village. Follow me, but stay behind me!"

They entered the village, and Drimm's pet shot away to attack the first bandit. It killed the Defias Pillager in short order and immediately proceeded to attack another. Drimm and Robert followed the huge bear, Drimm firing with his gun into the houses, whenever he saw a member of the Defias Brotherhood inside. In this way they proceeded to the western part of the town where they came upon a plaza with a fountain in the middle.

"This way," Drimm said, and he led the way into a shed built next to a larger building. It proved to be the entrance to the Dead Mines. Robert followed as they descended some steep mining shafts. After some confusing turns in the dark and another jump down, they came upon the entrance to the instance.

"Are you ready?"

"Yes," Robert answered.

"Good. Stay behind me. If you're attacked, just yell and I'll rescue you. Understood?"

Hunterino nodded in confirmation. At that, they entered the instance.

Afterward, Robert couldn't remember much of the adventure in the Dead Mines. It was rather dark, and he did nothing other than looting the corpses that Drimm and his bear left behind. They wound their way through a maze of tunnels, and he was disoriented from the start.

Several times, they passed through sets of huge doors that had been opened by Drimm before Hunterino caught up with him. Apparently, some of those passages were guarded by so-called bosses because Drimm ordered him to search a specific body for loot. Each time, it netted Robert a blue item. Not everything was useful, but he was still accumulating some vastly superior gear.

At some point, a path led downward to a multitude of mobs, which were Goblins instead of Defias bandits. Drimm ordered Hunterino to stand back while he engaged the Goblins. When the area was cleared, it took Robert several minutes to loot all the corpses.

While he was engaged in corpse picking, Drimm went ahead and cleared the next area. When Robert joined him, another doorway was already opened and another boss was down. After a while they found themselves in a huge cavern flooded with water. Robert couldn't discern whether it was an underground river or if there was another source for the water under this mountain. Maybe it was even connected to the ocean, which was close, after all.

In the middle of the cave floated a large pirate ship. It could be reached by a construction of wooden platforms crowded with a host of enemies. They were not only Defias, Robert spotted many Goblins as well.

Finally, they came upon Edwin van Cleef, the Bane of Westfall and the leader of the Defias Brotherhood.

"Ready?" Khalid asked.

Hunterino pocketed the loot from the last victim of Drimm's two-handed axe. "Yes."

Drimm cheered and sent his bear to attack Edwin van Cleef. He was accompanied by two body guards, who desperately tried to fight off the animal. Drimm fired a Multishot, hitting the three targets at the same time. They all went down at the same time.

"Let's see what he has got for you," Drimm said, indicating the dead Van Cleef.

When they searched the dead body, Drimm cheered.

"You're so lucky!" he said. Indeed, Robert received an extremely good chest armor piece called Blackened Defias Armor. As a bonus, he also got a sword called Crual Barb, that had an extraordinary attack power stat. It would improve his damage output.

Suddenly, Drimm jumped over the side of the ship on the other side. Sounds of fighting drifted up, and Robert sent Hunterino to the railing to see what was happening.

"Come here," Drimm said.

"What is it?"

"There's another boss beyond the main boss in this instance. His name is Cookie, the ship's cook. Unfortunately, he didn't drop anything special."

Drimm led him to a hidden path that led up and away from the ship. They took a turn, and suddenly they arrived at the secret back exit of the instance. They went through and found themselves somewhere up in the Dagger Hills.

"Well, enough for today," Khalid said. "You can use your hearthstone to go home. We're far from civilized Horde territory."

After Robert did so, he went to see Khalid in his room.

"Thank you very much for your time," he said.

"No problem. You can ask me for help anytime when I'm online. Sometimes I'm busy with my guild, so there are no guarantees."

Robert saw an opportunity. Should he take it? He swallowed, but decided to press on. "Of course. And I noticed that sometimes you go out for a couple of days."

It remained silent for a full minute. Finally, there came a reply. "Yes, I have family in The Netherlands. Sometimes I visit them."

"Oh, that's nice. Well, it would be great if you can give me a boost again when you're here and you have time!"

Robert went outside to call Rebecca, not taking any risk of being overheard by his friendly neighbor. He was floating somewhere between jubilant and exhausted, and couldn't wait to share his success with her. She must have been waiting for his call because she answered after a millisecond. However, she showed admirable restraint. "Well done. You can tell me later. Is he still in his room?"

Completely taken aback, Robert confirmed that he was.

"Great. Get your ass over there. Now. Thank him for his time."

Proudly Robert replied. "I already did."

But Rebecca wasn't satisfied. "Go back again. Chat. Ask questions. Play the fool. Whatever. Just create the precedent of you paying Khalid a social visit. You're going to be a regular visitor. He might as well get used to it. World of Warcraft is probably his favorite topic anyway, so talk about that. Now go!"

This time, it was a lot easier to knock on the door. When Khalid opened, he smiled in genuine welcome.

"I wanted to thank you in person for your time and the great tips," Robert said while he boldly stepped into the room.

Khalid still seemed a bit uncomfortable with his presence, but Robert didn't think it had anything to do with him personally.

"Like I said, no problem. I always like to help new players along."

"That's nice. Are you in a large guild?"

It was probably because he was looking out for it, otherwise Robert would certainly have missed it. But it was there, unmistakably. Just before Khalid answered, there was the tiniest hesitation. "No, not really. We're just a couple of level eighties who like to do difficult raids together."

"Do you play often? Or are you too busy with your studies?"

Khalid made a dismissive gesture. "My studies are easy. Still I don't play WoW all the time. Usually I play a little in the evening. Sometimes, when I feel like it, I also play during the day."

Robert was tempted to ask what else he did in his spare time, but decided against it. There would be plenty of opportunity later, when a natural occasion to broach the subject presented itself.

He stayed another ten minutes, discussing the best places for Hunterino to go for his leveling. Robert noted that Khalid had some different ideas than Rebecca that sounded quite viable as well. *Gaming isn't an exact science*, he reminded himself. *There are many different ways to the same goal. Even goals are often not clear in a game like World of Warcraft.*

Robert thanked his neighbor again for his time and help. He retreated to his own room and sat on his bed. He leaned his back against the wall, crossed his legs under his body, and closed his eyes. In this position he remained for at least ten minutes, reliving the last hour. He used his memory as a filter, sifting through everything that had happened and had been said. When he was done, he called Rebecca.

CHAPTER XVIII

A ndy entered the shop fifteen seconds after Khalid. Robert watched him from across the street, partially hidden by a tree. After Andy had formally joined their team, surveillance in real life had become a priority. They had been trailing the man for over an hour now, but nothing out of the ordinary had happened. Khalid had visited a supermarket, where his shopping made Andy sent a message that their suspect wasn't involved in terrorism but seemed to be running a juice bar.

Now Khalid was inside a tobacco shop that also sold all kinds of magazines, books, and candy. After several minutes, Khalid emerged again. He set off in the direction of the Rapenburg. Robert waited for Andy to exit as well before he followed the pair, trailing some thirty yards behind Andy. He received a text message from Andy: *two packs of Marlboro Light*. Surveillance turned out to be rather boring so far.

Khalid didn't look back once. He kept his eyes to the ground, seemingly deep in thought. He stopped twice to transfer his shopping bag from one hand to the other. When they arrived back at the house, he looked up and down the street. His eyes didn't linger on Andy, though. While Khalid turned the key, Andy passed him on the sidewalk, not even once glancing aside.

Robert heaved a deep sigh. He was content that their first surveillance had gone so well. He also felt strangely relieved that nothing out of the ordinary had happened. They had no real plan yet on how to react when something did happen. Robert also realized that it would be difficult to determine whether something was suspicious at all. What if Khalid had met with someone? What should they do then? Involuntarily, he touched the miniature digital camera he was carrying in his pocket, as if to remind himself of the course of action.

Andy had reached the next corner and turned around to look down the street. When he saw that Khalid had entered his house, he jogged back to where Robert was standing.

"That went well, don't you think?" It was apparent that Andy liked their cloak and dagger work. "Pity he didn't do anything."

Robert grunted. "It may seem fun now, but the challenge will be to keep this up for the coming weeks. Or longer."

With a shrug, Andy nodded. "Let's hope we learn something useful soon. Something we can take to the police."

The three of them had agreed to take their findings to the police anyway, as soon as Rebecca joined them. Her arrival was still three days away. Robert and Andy were preparing a briefing document for the police, feeling that committing their findings to paper in a structured way would be the best method to convince them.

They parted, as Andy had other obligations. If Khalid decided to go out again soon, it would fall to Robert to follow him.

Back in his room, he logged on to World of Warcraft. As expected, Khalid was online as well. The man seemed to spend nearly every free moment in the virtual world. Robert decided to leave Khalid and to concentrate on the task of reaching level sixty-eight as soon as possible.

He currently was in a zone called Netherstorm, a bizarre landscape that resembled the surface of a dead moon, inspired by the mind of a stoned graphic designer. It consisted of several immense chunks of rock that floated in space, connected to each other by bridges. The remoteness was broken by mind blasting Eco-Dromes rising majestically out of the dead rock. These Eco-Dromes were bubbles of contained atmosphere, where lush flora and fauna flourished in abundance. When stepping through the transparent wall of one of those bubbles, there suddenly was an impossible jungle. Of course, danger lurked everywhere. There were several so-called Mana Forges, where demons were undertaking some potentially dangerous experiments.

The quest line aimed at shutting those forges down one by one. He was at the last stages of level sixty-six by now and progressing fast, though not fast enough according to Rebecca. He estimated that he would reach the end of his time here in Netherstorm pretty soon.

It happened when he was turning in a quest. Gunslinger was about to enter the local town, when Drimm and Pharad landed at the Flight Master, who was stationed outside the main gate. It took a moment to register that it was really them. He held in and remained watching from a short distance.

The two level eighties didn't waste time. They summoned their own flying mounts and flew off in an easterly direction. There was no sense in trying to follow them. At his level, Gunslinger wasn't eligible for the epic flying skill, like the Grimstones were. Their flying mounts were twice as fast as Robert's own. With regret, he watched them go. Soon, they were nothing more than specs on the horizon.

In quick succession, several other members of the Hammer of Grimstone came online. Pharad and Drimm were now in a place called Tempest Keep. Robert scrabbled it down on a yellow paper. Shortly after each of the newcomers had come online, their listed position changed to that location as well. Robert remembered that Rebecca had once explained that at the entrance of many instances was a so-called summoning stone that could be used to summon absent party members. Apparently, this was what was happening now. They were going to do an instance together. As he couldn't follow them there anyway, he disregarded the group and continued with his own tasks.

He reached level sixty-seven a little over an hour later. The entire Hammer of Grimstone was still in an instance called The Botanica. Robert decided to stir things up a bit. He logged off and logged on again on the alternate account, bringing Hunterino into the world.

He took the flightpath to Ogrimmar and, while he was airborne, he tried to come up with the best approach to Drimm. He decided to keep up the ignorant façade.

"Do you know where One Thousand Needles is?" he asked Drimm, using a whisper.

It took so long for his neighbor to answer that Robert repeated his question a few minutes later. Finally, after one more minute, there came a reply. "Sorry, I was in a boss fight. 1KN is to the south of the Barrens. Just follow the road all the way."

"1KN?"

"One Kilo Needles. One Thousand. Just follow the road."

Fifteen minutes later there was a knock on the door.

"Yes!" Robert yelled.

The door opened and admitted Khalid. He took one step into the room and halted there, as if he had second thoughts about coming here. Robert smiled in welcome. He was pleased with this development.

"Are you doing okay?" Khalid asked.

"I gave up on the Needles place. It was too far away. Look, I'm in Stonetalon Mountains now." He pointed at the screen, which showed Hunterino on the borders of Mirkfallon Lake.

Khalid glanced at the screen, but didn't seem interested. He walked over to the window and stood there for a couple of minutes. He seemed to be studying the dead wall intently. When he was finished, he turned back to the room again.

"If you want me to help you with WoW, it must be in the next two weeks. When Cataclysm comes out, I'll be too busy."

Robert didn't know what to say for a moment. Why was the man telling him this? Was he simply being nice?

"That's a nice offer," he said in the end. "When does the expansion launch?"

"December seventh."

Involuntarily, Robert glanced at his watch to check the date. It was the twenty-fourth. *Rebecca comes tomorrow!*

"Well, if you can help me some, that would be great," he said. "So I have two weeks to reach level eighty?"

This evoked a hearty laugh. "No chance. That's going to take a lot longer than that. And I have to leave town for a few days before that."

Robert tried to hide how this news electrified him. He turned down his eyes and breathed in and out a few times. Looking up again, he tried to sound casual. "Really? Going somewhere interesting?"

Khalid seemed to be watching him intently, but his face showed no suspicion. "Not really, just a few days with some friends in the first week of December."

Desperately trying to pin down the exact moment, Robert said, "Until when do you have time to give me some help?"

"I'll be here until Friday. I'll be back the Tuesday after."

Robert nodded. "Okay, so we still have some time."

"Let's get started. I'll meet you in Sun Rock Retreat."

They played together for two hours. After their exploits of the day before, they had fallen into a kind of easy companionship, which was quite a surprise to Robert.

During this time, Hunterino went nearly two levels up. It went so well that Robert almost regretted that this wasn't his real account. They didn't speak much while playing. Khalid didn't waste time on idle chatter and limited the conversation to short instructions. Still he gave useful advice on the use of some abilities that Robert rarely, if ever, used. As in real life, one tended to stick with familiar things, without exploring new possibilities. Robert vowed to take a fresh look at his Spells and Abilities book as soon as he was back on Gunslinger himself. He was convinced that some of the things he was learning would improve his performance on Gunslinger as well

Rebecca called him near the end. He quickly told her what he was doing with Khalid.

"Well done!" she praised him. "This might help getting his account name and password."

According to her plan, he waited a long five minutes after Khalid had logged off and knocked on Khalid's door. It opened almost immediately. Khalid seemed to expect him.

"I wanted to thank you again for your time," Robert said. "And I wanted to ask you something."

Khalid stepped back, indicating that Robert could enter.

"What more can I do for you?"

"I wondered if you could show me how you play with Drimm. What your screen looks like and what kinds of new abilities I'm going to get when I progress."

Khalid nodded. "Sure. Give me a second to log on again."

Khalid started World of Warcraft again, and they had to wait a few seconds for the log on screen to appear. Unobtrusively, Robert edged a little closer to get a view of the keyboard as well as the screen.

Khalid had checked the box that saved his account name on the computer, so Robert had all the opportunity he needed to memorize the word. The username was a hotmail email address, just like Robert's own username. Unfortunately, it was impossible to discern the following word that Khalid gave in as his password. Khalid typed so fast, he could only see that it started with a G and that it contained two E's. He was able to note though, that it ended with a number combination, as simple as could be; 3-2-1.

He sat on the desk when the character selection came up. To his surprise, he saw that Khalid had three more characters on Sylvanas. Before he could take in any details, Khalid had hit Enter and the screen was replaced by the follow up screen that showed the loading of Drimm into the virtual world. He appeared in Dalaran, on a huge square called Krasus Landing. Until now, Drimm had been accompanied by a bear, but now he had a lion at his side. Robert commented on this, and Drimm explained that a hunter could have several pets, with different strengths and weaknesses. Pets could be stabled at a stable master, to be retrieved when the occasion demanded a pet with specific skills.

"Now I'll show you some of the things a level eighty hunter can do," Khalid said. He summoned an enormous dragon and took off in a southerly direction. "Dalaran is a no-flying zone," he explained. "The place we just left is the only spot where flying is allowed. It's like an airport."

He turned eastward, ascending endlessly to cross a ridge of high and steep mountains. Soon after, they entered a zone called Stormpeaks. It offered steep rocky mountains and large snow-covered plains. Khalid veered eastward and steered the dragon with Drimm on its back into a steep canyon and started to follow it at neck breaking speed. Walls of rock loomed over them as the dragon descended even farther and hugged the solidly frozen water of the river that once flowed here. For a moment Robert wondered about seasons in World of Warcraft. Would this river thaw and run again in several months?

They flew on until they reached an immense flat open area called the Foot Steppes. There was nothing ordinary about the Foot Steppes. In the middle of this plain a seemingly perfect round hole of sheer impossible dimensions was drilled into the ground. Inhuman was the word that came to Robert's mind. There was no telling how deep it was. The dragon perched at a safe distance from the rim of the hole and deposited Drimm in the snow on the ground. The hunter turned toward a large herd of Rhinos that Robert hadn't noticed before. They were all level seventy-seven to seventy-nine, including the three calves that were part of the herd.

"Only the bull is aggressive," Drimm said. "The others won't attack unless they're attacked themselves."

Robert nodded at the telltale colors, red and yellow, that lighted up under the cursor of Drimm's mouse. "Will a Rhino attack to protect her baby?" he asked.

"Possibly. You never know. They might also attack simply because you anger the bull. When you first encounter a new species, always be careful. Especially when they're moving in herds. Before you know it, you're stampeded by ten angry beasts."

While he was killing them one by one, aided by his lion, Khalid demonstrated several different tactics that could be used. Especially interesting to Robert were the tips he gave about how to transfer the aggro between the hunter and his pet. Again, he was learning from an accomplished hunter.

After twenty minutes of demonstration, Khalid announced that he had other things to do. Robert thanked him again and Khalid gave him a wide smile in response.

"No problem. You learn fast. It's a nice game, don't you think?"

It was obvious that the man was enjoying this opportunity to be his tutor. To his surprise, Robert found that he was actually starting to like him.

He smiled back. "Very nice. And addictive. I must be careful that it doesn't ruin my studies." With a pang, he realized that this was exactly what was already happening. If he didn't spend more time with his books, he'd be in trouble.

"Don't say that I didn't warn you," Khalid said. "But it's up to you!"

Back in his room, Robert sent a text message to Rebecca: *Account: AlMaud@hotmail.com*

CHAPTER XIX

"One of the most intriguing things that ever happened in World of Warcraft was the outbreak of the Corrupted Blood Disease in 2005," Rebecca said later that night. "I had just joined the game at that time."

It took Robert a moment to shift his thoughts away from Khalid to this new subject.

Rebecca continued, "Without warning, a lethal and contagious disease started to spread. It started in the big cities, but it quickly spread around the world. Thousands upon thousands of players saw their characters die, everyone panicked. After some time it was hard to find even a small village without dozens of corpses on the ground. Rumor had it that it was a programming bug. A little later there was talk that it was an attack by cyber terrorists. Blizzard tried to stop the spreading of the disease by rebooting the servers. That didn't help."

She had captured his imagination now. "What happened?"

"It turned out to be a virus which originated inside the newly added Zul'Gurub instance. The end boss had been given a special ability. He infected his opponents with a disease called Corrupted Blood that slowly drew away the health of a player."

"So Blizzard added the virus on purpose?"

"Yes, but it was never meant to escape Zul'Gurub. It was programmed in such a way that, upon leaving the instance, the disease was removed from a character."

Robert tried to process this information. "So what went wrong?"

"What happened was that a hunter got infected. His pet got infected as well. Then something happened that the program designers hadn't reckoned with. Before the hunter left the instance, he dismissed his pet. As you know, when you dismiss your pet, it just disappears. *It's simply not there anymore.* So when the hunter left Zul'Gurub, the disease was removed from his own person, but not from the pet. When he summoned his pet again, he was back in a crowded city. Only, the disease hadn't been removed from the pet. You can predict the rest of the story."

"Sure I can. The consequences must have been terrible," Robert replied in disbelief. "What happened next? What did they do about it?"

Rebecca laughed. "What happened next is what makes this so interesting. Blizzard tried to contain the virus by imposing a mass quarantine. Players were ordered to avoid certain areas, like the cities, while other places were designated safe zones. The programmers expected players to do as they were told, and the large majority did. There were others who ignored the quarantine or even seemed to enjoy spreading the virus. In the end, four million characters contracted the Corrupted Blood Disease."

A vision of millions upon millions of virtual corpses scattered around Azeroth came to Robert's mind. He found it difficult, if not impossible, to comprehend. Then a question came up. "Why are you telling me this?"

"Because we need something to make the police understand that they should take us seriously. Until now, they dismissed us out of hand because they regard WoW as just another computer game."

"And how is this going to help?"

"We're going to show them that many scientists take World of Warcraft seriously, exactly because it's so realistic. There have been several studies into the Corrupted Blood outbreak. Reports have been published in serious medical and scientific papers that all support the notion that this is the only realistic model available for studying and predicting behavioral patterns in case of a worldwide pandemic."

Right after ending the call, Robert searched the Internet for support of Rebecca's claim. He found several articles that linked the Corrupted Blood Disease to the study of pandemics in the real world.

Most notably, an American professor called Nina Hefferman received a lot of praise for an article she published in *the Lancet's Infectious Diseases Journal* in 2007.

He carefully read the entire article. He had to admit that the significance of the occurrence seemed to be much greater than a simple programming glitch in a computer game. Maybe it could help convince the authorities to take them seriously. He printed the article and also some of the various comments.

He looked at his watch and saw he had over an hour left of his 'shift'. After that, Andy would be standby to follow Khalid in case he decided to leave the house. With nothing better to do, he went back to the chore of completing the last level with Gunslinger.

The next day Robert took an early train to Schiphol Airport. He was excited at the prospect of seeing Rebecca again. When he arrived at the point where the passengers of Rebecca's flight were to emerge out of the baggage reclaim area, the screens with flight information told him that he had to wait another thirty minutes for the plane to land.

He sat on the ground with his back against the glass wall of one of the many shops. He closed his eyes and let his thoughts drift. They turned to Rebecca and how anxious he was to see her. How was she going to react when she saw him again? They hadn't seen each other for quite some time. Their only contact had been through telephone calls, text messages and, of course, World of Warcraft. He realized that he often visualized her as the Undead avatar Killermage from World of Warcraft.

His thoughts drifted back to the last weeks. Many conversations passed by in his head. Sometimes he had difficulties with the abrupt changes in her attitude toward him. She could swing from light-hearted and funny to businesslike and distant in a matter of seconds. How would it be to see her again? Was he falling in love with her? He just hoped their companionship would be as easy as it had been before she left.

He forced his thoughts away from this course and tried to empty his head. Instead of the void he was looking for, he was suddenly presented with images of himself and his parents when they arrived at this airport over two months ago. Who would have thought that his term of studying abroad would take such a turn? Suddenly, he was assailed by doubts about everything currently going on in his life. He envisioned the disappointment of his parents if he didn't pass the exams in Holland. There was no denying that he was lagging at his studies. On the other hand, what was he to do? Could he just walk away from everything they had discovered? Lives were at stake!

His stomach contracted painfully at all these thoughts and doubts flying through his mind. As if they had a mind of their own, his legs pushed him up and started to walk. The sudden physical movement helped to quell the tide of dark forebodings rising fast inside his chest. He walked up to a counter and bought a newspaper. Next, he ordered a *latte macchiato* and browsed the news.

When he looked up again, he saw that Flight U26923 had landed. Shortly after, the assigned conveyor belt started to move. The area for passengers was separated by a glass wall that was opaque at most places. He tried to get a glimpse of Rebecca between the other people, but didn't see her. He was still trying to see through a narrow band of transparent glass when he felt a knock on his shoulder. When he turned around, Rebecca was standing right behind him. She was carrying an oversized sports bag. Over her other shoulder she'd slung a laptop bag.

"Mr. Gunslinger, I presume?" she said with a wide grin.

Immediately, all the doubts he had been feeling earlier, blew away like a handful of dried leafs in a storm. One look at her face and tumbled hair was enough. With a stab, he realized that he had indeed fallen in love with this Scottish girl. They had gotten to know each other mostly by talking in chat channels in World of Warcraft, but did that matter?

He answered with a grin of his own and said "DING!"

It took her half a second to take in what he meant. Then she embraced him and gave him a kiss on the cheek.

"Gratz on reaching level seventy! When did it happen?"

She made no move to break away, so he held her like that for a few seconds. She reached a little over his shoulders. The smell of her hair was delicious. Making use of the opportunity, he kissed her on the top of her head.

"Right before I left to catch the train. I think it's really cool!"

She stepped back and held out her luggage to him. "If you're level seventy, you're certainly strong enough to carry the bag of a lady."

He took the sports bag and they walked in the direction of the exit. Rebecca asked him a thousand things about his conversations with Khalid, forcing him to remember nearly everything. When she was satisfied, she started to grill him over the briefing document he and Andy had prepared for the police. By the time they arrived back in Leiden, he had no more answers. Rebecca's questions weren't nearly exhausted.

He was relieved by Andy shortly after. As agreed, his Dutch friend was waiting for them in a coffee bar called De Bruine Boon, which was close to the train station.

He had the briefing document with him, and she made him translate it to her word for word. When he was finished, she went back to the killing of Benjamin Natale.

"Look," she said, producing a sheet of paper out of her computer bag. "I made a drawing on scale of Raynewood Retreat."

She put the paper on the table and gestured to Andy to hand her the drawing they had found in the newspaper. Now that they were side by side, the similarities were more obvious than ever. Still, she took the time to point them out one by one.

"There's something else I found on the Internet that's interesting," Rebecca said as she carefully folded the paper and put it aside. She reached into her bag again and this time produced a set of prints in a plastic binder.

"In 2008, a presentation was given at the DNI Open Source Conference that's of interest to us. DNI stands for Director of National Intelligence, by the way. As far as I could determine, it's a conference of the international intelligence community that's not held behind closed doors. It was held at the Ronald Reagan Building. The topic was 'Open Source Challenges.' Among the speakers were officials from Homeland Security and the CIA."

"Open source Challenges, like World of Warcraft," Andy interrupted.

She fixed him with a stare. "Exactly."

She tapped the binder. "One of the speakers was a certain Dr. Dwight Toavs, a professor at the National Defense University, according to the Internet. I was able to find and download the Power-Point of his presentation. In his speech he warned the audience for the threat of terrorists using World of Warcraft to communicate with each other."

She removed the prints from the binder and handed them over to Robert. He leafed through them with Andy looking over his shoulder, noting a map of the zone of Ashenvale behind a slide called 'Decoding the Scenario.' There were arrows on the map, pointing out the Zoram Strand and the neighboring zone Stonetalon Mountains.

Rebecca leaned over, flipped through the sheets, and asked them to read the one she pointed out. They obliged:

> *A simple little conversation in a small corner of a 'digital kingdom.'*
> *One of a million such similar conversations occurring at the same*
> *time on message boards and online games across the country.*

Next, she asked them to read another part, which appeared to be a transcript of the 'little conversation' the former sheet was referring to. Again, Robert read it out loud.

TALON238> Hey War, got your message. What's up?
WAR_MONGER> Leading a big raiding party next Thursday! I need to activate your Guild. You up for it?
TALON238> Yes, the warriors have been training and are organized. Everyone's at Level seventy and ready for action.
WAR_MONGER> Good. This is the big one. Lots of XP for everyone! And a ton of mobs to slaughter!

TALON238> That's what we've been waiting for. Where's the raid?

WAR_MONGER> A fun little romp through StoneTalon Mountains. You know the place?

TALON238> Sure, we scouted the area last year in a party, but left because the White Keep was too strong.

WAR_MONGER> Yes, but this time I want to hit the Keep! We'll take down the Master Mage and his little Gnome. PvP baby!

TALON238> Wow! To take on that Instance, you must have acquired the Dragon Fire spell?

WAR_MONGER> Yes. Last week. In my Inventory and ready to cast. But I need tanks and DPS's to support the raid and clear the guards.

TALON238> We're ready. We just got a shipment of Elite and Epic weapons last month. DPS's have tons of Mana. And the tanks are buffed.

WAR_MONGER> Excellent. The time for the raid is 11:30 am EST. Have everyone online and ready to roll. Rally on me and don't be late! The Alliance may be listening, so only communicate in Whisper mode.

TALON238> Of course. The whole Guild will be there and at your command. Where do you want us to gather?

WAR_MONGER> Come in southeast of The Zoram Strand. Clear out all the mobs. Then we attack the Keep itself and use the Spell. The Oracle says there are 110 Gold and 234 Silver inside. That's the real target!

TALON238> 110 234 Got it. This is going to rock the World!

WAR_MONGER> Remember, eliminate all castle guards patrolling the road to the Keep, and kill all other players in the area then get clear. The Dragon Fire spell will be coming through the south gates of the Keep soon after!

TALON238> Got it. The Horde can't wait to see it burn! The Gods willing, we'll succeed and dance on its burning rubble!

WAR_MONGER> No one will dance there for a hundred years after this spell is cast. The Gods and their magic are with us. The White Keep is vulnerable. Good hunting!

Right after he finished reading the conversation to them, Robert turned to what was called 'Decoding the Scenario.' In the next sheets, it was shown how the bad guys were actually planning a nuclear attack on the White House and how the information about coordinates, attack vector, avenue of approach, and timing were encoded in the conversation.

They remained silent for a few moments. Robert was first to speak. "What do you think?"

She shook her head. "No, I'm curious to know what you think. You've been playing for quite some time now, so you're no rookie anymore. So tell me."

He nodded at Rebecca. "Okay, my feeling is that it's total bullshit. And I'm not even level eighty yet."

"Why do you think so?"

"First of all, Talon238 says that 'all the warriors have been training and are organized.' That suggests that all the guild members are warriors, which is extremely unlikely. He also says that they're all at level seventy, which must have been the maximum level back then. At maximum level, you don't get experience points at all. It has become an obsolete concept. So why is War Monger talking about 'Lots of XP for everyone?' And why does Talon238 answer 'That's what we've been waiting for?' It's total bullshit from a WoW point of view."

Rebecca smiled warmly at him. "Good! What else?"

"Well, they're going to Stonetalon Mountains. I've been there myself, and also in Ashenvale, where the map is from. There are no instances in Ashenvale or Stonetalon Mountains. And there certainly is nothing that a level seventy should turn away from because it's 'too strong', let alone a whole party of level seventies. Hell, I'm level seventy myself now, and I could kill anything that lives in Ashenvale in seconds. And the White Keep doesn't exist. At least, not there."

Still smiling, Rebecca encouraged him with her eyes. Robert started to feel more comfortable. It was amazing how much knowledge he had gained already.

"They say that the White Keep is an instance, and that's indeed the only thing that it could possibly be. But then War_Monger says 'PvP baby!' which is complete nonsense. It's contradictory. Doing an instance has nothing to do with Player versus Player combat."

"Correct. Go on."

"I don't know about a Dragon Fire Spell, but I assume that a spell is mastered. It seems strange and illogical that a spell would be carried in someone's inventory. Then there's the mention of the 'shipment' of elite and epic weapons. I don't know what elite weapons are or if they exist at all, but I do know what epic weapons are. One thing is for sure. They don't arrive in shipments. They appear sporadically, or they can be bought, but usually can't be sent or transferred at all because they're soulbound to the player who picks them up."

This was rewarded by an even broader smile. "Very good. Anything else?"

He smiled back. Andy was looking at them with wide eyes. He was obviously out of his depth, trying his best to follow what they were saying.

"Yes, well, the rest is bullocks as well," Robert continued. "The raid is in a few days, but the tanks are buffed? Everybody knows that a buff exists for only two hours maximum. And the Alliance may be listening? That's ridiculous, because the Horde and the Alliance can't even talk to each other, let alone eavesdrop on each other. And a 'real target' of 110 Gold and 234 Silver isn't going to arouse any player at maximum level, let alone a whole guild. That amount of gold would be peanuts to them."

"So what do you think?"

"I think this scenario is utter nonsense. At least, from a WoW point of view."

Rebecca put a hand on his arm and left it there. She looked him right into the eyes. "I agree, and that's what I don't understand. This whole conversation is ridiculous. You haven't even pointed out everything. In fact, every single line screams 'this is bullshit' to the reader who knows anything about World of Warcraft."

Searching for a metaphor, Robert said "It's like reading a report about Iceland that says the people living there are all negroes, the climate is hot and humid, and that the country is so densely populated that it makes you feel crowded."

She laughed. "Nicely put! The question is why? Why is this report so faulty? Why is it so full of mistakes that it can't be taken seriously? Why did they do this?"

"Do you think the mistakes were made on purpose?"

"What else? Look, this Dwight Toavs. He's a professor, right?"

Robert nodded in confirmation. "At the National Defense University, whatever that may be."

"Exactly. This guy is about science. And scientists are thorough. They investigate. They check and double check their facts. So it's highly unlikely that a professor would present something so obviously and totally wrong. The twelve year old son of his neighbors could have told him so."

"But why would he do it? Why would he make mistakes in his presentation on purpose?"

Rebecca shrugged. "I don't know. My best guess is that it's because they were aiming for the reactions they got. I had a look at some forums. As expected, the presentation hit the WoW community within hours, with countless people commenting on it. Precisely because it's so much bullshit, people were shredding it and tearing it apart, not taking it seriously at all. Maybe that's exactly what they were aiming for."

"You mean they wanted it to be disregarded?'

"Yes!" She leaned forward with glittering eyes. "That must be it!" She hit him on the shoulder quite hard. Robert winced, but didn't pull away. "It's so obvious," she continued. "They didn't want to advertise the opportunities that WoW offers to criminals or terrorists. So they released a research report that would be viciously denounced as utter nonsense as a kind of smoke screen. They got their message across to the people who mattered, but otherwise managed to bury the research report under a stinking heap of ridicule."

Robert whistled. "Clever. If that's what really happened, those guys in the US are smart."

"They could be. It could be plain stupidity as well."

Robert nodded. "Either way, it shows once again that maybe we're not chasing shadows.

"We need to approach this as if we have to convince a jury," she admonished. "At what time do we have the appointment?"

"Tomorrow morning at ten o'clock," Andy answered.

"That means we have only tonight to rehearse our presentation. Robert, let's go to your place first so I can dump my stuff. Then we go somewhere else. Andy, can we use your apartment? We can't risk Khalid walking into the room of his new neighbor friend while we're discussing his doings."

With a big smile on her face Rebecca looked at Andy and said, "Who would have thought that our dear Robert would get friendly with a terrorist?"

Robert was about to protest when he saw her wink. He mumbled something inaudible in reply and stood to pay the bill.

They discussed their case till deep in the night. Finally, they agreed on the order in which it would be presented and on who would tell which part. It was past two a.m. when Robert and Rebecca went back to the ancient house on the square where Robert and Khalid lived. The cobble-stoned streets were silent and deserted, and they walked in silence as well.

In his room Rebecca forestalled any uncertainties about what was going to happen next. She took a toothbrush out of her bag and disappeared to the bathroom. She was away for over five minutes.

"Your turn," she said when she returned.

He nodded and left the room, to discover upon returning that she had produced a bright red sleeping bag and a thin travel mattress. She was just crawling into the sleeping bag when he entered.

He felt a mixture of relief that a potentially awkward situation had been averted by her, and equal disappointment about the way in which it had happened. "Don't you think it should be the other way around?" he asked. "You can take the bed, and I'll sleep on the ground."

She shook her head and smiled at him. "No way. I've slept in this thing often enough. Go get some sleep. Tomorrow is an important day!"

He stood in the middle of the room for a few seconds, unsure whether he should press the point. He decided to give in and started to undress. Rebecca turned her face to the wall.

"Sleep well," he said, a second before he turned off the light.

"Goodnight, Robert."

CHAPTER XX

She woke him at eight o'clock, teasing him out of his slumber with the smell of freshly brewed coffee. "Gratz with level seventy-three," she answered to his mumbled greeting.

He sat up straight. "What?"

She smiled down at him. "I couldn't sleep. So I decided to push on. We're running out of time. You need to be at eighty as soon as possible."

He felt a mixture of regret and elation. One part of him welcomed the extra three levels, another part chafed at having been cheated out of the satisfaction of achieving them for himself.

She seemed to read his feelings and put a hand on his shoulder. "You'll have time to explore the ground I've already covered for you later. Don't worry, it'll be all right."

He smiled back at her. "Yeah. Thanks."

They were brought to the same interview room as before. Only this time, Robert felt much more at ease. Maybe it was the presence of Rebecca, maybe it was the fact that they had really prepared for the occasion, or maybe it was simply because he felt so much more convinced about what they were going to tell.

The man they had come to meet motioned them to sit at the table. The last time, the female police officer had sat opposite them, making it clear there were two sides of the fence. This time, each of them sat at one of the four sides of the square table, making it a much more equal arrangement. Robert glanced again at the business card the police officer had given to Rebecca. *Sander Slingerberg*: what an impossible name to remember, let alone pronounce.

"I take it you have something important to tell me," Mr. Slingerberg began. He looked inquiringly at each of them in turn.

"Indeed," Robert began. "Last time you asked us to keep an eye on my neighbor and to call you when other suspicious things came up. By keeping an eye out, we discovered several profoundly disturbing things. For your convenience, we've put down our findings in a document. It's in Dutch. We'd like you to read it and discuss it with you."

On cue, Andy pushed the file across the table. "*Alstublieft*," he said in Dutch.

Mr. Slingerberg opened the file and flipped through the pages. It held five pages with an extensive narrative of everything worth mentioning about what they had seen and done. Also included were the maps of the murder site in Belgium, the CIA report, the PowerPoint presentation by professor Toavs, and some of the articles about the use of WoW as a research ground for infectious diseases. They had also included several screenshots to give an impression of the texture of World of Warcraft.

"Do I have to read all of this now?"

This time, it was Rebecca who spoke. "That's possible. But we can also give you a summary, leaving the details and proof for you to read at your leisure."

She got a slow nod in return. "That seems a good way to approach this. So which one of you is going to be the spokesman? Or spokeswoman?"

The three exchanged a glance. Rebecca nodded almost imperceptibly. Andy cleared his throat. "Eh, that would be me. We felt that it could best be done in Dutch."

The man looked at the faces of Rebecca and Robert. "Doesn't that bother you?"

"No, not at all," Rebecca ensured him. "As long as we can discuss things in English afterward."

Andy started by giving an outline of the magnitude of World of Warcraft and the many potential possibilities it presented for a criminal organization. To underline his words, he showed documents at the appropriate times, explaining their content.

From there, he took the policeman to the Hammer of Grimstone and the observations they had made. When he showed the maps concerning the murder of Benjamin Natale, Mr. Slingerberg took a full five minutes to study them. He asked some questions, which were answered by Rebecca.

Eventually, they came to the point how Robert had befriended Khalid and the latter's announcement that he would be out of town for several days during the first week of December.

When Andy had finished, Mr. Slingerberg said nothing for a while. He stared at the ceiling, tapping his fingers on the table. After what seemed like an eternity, he turned his attention back to them.

"I must admit that I have no experience whatsoever with computer games. However, after you were here last time, I did a little research into World of Warcraft. I read about it on the Internet and asked around. My conclusion is that what you're saying isn't impossible. Improbable, but not impossible. The point is, it's not up to me to decide whether your story is plausible or not. Another problem is, I know just as much as you, even less, about those attacks you mentioned. They happened outside my jurisdiction. One was in Belgium and the attack on the boat was in another area."

Robert sat forward, boring his eyes into the man. "We understand that, but we don't know who else to turn to. Couldn't you pass this information on? There must be something like an anti-terrorist department!"

Mr. Slingerberg nodded. "That's exactly what I was going to propose. Maybe we should have done that the last time you were here."

The three looked at each other with smiles. "Thank you very much," Rebecca said. "We appreciate that."

"I said I'll pass it on. There are no guarantees."

"I understand that," Robert answered. "How long do you think this is going to take? And what are we supposed to do in the meantime?"

"Fortunately, I have a certain contact I can use. So it'll be a matter of days, at the most. Until then, I propose that you keep doing what you've been doing. If you're right, something may be happening again, and it would help if you were able to get as much information as possible."

They parted with the promise that Mr. Slingerberg, or his contact in the Dutch equivalent of the Secret Service, would contact Andy or Robert as soon as possible. Walking home, they shared many smiles and congratulated each other again and again. Robert marveled at the feeling of relief he was experiencing. Now that they were getting closer to the terrorists, it was good to know they weren't alone anymore. He didn't doubt for a second the police wouldn't follow up on their information now. There was too much at stake, and with all the information they had provided, they just couldn't fail to investigate further.

CHAPTER XXI

B ack home, Robert prepared to attend class while Rebecca started to fiddle with the plug of the Internet connection. She had her notebook on the desk and was busy converting the mono plug into a duo connection.

He watched her, amazed at how competent she was with all things technical. He remembered how easily she had set up a connection with a webcam earlier, allowing him to be a part of the world view of her Alliance rogue in Edinburgh, hundreds of miles away. She seemed to read his thoughts.

"This is only child's play compared to what we're going to do next. Have you thought about a way to get the master key yet?"

He nodded and held up his own house key. While holding it aloft, he proceeded to tell her what he'd come up with. She looked doubtful. "It may work," she conceded, "but it has a distinct disadvantage. It takes an unknown quantity of time right after he leaves before I can start working."

"I know, but do you have a better idea? Look, when he goes away we'll have all the time we want. If we want to move earlier, it's going to be tight."

"Yes, I know. Just make sure that you're ready the moment he leaves!" She tossed him the plug she had removed from the wire. "So get back as soon as possible!"

***

When he returned at the end of the afternoon, Gunslinger was at level seventy-seven. He sat next to Rebecca, who was piloting his hunter toward Icecrown.

"At level seventy-seven you're permitted to fly in Northrend," she explained.

He nodded. It had been an unpleasant surprise to discover that a player had to learn Cold Weather Flying to navigate the arctic skies, a skill which only became available at level seventy-seven. With envy he studied the terrain he hadn't been able to explore by himself.

"How the hell did you manage four levels in five hours?"

"More like three levels, because I was already at the end of seventy-three this morning," she downplayed her achievement. "For the rest, I did some cheating."

"Cheating? I thought cheating was impossible?"

"Well, not real cheating. Let's just say that I spent tons of gold to rake in as many experience points as possible."

He was curious now. "What did you do?"

She gave him a nudge and a triumphant smile. "I bought the services of four level eighty players for the entire afternoon. Not everybody is rich, so let's just say I made them an offer they couldn't resist. They boosted me through no less than six instances and helped me complete some rewarding group quests."

She logged his account off and shoved the other laptop in his direction.

"Let's see if we can make level eighty before tomorrow morning. Gunslinger and Killermage together."

He pushed the computer back at her. "Not without some fuel." He produced two bottles of Margeaux and a small plastic bag.

"Cheeses!" she exclaimed at the smell coming from the bag.

"Also olives, pâté, and Parma ham." He grinned.

She looked him in the eye. "I could get used to having you around."

Robert held her gaze and nodded. "Same here."

She was the first to break the contact. "Let's do this."

In the end, the two bottles of Margeaux didn't carry Gunslinger all the way to level eighty. Only at five o'clock in the early morning and on the fumes of the last dreg of an extra Peymorol, a quite acceptable Bourgogne, did the death throes of a Scarlet Crusader accompany the characteristic sound of the achievement of reaching the final and ultimate level.

They were sitting side by side at his desk, their laptops plugged into the Internet connection Rebecca had split so expertly earlier. They had been working together as a team, tackling quest after quest together. Icecrown was the least attractive part of Northrend Robert had seen so far. Other parts of the continent were often cold, harsh and isolated, but Icecrown was simply dead. Nothing lived there, nothing grew. The ground was solid ice, a kind of glacier that had been broken up at places to accommodate some monstrous constructions. All that moved were the Undead scions of the Lich King, the ultimate evil personage who ruled this place.

Exhausted and jubilant, Robert fell back in his chair.

"Yes!" Rebecca exclaimed, bouncing out of her chair and hugging him. "We did it!"

He hugged her back, exhilarating in the smell of her. The mixture of wine, stale cheese, and sweat was the most intoxicating he'd ever breathed. After some time she drew back a bit, so she could look at him. Their eyes locked. Smiling softly, she cupped his face in her hands, and he saw her mouth approaching his. Then they heard it.

The door across the corridor opened and was closed again. Footsteps swiftly descended the stairs.

Before he knew it, she was up and at the door. She opened it and soon they both heard the front door shutting. The house became silent again.

"Damn, if only we had that key now," she exclaimed. She was all purpose again. "And we can't even follow him now that he's already gone. Who knows what he's up to, in the middle of the night!"

He shrugged. He didn't share her disappointment about the key. That would come. And he didn't particularly relish going out at this very moment. But he did curse Khalid for breaking their moment from the bottom of his heart.

The next morning they started to upgrade Gunslinger's gear. Now that he was level eighty, there was a wide range of exceptional epic gear available that would boost the strength of his character to new heights. Some of it could be bought, some of it could be crafted, but most of it had to be earned. If they were to be on a par with the Grimstones, they had work to do.

Every item in World of Warcraft had a certain item level. Since there were no less than twelve 'slots' on his person to be outfitted, they had a long way to go. The people organizing a raid typically scrutinized each would-be applicant before admitting them into their group. There was no way that Gunslinger was going to be accepted in any group with hard core players like the Hammer of Grimstone.

The easiest way to accumulate gear was to run as many instances as possible. Completing these at heroic setting earned a player emblems, which could be used to purchase epic gear items. There was a feature that allowed a player to queue for instances, but one could complete each instance only once a day, and there simply was only a limited number of instances available.

Rebecca explained to him that they would run the maximum number of instances each day, to gain as many emblems as possible. To improve his gear even further they would also go for the epic Player versus Player gear. "Not a bad idea anyway, as on this Realm open Player versus Player combat is allowed, so there's always the risk of being attacked by players of the Alliance. When Cataclysm arrives, every player and his dog will be out there in the open, and it's going to be a massacre. Horde and Alliance will be fighting each other probably even more than concentrating on new quests and territories."

Instead of fighting they started off by raiding the auction house. This was mainly a matter of spending a lot of gold.

"I leave it all to you." He relinquished the task of deciding what was best for him.

"Aye aye, Sir!" she replied. "You know how girls like to shop!" And Killermage was off, doing exactly that. He went to stand behind her so he could look over her shoulder at what she was doing.

He winced at how much gold they were burning. She still had a little over sixteen thousand gold left. Considering what had been spent already, not forgetting the fortune that had already been spent on gear, training and mounts for Gunslinger, she must have brought something like forty thousand gold with her when she moved to the realm of Sylvanas.

"Actually, forty-five thousand," she replied when he asked her about this.

The magnitude of that sum was so overwhelming that it took a few moments to sink in. In his guild there were often discussions about gold, and he knew nobody who came even close to having amassed such a fortune. Most of the level eighty players had to go through a daily routine of grinding the same quests to produce an income maybe a little over two hundred gold per day. This gold was needed for repairs, food, and, of course, for the occasional extra costs of enchantments and gems.

"How in the world did you get so much gold?"

She looked at him with a coy expression. "That's my secret. As you're so special, I'll share it with you. Some of it, at least."

He looked expectantly at her. "Please, enlighten me!"

"You know, right across from the bank in Ogrimmar, there's a large building. Did you ever notice that?"

"You mean the auction house?"

She rolled her eyes up in her face, mocking him with an incredulous expression. "You mean, you mean, you already know!"

"Oh, come on!" He gently pushed her. "Stop making fun of me. Tell me your secret!"

"I'm serious. The auction house is the answer. Anyone with half a mind and a little guts can easily earn a thousand gold a day by trading smartly."

Before he could press her for further details, she pointed at his own computer, telling him to get on with it. Grumbling a little, he obliged.

Around noon, Khalid returned. They were so immersed in their virtual world that they only noticed when they heard his door slam shut. Twenty minutes later, there was another sound from the corridor. This time, they were prepared.

Robert put a finger to his lips, urging Rebecca to silence, and opened his door a little. Through the crack he could see the disappearing back of Khalid.

"Go!" he whispered, gesturing urgently. She grabbed her coat and hurried after the Egyptian, careful to stay out of sight. At the same time, Robert called Andy to inform him that Khalid was moving and that Rebecca was on his tail.

She was back half an hour later. She reported how she had followed him straight to the faculty of Art History, where he joined a class that would run for two hours. Andy was sitting down the hall next to the coffee machine.

They discussed whether this was enough of a window to try to sneak into his room, but judged it was too risky.

"At least this calls for a break," Rebecca said. She stood and stretched, yawning at the same time. "You want some tea?"

Without bothering to wait for an answer, she knelt by the small low table and started fiddling with the electric water heater. "Amazing, I'm at home already. Do you want a biscuit as well?"

He watched her from where he sat at the desk, marveling at how much he'd become attached to this girl. They had been apart for quite some time. Now she was back, it felt as if that episode hadn't happened at all. He found it difficult that she could be so unpredictable. Their intimate moment of last night, when he'd been so sure that things were finally happening between them, had been with him all day long. In fact, at times he found it hard to concentrate because his mind kept wandering back to that moment. She seemed to have forgotten it. She acted as if it never happened, as if they hadn't been a heartbeat away from kissing.

Rebecca seemed to feel his eyes on her, because she turned around suddenly. She caught his gaze and held it. With an absent gesture she removed one of the stubborn strands of dark hair out of her face. She nodded slowly, more to herself than to him. He wasn't sure what she meant by that, but it felt good.

"We're going to get them!" He didn't know where the words came from, but they were out of his mouth before his conscious thoughts caught up with them.

Again, she nodded. A serious look came to her eyes. "Yes, we should focus on that. We can't afford to let more people die."

The tea and biscuits were the fuel for the next stage.

"This was the easy part," Rebecca warned him. "We acquired everything that we could buy for gold. Buying things is always the fastest way, provided that you have the gold to spend. We'll keep monitoring the auction house. If more things come up for sale, we'll buy them, but don't count on it. The rest of your gear will have to be earned with a lot of sweat and blood."

At seven o'clock Andy called to tell them that Khalid had entered another class.

"Damn, we need to get his schedule," Rebecca exclaimed. "If we had known this in advance, we would have known that we had ample time to break into his room!"

"Working on it," Andy replied. "I'm busy charming the secretary of the faculty. You know how irresistible I am."

They shared a laugh at that, and Andy signed off to have dinner with his fraternity, explaining that this was their weekly drinking eve but that he would stay sober.

From that moment on, they entered a routine of complete madness. To purchase the gear he needed, Gunslinger would have to fight in countless battlegrounds to earn honor points, which could be exchanged for gear. Rebecca had made an estimate of the number of battlegrounds that Gunslinger would have to compete in. According to this estimate, he was going to be in battle for nearly three days in a row.

Battlegrounds were places where armies of the Horde and the Alliance met each other in open combat. There were six of them, right on the brink between different servers. This meant that players from different servers joined together for battle. Robert suddenly found himself fighting shoulder to shoulder with players whom he would never meet outside the battleground.

Rebecca guided him through his first steps in the different battlegrounds, that each had their own objectives. In Warsong Gulch the opposition's flag had to be captured, in Arathi Basin resource nodes had to be captured and defended, the Eye of the Storm was a combination of those two, while in Alterac Valley the objectives were a lot more complex. The Isle of Conquest soon became Robert's favorite, while he quickly learned to hate the Strand of the Ancients.

The Player versus Player combat in those battlegrounds was incomparable to 'normal' gameplay, with its own challenges and demands. It was incredibly fast paced, and real players were much more versatile than computer-controlled opponents. It required another mindset, lightning reflexes, and some different skills.

Her introduction was certainly useful, and she spent four full hours sitting next to him and supplying him with tips and advice. After that, he was stiff and tired. Rebecca took over and suggested that he'd go out to buy some food.

They ate pizzas behind the computer. When they finished their dinner, they heard Khalid return to his room. Five minutes later, Andy entered. He had two six-packs of beer with him. He shared the beers out and sat on the ground with crossed legs. At that time, Robert had taken over Gunslinger again. He was playing and joining the conversation at the same time. Andy and Rebecca were sitting against the wall with cans of beer in their hands, chatting and laughing. The mood in the room was improving by the minute.

When Robert felt he couldn't lift another finger, Andy insisted on doing his part. Even though he had no experience at all, Rebecca started to give him basic instructions on how to play Gunslinger in Player versus Player combat. Andy was eager, and soon he was whooping and cursing as he was killing and being killed. Rebecca was next to him, cheering him on.

Robert sat on his bed and watched them for awhile, but he was getting drowsy, and soon he couldn't keep his eyes open any longer. He tried to fight it, but the fatigue couldn't be denied.

He woke up in the middle of the night, finding that someone had covered him. The lights were out, but the room was illuminated by the harsh glow of the computer screen. He didn't move, watching how the ever changing brightness and colors played on Rebecca's face. She was wearing one of his white T-shirts and her legs were bare. The only thing that moved were her fingers that raced over the keyboard as if she was playing a piano. She was so beautiful, strong, and girl-like at the same time that he felt his body suddenly ache for her.

When the battleground ended, she looked over at him. Seeing he was awake, she came over and knelt at the bed. She put her hand out and gently stroked his hair.

"Sleep now," she whispered. "I'll finish one more battleground, then it's done for today. We have many sleepless nights in front of us, so we need all the sleep we can get."

"Are you sure? Do you need help?" His voice croaked, the result of too much beer and the time of night it was.

She smiled down at him. "No. Sleep now."

He drifted off again with the feeling of her hand on his head.

CHAPTER XXII

Over the course of the next two days, Gunslinger's performance in battlegrounds improved. Once Robert mastered the basic skills, he gradually became an adequate fighter, though not yet ready to face the members of the Hammer of Grimstone after the launch of the new expansion.

The three of them managed to keep Gunslinger busy almost twenty-four hours a day, turning over the keyboard after several hours. In this way they completed as many battlegrounds and instances as possible, collecting a mass of emblems of Triumph and emblems of Frost, that could be used to buy superior gear later. Mostly it was Robert who was in charge, because he was, as Rebecca called it, 'the one who had to do it in the new expansion'.

Meanwhile Hunterino wasn't sleeping; Robert kept playing with Khalid now and then. He had introduced Rebecca to him, explaining that Rebecca was his long-time girlfriend. He told him she was over from Scotland for a visit, so he didn't have as much time to play with Hunterino as he would have liked. He expressed his regret at not being able to play more often with Khalid, as the Egyptian was to leave for a few days soon.

Khalid seemed to think nothing of it. He was busy playing WoW as well. Together with four members of his guild, he played the instance of the Blood Furnace over and over again. This in itself was strange behavior as it wasn't even a level eighty instance, but designed for players of level sixty-four. The so-called heroic version was tuned for players of level seventy. Rebecca knew that place intimately, and she racked her brain for a possible reason for them to do that. The grounds of Raynewood Retreat and the ship at the Cape of Stranglethorn had been clear training objectives. The purpose of raiding the Blood Furnace over and over again eluded them.

Khalid kept to his room most of the time. He did go out several times, trailed by Andy, but nothing out of the ordinary happened. The day of his announced departure approached with nothing out of the ordinary happening.

On the afternoon of December second, several things happened at the same time. At the moment Rebecca returned from the bathroom, Khalid exited his room. He was dressed in a heavy dark colored winter coat and was carrying a big canvas bag.

"Hi, are you going somewhere?" Rebecca asked innocently.

It was obvious that Khalid wasn't in the mood for idle chatter. He murmured an affirmative, without meeting her eye, and turned away from her. With long strides he walked away.

"Well, have fun!" she called to his retreating back. Right after that, she sent a text message to the already waiting Andy, saying that Khalid was on the move. Robert, who had heard their voices through the door, rushed over and handed her jacket and bag to her. She hurriedly shot on the jacket and put on a cap before running down the corridor. Just before she reached the stairs, she turned around and blew him a kiss. A second later, she was gone.

Since they knew in advance that Khalid would be leaving on this day, they were fully prepared. Andy had borrowed his mother's car and had it waiting around the corner. As soon as Rebecca was close enough behind to follow Khalid herself, Andy rushed to the car and drove to the mini ring around the inner city center. He quickly reached a point where he could choose from several directions and parked to wait for further instructions.

Rebecca trailed a fair distance behind Khalid. The weather was typical for this time of year. At a temperature of about forty-three degrees Fahrenheit, a grey cloud cover sprayed a continuous faint drizzle on the world below. At one point she saw him looking over his shoulder, and she moved quickly behind an elderly couple with a white oversized umbrella.

When she saw he was headed to the train station, she quickened her pace. Still, she nearly lost him in the hall of the station. It was only by luck that she spotted him stepping away from one of the big yellow automated ticket dispensers. She hid behind one of the machines herself, while she watched him study a timetable. Her eyes followed him to the stairs to track nine.

She speed dialed Andy. "He's taking the Intercity in the direction of The Hague."

"That's the international train," the Dutchman replied. "It runs all the way to Brussels in Belgium."

Without hesitation, Rebecca started punching the buttons of the ticket machine. She groaned when she saw the amount for a ticket to Brussels. She paid with her debit card and went up to the tracks. She spotted Khalid leaning against a metal pillar near the end of the platform.

Stepping back between a cluster of other passengers, she called Robert to update him on the situation. Meanwhile, Andy had reached the motorway. He pointed his mother's car, a compact VW Golf, in the direction of The Hague. He estimated that he'd be hard pressed to keep up with the train as it followed its course from The Hague to Delft, Rotterdam and Bergen op Zoom at the Belgian border, but that it wasn't impossible.

Robert was still on the phone with Rebecca when the second thing happened. He heard the telltale beep which meant that he had another call waiting. He looked for the number and saw the caller was anonymous. He ended their conversation and answered the call.

"Ernest Fitzgerald," a man introduced himself with an unmistakably English accent. "Is this Robert Barnes?"

"Speaking. How can I help you?"

"I'm working with the AIVD, the Dutch equivalent of MI6. We've been given some information on a possible line on the terrorists that call themselves The Hammer of Righteous Justice. This information originated with you, correct?"

Robert felt his heart make a jump in his chest. *Finally!* Suddenly, his throat felt as dry as barn paper. His affirmative came out as a croak.

"When can we meet?" Fitzgerald asked without any further preamble.

He thought furiously. There was no telling when Andy and Rebecca would return. Their trip could take them all the way to Belgium and maybe even farther. Making a decision, he answered that he was available immediately.

This obviously pleased the man. "We'll be at your place in an hour."

At the end of this hour, the train carrying Rebecca and Khalid was traveling through the endless flat pastures of the province of Noord Brabant. Andy was slightly ahead of the train and nearing the Belgian border. Rebecca was seated in the compartment next to Khalid's and was keeping them updated by text messages. So far, their quarry hadn't moved. He was reading a book and seemed totally unaware of his surroundings.

When the buzzer rang, Robert had just finished tidying his room. It was a small place, and now they were living there with the two of them it kept turning into a mess, no matter how hard Robert tried to maintain order. Rebecca didn't seem to mind as she was only occupied with getting the Hammer of Grimstone.

Half a minute after he pressed the automatic door opener, he met two men halfway down the stairs. They both wore suits, complete with tie, which was uncharacteristic for the Dutch. Robert had noted that even many Dutch politicians had abolished their ties.

They shook hands in the corridor. Ernest Fitzgerald was younger than expected, probably in his mid thirties. He judged the other, a Dutchman by the name of Sjoerd Broersma, to be closer to fifty. Robert invited them in and indicated where they could sit. Suddenly, the room seemed even smaller than before. Nobody said a word while he prepared coffee. He was interrupted by the familiar beep of an incoming text message. Robert reached for his phone. It was an update from Rebecca, telling they just crossed the border and were in Belgium now. He couldn't suppress his excitement any longer.

"You must send people to Belgium at once!" he said urgently. "Khalid is on his way there and we're following him!"

Fitzgerald didn't answer but held his hand out to receive his cup. He stirred some sugar through his coffee and fixed Robert with a stare.

"Very good that we could meet on such a short notice," he said as if he hadn't heard Robert at all. "Let me first explain something about the confidentiality statement you'll have to sign before going any further."

This caught Robert off guard. "What do you mean?" he asked.

The man coughed. "Well, we're keeping our investigation into this Hammer of Righteous Justice strictly confidential. No word to the press about our progress, no matter how they hammer us for an update." Fitzgerald produced a faint smile at his own choice of words, before continuing seriously: "This is an international investigation, with multiple foreign services involved. We want to nail those bastards."

"Forgive me for saying so," Robert said cautiously, "but I have the feeling that you're not close to them yet."

Again, Fitzgerald stared at him. "Who knows," he said after a few seconds. "Still, the question remains, can we trust you?"

"You can trust me."

"Hm. I suppose we'll have to, don't you think? Now, will you promise not to disclose anything we discuss today? To anyone?"

Robert hesitated before answering. "That depends," he said slowly, "on whether 'anybody' includes Rebecca and Andy too. We're in this together."

Now it was Sjoerd Broersma who answered. His English was heavy with the characteristic Dutch accent. "You may share this conversation with them."

"In that case, I promise not to disclose anything to anyone, except for Rebecca and Andy."

"All right. Let me start by saying that we don't discount the possibility of World of Warcraft, or any other online game for that matter, being used as a possible communication channel for criminal organizations. As you already clearly stated in your briefing document, it's perfectly suited for the purpose. It's anonymous, accessible from anywhere, and totally secure."

Robert nodded. He briefly wondered why the man was stating the obvious. When he didn't respond, Fitzgerald continued, "Either way, if it's true that the Hammer of Righteous Justice is using World of Warcraft as their means of communication, and even as their base of operations, that makes them the first. There have been some worries about this, but we haven't seen it actually happen. Yet."

"Until now."

"Maybe. I don't say it is, I don't say it isn't."

Robert was getting a bit irritated. Did they believe him or not? If they believed him, what were they going to do about it? People were dying!

"So what are you going to do about it?" He jumped to the conclusion his brains had reached a second before. "I believe it's time to take action."

"Maybe. It's no use to take action when it doesn't lead to results. We could arrest your neighbor now, but what would we gain by that? Would he confess? Would he give us the names of his accomplices? Would he give us the name of his commander? Would he tell us where and when to find them? And would he tell us what their next target is?"

Robert shrugged. "No."

"And that," Fitzgerald raised a finger at him, like a professor addressing a particularly stubborn student, "is why the national security is in our hands, and not in yours."

The rebuke stung, but Robert had to admit that the man made a point. "So what's going to happen next?" he asked.

"First, we're going to establish that we're indeed onto something. We usually do that by observation. We're going to follow your man wherever he goes. We'll see who he meets, who he talks to, and we'll check those people out. If necessary, we'll start observing those people as well. And we'll tap his phone of course."

A look passed between the two officials and now Sjoerd Broersma took over. The Dutchman finished his coffee and used his index finger to brush some springy grey hairs from his forehead. "We were especially intrigued by how you connected the brutal attack on the *Droesem* to the Hammer of Righteous Justice."

"The *Droesem*?"

"The ship attacked in the harbor of Enkhuizen at the IJsselmeer."

"Ah yes." Robert looked expectantly at Broersma. When nothing more was forthcoming, he continued, "The connection was logical. We knew they were going to attack a ship, because we observed them rehearsing exactly such an event. When we heard about the attack you just mentioned, we put one and one together."

Again, both men remained silent for a short while. Then, with a sigh, Broersma reached into his pocket and withdrew a paper. He slid it over to Robert, blank side up. When he turned it over, Robert saw it was a blow up of a photograph. The picture showed a painting, mounted on a wood-paneled wall. The painting was clearly visible. It was ghastly. It showed the head and torso of a bearded dark-skinned man. The head was in an unnatural position, lolling sideways as if all the muscles and sinews had been severed. Any doubts about the fact that the person was dead were dispelled by a thin rivulet of blood that trickled from the slack mouth.

Robert shuddered. "What's this?" he asked. "Why are you showing this to me?"

"Gruesome, isn't it?" Fitzgerald said. "But take another look at the picture. You'll see why this is important."

When he looked again, he immediately saw what he'd missed the first time. He'd been too shocked by the dead man in the picture. He nodded and handed the paper back to Broersma.

"I presume that you found this on the ship?"

The Dutchman nodded. "Neatly fastened to the wall. The police missed it at first, but finally someone wondered about the strange painting. Then someone noted that the dead face belonged to the owner of the ship, who was lying only a few feet away in a similar pose. And when they read the signature on the painting, we were called in."

"*The Hammer of Righteous Justice*," Robert breathed.

"Exactly."

"Why? We wondered about that. The papers said the boat belonged to a drugs dealer and that this was nothing but a liquidation in the criminal circuit. A gang war."

"In a way, that's not untrue. Jahal al Haddouti, a Saudi Arabian, was certainly running a drug trafficking business." He held up the photograph again, indicating he was talking about the dead man. "He was an important link in the export business of Afghan heroin to Europe. On the surface, he was just that. But two months ago, we found out that the profits were laundered in Luxembourg and Germany, then transferred to a bank account that we'd been watching lately. Money from this account had been used to purchase explosives for a particularly devastating suicide bombing in Pakistan."

"I see." Robert was trying to come to grips with the sudden broadening of the scope of what they were dealing with. "So, this man was a terrorist as well? Why was he killed then?"

"Good question. And the answer has us worrying. When we found out about all this, Jahal al Haddouti was quietly brought in. We surprised him at one of the rare occasions that he wasn't surrounded by his body guards. We picked him up while he was visiting his mistress."

At this point, Fitzgerald took over. "Much sooner than we expected, Al Haddouti broke. It seemed he had gotten so accustomed to his luxury life, that he just couldn't stomach the prospect of a lifetime in prison. Unlike many terrorists, he was in it for the money, not for some higher religious goal. He couldn't give us very valuable information, because he was only a middle man after all. Still, he cooperated much better than expected. To top all that, we were able to close a deal. In return for his freedom, he would continue his business as usual for six more months, giving us full disclosure on all his transactions, clients and contacts. At the end of that period, he'd be able leave the country unhindered and vanish."

"So he was killed because he was turned?"

Fitzgerald nodded. "And they weren't subtle about it either. By leaving that painting behind, they sent us the message they knew exactly what had happened."

Robert served another round of coffee. Now it was his turn to talk. Again, he wanted to start by telling how Andy and Rebecca were on Khalid's trail right at that moment. However, the two men insisted he told everything from the beginning. This he did, even though it was sometimes hard to keep focus because of the many questions they had. They also wanted him to show World of Warcraft to them, which he did. He started by taking them to the relevant places. They were especially interested in the ship. Afterward, they spent some time randomly navigating several zones and cities. While they were online, Rebecca called to check in. He told her he was still talking to the AIVD and put her on the speaker phone.

She introduced herself and got straight to the point. "We lost him. He got out at Antwerp Central Station, and I was able to follow him right through the main exit and onto the plaza in front. Andy wasn't here yet, he was having trouble getting into the city. Khalid went down into the parking lot underneath the station. He had a car waiting for him! He just went up to it and drove away. There was nothing I could do."

Fitzgerald cursed. "Did you get the license plate?"

"Of course!" she said indignantly. "It was a dark blue Toyota Corolla with Belgian plates."

She read off the plate number and after Broerse had written down the combination of letters and numbers, he left the room. Fitzgerald asked her more questions about the trip, but when it was clear that nothing out of the ordinary had happened, they ended the call. Rebecca and Andy would drive home by car and expected to be back in the evening.

Broerse returned and they continued their questioning. When Robert was at the end of his narrative, he felt utterly exhausted.

"You've done well," Fitzgerald said. "It took guts to proceed when the police turned you down. We can only thank you for that."

Robert nodded. "Will you take over from us now?" Speaking the words, he suddenly realized he didn't really want the adventure to end.

Again, a look passed between the two men. "No, not yet. We're going to ask you, the three of you, to cooperate and continue like before. Well, not exactly like before, but close. A lot seems to revolve around World of Warcraft, and we have no experience whatsoever with the game. On top of that, you've befriended him, and that may be the best way to get information. Will you help us?"

Feeling relieved, Robert said he would. "So, what will happen next?"

"We're going to put surveillance on Khalid as soon as he surfaces again. And we'll obtain permission to get access to all kinds of information, like his phone bills, credit card statements and the like. Maybe even to enter his room. Apart from that, we're going to see if it's possible to get information from Blizzard Entertainment on the accounts of the Hammer of Righteous Justice through our colleagues in the United States. That may take some time, but it may also give us some valuable information like IP addresses that lead somewhere."

Robert quickly explained what Rebecca and he had planned. A pensive look appeared on Fitzgerald's face, but it was Broerse who answered. "You'll understand that we can't officially endorse such an action. If I were to know what you intend to do, it would be my duty to tell you to refrain from it. Therefore, I have just forgotten what you said a minute ago. You understand that we're not responsible for anything you do as a private citizen?"

Keeping eye contact with the Dutchman, Robert nodded. *They were still on their own.* "I would never do anything that goes against the law," he said solemnly.

With the promise they would be in touch, the two men departed. Alone again, Robert didn't know what to do. He logged on to WoW but found that he wasn't in the mood. He knew he should call Rebecca and Andy, but the prospect of more talking daunted him. All those long days and nights playing World of Warcraft, in combination with the tension of dealing with dangerous terrorists, suddenly took their toll. With a deep sigh, he put aside his fatigue and made the call after all.

CHAPTER XXIII

Even though they knew they were alone, Robert and Rebecca stole soundlessly into the room. The place smelt stale and dank, as if it had been unoccupied for weeks instead of a mere twenty hours. Khalid always kept his curtains shut, allowing even less of the cigarette smoke to escape through the small window opening. Two full ashtrays were on the desk; another was right next to the bed. A mountain of clothing was piled high on a chair, probably waiting to be taken to a laundry service. One corner was taken up by a small pile of books that balanced perilously on an empty cardboard box. Rebecca carefully fingered the uppermost book. It was about Johannes Vermeer, the famous Dutch painter. At first glance, all the books seemed to be related to the subject of Art History, which Khalid was studying.

"Let's start," Robert mouthed silently. The chance that they would be caught was negligible, still he wanted to be out of there as soon as possible.

She nodded and took the tiny camera out of the plastic bag she was carrying. Since Khalid's room was an exact copy of Robert's, albeit in mirror image, they been able to test and practice the set up endlessly. They worked quickly and efficiently.

Rebecca lithely clambered onto the desk that was right against the window sill. She took a moment to balance herself, then positioned the camera on the small wooden ledge just above the extreme left hand top corner of the window. She made it so that it was mostly hidden by the curtain. She held out her hand, and Robert handed her two strips of transparent tape. She stuck one to the back of her hand

and used the other to fasten the webcam. The other piece of tape was used to secure it in place. After a last check, she switched it on.

Robert was kneeling on the ground with Rebecca's laptop. It took far longer than expected for the Bluetooth connection to be established. After some time of fruitless waiting, he got a failure message.

"It isn't connecting!" he whispered urgently.

With a barely suppressed curse, she jumped down from the desk and kneeled beside him. Her swift fingers ran over the keys. After two attempts, she sat back. With a pensive look on her face she stared at the ceiling.

"Check the relay unit," she ordered.

With a nod, Robert scrambled to his feet and went back to the hallway. There were two lights fastened to the ceiling, one of which wasn't working. He stretched and reached up to the defunct one. With a few turns he unfastened the opaque crystal ball and removed it. Inside was the tiny device they had put inside earlier. He turned it over in his hand and saw it was switched off. "Idiot!" he murmured to himself.

"Check again!" he called softly to Rebecca.

Just when he had put the crystal ball back where it belonged, Rebecca appeared in the doorway. She gave him a thumbs up and turned back into the room.

With a nimble jump, she was on the desk again. He kneeled by the computer and looked at the screen. It showed the table top in amazing detail.

"A little to the left," he instructed. She tweaked the camera until Robert indicated that it was right. Once it was accurately aimed at the spot where Khalid usually placed his laptop, Robert used the arrow keys to test the zoom of the camera. Satisfied, he closed the laptop.

"Ready? Let's get out of here!"

She gave him a broad smile and held up her hand for a high five. He met the gesture, and they stood like that for a minute, surveying the room. Only when they were satisfied that it looked exactly like how they found it, they left the room. Robert secured the door behind them, making sure it was locked.

"We still don't know the meaning of the word AlMaud," Rebecca mused half an hour later. She was lounging at the desk in a relaxed pose with her feet on the table top. With one hand she was idly clicking through endless pages with Google search results.

"There's no end to the references to Orchids. People in France are called Almaud, a rapper uses the name, there is a castle in Spain. Hell, we'll never know what the word means."

Robert lay stretched on the bed, his hands behind his head. "Maybe there is no meaning," he said. "It could be just that. A word."

"Nah, I don't believe that. There must be a meaning. It might lead us to his password."

She typed something in the search bar and hit Enter again. By her expression, he could see she had hit another blank wall.

"What did you try now?"

"I typed *What is the meaning of the word AlMaud.*" She shrugged. "Doesn't really shed any light. Listen to this search result:

Rose Mkamth the Almaud Love, love leaves. Why not preventing and responding... Requests blessings beloved meaning. You HE filled life. All souls who HE...

Disgusted, she pushed the mouse away and swiveled around to face him. "We'll have to wait until Khalid returns, then we'll find out soon enough. It's just that I'm a bit impatient."

With a grunt Robert heaved himself up from the bed and came over to her. He took the mouse and flicked back a few of the pages she had been watching. Suddenly, something clicked in his brain.

"Do you still have that text message I sent you?" he asked.

She gave him an uncomprehending stare. "Sure. What for?"

"Just get it."

After some searching in her inbox, she presented him the phone with the text message on the screen. *Account: AlMaud* he read.

"I'm not sure that's right," he said slowly. "Maybe I made a mistake. I think it was written differently, with a T at the end."

He reached over and typed *What is the meaning of the word Al-Maut.* After he hit enter and the results came up, they were both silent for a few heartbeats, digesting the information. Rebecca was the first to speak: "Well, that settles it, I guess. An account name with a meaning!"

"Just like you thought," he replied. With his index finger he tapped the screen, indicating the very first search result:

Alamut is from the Arabic word almaut, meaning death. Notice the closeness of the Latin and English mort with the Arabic maut.

"Did you read the fifth one?" Rebecca pointed a little lower:

19 Mar 2003 ... The meaning of Jihad Dictionary of Islam defines Jihad as: "A religious ... He and his followers captured the hill fortress of Almaut in ... According to it, Jihad is "the most glorious word in the vocabulary of Islam ...

He just nodded and didn't reply. They were both reading the various excerpts from web pages unearthed by the search engine in response to their query. Exactly at the same moment, they arrived at the bottom of the screen. "Holy shit!" Robert exclaimed loudly.

Rebecca just whispered, "I'll be damned."

The header read *Pedestrian Infidel: Islam's twelve Steps to Destroy Dar al-Harb (Land...* and was followed by one of the characteristic short jumbled texts. It was there that they found it:

*31 Oct 2005... in Iran one by one, and finally **Almaut** itself fell in twelve-hundred fifty-six... **World** of Warcraft Gold, do you know they have the same **meaning**, Both of...*

Impatiently, Robert clicked on the link. The screen went blank and, after a long wait, they were presented with an error message: *Oops this link appears to be broken!*

Two days later they got a call from Ernest Fitzgerald. They had nothing new to tell him. After some prodding, Fitzgerald grudgingly divulged that the car in which Khalid had driven away in Antwerp was a dead end. "Leased by some postbox company from Dubai, paid for in advance," he explained.

"It does prove that he's not just an innocent Art History student on an exchange program," Robert interjected. "Normal people don't drive around in cars rented by front companies in the Gulf."

"That's right, usually they don't."

After promising to notify him as soon as Khalid returned, Robert ended the call.

"At least, that settles it," Rebecca said. "We were right from the beginning. That Fitzgerald should show some gratitude. Without us, they'd still be in the dark. Now, thanks to us, they have something to work on."

CHAPTER XXIV

Khalid came back sometime during the night. It was Rebecca who noticed. She went to the bathroom early in the morning, and out of habit she checked the tiny woolen thread they had attached at the bottom of their neighbor's door.

Her gentle prodding forced Robert to open his eyes. His sleep clogged mind didn't take in what she was trying to tell him at first. All he registered were her tousled curls and deep brown eyes that were far too close to his face for comfort. The second thing he noticed was her smell, the unrefined fragrance of her body, just roused from sleep and nothing but pure Rebecca. He smiled, and his spirit leaped out of his eyes, reaching out to her. His reaction was so genuine and coming from so deep within, it seemed to take her by surprise. Involuntarily, she withdrew a little.

The intensity of the hurt he felt surprised him. He cursed himself for laying his feelings so bare to her, for making himself so vulnerable. Again, he promised himself to take some time alone to examine his feelings for this girl, and determine what he should do. He was obviously attracted to her, had even fallen in love with her, but what were her feelings for him? Her attitude toward him swung from intimate to distant and sometimes to businesslike. It suddenly occurred to him that their relationship had been easier while she was still in Scotland and they only met each other in the virtual world. Now that she was sleeping no more than a few feet away from him every night, he felt more tension than before. He definitely needed some time to think things over. He didn't want to lose her friendship, but it wasn't easy to consider matters of the heart when there was a dangerous terrorist lurking at the other end of the hallway.

A hot shower helped to shrug his heartache off. When he returned fully clothed, Rebecca was behind her own computer, staring intensely at the screen. He stood behind her and shared the view of Khalid's room. It was dark in there, and very little could be distinguished. Rebecca panned the camera all the way to the left, but Khalid's bed was just out of range.

"Weird to be spying on someone in this manner," she remarked absentmindedly. "Maybe it's a good thing we can't watch him in his bed."

"You're right. Could you put the camera back in the neutral position, else he hears the whirring."

They had bought the camera with the quietest electrical motor available, but it still made a little noise when activated. They had tested it beforehand, and both agreed that it was highly unlikely that he would hear it. Now that it was all for real, he felt it was better to avoid any risk. Suddenly, fear gripped him. They were dealing with a ruthless terrorist organization, with people who killed as easily as he swatted a bug. *As easy as I kill other people in WoW myself.*

"Shouldn't we call our friends at the AIVD?" he asked.

"Nah. It's not even six o'clock in the morning. Let them sleep."

"Are you sure?"

She looked at him as if daring him to admit he was afraid. "I'm not sure. But nothing is happening. He's asleep. Besides, they're probably watching this house already."

A sudden insight flashed in his mind. "You don't really want them involved, do you?" he asked. "Honestly?"

This time, it was Rebecca who looked away. It took some time before she answered. "I don't know. I mean, it was our investigation. It was, still is, exciting to be on the trail of something big. I'm not sure I want it to end."

Before Robert could answer, she hastened to add, "I do want it to end. I really do. I mean, the killing must end! But I must admit I like what we're doing. It gives a purpose."

He considered what she'd said. What she tried to express wasn't entirely unlike his own feelings. "All right. But we'll make the call at nine o'clock."

Half an hour later, the lights in the other room went on. They were alerted by the sudden brightening of Rebecca's computer screen. While Robert and Rebecca hurriedly seated themselves on the front row, Khalid walked into view. He was barefoot and only dressed in boxer shorts and a T-shirt. They watched him light a cigarette and sit at the desk. For a second, he looked straight into the camera. They both held their breath, but there was no reason to worry. He reached behind him and heaved a bag onto his lap. He unzipped the bag and got his laptop out. He put it on the desk, exactly at the spot they had chosen as the focus point of their little camera.

"Yes!" Rebecca cried out, immediately putting her hand for her mouth. In her enthusiasm, she punched Robert on the arm.

"Ouch!"

"Don't be a sissy. Come on, let's concentrate!"

They both sat forward, eyes glued to the screen, and witnessed how Khalid booted the machine. Not surprisingly, he launched World of Warcraft.

It went fast. With the practiced movements of one who had entered the same information in the same box countless times, he rapidly punched in his password. It was done quickly, there was no way they could decipher the word nor the combination.

The information was duly verified by Blizzard and the character selection sheet came up. Khalid immediately hit the Enter key, making it impossible for them to distinguish exactly how many different characters he had, or what they were called.

The other computer made a sound. Robert looked over. *Drimm has come online* the text box announced. The social window told them he was in Dalaran. Indeed, at the same time, on the other monitor, they saw the level eighty hunter appear right in front of the entrance to Sunreaver Sanctuary.

Rebecca pushed the computer with WoW away and turned her attention back to the one showing Khalid sitting behind his desk, now steering Drimm to the side garden with the fountain, all part of the secluded Horde section in Dalaran. Here were the portals to all the major cities on the other continents.

"He's going to Silvermoon City," Rebecca said immediately. "The portals to Undercity, Ogrimmar and Thunder Bluff are on the other side." True to her prediction, Drimm emerged in the home city of the Blood Elves. They watched how he proceeded along the endless corridor like streets.

"He's going to the auction house," Robert said.

She nodded. "That figures. He's been offline for several days, so checking the status of his trading business is the logical first thing to do."

They watched Khalid a few more minutes. When it became apparent that nothing more was happening, Rebecca ended the current recording and started a new one. That done, she opened the explorer and looked up the file that held the images on the hard disk.

The quality of the recording was exactly the same as the live images they had just been watching. By using some special program, Rebecca managed to add more light and brightness and to enhance the detail level. She fast forwarded to the point where Khalid gave in his password, freezing the recording at the moment that the log-on screen appeared. Everything on Khalid's computer was clearly readable, including the account name.

"You were right, the account name is AlMaut and not Almaud," she said. "It's a pity that the password is protected from prying eyes like ours. Anything you type is shown on the screen as an asterisk."

Robert sat forward. "Yes. But we can watch the strokes on the keyboard."

"That's right. Now let's see if we can decipher his password. I'm going ahead real slow, so pay attention!"

The video played at a speed of one frame rate per second. They watched Khalid's right middle finger descend excruciatingly slow onto the keyboard. The first letter he hit was the G.

"I told you it started with a G," Robert said smugly. "The next letter is an E, and there's another E in the word as well. It ends with 3-2-1."

"Just watch," she replied, writing down the first letter on a scrap of paper.

The second letter was indeed an E, entered with the index finger of the left hand. At the third letter, it became more difficult. It was done by the right middle finger again, but it was hard to distinguish exactly which letter it was.

"It could be the G again, but I'm not certain," Robert said. "It may be that he shifted his hand a little."

Without answering, Rebecca picked up the mouse. A few clicks later, they were looking at the same motion again.

"It's still not clear. It could be a G, but also an H. Maybe even a B or a N."

"I agree. This is harder than I thought. It's a pity that his hand is blocking the view of the keyboard."

Robert nodded. "Can you show it again? Even slower?"

"Sure. I can even zoom in a little more at the keyboard."

On the screen, Khalid bent over a little and started typing. Rebecca froze the motion. "No doubt about it. That's a G. Notice how he really punches the letter. The poor keyboard must hurt."

She clicked again, and the jerky movements continued. They could clearly see the man enter the second letter: E. Instantly, he was frozen again.

"Now concentrate on the hand, not on the finger," Robert advised. He nodded for her to continue.

Before their eyes, from one frame to the next, Khalid's hand made a slight movement to the right. It seemed that he moved a little to the bottom as well. Robert stared at the keyboard, looking at the position of the keys and thinking. "My guess is as good as yours. It could be another G, even money on an H, but maybe a B or a N."

She froze the picture again and wrote down the possibilities he'd just named. That done, they continued with the next letter. The immobile Khalid on the screen came to choppy life again. They watched how his left hand produced the next letter. This one was easy: another E. She halted the video again and wrote it down.

"So now we have GEGE, GEHE, GEBE or GENE," she said. She looked at the words for a minute, trying to make something out of it.

The next letter was a N. This time it was clearly visible how Khalid shifted his right hand a little to the right. The camera clearly registered how his finger pressed the key. The N was followed by an unmistakable A. They were looking at a frame that showed his left index finger pressing the A, all the way to the left of the keyboard. The note now read GE(GHBN)ENA.

"This is almost too easy," Robert laughed.

"I'm not so sure. In fact, I don't know if there's a restriction to the number of times you can give in a wrong account number. It wouldn't do if we disabled his account by entering the wrong code three times. That would certainly alert Khalid to the fact that someone is trying to hack his account. Besides, we're not done yet."

She activated the video again. It was as easy as Robert thought. They watched Khalid enter three digits, the same numbers that Robert had noticed when he was standing next to the man when he was logging on a few days ago.

"GEGENA321, GEHENA321, GEBENA321 or GENE-NA321," Rebecca said. "Something tells me that this word also has some meaning, just like the word AlMaut. Probably another Arabic word. All we have to do now is find the right one."

For the next hour, they tried various options on the Internet, but found nothing that seemed right. All the words seemed to exist in some way, either as the name of people, pop bands or geographical locations.

At nine o'clock, they went to Andy's place. Robert called Ernest Fitzgerald, putting the phone on speaker. If the man was aware of the fact that Khalid had returned, he didn't reveal it. He just thanked Robert for notifying him.

"We may have cracked his password for World of Warcraft," Robert told him proudly.

This evoked more interest. Fitzgerald wanted to know exactly what they had done, not commenting on whether it was legal or not. He asked many questions, and they found themselves recounting in detail everything they'd been doing for the last hours. Several times he asked Robert or Rebecca to repeat something because he was writing everything down and couldn't always keep up with them. At the end, he gave them an email address to send the video file to.

"Our people will take a look at it, too. We have several specialists in this kind of thing. I also want a linguist to have a crack at those words."

He signed off with the announcement that he'd be unavailable that afternoon.

"If anything comes up, it'll have to wait until tomorrow morning. So be careful. I can't say that I'm happy with the risks you're taking. Promise me to sit tight. Don't expose yourselves. This isn't a game. You're definitely not equipped to deal with these people. Is that understood?"

He waited until they had all given their assent. Only then he thanked them for the information and said goodbye.

At noon, Andy came over to them. The camera still showed Khalid behind his desk, playing World of Warcraft. They had watched how he got dressed a little over an hour ago. He hadn't even showered nor eaten anything.

By that time, all the Grimstones were online. They were each going their separate ways, doing things that were apparently unrelated to each other. Many were hanging around in the various cities.

They observed some of them for a while. It seemed they were doing nothing but some innocent trading at the auction house.

"They're all preparing for the big moment," Rebecca said. "Tomorrow the new expansion is in the stores, and the new world of Cataclysm is ready for exploration. Reaching level eighty-five as soon as possible is the goal."

Robert had been reading up on all the available information on the expansion during the last few days. There was a host of information available on the Internet. Prior to the launch, Cataclysm had been open to a small group of players on the Public Test Realm. This meant that people could try out the new content in an enclosed environment and give their feedback as well. To the developers, this provided valuable information, not only on the inevitable bugs, but also on how people experienced things. The people who had been playing on the Public Test Realm had put a lot of their findings on the Internet and additionally uploaded many pictures and screenshots.

Andy had taken up the task of breaking the password. He was sitting on the edge of Robert's bed with a laptop on his knees. Now and then he scribbled furiously on a sheet of paper. After some time, he threw them away disgustedly.

"Can't we get him to log on again?" he asked. "Maybe if we have another recording, it'll become clearer."

"We've been thinking of that, too," Rebecca said. "But short of barging into his room, we can't think of a way to force him to log off."

"We could accidentally trigger the fire alarm?"

Seeing the sudden interest on Rebecca's face, Robert put up a hand. "Easy now. we shouldn't force our hand. Remember what Fitzgerald said. Let's keep our heads down."

Finally, at four o'clock in the afternoon, Khalid interrupted his gaming. Their interest in watching the immobile figure at the desk had waned long before that moment, so it could happen that they were alerted by the sound of his door opening and closing.

They all held their breath until the sound of footsteps had receded down the stairs.

"Go!" Rebecca commanded Andy. "Hurry or you won't catch up with him!"

Their friend was already halfway to the door, putting on his coat at the same time. He winked at them and was gone.

He was back forty minutes later. All three crowded around the computer screen that showed how Khalid got out of his thick winter coat and seated himself at the desk again. Andy quickly brought them up to date: "He went to the big supermarket at the *Hooigracht*. He bought milk, orange juice, bread, cheese, tomatoes, and a whole lot of candy bars. On the way back he stopped at the tobacco store he always visits and bought a carton of Marlboro Light. He didn't talk to anyone but the girl at the counter of the supermarket and the shop keeper of the tobacco store."

Instead of turning back to the computer, the man on the screen started to prepare a sandwich. He shoved the computer aside and put a plate in front of himself. Robert realized again how weird it was to spy on someone who was totally unaware of the fact that he was being watched. When he had made a double cheese sandwich, Khalid took a large bite and turned to his computer. With the same deft movements as before, he logged on to his World of Warcraft account. As soon as he was finished, Rebecca saved the file.

This recording wasn't as good as the first. The computer had been turned slightly, deteriorating the angle of the camera. The motion of the left hand had become practically undistinguishable. The other hand, the one they were most interested in, was still visible.

Like they had before, they watched the process in extreme slow motion. Robert felt disappointed that it didn't become any clearer what the third letter of the password was. Rebecca and Andy didn't share his disappointment. "I think we can discard the letter N on the basis of what we just saw, so that does bring us a little closer," Andy said.

"Crossing off the N may be more important than just reducing the possibilities by one," Rebecca added. "I looked up the policy on password protection. You can enter two wrong passwords before your account is disabled. After that, you have to reset your password, for which the linked email account is necessary. We can't afford that, not only because we can't access Khalid's email, but simply because we can't give away what we're doing."

Andy interrupted her. "We only have three possibilities left now. So we should be able to hack into his account without risk!"

"Nothing is without risk," Robert said. "I'm not so sure as the rest of you about this. For now, our friend is doing some battlegrounds." He nodded in the direction of the screen, which showed how Drimm was just emerging out of the cave at the beginning of Alterac Valley. "I think I'll join him."

He sat down and started WoW on his own computer. Shortly after, he was in the queue for a spot in Alterac Valley.

While Robert was doing battlegrounds, sometimes fighting in the same team as his neighbor, Rebecca and Andy immersed themselves in the possible meaning of the password again. They scouted endless Internet pages and rewound the two recordings of Khalid entering his password again and again.

At dinnertime they ordered pizzas. While they ate, they discussed the next steps.

"We won't have much opportunity to hack into his account the upcoming days," Rebecca said. "As of tomorrow morning, he'll be playing WoW more or less nonstop. My guess is that he won't rest until Drimm is at level eighty-five."

"We can do it at night," Andy suggested.

Robert scowled. "We can also let the police do it. What will happen if those terrorists find out about this?"

Both Rebecca and Andy looked at him in surprise. "Are you scared?" Rebecca asked.

He answered without hesitation. "Yes, I am. Scared to death, if you really want to know. And you should be scared as well. We have every reason to be afraid."

It was Andy who nodded first. "Robert is right. Maybe sometimes we forget what we're doing, who we're dealing with. We mustn't take any unnecessary risks."

After these words the spirit left them a little. They all went back to what they had been doing, Rebecca and Andy watching the recording and arguing over the password and Robert playing battlegrounds.

At 22:00 hours Robert alerted them to the fact that Khalid had just logged off. The others had just agreed the password was most likely GEHENA321.

"He's going out again," Robert said urgently. "Look, he's putting his coat on!"

Andy looked out of the window at the cold December night. It wasn't raining for a change, but an unfriendly wind was blowing through the streets. He sighed, obviously not pleased at the prospect of going out.

"I'll go after him," Rebecca suddenly announced. "I need some fresh air. You guys be prepared to enter his account as soon as he has a distance of five minutes away from the house."

She left the building twenty seconds after Khalid. Two minutes later, she sent them a text message saying that her quarry was going in the direction of the city center. Shortly after, she ordered them to give the account a try.

Robert took a deep breath and sat up straight in his chair. He positioned the computer again, so everything was right as it should be.

"We have two tries," Andy said encouragingly. "Maybe even three if we want to take the risk."

"Yes I know. So what's our first try?"

"GEHENA321," Andy spelled.

Robert slowly entered this into the box, careful not to make a mistake. He glanced up at Andy, who had been looking on, for confirmation. At his nod, he clicked on the Enter button.

The information you have entered is not valid. Please check the spelling of the account name and password. If you need help in retrieving a lost or stolen password or account.

"Damn!" Andy exclaimed. "I was so sure it was GEHENA!"

Impatiently, Robert drummed his fingers on the table top. "What's your next bet, mister Code Cracker?"

"That's difficult. I was so sure the middle letter was an H!"

"We crossed off the N, so that leaves us with two possibilities. Tell me which one it is."

Andy shook his head. Clearly guessing, he said: "B. The word is GEBENA."

Nodding, Robert entered the word and added the three digits at the end. He pressed Enter again.

This time, they both cursed as the error message came up. "One more chance left," Andy said. "Let me think for a few moments more!"

At that moment, Robert's mobile rang. It was Rebecca.

"I think he's going to the train station," she said. "Have you cracked the code yet?"

He quickly explained how they were having no luck at all. Rebecca agreed that GEHENA had been her personal favorite as well.

"Did you consider double input as well?" Robert asked.

"What do you mean?" the others both asked at the same time.

"Well, you guys were so busy with the password and Internet that I presumed you took a look at that as well. I'm talking about the possibility that he pressed the same button *twice*."

Their silence told him enough. Andy was looking at him as if he was seeing him for the first time. With a jump, he was at the other computer, where Google was still open.

"My God!" he exclaimed. "Look at this!"

Robert walked over as well, holding the cell phone in the air. "What? What?" Rebecca's thin electronic voice could be heard asking again and again.

On the screen the answers to the question *What is the meaning of the word gehenna* were displayed. Robert immediately saw what Andy meant.

"It's GEHENNA instead of GEHENA," he told Rebecca through the phone. "In combination with the word Death as account name, this must be it!"

He read the search results out loud: "*Gehenna: Place where the dead are judged, the abode of the wicked...*"

"What are you telling me?" she asked.

"Apparently, the word Gehenna is derived from the ancient Greek language," he explained. "What's more important, it means 'hell' in a lot of languages and is used in a lot of books. Also in Arabic, by the way."

"Okay, I'm convinced. *Account name: Death. Password: Hell.* That must be it. I think you should try it!"

Swallowing, Robert sat back behind the computer again. He carefully typed each of the individual letters. At some point he brushed another key by accident. To make sure he hadn't messed up the word, he started again.

When he was ready, there was a deep silence. "Shall I do it? This is our last chance. If we're wrong, his account is disabled."

"Do it!"

Robert hit Enter.

It was the right password. They were validated in a few seconds and promptly arrived at the familiar screen.

"We're in!" Andy exclaimed. Rebecca cheered through the phone.

Robert selected Drimm and clicked on Enter World. A few seconds later, he was looking at the back of the hunter. He was in Ogrimmar.

He looked at the screen a few seconds and whistled.

"Rebecca?"

"Yes?"

"Did you say he was going to the station?"

"That direction, yes. We're close now."

"Well, he's going to take the train, believe me. And so are we. We're all going to Rotterdam!"

He pointed at the bottom of the screen, where the message box was taken up by a text in green color that signified an official guild communication.

"Look, Andy!" he said. The Dutchman read the text out loud, so Rebecca could hear it as well:

Guild message of the day: Cataclysm launch party! Binnenwegplein Rotterdam. Be there at 23:00. Meeting point Bram Ladage.

Andy started to laugh. At Robert's questioning look, he explained that Bram Ladage was a popular chain of snack bars. "Well, maybe they just like some French fries to go with it,' he said.

CHAPTER XXV

It was a ten minute walk from the train station of Rotterdam to the center of the shopping district. They were chilled to the bone by the time they arrived at the square. To their surprise an immense crowd had descended on this spot in the middle of the night. At least several thousand people were assembled outside the entrance of one of the largest electronics stores in the Netherlands. They were patiently waiting for midnight to arrive and their turn to be among the first to purchase the new expansion to World of Warcraft.

Bram Ladage was indeed a snack bar. It was right in the middle of the square. For the occasion, it was open at this time of night. Robert guessed they had hired extra personnel to keep up with the demand. They were doing a healthy business.

When the three of them drew closer, they saw that what had appeared a mass actually was a long queue. Fences had been placed to create a long mazelike corridor, just like at amusement parks.

"Ouch, this is going to be a long wait," Andy said. "It's going to take at least an hour to reach the front."

Rebecca looked at her watch. "I don't think we're going to stand in line," she said. "Our priority is to find the Hammer of Grimstone."

After a short discussion, they fanned out among the people, circling the pack of humanity. It was immediately clear that it wasn't going to be easy. Many people wore hats and scarves or had the lapels of their coats turned up to protect their faces.

"This isn't going to work," Rebecca said twenty minutes later, shivering from the cold. "We'll never find them among all these people." She checked the time again. "It's only eight minutes to midnight."

Behind them, the crowd cheered. All kinds of entertainment made the time pass quickly. In front of the crowd was a small stage where a man with a microphone was keeping everyone's spirit up. There had just been a 'dress as your favorite WoW character' contest, and now it was announced that a quiz about WoW lore was starting.

In the end, they decided that Rebecca and Andy would position themselves near the exit of the store, where the lucky people who had obtained their copy of Cataclysm would emerge as soon as the sale started. Robert would join the queue to see if he could spot them from within the writhing mass. The endless line snaked all over the square between the fences. There was a fair chance that he'd spot them somewhere along the line.

It happened the other way around. Midnight had come and gone with a lot of fireworks and cheers. Groups of around forty people at a time were allowed to enter the store, where they were handled efficiently, judging by the swift turnaround time. Soon, the long line of waiting people came in motion, taking the slowly shuffling Robert deeper and deeper into the melee.

Suddenly, he felt a tug on his arm. When he looked up, he found himself looking straight at the face of Khalid. He was at the other side of the fence, in a line that went into the opposite direction. If the man was surprised to see him, he hid it well.

"Hello, I hoped I'd see you here!" Robert reacted, just like he had rehearsed several times. "I went by your room tonight, but you weren't there."

"Really? That could be."

Robert looked behind his neighbor at the group of men who were obviously part of Khalid's entourage. They were in their mid twenties to early thirties. All had a Mediterranean look, with dark eyes and black hair. The most common feature amongst them were the coats they were all wearing. They all seemed to be from the same make, with dark colors. *The Hammer of Grimstone. The Hammer of Righteous Justice.*

Several of the men were looking curiously at him, which made Robert more than a little uncomfortable. One stepped forward. He was a bit taller and older and carried an air of authority. Robert wondered if he was looking at Pharad.

He asked something of Khalid in a language Robert didn't understand. Khalid took his eyes off Robert to look at the man. "Robert lives at the same place as I do," he replied in English. "He's from England. Also a WoW addict, but a recent one."

The man nodded. Also in English, with a thick accent, he said, "How do you do. Nice to meet you."

Without another word he turned away, making it clear that the conversation was over. Khalid nodded at Robert and turned away as well, engaging one of the other men in conversation. For a second Robert didn't know what to do. At that moment, the queue started moving again, rapidly widening the distance between him and the Hammer of Grimstone. As soon as he was sure he was out of sight, he sent a text message to Rebecca's mobile. Pressing the little buttons, he noticed that his hands were shaking slightly.

She shared his mixed feelings about the encounter.

"They're way ahead of me," he replied. "I think they're fifteen minutes away from the store."

"We'll pick them up upon leaving the store and do the job," was her short reply. A little disappointed that Rebecca had more or less decided that the covering of the Grimstones was over for him, Robert decided to stay in the queue.

Robert's guess was right on the mark. A little over fifteen minutes later, he saw how Khalid and the other men were among the next group to be admitted to the store. He quickly counted the number of men he judged to be the companions of his neighbor. There were nine of them.

He updated Rebecca and Andy by text message. Almost immediately, he received a response confirming they had seen them enter as well.

The night may have been icy cold, but he noticed that he was sweating underneath all the clothes he was wearing. The tension was almost unbearable. It occurred to him how stupid and unprofessional it was for the AIVD people to be of reach for an entire day. The man should have given them an alternate phone number in case of an emergency, or in case of a development like this. Wasn't it madness that they should be the ones to handle this? He swore he would get that Fitzgerald if something happened to Rebecca.

He didn't see them leave the store, but he was notified by another text message from Rebecca. They had spotted them when they left the store. Andy had even managed to take some pictures of the group while they were standing in the lobby, backlit by the bright illumination from inside. While Robert shuffled closer and closer to the front of the line, his friends kept him abreast of what was happening. The group had split up shortly after leaving the store, and so had Rebecca and Andy. She was following the big man whom they presumed to be Pharad. Andy was on the tail of two of the Grimstones who seemed to stay together. They were going in the direction of the train station. Pharad was going in the opposite direction.

Right at the moment that he pocketed his change from buying two Cataclysm expansion sets, he got the message that Rebecca had nearly lost her target, but had picked him up again by pure luck when he reappeared out of a small café.

With nothing better to do, he looked for a pub to sit down and wait. He found one in a side street just off the square and seated himself at a table in a corner. He ordered a beer and put his cell phone on the table. Soon it lit up again. Another message: Andy had just gotten on a train.

The man who called himself Pharad in the virtual universe of World of Warcraft walked purposefully through the Dutch city. Rotterdam was close to a modern city as is so common in the United States, a spacious city center of tall modern buildings and even some skyscrapers worthy of the name. Most cities of any note in the Netherlands had old city centers, often dating hundreds of years back. Rotterdam, too, used to be famous for its magnificent historical city center, until the invading German army bombed the inner city in 1940 in a successful effort to force the stubborn neighboring country to surrender. Nowadays, only a few old lanes remained as a testament to the city's stately past.

The stocky man knew exactly where he was going. He crossed the four lanes of the Westblaak without waiting for the pedestrian traffic light to turn green and ducked into the dark gallery that encompassed a large office building.

Rebecca trailed some twenty yards behind, keeping as much to the shades as she could. The man looked around once or twice, but didn't seem to notice her. When he reached the end of the building, he lit a cigarette before crossing a small street. A peculiar smell reached her nostrils. It wasn't the smell of ordinary tobacco, neither of a joint. It was sharp, spicy, and distinctive. She didn't mind, as it gave her a beacon to follow.

In this manner they reached a large crossing. The man didn't continue in the same direction. He turned left. Rebecca did the same a little later. She immediately saw that her quarry had quickened his pace as the distance between them had suddenly nearly doubled.

They were on a beautiful wide avenue. Majestic old houses flanked either side of a broad canal. Perfectly kept lawns with a width of at least ten yards formed the banks of the waterway. Rebecca left the paved walkway and stepped onto the grass and into the darkness. She could see Pharad clearly as he was walking in the illumination of the streetlights. Silently, she started to run.

Just when she thought there was no end to the street, it suddenly ended. She was alerted to this because the man she was following suddenly disappeared. Confused, she halted, unsure if she should move toward the point where she had last seen him. She strained her ears, trying to catch a sound.

Hearing nothing, she backtracked some twenty yards and crossed over to the paved walkway, starting to walk down in the direction where he had disappeared, acting as if she was just another pedestrian. Soon she reached the point where she had lost him. Now, she saw that the walkway ended in stairs leading up to a large road that crossed the street she was on. The streetlight at this point was broken. Fear gripped her. If something happened to her now, nobody would notice. Pushing that thought to the back of her mind, she mounted the dark stairs and emerged onto the brightly lit road above. Even though it was a four lane road, it was deserted. No cars, no pedestrians. She cursed. How could she have lost him in no more than a minute?

Suddenly, her eyes were drawn to a motion on the other side of the street. She squinted in an effort to penetrate the darkness on the other side of the street. She wasn't sure, but it seemed as if someone was walking there. Since there was no alternative, she certified that there was still no traffic, then sprinted to the other side of the crossing.

She saw no one. Slowly, she continued down the street. She found herself in another part of the city, much seedier than where she was before. She passed several rundown bars and nightclubs on her right, some of which she suspected were actually brothels. Strangely enough, on her left were also some obviously upscale restaurants and shops. After two hundred yards she came to another crossing.

Rebecca hesitated. Which way should she go? She was just about to follow the main road, when she caught a whiff of the peculiar cigarette scent. It was brought to her by the wind that blew into her face from the sharp right.

This street was much narrower than the other one. It was a lot darker as well, even though this was clearly a neighborhood where people lived, not some industrial area. She passed many houses with multiple mail boxes, indicating that each was inhabited by several different people and families.

She found the place where he lived by accident. Apparently, she had made good most of the distance between them, because she suddenly heard the sound of a door slamming shut only some ten yards farther down the street. She halted in midstride, her heart in her throat.

When it remained silent, she stole closer. It was an old derelict house, with a door that had once been dark green. All the windows were closed, with role curtains drawn all the way down. Again, her nose picked up the strange cigarette smell. It seemed to come from behind her. When she looked, she saw a squashed cigarette lying on the ground, the tip still faintly glowing. With some distaste, she picked it up and held it to her nose. From up close, there was no doubt. It was definitely the same smell as before.

She looked at the door again, realizing that she had just stalked the leader of a dangerous and extremely violent terrorist group to his lair. The audacity of what she had done suddenly dawned on her. She memorized the house number and slowly backed away from the house, as if it were a dangerous beast that could jump on her if she made a wrong move. When she was some distance away, she stored the name of the street and the house number in her phone. Then she started running.

Andy checked in more than half an hour later. He reported another success. The two men he had been following lived together in the same house, a fairly new standard single family home in a town called Gouda, some fifteen miles away from The Hague. The pictures he had taken of the Hammer of Grimstone with his mobile phone were of unusual good quality. He promised to send them by email the moment they finished the call.

Unfortunately, he was stranded in that strange town, because no more trains were running until the next morning. Robert suggested he called a taxi.

"That Fitzgerald is bloody well going to pay for that!" Andy said grumpily. "Do you have any idea what taxis cost in this country?"

Robert and Rebecca took the night train back to Leiden. When they finally got home, they were totally exhausted from this day full of tension and unexpected happenings. Before going to sleep, they checked on their neighbor. His room was dark, and the camera showed nothing. If he was in, he was asleep.

"They're probably going to storm the new expansion early to-morrow morning," Rebecca guessed. "Let's be prepared."

She opened the two boxes and withdrew the software CD from each of them. Robert took one and started the installing process on his own laptop, while she did the same on hers. Satisfied that it would run until the end without their support, they quickly undressed and made ready for bed.

CHAPTER XXVI

"**M**y God, it's incredibly busy!" Robert exclaimed. They were sitting side by side at the desk, with their laptops in front of them. They had just completed the installation and registration procedure and were ready to enter Azeroth after the effects of Cataclysm.

It was early in the morning, not even six o'clock. Their alarm had gone off only ten minutes earlier, but they weren't sleepy at all. Robert was thrilled by the prospect of finding the virtual world as he knew it completely changed overnight. At least, to have all the new additions, changes and possibilities actually working and accessible. Much of the new content had been added by way of massive patches shortly before the release. Many of the changed territories could already be visited in the days before Cataclysm launched, but only in the old fashioned way. Now, it all lay wide open to be explored, including numerous new and exciting zones that had been added to the existing world. Even new races had been added.

He was looking forward to all the new challenges. Even more exciting was the other task ahead, to try to merge with the Hammer of Grimstone in their rush to level eighty-five.

He looked over at Rebecca. Like him, she hadn't showered and dressed. She was wearing one of his shirts, buttoned only halfway up. Her bare legs were stretched underneath the table. She looked absolutely fabulous. She caught his stare and smiled at him.

"Concentrate on WoW, mister," she instructed, not unkindly.

He felt his cheeks flame. "Sure," he mumbled.

"This won't do," she said, standing. She bent over and suddenly was closer to him than she had ever been before. Her lips lightly brushed his in a fleeting touch that burned nevertheless like a glowing smith's tool. Robert was stunned. She ran her hands through his hair. Her eyes shone with a new tenderness.

"Later," she said softly. "We have work to do."

Before he could muster his wits, the screen of the extra laptop suddenly lit up. They both turned their heads. On the screen, Khalid walked in and out of view. A second later, they heard his door open and his footsteps going in the direction of the bathroom.

Robert silently cursed the man. This was the second time he interrupted such a moment between Rebecca and himself. Couldn't he wait another five minutes? Only one?

He took a breath. "I'm ready."

He had been online at this time of day before. Usually, the number of players around in the early morning was negligible. Today, however, many people were preparing to set out for new territories.

Gunslinger and Killermage were hovering over the imposing gates of Ogrimmar, looking down on the city in wonder. Like them, many people were trying out the new feature of flying in Kalimdor and Eastern Kingdoms. Before, the two old continents could only be explored from the ground. That had changed with the new expansion.

They joined several others in exploring the Valley of Strength from the air, swooping around the buildings like madmen. Robert tried to define the difference he was experiencing. The city had been changed, there was no doubt about it. The zeppelins now departed from inside the city for example, instead of from the two towers that used to be some distance outside the walls. He could see other obvious changes as well, even though he would have recognized the place as Ogrimmar any time. If he had to define the change, the greatest improvement was the way it all felt. It seemed as if the light was brighter and details appeared more distinct. The texture of the world had become fresher and more pronounced, as if a tropical rain had removed all the dust leaving a reborn world. Which it was, of course.

"It's wonderful, don't you think?" Rebecca said. "I can't wait to explore it all. It must be something, to see all those places that have changed completely. Especially from the air!"

He started to type a message to her, but suddenly realized the futility. They weren't even three feet apart. "Are we going now?"

She shook her head. "We want to keep close tabs on the Grimstones. We don't know where they're going. Once we lose them, it may be impossible to trace them again."

She opened the map of Azeroth that looked more or less the same as before. As she zoomed in on first Kalimdor, then Eastern Kingdoms, the changes were immediately apparent. "Those are the two areas we must be watching," she said, pointing them out. "Vashj'ir in Eastern Kingdoms and Mount Hyjal in Kalimdor. Those are the two so-called starting zones for the road from level eighty to eighty-five. Assuming that they want to level their existing characters to eighty-five, instead of starting a new character with one of the new races."

"Shouldn't we split up? That way there's always one of us to follow them if they take any of the two zones to kick off."

She looked at him for a long moment, considering. "That's a good idea. You go to Vashj'ir. I'll just stay here for now and see what happens. Meanwhile, I'll check on the profession trainers. See you later!" With these words, she steered Killermage away.

Robert watched the Undead mage disappeared behind a tall building. He smiled at Rebecca, and she winked back.

It wasn't easy to find the way to Vashj'ir. Rebecca told him there might be a quest he had to complete first. He couldn't find the quest giver, though, so he started to pay attention to the chat channels. With some relief he discovered he wasn't the only one fumbling around. The upside was that there were as many people advertising how and where they had found it as there were people asking what to do.

Following the most frequently posted directions, he found the Warchief's Command Board in Ogrimmar and subsequently flew to a new harbor east of the city. There he joined a multitude of other players on the docks in watching a spectacle of Horde soldiers of some unit called Hellscream's Vanguard prepping themselves for going to war with the Alliance. After some time a mercenary ship arrived. He boarded, along with some fifteen other players and the soldiers.

The boat departed and he amused himself by watching the continuing scripted entertainment. The fierce battle talk of the commander of the Horde forces was interrupted by one of the crew members going insane and jumping overboard, causing much distress and grief of some of his fellow shipmates. It was all obviously designed to provide some background to the events he was about to join. In short, a new island had appeared just off the coast near Stormwind and the Horde was going to grab it. A foothold within striking distance of the Alliance capital would surely tip the scales in favor of the Horde.

It would never come to that. In mid-sea they encountered the floating wreckage of another ship and before anyone could investigate, huge tentacles rose out of suddenly churning water and grabbed for the unfortunate passengers on the deck of the ship. Gunslinger was taken as well, and Robert immediately lost control over his digital alter ego. The poor hunter was tossed high up in the air, followed by a plunge into the water. Like watching a movie, he witnessed how his unconscious hero slowly sunk to the bottom of the sea. All around him floated bodies of other castaways, players and NPC's alike, going the same way.

It became even worse when some scaled monster appeared out of nowhere and attacked him. Gunslinger still didn't respond to any of his commands, so there was nothing Robert could do to wake him up and save him. Then, suddenly, the attacker slashing at Gunslinger exploded in a bubble of gore and tiny pieces. A friendly non-player character approached the hunter and enveloped him in a protective bubble of air. Having ensured his immediate survival, the unexpected rescuer tucked the huge Tauren under one arm and started to swim away.

As there didn't seem to be anything he could do anyway, he glanced at the spare monitor. Khalid was at his computer as well now, dressed more or less like himself. Looking back at his own screen, he read *Drimm has come online*. Robert clicked on the social tab. The window now showed three members of the Hammer of Grimstone online, including Drimm. The others were Pharad and Gilead. They were all in Ogrimmar. Killermage had returned there as well.

"Three of them, all at your end in Ogrimmar," he said.

She nodded. "They'll be busy for awhile. They have to reset their Talents as we did, and I bet they'll do some sightseeing as well."

She hesitated. "But maybe not. I think they're going as a team. Drimm is a hunter, Pharad is a warrior, and Gilead is a priest."

"A DPS, a tank and a healer," Robert filled in. "They should be able to tackle almost everything."

"Indeed. Especially since they're heavily geared already. But not everything, and we're going to be around when they look for help. Now let's make sure of where they're going. There's no telling yet, so be prepared."

"Are you coming as well?"

"In a minute. I'll keep watch here a little longer. You never know!"

Robert turned back to his screen and noticed that control of Gunslinger had been restored to him. He found himself in the hold of a sunken ship. The intruding water was being held at bay by an air bubble. Apparently, his savior had managed to deposit him in a safe spot. Next to him was a quest giver. One click later it was explained to him that even this sanctuary was under attack by some species called Naga. He was sent out into the water to collect some fish and a specific shell. With nothing better to do, he obeyed these orders and swam out. There were so many other players about hunting for the same specimens, that it took quite some time before he was able to complete the mission. He had to return to the air bubble twice because his breath ran out. When he finally managed to collect all of the required items, a spell was cast upon him that granted underwater breathing, solving one major issue in surviving in this submerged realm.

"They're coming your way," Rebecca said suddenly.

He switched his gaze to her computer screen and saw how she was trailing the three members of the Hammer of Grimstone to the docks. He nodded. "I'll wait for them," he said.

"Great. I'll stay a bit and see if any others pop up."

Robert picked up the next quests and swam out of the wreckage. Now he didn't have to worry about his breath anymore, he simply took up position some distance from the sunken hull. He had a good view of the players entering and leaving the vessel. The next task he had been given was to save some other people, like he himself had been saved. Some were floating nearby. He managed to complete this quest while the Grimstones were watching the spectacle on the docks, a continent away.

"The ship is on its way." Rebecca announced.

A little later Robert saw another bunch of players materialize. Drimm, Pharad, and Gilead were among them. He selected Drimm with his cursor and tapped Rebecca on the shoulder. She leaned over to look. Again, her proximity sent a warm glow through his body, starting in his stomach and ending in his throat.

She nodded in confirmation. "Stick close to them," she instructed.

"You bet!"

When they too completed their quest to gain the underwater breathing effect, the three Grimstones didn't waste any time looking around and went about their next task immediately. This shouldn't have surprised Robert, because they obviously hadn't taken the time for a sightseeing tour of Ogrimmar either. Still, he wondered about it. There was so much to see and so much to marvel at!

Under the pretext of a major natural disaster, almost every single zone had been overhauled. The story was that an ancient evil had awakened, causing massive earthquakes and volcanic eruptions all over the world. The world as it was known was torn asunder. Entire towns disappeared under the sea, while new lands emerged from the sea bottom at other places. Gadgetzan, once a dusty town in the middle of a blistering sand desert, had now become a sea port, while the Barrens had been divided into two different zones by massive shifts of the tormented earth. Also, some areas that had been closed off before now had become accessible. The zone called Vashj'ir, where he was now, was one of those places. It was an alien place. All the while that he had been keeping watch for the Grimstones, he had been gawking around in wonder as well. It was like a gigantic aquarium, with all kinds of sea life moving about. Some was dangerously aggressive, some not. From where he was hovering, he could see other players engaging crabs and naga, sometimes in heavy battles, and moving on to other places after some time. Obviously, one was sent elsewhere after completing several quests at this spot.

"Welcome to Cataclysm." He smiled at Rebecca. She had come to stand behind him and was looking at the underwater realm with a stunned expression.

"I'll be right over," she announced. "Three more of them have logged on and I think they're departing for Mount Hyal now. They too are a team of DPS, healer, and tank. I think I'll just follow them to make sure, then I'll join you."

Robert nodded and maneuvered Gunslinger to follow the three Grimstones unobtrusively inside. They had just completed the same quest as he already had. They were easy to spot among the many other players, because the color of their name tags stood out due to the fact they were in his friends book.

Copying the members of the Hammer of Grimstone, he talked to the same captain of the Ogrimmar forces who had been on board of the doomed ship. He had survived the ordeal as well. The character told him to go out and kill naga and search for food.

To his surprise, he saw that the objectives lit up on his map. How could Quest Helper have this information already?

"Quest Helper has all the data from the Public Test Realm," Rebecca explained in answer to his query. "It'll be imprecise sometimes at first, but basically it has all the information you need, just like you're used to."

Pharad, Drimm and Gilead watched the melee for a minute. Robert thought they were discussing where to start, which quest to do first. Suddenly they started moving, swimming over to where the naga were. He followed.

It soon became clear he needed Rebecca with him, if he was to keep up with the three Grimstones. The challenge wasn't so much to kill the poor creatures, as well to find enough of them alive to kill in the first place. At least ten players were after the same prey. The three Grimstones had fanned out, covering a large area, enhancing their chances of catching the scaly humanoids. Being in a group together, they had the invaluable benefit of sharing the kills between them. A player alone actually had to kill each and every of the required number. In a group, the kills of each of the individual group members were added up.

When he saw the Grimstones return to turn in the quest, while he had only one third of the objective completed, he reached out and pulled the sleeve of Rebecca's shirt.

"This group is definitely going to Mount Hyjal," she said right at that moment. "Maybe I should follow them."

"No way. I need you here, pronto!" he said urgently. "If you don't help me now, we'll never catch up with them!"

They met at the wrecked ship shortly after.

"They're already off to another location, and you still have to complete the very first quests," Robert said with a note of panic in his voice. "It's going to be difficult to catch up."

She scowled. "Sorry, I made a mistake. I didn't realize how close this was going to be. Let's get kicking then. I'll do those quests you just finished. You look around and try to find out where they are now. We need to keep them in sight.

He couldn't locate them however, so he returned to help Rebecca with her tasks. Soon, she'd caught up with him so they were at the same stage of the quest line. Unlike they were used to, the quests were all part of a linear chain. They were playing their part in the unfolding story of whatever was happening in this sunken land. It was impossible to skip even a single quest.

Their sojourn at the sunken ship ended with a battle against a host of naga that struck at the hideout in a coordinated attack. Unexpectedly, they were quickly overwhelmed by superior numbers.

There were simply too many enemies attacking them at the same time. Right at the moment that Gunslinger would have died,. He was grabbed by an enemy. This was a new feature of Cataclysm. Every so often, at certain stages of a quest chain, the game took over and showed what happened next through a short movie. In this one, they were abducted by naga and taken away from their current location. Fortunately, they were saved by someone from a new faction called the Earthen Ring. They were brought to a location where more of these people were gathered. They had many quests to offer, which led up to them taming a sea horse and acquiring the animal as a mount after they succeeded. When they had completed all the quests on offer, they were sent to find another location, which proved to be the inside of some cave. Here, they found more Earthen Ring, a flight master, an inn keeper as well as Drimm, Pharad and Gilead. They were just leaving the cave when Robert and Rebecca entered.

"Let them," Rebecca ordered, "we have to overtake them in their questing and we don't accomplish that by running after them like headless chickens."

At this point, many other people were more or less at the same stage as they were. But Robert and Rebecca, as well as the three people they were following, were working as a team and were outfitted with vastly superior equipment. This advantage was waning, however, because some of the gear they were receiving as quest rewards nearly equaled the epic gear they were wearing. It wouldn't be long before they would discard some of their former gear in favor of new stuff. Nevertheless, they drew gradually ahead of the mob of ordinary people, and when their quests took them out of the starting area and into the wide open sea bottoms beyond, they had the world more or less to themselves. Vashj'ir was divided into three different areas, each of them easily as big as an entire zone as they knew it before Cataclysm. They had started in an area called Kelp'thar Forest, and now they moved into the Shimmering Expanse. Playing in this underwater territory was interesting in another way. Normally, a player was always on the ground when performing actions or fighting enemies. Flying mounts could be used for traveling, but apart from that, everything took place on the ground. WoW was a two dimensional game in that respect. Vashj'ir however, did away with the concept of flying. Everything happened in the sea water, at different depths, which meant that an extra dimension was added. This took some getting used to, but offered unexpected possibilities as well. Targets could also be attacked from above or from below. There were simply many more tactics a player could choose from.

At nine o'clock Robert became hungry. They had just wormed their way into the bowels, even the brain, of an enormous creature called Nespirah. The beast was so big, that it took up a significant part of the map. Except for the fact that walls were made of tissue, it was more like a monstrous building than like a living creature. It was clear that they were about to embark on a new series of quests aimed at saving the animal from some mutual enemies. The Grimstones were there as well, not more than a few feet away. They had been gaining ground on them slowly, and Rebecca estimated they were only two quests behind them now. One, Gilead, was looking in their direction.

"I wonder how long those guys can go without food?" Robert said, looking over at the monitor that showed Khalid. He was still in the same position as before. The other group of Grimstones had been joined by a fourth member by now and was busy in Mount Hyjal, the other starting zone. He imagined they were following the same protocol, blasting through the quests.

Robert's question was answered sooner than he thought. Right before his eyes, the Grimstones sat on the ground, immobile.

"They're logging off!" he exclaimed. To underline this observation, the monitor now showed Khalid getting up and walking to the door. One by one Drimm, Pharad and Gilead shimmered briefly, became transparent and evaporated. Rebecca stretched. She stood as well and bent her arms and legs.

"Let's finish the two quests we're behind and do the same," she said. "We have to get a shower, and we have a phone call to make. Our official friends must be interested in what we have to tell them."

They were. Robert talked to Fitzgerald while Rebecca was in the shower. The man was extremely pleased with the information they had gathered, but not so pleased with the risk they had taken. Robert pointed out that they had tried to contact them. He jotted down the email address he had to send the photos to. They agreed to meet the following morning. Right after the call ended, he emailed the pictures Andy had taken of the Grimstones to the email address.

Meanwhile, Khalid had gone out briefly. Robert met him when he himself returned from the shower.

"So, you went out to buy some groceries?" he asked, pointing at the plastic bag Khalid was carrying.

He got a nod in return. "Yes. Funny that I met you last night in Rotterdam."

Robert hid his face behind his towel for a second, pretending to rub his wet hair. He thought furiously.

"Yes, it would've been nice if you and I had gone together. You see, I joined a guild a few days ago with many Dutch people in it. They said they were all going to the launch party, so I thought I should go as well. Unfortunately, I didn't see any of them."

"Ah. Well. Yes, that can be awkward."

Robert produced a cough. "I think I caught a cold last night. That would be the perfect excuse to play for a few days."

This got a smile in response. Again, Robert realized that Khalid seemed, in fact, quite nice. Incredible that this young man was a terrorist. He asked, "Have you started playing Cataclysm yet?"

"Yes, I started this morning with a few of my guild. We're trying to keep ahead of the mass invasion that will start this afternoon."

"I see. Well, have fun!" Robert terminated the conversation. "I'm getting a little cold like this."

One hour later, they joined the Party of Pharad, Drimm, and Gilead. It happened quite naturally. They had been in each other's way for some time, like two flights of golfers who were way too close to each other and were trying to play the same hole at the same time.

Half an hour earlier, in the magnificent Ruins of Vashj'ir, Rebecca had strayed a bit and been attacked by a band of Alliance players. These seemed not to be questing, but having their fun picking on solitary Horde players instead. She had a hard time holding her ground against the superior numbers, but the Hammer of Grimstone unexpectedly stepped in to help. Together, they drove the Alliance players off, killing three of them.

It was a natural act, as Horde players were supposed to unite against the Alliance whenever called for. Nevertheless, she thanked them for their support, and they acknowledged her politely.

After that, it happened three times in a row that one group killed an objective just before the other group could, making the others wait for long minutes for the mob to spawn again. Apparently, the three Grimstones had evaluated their gear and game play, and had decided that more could be gained by joining forces.

It was Gilead who addressed Robert, asking him to join their party. They shared a triumphant look between them. Rebecca put her fists in the air, like she had just scored match point in the Wimbledon final.

"Sure, better than being in each other's way all the time," he replied casually to Gilead.

The familiar sound heralded the invitation. *Gilead invites you to a Party* his screen read. He pressed Accept. A split second later, the same happened on Rebecca's computer.

"Welcome," Drimm said in the Party chat.

"Thank you," Rebecca replied. "Now let's go before all the losers arrive!"

All that could be heard was the sound of Pharad laughing.

CHAPTER XXVII

There wasn't much talk on the party channel. Not that this was necessary; all players were experienced and knew what they had to do.

Robert enjoyed doing the quests enormously. He was deeply impressed by the designers and programmers at Blizzard Entertainment who had succeeded in creating such a realistic world again. In Outland, he had sometimes felt that they had overdone the fairy tale texture of the surroundings. Northrend had been a lot better in that respect. Their experiences today were surpassing everything he had seen before. He shared his feelings with Rebecca, who nodded in agreement and gave him a smile.

"I noticed it, too," she said. "It gives me the same vibes of wonder I remember from when I started playing a long time ago. Even though it's different and clearly changed from the Kalimdor and the Eastern Kingdoms as we knew it, they've succeeded in hitting the right note again."

Robert didn't have much experience with playing in a large group, but with Rebecca's aid and advice he acquitted himself really well. They went through the various quests like a warm knife through a roll of butter. The afternoon was waning when they were finishing up the last quests that had taken them to the Abyssal Breach. They were almost at the end of their sojourn in Mount Hyjal. The story line they'd been following had just ended with a dramatic cinematic. Now, they found themselves on the sea bottom, staring down into an abyss that seemed to descend all the way to the core of the earth. Each of them had reached level eighty-two in the last ten minutes.

Pharad suggested they enter the Throne of the Tides, a new dungeon that was supposed to be located somewhere far below in the swirling hole they were looking into. Rebecca and Robert exchanged a look.

"It's going to be late anyway," she said with a shrug.

They swam out into the whirlpool and were taken by the current, to be sucked down with spectacular force to unfathomable depths. Yet, their perilous journey ended with them being brought uninjured right in front of the instance.

From the moment they entered, Robert had more trouble than before. After they had taken some kind of elevator, they entered a hallway crawling with naga and murlocs of the Elite kind. He was tasked by Pharad, who'd assumed the role of commander of their group, with using his traps to keep certain enemies, marked by him, temporarily out of the fight. He found it hard and failed the first times. His inexperience with raiding instances worried him.

The fact that they all fought the encounters for the first time made it extra hard for all of them. Robert's inexperience didn't pose too many problems.

The three Grimstones and Rebecca were such experienced players that they swiftly got a handle on the encounters with their opponents. They fought their way to Lady Naz'jar, the first real challenge. Even though Robert nearly died twice because he didn't move away soon enough when the awesome elite naga cast something nasty called Vortex, they defeated her without suffering any casualties. The healing skills of Gilead were impressive.

The next encounter had him sweating even harder. After a short cinematic they had to face Commander Ulthok, who didn't seem to like Gunslinger. His hunter was grabbed twice by this so-called boss and flung helplessly around the room. Robert cursed in terror and nothing Rebecca said could soothe his panic. The experience didn't kill the hunter, though, so he simply clung on and tried to hide his embarrassment.

When they finally came upon Ozumat, the end boss of Throne of the Tides, Robert was as tense as a violin string. A faint sour smell of sweat was drifting up to his nostrils from under his shirt, adding to his discomfort. To make things worse, this encounter surpassed his most frightening nightmares. The fight had three different phases. It wasn't just the frightful Ozumat they had to face, but numerous other enemies spawned during the fights and had to be taken out. He constantly had to refocus his attention, following Pharad's orders.

After what seemed like an eternity, victory was finally theirs. Robert felt completely drained. He sagged back in his chair, and when Rebecca leaned over and ruffled his hair, all he could manage was a faint smile.

"I never want to do something like this again," he sighed.

"Oh come on, this was fun!" she replied. "Now cheer up because you just won a nice piece of shoulder equipment!"

It was nearly eight o'clock in the evening when they got out of the Throne of the Tides by returning to Ogrimmar through one of Rebecca's portals. By now, it had gotten even busier in the city. Countless players had bought the extension in a shop during the day and were taking their first steps in the remade world.

"I'm taking a break," Pharad suddenly announced. "We have a safe lead on these multitudes."

Robert looked questioningly at Rebecca. She gestured her own indecision. Should they try to prolong the cooperation?

"What is the rest doing?" she asked.

"If he stops, we stop," Gilead said.

"Shall we meet again later?"

"Maybe. We'll see," Gilead answered noncommittally. "Thank you for playing."

"Thank you for playing," Robert and Rebecca replied at the same time.

A few moments later the three Grimstones went offline, leaving them alone in the party.

"Well, we do have an appointment tomorrow morning," Robert said.

"You're right. Let's go out to call Andy and update him."

Andy had been in class all day. "You're falling behind," he accused Robert immediately after picking up the phone. "I told the professor you're still sick, but that won't hold up for long. You need to show your nose around again."

On seeing the expression on his face, Rebecca looked questioningly at him. He waved her concern away. "I know. What choice do I have?" he answered.

Andy grunted, not convinced. "Those terrorists are bad enough. You shouldn't let them ruin your study as well. Rebecca can keep tabs on them. You don't need to do everything yourself, you know!"

The next morning, even Khalid seemed to be studying. He wasn't playing WoW as they expected. The monitor showed how he had put his computer aside and was reading a book, scribbling on a notepad now and then. Maybe it was Robert's unease about his own failure to spend enough time on his studies that fed the thought, but somehow he didn't believe that Khalid was actually spending time on his Art History subject. Something stirred in his brain at that. It flashed through his mind before he could get hold of it. He sat on his bed, trying to recapture the thought. He felt it was important somehow, an insight just beyond his grasp.

Rebecca looked bemused at him. "What's going on?"

"Nothing," he replied. "Just something that came up in my mind, but was gone the next moment. Just like a dream that you can't remember exactly and that you can feel slipping away when you awake."

At that moment, there was a knock on the door. Involuntarily, they both looked at the monitor first. Khalid was still at his desk. Shrugging, Robert went to the door. It was Andy.

"Shouldn't we be going?" he asked while he stepped into the room.

Rebecca looked at her watch. "It's a little early, but maybe we should go. The sooner we're back, the better, because I want to be there when the Grimstones start again."

Their appointment was at the Holiday Inn on the outskirts of Leiden, just off the motorway. Fitzgerald and Broerse were already there when they arrived. Broerse was on the other end of the lobby, walking nervously up and down and talking frantically into his mobile. Robert made the introductions.

"Good job," Fitzgerald complimented Rebecca and Andy, whom he had only talked to on the phone. "Your photos were helpful," he complimented the last. He cast a glance at his colleague, who gestured that his phone call was important.

They sat down. Fitzgerald ordered tea all around.

"First of all, I'd like to apologize for our absence last night," the Englishman began. "I should have left a phone number for you to call in case of emergency. Nevertheless, I think you all deserve a compliment for the way you handled things without us. You've given us something we were desperately looking for, some addresses and," he looked at Andy, "some photos showing the terrorists."

They looked a little embarrassed under all this praise. Rebecca was the first to say something. "Well, we *were* a little disappointed that you just vanished without leaving a number to call and we *were* rather scared when we had to follow those terrorists all by ourselves through the night. I wonder, why didn't you already have Robert's house under surveillance? Why wasn't there a team waiting to follow that creep?"

Fitzgerald laughed at her half-teasing tone and, with that, the ice was broken. He leaned forward, and his eyes took on a serious cast. In a hushed tone he replied, "Because not everyone was convinced yet. Let's just say that some people at certain positions had some difficulties in believing that a couple of students had actually tracked down the Hammer of Righteous Justice through a computer game."

He sat back and fixed each of them with a stare. "But thanks to Andy and his remarkably sharp photographs, that changed. The man you call Pharad has been identified as Muhammad al-Moutti, one of the most wanted terrorists in the world. We thought he was dead, but that assumption was proven wrong by you."

These words fell into an abyss of silence. Robert, Rebecca, and Andy exchanged glances, bewilderment showing in their eyes.

Rebecca was the first to speak. "Who is he?" she asked in a quaking voice. The revelation that she'd been walking right behind one of the most dangerous people on the planet some sixteen hours previously had her trembling all over. Robert noticed how pale she had become, and he put his arm protectively around her. She responded by pressing herself against him.

Fitzgerald looked sympathetically at her. "You've been brave," he said softly. "You did something that even the most hardened professionals wouldn't undertake lightly. And you succeeded far beyond expectation. You have given us his home address. Even now, one of our teams is taking up positions around his place."

Andy sat forward in an attempt to catch the attention of Fitzgerald. When he saw he had it, he asked what al-Moutti was sought for.

"I have been reading up on his file right from the moment the identification was confirmed. Let me tell you what I know. He's believed to be Iranian by birth, though little is known of his origins. He used to be the commander of all al-Queda activities in southern Iraq until three years ago. In that capacity, he was responsible for countless deaths. His specialty is believed to be the organization of suicide bombings. Before he reached that exalted station, he was an instructor in a terrorist training camp in Pakistan, just over the border with Afghanistan."

Clearing his throat, Fitzgerald looked over at Broerse, who was still on the phone.

Noting the unsaturated interest on their faces, he continued, "Al-Moutti disappeared from our radar three years ago. We thought, even hoped, he might have been killed, but there was a tiny blip on the radar half a year later.

A suspicious truck was attacked by NATO troops in the south of Afghanistan. The truck happened to be a transport vehicle for Taliban troops, and a fierce firefight ensued. The NATO commander asked for air support. He got it in the form of two Apache helicopters that minced the Taliban with rockets. Twelve Mujahedin fighters were killed, two managed to get away. One of those fugitives was seriously wounded and was found bled to death the next day."

"What does this have to do with Pharad?" Robert asked.

"The dead man found was, according to a source deemed reliable, his brother. What's more, in the cabin of the truck a woman and her infant son were found. Apparently, they were both killed by the fire-fight. Because such a prominent leader might be involved, a scientific team was called in to confirm the information. They never proved that Muhammad al-Moutti was there. But a DNA test revealed both a kinship between the woman and the infant as between the brother and the infant, though he wasn't the father."

"It was Pharad's son!" Rebecca said excitedly.

Robert couldn't help but feel sorry. War was a terrible thing. He looked at Fitzgerald, who nodded.

"Yes. Hence, the woman was presumably his wife."

"What happened to Pharad then? What did he do?" Robert asked. He found that he couldn't stop calling the man by his WoW name, even though he now knew what he was called in real life.

"We were told by another source that he was so devastated by his loss, that he volunteered to do himself what he had been putting other people up to for so long, become a living bomb. Since we never heard from him again after that, we assumed he had already blown himself up somewhere. You see, there's rarely enough left of any suicide bomber for positive identification, nor is there always the time nor inclination for very thorough research."

Rebecca had pulled herself together during Fitzgerald's narrative. Now she sat up straight, tossing her shoulders to free herself of Robert's arm.

"What does it mean that he's surfaced here in the Netherlands?" she asked.

It was Andy who answered for the Englishman. "Isn't it obvious?" he asked. He turned to Fitzgerald and looked him straight in the eye. "Those NATO troops were Dutch, weren't they?"

When he got a nod in return, he continued in an ominous tone, "The Dutch were one of the most prominent foreign armies

240

in Afghanistan until recently. They were in command of an entire province. They had many ground troops, but also F16's and Apache helicopters deployed over there. On top of that, until last year the Secretary General of NATO was a Dutchman. That alone makes Holland a prime target for Muslim terrorists. Now we have one of the deadliest terrorists in the world with a personal grudge. The Dutch killed his wife, his son, and his brother. He's here for revenge."

The sudden voice from behind them made everyone jump, even Fitzgerald. Without anyone noticing, Broerse had finished his call and had come to stand behind them. Apparently, he had heard Andy's words.

"He's not only after the Dutch," he said. "That may be his ultimate goal, but he's still furthering the goals of his superiors in other places as well." He held up his mobile phone significantly. "I just got word that The Hammer of Righteous Justice struck again only one hour ago. A suicide attack just cost the lives of numerous people in Antwerp."

Fitzgerald seemed to have forgotten them. "How do we know it was them?" he asked of his Dutch associate.

"Another painting. It was found in a locker at Brussels central train station after an anonymous tip. According to what I heard, it's even more graphic and ghastly than what we've seen until now."

"What happened?" Robert asked.

"A bomb went off in one of the narrow streets of the diamond quarter of Antwerp. To be more precise, the Jewish street." He looked closely at them. "Have you seen them doing anything in that computer game of yours that has any bearing on that, now that you know this?"

Robert just wanted to give a negative answer, when a stern look from Rebecca silenced him. "Yes, we have," she said softly. She looked at Robert again. "Don't you remember?" she asked of him. Her eyes were filled with pain. "We wondered what they were doing in the Blood Furnace. Now we know!"

Robert tried to recall what he knew of that instance, but no connection came to mind. He shook his head. "Apart from the fact that we know that Khalid went to Belgium only a few days ago and returned yesterday, I don't see any connection."

"Yes you do. Think of the Blood Furnace. They were doing it over and over again! Do you remember what it's like when you've defeated the first boss, called The Maker, and you progress through the door behind him? That corridor you enter next is just like that alley in Antwerp. I've been there." She frowned. "But that isn't right. In the Blood Furnace, you're faced with a messy fight with many, many enemies. That's nothing like a suicide bombing."

Broerse was looking at her as if she had just put water on fire. His head was bobbing up and down like a madman's. "It was no suicide bombing," he said. "It was like you just said. Three heavily armed people entered the crowded street after the bomb went off and started shooting. It took the police over an hour and five casualties to take them down. Eighteen civilians were killed, and many more were wounded."

They were all stunned by the news. Andy started wondering loudly why they assaulted Antwerp as it wasn't part of the Netherlands, when suddenly, in the background, near the bar, a television was turned on. Automatically, they turned their heads. *Breaking news, mass killing in Antwerp* was painted in large letters on the screen. Robert felt nauseated.

"Now we know why there were only seven members of the Hammer of Grimstone online yesterday," he said.

CHAPTER XXVIII

The landscape was covered with snow. He cautiously moved up the slope, aware that if he made a misstep, he could easily tumble to his death. Each footstep was accompanied by a loud crunch as it left an imprint in the snow.

Drimm didn't look back. In fact, he wasn't concentrating all that hard. His mind was occupied by the loss of three of the members of their group. Of course, he had known beforehand that it was going to happen. And he had known all the time that it *could* happen; he had known only for a week that it was actually *going* to happen. It could have been him, couldn't it?

His mind kept returning to the three men who were dead now. They had been through a lot together. Their group had trained for many weeks in Africa, Asia, and even in Europe, and they had learned how to work together and how to depend on each other. He wondered again how each of them had received the news that they were selected to sacrifice themselves, and how they had felt in those last moments, just before they were committed, just before the point of no return. Involuntarily, he shivered. He, too, had pledged his life to the cause and to their leader. If he was asked to, he would be honor bound to sacrifice himself without hesitation.

Drimm reached a stretch of flat surface on the mountainside at a dizzying altitude. He turned around for a look at the broad colorless expanse of the Dragonblight. The land was far more than just a blur of featureless white with some dark patches. One of the few things that could be distinguished was the massive Wyrmrest Temple, rising majestically out of the frozen soil. On the foot of the mountains he had just climbed, the Mirror of Dawn was discernable. The surface of hard deep blue ice on this frozen lake had somehow remained unblemished by the snow cover that blanketed the land mass of the Dragonblight. Only the bones of a gigantic dragon carcass marred its ice cold perfection. In the far distance, he could even make out the mountains on the other side of the zone that separated Dragonblight from Icecrown.

Again, thoughts of his fallen comrades invaded his mind. He wondered what they would have thought of Cataclysm. He knew how much Caliburr had looked forward to the new expansion. With a sigh, he forced the melancholic thoughts out of his head. One of the things he had learned in the past years was how useless it was to dwell on issues that couldn't be changed.

He had come here to find some rest in his head before he continued the frenzy of questing and leveling again, and, more important, before they started the last few days of the preparations for their next mission. It was going to be their final act in Holland, the crown on their work here.

He couldn't find his much needed rest in the other parts of WoW, now that Cataclysm had turned everything upside-down. There was something unsettling about having the world changed so much. The familiarity of the game, and the knowledge that he was always in control, had become an anchor is his life. As Northrend was the only Azerothian continent unchanged by Cataclysm, he had come here to think.

A giant Magnataur was just coming out of a large cave in the mountainside and passed right below the ridge on which Drimm was perched. From his vantage point, Drimm could see most of the inside of the cave. A cozy fire was burning, and in its illumination he could see some furnishings and even some decorations on the rock wall. Dregmar Runebrand obviously lived in some comfort.

He knew this mob, of course. Killing it was part of a quest chain that ran out of Wyrmrest temple. It normally took a group of three people to bring the elite Magnataur down. Even though the creature, half human, half beast, had over a hundred thousand hitpoints, he could easily kill it if he wanted to. He watched Runebrand as he ambled up a slight rise and walked right up to the point where the abyss beckoned. Just like Drimm himself had done only minutes before, Runebrand took his time to gaze out over the Dragonblight.

He checked his watch. Pharad was late. His social window told him that the people they had been playing with yesterday, Gunslinger and Killermage, were online and somewhere in a place called Deepholm.

Strange that Gilead wasn't online either. They had a clear appointment to rendez-vous at this time. It was unusual for any of them to fail to show up.

At that moment he heard the sound that told him that someone he knew had come online. He glanced at the bottom of his screen and felt a sudden tightening in his belly. He nodded to himself. Under the circumstances, and especially in his present mood, maybe this was to be expected. Without preamble, the newcomer invited him to a party. He accepted. It was just the two of them.

"Can you come to the Quel'Danil Lodge?" He was given an order: this was definitely not a polite question. He had met Jinn only three times before, always to receive instructions while Pharad was absent for some reason. He had often wondered about the true identity of this character. Who was this person, so obviously in their leader's confidence? At some point he had suspected that Caliburr could be this force in the shadows. But Caliburr was dead now, so that guess was proven wrong in the most convincing way.

Drimm acknowledged the request, and the party was disbanded immediately. With a sigh, he took one last look at the landscape and used his hearthstone to leave.

Drimm prided himself on his bibliographical knowledge of World of Warcraft. Most players wouldn't have known immediately what or where the Quel'Danil Lodge was. The lodge was one of at least twenty different areas in the Hinterlands, a quiet backwater and in turn only one of the many zones in the entire game. He knew immediately what and where it was. He fleetingly wondered how much this zone had been effected by Cataclysm.

Before Cataclysm, he would have had to use a flight master to get there. Now, he just summoned his own flying mount and flew northward from Undercity.

The Quel'Danil Lodge was an Alliance friendly place and therefore the objective of some Horde quest givers. It was exactly like what could be expected from a wildlife hunter's lodge in the wilderness of Africa. It consisted of a main building at a small lake, with several smaller outbuildings where guests could sleep.

When Drimm arrived, the inhabitants of the lodge were already dead. The elven corpses were scattered all over the grounds and the inside of the main building. He entered and walked through the lodge until he emerged on the terrace at the back. He noticed Jinn immediately. He jumped down from the terrace and walked up to the Troll mage standing in the grass at the edge of the small lake.

"Here I am, as you requested."

A trade window opened, and he received a document. He accepted it, without reading it first.

"Now you have your orders. P will contact you. Be careful. Something is amiss."

With these words, Jinn started to cast a spell. A few seconds later, he disappeared, leaving Drimm alone at the edge of the silent lake in the wilderness. He sat with his feet in the water and started to read.

CHAPTER XXIX

"I just don't get it," Rebecca said when they finally got the message that Drimm had logged off. He had remained in the Hinterlands for over an hour. Now none of the Grimstones was online. "They were so eager to kick off with Cataclysm, and now they aren't playing anymore."

"Maybe they're focusing on other priorities," Robert said. "Like planning their next attack."

"That could be. Have you considered how weird this all is?" She made Killermage sit on the ground and turned to him. "Do you realize that it's most likely that some of the people we saw in Rotterdam, are dead now? And that they killed at least eighteen innocent people in the process?"

Robert nodded. "Imagine going to Rotterdam to buy the new expansion, knowing all the time that you won't be playing it. Because you're going to your death shortly. Voluntarily."

Rebecca looked at the window and shivered. It was comfortably warm in the room, but outside the temperature had dropped and heavy rain beat on the glass of the window. She was sitting in the swivel chair at the desk, dressed in a simple white jersey and faded jeans.

"Not getting to play would be the least of my worries," she replied. "I can't place myself inside the mind of someone who would do something like that. Killing all those innocent people for some religious purpose? Letting myself be killed? You must be strange and warped to do such a thing."

Robert nodded with a grimace. "Drimm was certainly acting strange as well. And he didn't go to Undercity to visit the bank. He was out of there too soon. By far."

They had followed the progress of the Tauren hunter through their social window and seen that he had left the underground city of the Undead almost immediately after arriving there. He had taken a flight to the Hinterlands and remained there for a long time.

"The Hinterlands is a strange place to go for a level eighty-two," she confirmed. "There's nothing to be done there, apart from examining the damage caused by Cataclysm. Why would he go there of all places, while he's in the middle of leveling to eighty-five in brand new zones?"

Robert looked questioningly at her. "What should we do now?"

She frowned, then looked up with a tight smile. "We do what we did before. We switch to real world surveillance. Let's activate the camera!"

She wheeled her chair over to the other computer, on which the software of the little camera was installed. The image of the other room didn't come up at the tap of a key. Questioningly, Rebecca hit a few more keys.

"The power is off." Robert had come to stand beside her. He pointed at a flickering yellow light at the base of the laptop computer.

"I can see that!" she snapped back. "Somehow," she directed a sharp glance at him, "the power cable has become unplugged. So the computer went in power save mode."

The computer whirred back to life, taking a minute to restore itself to the point where it had shut down. Their window onto Khalid's room opened again.

They both froze at what they were seeing. Khalid was standing in the middle of the room, carrying an enormous backpack. He was looking around the place in a way that couldn't be misunderstood. He was leaving. For good. They watched him finish his survey and step to the door. At the same time, the sound of the door opening and shutting reached their ears as well. They remained motionless until the heavy footsteps of their former neighbor had dwindled down the stairs.

Rebecca reacted first. She snatched the telephone and frantically looked up the number of Broerse. A snarl of frustration escaped her when she reached his voicemail. She dropped the device and turned back to her computer. She clicked a few times, then sagged back with a defeated expression. Robert looked at her uncomprehendingly. "What's the problem?" he asked.

"Look for yourself," she answered, pointing at the screen.

He moved over and looked. It took a few seconds before it sunk in what she meant. When he finally understood, he actually felt the blood drain from his face. He stared at Rebecca with blank eyes. The social window, which until now had always displayed the status and whereabouts of the Grimstones, was empty.

"How can this be?" he stammered. "Where have they gone?"

In answer, she reached over and clicked on the log to the left side of the bottom of the screen and scrolled up.

"There it is", she said, tapping the monitor. "They all went at the same time."

Friend removed because the character no longer exists Robert read. He scrolled upward and saw the message repeated several times.

"What happened? Did they just delete their characters?"

Rebecca laughed at him. "Of course not, silly! I bet you a hundred to one that they moved them to another server."

Seeing the blank look on his face, Rebecca elaborated, "Remember what I told you about the many different servers? They moved their characters to another server, just like I did with my mage and my rogue. I moved them to Sylvanas so I could be with you and the bad boys. You pay a little money, that's all."

With a slight nod, Robert signaled his understanding. His brain was working at lightning speed. "The question is, why would they have done that?" he said hesitantly. "Do you think they found out about our surveillance?"

She turned serious again. "Good question. It could be merely a precaution. Or maybe not. Still, we need to find them again."

"How are we going to do that?"

She answered with her face already turned to the computer. "That depends on how thorough they've been." Her fingers flew over the keyboard. With a sigh, she suddenly slumped back. "Damn!" she exclaimed. "It's as I feared. They also changed their names!"

Robert took the two steps that brought him behind her, so he could look over her shoulder. Rebecca had the Armory on the screen, the database in which every single WoW character over level ten could be found. She had searched for 'Pharad,' but the character wasn't displayed.

"I already checked all the others. They're not to be found."

"So what does that mean?"

"It means that they changed the names of the characters as well. Another service provided by Blizzard in exchange for a few dollars."

Suddenly, she slammed her left fist on the table. "Damn, we're forgetting something. Maybe he didn't change his password. We could still hack into the account!"

Immediately, she brought up the login screen of WoW. She entered Khalid's username and password and hit enter.

The information you have entered is not valid. Please check the spelling of the account name and password.

They swore the same oath simultaneously. "How are we ever going to find them again?" Robert asked desperately.

She grimaced. "By investigating the entire haystack. We know the needle is in there, and we know what it looks like."

With a frown, Robert asked, "Do we?"

"Yes, we do. Assuming that they formed a new guild on their destination server, we should be able to find them. We know their races and classes and we know what gear they're wearing. We need to be quick about it, because they'll start playing again and level up to eighty-five. That means they'll upgrade their gear and weapons, making it a lot more difficult to identify them. Probably even impossible."

"Their high-end gear is going to be the giveaway," Robert mused.

She snapped her fingers with renewed energy. "Exactly! Because they're such super heroes, they're wearing vastly superior stuff. It'll probably take until they actually reach level eighty-five before they'll substitute the final items with new ones. Until that time, we can identify them by their gear."

Frantically, she started to rummage in a stack of printouts balancing precariously on the window sill. Cursing because she didn't find what she was looking for, she went through the papers again, slower this time.

"Yes, here's one!" she suddenly exclaimed. "And one more!"

Robert craned his neck to see what she was holding. Noting his interest, she handed one of the papers over. It was a screen print of the Armory file of Drimm they had made an eternity ago.

"We know that the gear they're using now is still exactly the same as the gear they had when we first looked at them. That may be enough to find them. I hope."

CHAPTER XXX

The hunter who used to be called Drimm was still marveling at his new perspective on the online world. He had been a member of the Horde since the beginning. Khalid never felt the compulsion to start an Alliance character simply to see what the other side was like. The Horde side suited him. He preferred its often rough and primitive towns to the neat and polished cities of the Alliance.

Sylvanas was a PvP server, allowing the players of the opposing factions to attack each other at will. He had certainly killed his share of Alliance players. Together with his achievements in battlegrounds, his count of so-called Honorable Kills was a little over 65,000 Alliance players.

Now, thanks to a relatively new feature of Blizzard, Drimm had switched sides and had become a member of the Alliance himself. Considering his past, it was a good thing he had changed his name as well.

His former Tauren appearance had been replaced by that of a sleek Night Elf. His reputations had been transferred as well, only now reflected his standing with the states, cities, and races of the Alliance that were the counterpart of their Horde equivalent. Suddenly, he was welcome in the Alliance cities of Stormwind, Ironforge, and Darnassus, the capital of the Night Elves.

For now he remained on familiar ground. Dalaran was open to both Horde and Alliance. However, the Silver Enclave where he'd been ordered to go, was a secluded area where only members of the Alliance were welcome.

The Beer Garden was there, off limits to the Horde, at the back of an inn called A Hero's Welcome. As most people were discovering the new opportunities of Cataclysm, Dalaran was nearly deserted. Lively streets and squares that had been thronged with people only days ago, now looked desolate and sad. Even the Beer Garden was empty except for the two of them. They were seated next to each other on one of the long wooden benches. The table in front of them was empty. Looking around, he saw that it really was a garden. On television he had seen impressions of such places during the *Oktoberfeste* in Germany.

Khalid barely suppressed a smile. Wasn't it funny, meeting in a place like this? His religion forbade the drinking of alcohol, and even his WoW characters abstained as much as they could. He only used to make an exception for Rumsey Rum Black Label, back when having a Twink still was fun and worth the effort.

He looked at his companion again. Oddly enough, he had no idea who he was talking to. He had simply followed the orders he had been given, changing faction and renaming his character, then leaving the place where he had lived for the last few months. At Amsterdam central station he went through the rehearsed routine to shake off anyone possibly tailing him. Now he was staying at a hotel just across the German border. The room had been paid for in advance. As promised, there had been a clean laptop computer waiting for him. The World of Warcraft software had already been installed. He had used it to come to this meeting.

"We wait," the level eighty Gnome deathknight repeated. Khalid made his character nod. Right at that moment, a motion drew his attention. He turned around and saw a Human warrior emerge from the arched doorway that separated the inn from the garden. He approached their table and sat on the opposite bench. At the same instant, the presence next to Khalid shimmered and vanished. There were just the two of them now.

"Pharad?"

"Don't ever use that name again. It doesn't exist anymore. He doesn't exist anymore."

Khalid swallowed. Much had happened during the last few days. Not being singled out for the operation in Belgium, the subsequent loss of several members of their team and most recently, the sudden transfer to this hotel room in Germany, not to mention the order to effectively destroy Drimm, the character that had been with him for nearly five years. Drimm had many friends and acquaintances outside the Hammer of Grimstone. His sudden disappearance had been an act of dying in its own way. He wondered what people would think. Were they talking about him, wondering what had happened to him? Only now, he looked at the name of the warrior on the other side of the table. He was called Malak. Angel. He grimaced.

"Why?" he asked.

"We've been compromised," Malak answered. "My place was under surveillance. By professionals. They were good, but not good enough." He laughed. "I think they're still staking out the place!" It remained silent for a few moments. "Are you sure you weren't followed?" he continued.

Khalid nodded. "Yes. Hard to tell if anyone was on my tail in Leiden. I assure you I was clean when I left Amsterdam. I exited at two places in between to make sure. Negative."

"Good. Now, I want you to think about the last few weeks. Did anything happen, *anything*, that could explain how our cover was blown? Anything out of the ordinary that might have given us away?"

"I will. Please tell me, why did you make me change faction?"

"Because of something you said. Do you remember when we were at the Tower of Eldara? You told me the next day that you saw a player near us? A Horde player, watching us?"

Khalid nodded.

"I chose that spot because nobody ever goes there. Nobody. Ever. What were the chances that someone else would be there at exactly the same time?"

"Well, it could happen. People do try to discover the world."

"Right. They do. But who gets it into his head to go to Aszhara? Who would ride all the way to that deserted and utterly pointless location? Besides, everyone knew that discovering that zone was a waste of time anyway, because it was going to be completely overhauled with the launch of Cataclysm! The all-important question is, why would a Horde player hide? That's the main concern. Sure, if it had been an Alliance, hiding from a dozen hostile level eighties would have been a sensible thing to do. Not for a Horde."

Khalid shrugged. "It could be. It could be nothing."

"Indeed. But I have this feeling. The feeling of being watched. Inside World of Warcraft. I never had it before. The problem is, I can't pinpoint it. Don't you know how you automatically learn to recognize the names of players and guilds that cross your path? The regular players? I mean, there are always other players around, and you just *take notice*. Well, let's say that I've been seeing the same name out of the corner of my eye just a little too often."

Khalid thought about that. He didn't share the feeling of being followed. Still, he knew enough of Pharad, now Malak, to trust his instincts. He was alive because of them.

"Anyway, nobody knows who we are now," he replied.

"Indeed. For now. There's no telling how long WoW will remain secure to us."

"We only need five more days," Khalid interjected. "Then it's all over one way or the other. Afterward, we can build new characters on new accounts. Or maybe even in another game, like Everquest."

Malak stood from the table. "Correct. First we'll make the world tremble. And we'll make the people who betrayed us pay. In blood. So keep your eyes open. And think carefully about what I asked you." With that, the other man traded him a document, giving the details of their next rendez-vous. Then he turned away and walked out of the garden.

Sixteen hours and nineteen minutes later, special assault teams simultaneously hit the addresses in Rotterdam and Gouda. Road blocks had been set up in the area, snipers were on the roofs of surrounding buildings. Even though nobody had seen the subjects leave, both houses were deserted. Not a scrap of useful evidence had been left behind. The Hammer of Righteous Justice had slipped through the net.

The raids were witnessed however, by ordinary looking men wearing inconspicuous clothing. They watched from among the inevitable crowd of curious onlookers, swaddled in huge shawls to protect their faces from the bitter cold. They left before any of the other people did.

CHAPTER XXXI

Rebecca's suggestion to ransack the database of the Armory for the Hammer of Grimstone didn't work out. The interface wasn't suited for the kind of search they needed to undertake. Nevertheless, they tried for many hours before finally admitting that their efforts were futile. They were never going to find them this way.

To make things worse, with every second that ticked away, the chance that one or more of the members of the terrorist guild acquired new equipment became bigger. The entire effort was based on the assumption that the Grimstone's gear was so superior that they wouldn't substitute all of it until they actually hit level eighty-five. They were coming across an increasing number of people who had reached the new pinnacle by now. There was no sense in keeping up the search of the haystack, if they didn't even know what the needle looked like anymore.

***

They weren't the only ones to swallow bitter defeat. Frustration and anger rose with each level that the matter, and thus the failure, was kicked up the chain of command. What had started as an internal issue of the Dutch was now a priority of the international anti-terrorism community. With the identification of Muhammad al-Moutti as the commander of the Hammer of Righteous Justice, it had become more than just a blip on the radar of Homeland Security.

Accusations and recriminations flew across the Atlantic. The Dutch resented the way in which they were held responsible for the failure to apprehend the terrorists. There was no doubt however, that the entire handling of the Hammer of Righteous Justice had been a cock-up from the start. While the investigation was going nowhere, the input of the English student had been dismissed out of hand. Only much later had it been acted upon, and even then only half-heartedly. Most criticism however, was directed at the decision to leave the important task of investigating the doings of the terrorists in the virtual world to amateurs. Somehow, they must have made a mistake that had put the terrorists on alert.

Robert, Rebecca and Andy were told in no uncertain terms that they were off the case. This happened after they had been taken to a modern office building in the nearby city of The Hague, where they were questioned for over six hours. From the unexpected appearance of three men in dark suits at his door, to the end, it felt like an arrest.

They were separated during the questioning. Robert was taken to a medium-sized conference room. He was seated at a large table and made to wait for twenty minutes before two men and a woman entered. They took him slowly through everything that had happened since the moment he first laid eyes on Khalid. This was frustrating, because all this information had already been shared with Broerse and Fitzgerald. When he thought they were finally finished, they started all over again, right from the beginning. At some moment he asked for Broerse and Fitzgerald, but they dismissed his question completely.

After several hours, he was faced with two new people. They asked a series of specific questions, presumably to verify some of the details that had been divulged by Rebecca and Andy.

By the time they were reunited again, it was nearly midnight. Robert was the last to be brought to a deserted cafeteria somewhere in the building. His friends were already sitting at a square table. Andy was slumped in his chair, his eyes downcast. Rebecca was stirring some hot substance, presumably coffee, in a styrofoam cup. She met his eyes briefly and winked. His spirit lifted.

The next day, a computer expert came to Robert's place to verify that their camera hadn't made any recordings of Khalid's last hour in his apartment. He didn't say much beyond introducing himself, but managed to convey his disdain for their set-up by much sighing and shaking of the head. The man was their age, maybe a little older, but he carried himself with the air of an accomplished professional. He sported a slim little pointed beard, much like a pirate out of a movie. The tip of a tattoo on his wrist peeked out from underneath the sleeve of his shirt.

When he was finished, he obviously wanted to take the extra laptop computer with him. He actually went so far as to put it into some special bag, when Rebecca put a stop to that. While Robert had been feeling deflated and dejected since the night before, she had been getting angrier by the minute. He had been watching her simmering anger build up with some trepidation, so he wasn't surprised when she erupted. All her frustration poured out, aimed at the poor technician. She tore the computer bag out of his hands with such force that he relinquished his grip by pure surprise alone.

"What the fuck do you think you're doing?" she yelled in his face. Robert saw the man flinch and take an involuntarily step backward. Computer Whiz started to say something, but Rebecca wasn't interested.

"Do you have a search warrant?" She poked him in the chest, forcing him another step back. "Well, answer me!" Another poke. "Do. You. Have. A. Search. Warrant?"

"Eh, no," he stammered. All his former bluster and bravado was gone now. "But I thought, I was told-"

"You were told that those stupid amateurs would cooperate with anything, right? You were told to take anything you deemed necessary, right? You were told not to pay too much attention to us, right?"

Robert could see in the man's eyes that Rebecca's remarks had struck home. They were being pushed out of the way, and the taking of their computer equipment was part of the process. She was right, nobody could take his property away like that. The irony was that, if the man had only asked politely, he wouldn't have objected at all. Now, fueled by Rebecca's anger, and a wish to stand by her, he supported her with a fierceness that surprised even himself.

"That computer belongs to me," he snapped. The man's terrified eyes flicked his way. He took another step backward and was now almost touching Robert's bed. "And this room as well," he continued. "You have exactly ten seconds to remove yourself, or you can explain to the local police why you trespassed and why you had my computer in your bag!"

A bead of sweat rolled down the man's face. Fascinated, Robert followed its descent along his cheek and watched it disappear inside the thin hairline of the man's beard.

Rebecca chose that moment to step up again. She raised her finger and made another move. It was too much. The technician tried to turn and flee the room, but he was unaware of how close he was to the low crossbar of Robert's bed. His legs touched the wood and he lost his balance, stumbling backward onto the bed. His head hit the wall with a hard bang. Robert could see the pain ignite in his eyes.

Rebecca was relentless. She grabbed the man by his shirt and hoisted him upward with almost inhuman strength. Robert stepped in and helped her pull the man upright. Together, they shoved him toward the door.

"Get out and tell your bosses that we appreciate their gratitude for all our efforts and the time we spent," he spat. Suddenly, he was as angry as Rebecca, just by thinking of all the valuable time that had been wasted. "All of that because you were too stupid to believe us for weeks. Now go, and take your superior self out of here!" With a mighty shove, he pushed the man through the door and nearly down the stairs. Rebecca threw the door shut with satisfying force.

They were both panting with the physical effort and the emotion. The footsteps of the poor computer expert could be heard receding down the stairs. He looked at her and smiled wanly. She met his gaze, and he would have sworn that he saw the color of her eyes change for a second. Her eyes were usually dark brown, but now she looked at him with such intensity, he would have sworn that he saw them turn black. He didn't know what was wrong with her. Was she angry with him? He started to say something, but found that he couldn't. His throat was locked. He had once read that certain snakes immobilized their targets simply by looking at them. He felt like a little mouse at that moment, hypnotized by the eyes of Rebecca.

As in slow motion, he saw her reach out to him with one arm. Her hand locked behind his head, and she drew him toward her with unsuspected strength. Their mouths locked with such force that he was surprised he didn't taste blood when he finally found the strength to kiss her back. At that, she turned frantic. Her breathing became ragged, and she started to pull at his shirt. When she couldn't get the buttons undone fast enough, she ripped it open. He heard a moan, and only then realized that it came from himself. She stepped away from him and started to tear the clothes from her own body. Her T-shirt snagged in her hair, but when he tried to help, she pushed his hands roughly away. She finally got the piece of clothing free and threw it away. It landed at the side of the room on his wine cabinet. His breath caught in his chest. He felt his legs go liquid. With some effort, he remained upright.

She looked up and smiled. They kissed again, and he held her like that for what seemed like an eternity. Eventually, she broke away and pushed him backward on his bed.

The world exploded in more colors than he ever believed existed in the universe.

The next morning, Robert discovered a message from Khalid in his mailbox.

CHAPTER XXXII

It was by pure chance that he logged in with Hunterino, the character he had been using to interact with Khalid's Drimm in World of Warcraft, instead of Gunslinger. He had been awake for over an hour, not daring to move because he didn't want to wake Rebecca. The bed was too narrow for the both of them. In the end, he got up slowly and carefully switched on his computer. He was so preoccupied with beautiful Rebecca, who was slumbering only a few feet away, that he accidentally logged on with the wrong account.

This launched Hunterino into the virtual world. His eyes immediately focused on the icon in the upper right of screen, signaling that he had new mail waiting. By moving his cursor, he saw that the letter was from Drimm. This jolted him wide awake.

He hurried toward the nearest mailbox and retrieved it. Even before he started to read, he made a permanent copy of the letter.

Dear Robert,

You have probably discovered by now that I had to leave suddenly. I had to go home because my father is ill. I also need to concentrate more on my study, so I terminated my account of WoW. Sorry, but I can't help you anymore.

I wish you luck and success.

Regards,

Khalid

Rebecca wasn't asleep anymore. She was standing behind him. With both arms around his neck and her cheek pressed to his, she read the message as well. They stood like that for quite some time, each coming to grips with the happenings of the last few days. Robert felt at peace. He let the events catch up with him, his brain processing them at their own pace. His thoughts turned to his parents and his brother, whom he hadn't talked to for longer than he should have. So much had happened that he hadn't shared with them. How was he ever going to explain the excitement, the fear, and turbulent encounters in and out of the virtual world, and their failure to achieve anything in the end? The brusque way in which they had been tossed aside by the authorities? Still, there was a sense of liberation in the fact that the Hammer of Righteous Justice wasn't their responsibility anymore. The knowledge that lives were at stake, and that they might be the only ones standing between the terrorists and the next act of senseless violence had weighed heavily on him. Now that the burden was lifted, he realized how much they had been driven by simple fear. He felt strongly, however, that the girl next to him was worth every single second of the past weeks. Rebecca was another thing that had changed in his life. A good thing, he thought. He leaned back into her, luxuriating in the press of her soft breasts against the back of his head. In response, she stroked his head. Her fingers whirled through his hair, tugging softly at the ruffled strands.

He turned around and kissed her flat stomach. Rebecca gently pulled him back to bed. He went willingly.

The thought came to him an hour later, while he was in the shower. He digested it, turning it over and over in his mind, willing himself to visualize the various screens of WoW's login interface. When he reached the conclusion that his hunch was on the mark, he abruptly shut off the water and strode back to the room, not even bothering to towel his wet body.

"Listen!" he nearly shouted when he entered. Rebecca, who had showered before him, hadn't dressed yet and was wearing one of his white cotton T-shirts. It was too large for her, and fitted like a mini dress. She looked incredibly sexy. She turned toward him, and he noticed only now that she was on the phone. She motioned at the device, indicating that she was trying to terminate the call. Almost quivering with excitement, he waited until she finally hung up.

"Khalid's WoW username is an email address, right?" he asked without preamble.

"Yes, all usernames are email addresses these days. It wasn't like that before, but they changed that some time ago."

Robert nodded vigorously. "Whatever. The point is, he uses a Hotmail address, like we do. I set up an account specifically for my WoW username, because I didn't want any spam or advertisements in my regular email. I believe you did the same, because you use another account for your other emails, isn't that correct?"

"Yes," she replied, gesturing for him to go on. He could see she was already catching up with him.

"Well, let me guess," he continued, "do you have the same password on your dedicated WoW email account as on the one you use for logging on to WoW?"

"Yes!"

"Exactly, so do I. Now-" With these words he hesitated for a moment. "Just suppose that Khalid also used one single password for both his dedicated email and his WoW account. And suppose he didn't change the password on his email. That he forgot, or simply didn't bother. What would that mean?"

Rebecca frowned. "That would mean that we could access his email. Through that, we'd be able to hack into his account after all. We could request a new password. There's a procedure, in case someone forgets it. I believe the new password is sent to the email address attached to the account. If we can access that email, we can pick up the new password. He wouldn't be able to log on the next time he tried, because we changed the password. So he would know that someone messed with his account. Khalid would have to do the same thing as we did to get his account back."

"That's what I thought. Would there be some way to cover up what we did?"

She concentrated deeply. A thin line appeared above her eyebrows as she thought it through. "Not really," she said finally. "We could erase all our tracks. That would leave him guessing as to what happened exactly."

They dressed first and had a cup of coffee. And another. They didn't say much, both feeling the tension building. When there was no more reason to postpone the moment, they sat at the desk side by side. Rebecca was at the keyboard.

"We just log on and log off, nothing else!" Robert repeated. "We see if it works and that's it."

"Yes, don't worry," she replied, clicking on the bookmark of MSN Live Hotmail. The familiar blue screen immediately popped up. Rebecca's own email address was displayed as default in the appropriate box. Carefully, she erased it and typed in the email address of Khalid, the same one he used as his username for WoW. She studied it for a few seconds, making sure she typed it right. After that, she proceeded with the password. She hit the keys one by one: GEHENNA321. She pressed the button to log on. It didn't work. In red, a warning appeared: *The email address or password is incorrect.*

Robert's reaction was one of equal disappointment and unexpected relief. He released the breath he had been holding. It was over. Now they could finally put it to rest.

"Well, that was it," he said. "At least we tried."

"No, it isn't over," Rebecca replied. "Not yet anyway. Don't forget, passwords of Hotmail are case sensitive. I used capitals. Let's try again with lower case."

She followed the same procedure again, but now she entered gehenna321 in the password box instead. She clicked on the button again.

They were in. *Hello Drimm!* large letters read on the upper left side of the screen, above several file folders. Rebecca clicked on the inbox. It was empty.

Shocked, Robert reached over and took the mouse out of her hand. He pointed the cursor to the upper right corner and clicked on the log out icon.

They simply looked at each other for long seconds. Robert released the mouse and found that his hands were shaking.

Andy was totally opposed to their plan. He argued vehemently that they had been officially called off and that it wasn't their responsibility anymore. He also didn't want to go through another session with the AIVD like the one they had to endure the night before.

"It's over," he repeated for the third time. The three of them were sitting at a quiet table in the back of Einstein, a large pub at the Nieuwe Rijn, one of the charming canals in Leiden. He looked from Rebecca to Robert. "Besides, I know someone who really needs to push on with his studies. I know a guy who missed over half of his classes already and who's going to fail spectacularly at the upcoming examinations and tests!"

Robert looked down. He fingered the remains of the milk out of his empty coffee cup. Andy was right, of course. He had felt some liberation at the knowledge that their hunt for the Hammer of Righteous Justice was over. All avenues had seemed closed. It was easy to give up in the face of total defeat. It was a lot harder now that they had possibly found a new opening.

"I'm not so sure it's that simple," he said softly. "Rebecca and I talked about this. The question is-" he looked up and fixed Andy's eyes with his own before continuing. "Do we trust those assholes who badgered us yesterday? So far, they haven't shown any affinity nor aptitude with what we've been dealing with. They don't understand WoW at all. Suppose we gave this to the AIVD; what do you think they would do with it?"

"I don't know and I don't care!" Andy was getting angry now. "Don't you understand that you could get killed? We're dealing with terrorists! And those intelligence guys? When you're lucky, they'll only throw you behind bars for interfering with an official investigation. Hell, maybe they'll stick something like endangering national security on you!"

Rebecca shook her head. "I understand how you feel," she said. "Can you so easily forget why we decided to push on by ourselves in the first place? Yes, you're right that we're dealing with dangerous people. Remorseless killers, professionals. Religious fanatics, for all we know. But isn't that exactly why we're here? To stop them, when no one else will?"

Now it was Andy's turn to look down. When he looked up after maybe twenty seconds, he caught Robert and Rebecca exchanging a look. Suddenly, he smiled broadly, and the tension broke a little.

"Admit it, you did more than just talk last night!"

To Robert's surprise, Rebecca actually blushed. He took her hand and looked back at his friend. "Yes, we did," he said happily.

"Congratulations! I was wondering how long it would take!" Andy seemed genuinely pleased. "Even a blind man could see the sparks between you two. All the more reason not to get yourselves killed, I'd say."

Rebecca reached over the table and took Andy's hand in her free one. She suddenly had a serious, even solemn, air about her. "I wouldn't be able to live with myself if I let other people die because it was easier and safer for me to walk away. If I can't even be true to myself, how could I ever be true to Robert?"

She squeezed both their hands. "Well, what do you say? Are you with me? Are you with Robert?"

"I'm with you." Andy sighed. "And I'm not even the one who gets kissed by the beautiful girl. I must be crazy. Damn you!"

Rebecca squeezed his hand even harder. "You're great!" she said. She bent over and kissed him squarely on the lips before releasing him.

***

"Gold sellers are one of the biggest problems of World of Warcraft," she lectured a little later. They were back in Robert's room, in front of the computer screen. Both men were turned toward Rebecca. "They are the people who keep whispering to you in broken English, asking if you'd like to buy some gold."

Robert nodded. He had been approached often enough. Even Andy, who hadn't been online all that much, affirmed his experience with the phenomenon.

"They also advertise in the Trade Channels, even though that has become less frequent recently. Blizzard probably found a way to stamp that out. Blizzard tries everything it possibly can to eradicate the problem."

"Why is it such a problem?" Andy asked. "I mean, buying virtual money for real money seems like cheating to me, but why is it forbidden?"

"Good question!" Rebecca praised him with a wide smile. "The cheating is certainly one side of it. The main problem lies in the way the gold is collected."

"Why? How do they do it?"

"One way, the honest way, is by actually earning it. Imagine countless offices in China, where scores of Chinese worker bees toil endlessly behind computer screens, fourteen hours a day, seven days a week. They hunt animals for endless hours, putting the skins and the meat on the auction house. Or they mine for minerals and metals, or repeat the same daily quests over and over again on different servers. There are many ways to make gold, if you're willing to put a lot of time into it. For a few lousy dollars an hour, thousands of Chinese perform the dull labor that most regular players don't have the time nor inclination for. This has become quite an industry over there."

Robert had actually read an article about this not so long ago. Still, he didn't understand what she was getting at. "What does this have to do with us?" he asked.

"The farming and the grinding have many reverse effects on the game's economy," Rebecca continued. "For instance, the market prices for many commodities are influenced significantly by the influx of too much supply for the average demand. Prices go down and inflation kicks in. As a consequence, players can't make as much gold on the market as they should. Many players have problems earning enough gold."

Andy whistled. "And so they go to the gold sellers!"

"That certainly happens. The majority of the players doesn't want to cheat, but there are more than enough people who don't mind. They're just lazy. Or greedy." Her contempt carried clearly in her voice. "Some people just like to show off their Mechano-hog of sixteen thousand gold, even though they wouldn't know how to get that kind of gold in the first place."

"What does all this have to do with our hacking into Khalid's WoW account?"

"During the last year or so, the gold mafia shifted much of their focus from earning gold to stealing gold. We're going to make it look like that."

The two men looked uncomprehendingly at her. "They steal WoW accounts and suck them completely dry," she explained. "Sometimes they try to trick you into giving them your username and password by impersonating Blizzard personnel. Or they set up official looking websites, with the sole purpose of getting people to enter their personal information. Mostly they work through clever little virus programs."

She laughed at their rapt attention. "You can pick up those viruses on all kinds of WoW-related websites," she continued. "You both know there are thousands upon thousands of websites dedicated to the game. Most viruses are so-called key loggers. They simply record your keystrokes while logging on to WoW and send that information back over the Internet. As easy as that."

"And what do they do, exactly, when they have that information?" Andy asked.

"Let me show you." Rebecca straightened the laptop in front of her and summoned the official website of World of Warcraft. She selected account management and followed a few easy steps to the point where she could request a new password. It was telling that this was referred to as a service 'in case of a lost or stolen password'. Apparently, the theft of accounts was as common as Rebecca had described. She confirmed the request for a new password and received a message that the new password was sent to the email account.

Next, she opened Hotmail in a new window. She logged on, using Khalid's information, and sure enough, there was an email from Blizzard in the inbox. She opened it. In the email was a link that had to be followed. It brought them to another section of the World of Warcraft website, where they could change the password. Rebecca did so, changing it to *hello123*. Next she switched to the other window, where another email from Blizzard had arrived. It confirmed the request for a new password and warned that this could mean that the account had been hacked. It also gave directions to Customer Support if this was the case.

Grinning, she selected both emails and deleted them. Immediately after, she went to the folder where the deleted items were stored. She deleted the emails again, erasing them permanently.

She didn't close the email immediately. Quickly, she opened each of the few file folders of the email account, checking for emails that might be important. There was nothing but emails from Blizzard, with announcements and the like. It was clear that this account was set up solely with the purpose of providing a username for World of Warcraft and a valid backup email.

"Okay, let's do it," Robert announced. He had taken the other laptop and had the login screen of World of Warcraft in front of him. He had already entered Khalid's account name and his fingers were hovering over the keyboard, ready to pounce. They shared a look. Andy shrugged. "We already screwed up his account, so let's make use of it!"

Robert typed *hello123* and only seconds later they were looking at the character selection screen. The preselected character was a level eighty-three Night Elf hunter named Argus. Rebecca clapped her hands. "They didn't move to another realm," she exclaimed. "They just did a faction change. They switched from Horde to Alliance. No wonder we couldn't find them. We didn't even think of that!"

She pulled Robert's computer toward herself, holding out her other hand to him. With a shrug, he handed her the mouse.

"Get me a pen and a notebook," she ordered. Robert stood and just as he returned with the requested items, Argus the Night Elf hunter entered the world. He was in Dalaran, in front of the entrance to the Silver Enclave. She opened the social tab. Argus a was member of a guild called Sphyrnidae. There were seven guild members. None was online.

Rebecca furiously started to copy down all the names.

"Can't we just make a print screen?" Andy suggested.

"Sometimes I put my trust in old fashioned technologies," she replied without looking up from her work.

Meanwhile, Robert used the other computer to look up the profile of Malak, who was the guild leader according to the guild info tab. He took the profile of Pharad they had made before in their futile efforts to locate the lost guild. After a quick comparison, he announced, "The guild leader is a Human warrior with matching gear. It's Pharad, one and the same. There's no doubt about it!"

Rebecca nodded at this confirmation. She was done with copying the names and closed the window.

"What do you think of the guild message of the day?" she asked them.

"I didn't see it," Robert confessed. Rebecca reopened the tab and showed it to them. *ArenA practice every day from 11:00 to 13:00 and 18:00 to 20:00*

"What does it mean?" Andy asked.

This time, it was Robert who answered. "Arena fighting is a kind of player versus player combat. You participate as a team, and you fight against other teams. The fights take place in special arena areas."

"Correct," Rebecca supplied. "It's the real hardcore player versus player combat. Up close and personal. You can't compare it to fighting in battlegrounds. Every fight is recorded, and points are awarded or subtracted after each fight. All teams and players have rankings. The year is divided in Arena Seasons. At the end of each season, prizes are awarded to the best teams and players. There are even tournaments around the world where the best teams engage each other. Spectators follow the fights on big screens. If you want to attend, preorder tickets now, because they're usually sold out."

"So are these guys into this?" Andy asked.

"They used to be," she answered. "Drimm was in a five player team as well as in a three player team. All teams were made up of members of the Hammer of Grimstone. Now they switched to the Alliance, those teams must have been disbanded." She clicked on Argus' PvP button and opened the Arena tab. He wasn't part of any Arena team currently.

"You can practice without being in a team," Robert said. "There's an option to enter non-rated combat."

Rebecca turned to him, surprised.

"Yes, I tried it once," he said defensively. "Just to see what it's like. But it was too hard."

"Whatever," she answered, glancing at her watch. "We have less than ninety minutes before the evening practice starts, whatever that is. I don't think we want to be online when the rest appears. Let's get started to irritate the hell out of Khalid and his guild!"

The cover-up operation was a lot of fun. They stole or simply sold off every single piece of property that Khalid possessed. There was plenty. The man not only possessed a stunning cash fortune of over eighty thousand gold, his bags were brimming with valuable stuff. They sold the 'soulbound' items that couldn't be removed from the character, together with the items that weren't so easy to sell on the auction house, to the shopkeeper of the Wonderworks in Dalaran. When they were finished with the items he was wearing and carrying in his bags, they went to the bank building and emptied Khalid's considerable bank account.

Next, Rebecca flew the now completely stripped hunter to Booty Bay. Simultaneously, Robert brought Hunterino by ship to the same place. He was logged on with the alternate account because Rebecca thought it was safer not to use his real account for the execution of the theft. They didn't know how thoroughly Blizzard was going to investigate the matter. It wouldn't do to have Gunslinger suspended for complicity in theft. Hunterino was expandable.

In Booty Bay, at the backside of the town, the Blackwater auction house was located. It was special, because it allowed players of the different factions to trade with each other. In other words, a Horde player could bid on an auction that had been posted by an Alliance player and vice versa. In return for this unique service, the Blackwater auction house charged an outrageous commission of fifteen percent per transaction.

Hunterino put up an auction of a completely worthless piece of equipment. He auctioned a Broken Sword, setting the buy-out price at 86,500 gold. A few seconds later, he got the message that his auction had been successful. *Incoming amount: 86,500* his screen read. That much gold was roughly the equivalent of fifty million Euros, dollars, or whatever currency one could amass a fortune in. It was completely off the charts. He laughed hysterically.

"That must have been the most bizarre transaction in the history of WoW!"

"We're not ready yet," Rebecca said smiling. "Are you ready for some bargains? Let's start with eleven stacks of Eternal Fire. They're up for ten Copper each!"

Robert typed *Eternal Fire* in the search box. For the total price of one silver and ten copper he purchased Eternal Fire with a worth of two thousand gold. In this way, Rebecca squandered all of Khalid's remaining assets. Hunterino greedily bought everything she put up for ridiculous prices.

Just as they were finishing, they were alerted to the appearance of two of Argus' guild members at the same time. Robert looked at his watch and saw to his surprise that it was already nearing half past five in the afternoon. They had been busy for over an hour. The announced Arena training would commence in than half an hour.

"What do we do now?" he asked, directing the question at Rebecca. He was still feeling a little giddy from what they had just done.

Rebecca shrugged and looked at Andy. Their Dutch friend had glittering eyes as well. "Maybe it's best to log off?" he offered. "The question is, what would real hackers do?"

Right at that moment, Argus received an invitation to join a Party. The invitation came from Malak, the guild leader, a.k.a. Pharad, a.k.a. Muhammad al-Moutti.

They all stared at the window that had appeared in their screen. It offered two options, Accept or Decline.

"That's obvious," Rebecca announced and resolutely pressed Decline. "Ordinary hackers ignore all whispers and invitations. They are focused on one thing only: making money!"

"That should set off all their alarm bells," Robert mused. "What will they do now?"

The answer came almost immediately. The Party invitation popped up again.

"He must think Khalid accidentally hit the wrong key. It happened to me often enough. But I don't think he'll still think that after this!" With relish, she declined the invitation again.

[Malak] whispers: what's wrong?

They looked at each other. Suddenly, all their former bluster and glee were gone. Each realized that they had just been addressed directly by Muhammad al-Moutti, one of the most dangerous people on earth. A minute passed, during which none of them moved.

[Malak] whispers: argus, is that you? verify your identity code five.

"They must have a protocol to ensure that it's really one of them," Rebecca said.

Robert stood, unable to bear the tension. He was thinking that maybe they had pushed it too far. How smart was it to anger these people deliberately?

Rebecca must have been thinking almost the same. "The best thing to do is to behave like ordinary robbers," she said. "And unfortunately for Pharad & Co, that means that they're going to get robbed as well!"

She moved Argus a few feet to the right, and clicked on the guild bank. "As I hoped," she said. "Our friend has full access to the guild bank account." She started to systematically transfer items from the guild bank to the empty bags of Argus.

"The guild bank works more or less in the same way as a personal WoW bank account," she explained while she worked. "The main difference is that it can be accessed by multiple people. A guild leader controls the access the other members of the guild have."

Soon, the bags of Argus were full. There was still a tremendous number of items left in the bank. The Sphyrnidae account held several tabs, each of which was completely filled with all kinds of different things, most of them rare and valuable. It was a treasure trove of expensive potions, flasks, food, gear and materials.

"Now, how are we ever going to get rid of all this stuff?" she mused. "I think we must hurry, so there's no time to put it all on the auction house as we've been doing until now."

"Destroy it?" Andy suggested.

"Too slow. I have a better idea."

Rebecca walked Argus over to the mailbox. "Do you see that level twenty-eight rogue over there?" she asked, tapping the screen with her finger, indicating a random low level player. "He's going to be rich!" She entered the rogue's name as recipient of her mail and started to send him the contents of the guild bank. "I wish I could see that person's face when he checks his mailbox the next time!" she said smiling.

When she was done, she turned her attention to the guild bank again, quickly and efficiently refilling Argus' bags.

"Shouldn't we take the cash as well?" Andy asked. He pointed at the bottom of the screen.

She slapped her forehead. "How could I be so stupid! Of course, that should have been the first thing we did!"

"Auction house, minor health potion," Robert announced. "Giving away that much gold might be a little over the top."

"And a waste!" Andy said.

With a nod, Rebecca moved Argus over. She looked up the item Robert had mentioned and quickly found the auction. She paid 9,000 gold for the potion actually worth maybe fifteen silver. The money would flow to Hunterino, with a deduction of the fifteen percent fee of course.

"What do you think Pharad is doing now? Andy asked. He checked his watch. "We haven't heard from him for more than five minutes."

As if in answer, a message appeared on the screen. *You have been kicked out of Sphyrnidae* it read.

"Damn!" Robert sighed. "He threw us out of the guild. We can't really blame him. It's the fastest way to cut off our access to their bank."

"Yep, they must have verified that Khalid's account has been stolen." Rebecca leaned back in her chair and stretched. "They probably contacted Khalid directly. I bet he's somewhere behind his computer trying to get his account back."

She was right. Khalid was in his hotel room in Germany, staring in disbelief at the fading illumination of the little screen of the cell phone that had come with the new computer. At first, when he couldn't access the game, he blamed it on a faulty Internet connection. It happened sometimes. When he verified the connection, he had to admit it was something else. Had he forgotten his password? Had he really been so stupid? He couldn't believe it. He cursed the order to change the familiar one.

Now he knew his account had been hacked. His leader had just confirmed that Drimm, he still thought of his beloved hunter by that name, was walking around in the virtual world, with someone else at the controls.

Khalid was livid. He couldn't remember ever being as angry as he was now. How could this have happened? The only explanation that made sense to him was that the firewall protection on the new laptop computer had been inadequate, allowing a key logger to slip through. His angry fingers jabbed at the keys, looking for the details to contact customer support. There was a toll free phone number to call in case of a stolen account. He dialed the number and was told to wait. While holding, he surfed to the Armory. He accessed the profile of Argus. The Armory was updated continuously, making it a live database of each WoW character. Sure enough, the level eighty-three Night Elf hunter was completely naked. He kicked the wall in frustration.

[Malak] whispers: Whoever you are, you just made a big mistake. You have no idea what you have done. This is not over.

Of course, they didn't reply.

"Idle threat," Rebecca said dismissively. "For all they know, we're some anonymous poor peasants operating out of China or India."

The next instant, there was a puff of smoke and, on the spot where Argus had been standing, a small penguin was suddenly skittering around. "What the f-' Robert began, but Rebecca silenced him with a hard slap on the arm. It hurt.

"Log off!" she yelled hysterically at him. "Shit, shit, shit! Log off, now! NOW!"

When he didn't react, paralyzed by her sudden outburst, she shoved him out of the way. She took control of Hunterino and quickly moved the level twenty-two hunter away from the auction house area. She ran up the wooden ramp and turned into the inn situated around the nearest corner. Once inside, she logged off.

On the other computer screen, a level eighty Troll mage walked into view. His name was Jinn. He looked at the penguin that used to be Argus. He started to cast a spell. Little sparks of fire danced at the tips of his fingers.

"Pyroblast, Presence of Mind, Pyroblast," Rebecca muttered absentmindedly.

After what seemed like an eternity, a huge boulder of fire leaped at the penguin. On impact, Argus was restored to his original form. The ball of fire had eaten away nearly half his health. Worse, he was actually on fire. Flames cackled *within* his body, eating away more of his precious health. Even if he had wanted to, there was no way the hunter could have defended himself. All his weapons and gear had been sold. He didn't even have a small skinning knife left. He was totally defenseless. Under the circumstances, it didn't matter at all that he was three levels higher than his attacker. Almost immediately after the first, the mage released another Boulder of Fire, similar to the first one. It hit the poor Night Elf squarely in the chest. He let out a shriek and tumbled to the ground. Argus was dead. The mage called Jinn walked up to the corpse and spat on it.

A nervous Rebecca exited Khalid's account. Robert had never seen her like this. Her hands were trembling and her face was as white as a sheet. Her hair was all sweaty.

"What's wrong?" he asked.

She looked away. "We made a mistake by bringing Hunterino into this. I thought I was being clever, using an account that we weren't playing with anymore. I was concentrating too much on the consequences of getting caught by Blizzard. You see, when Blizzard catches someone doing what we just did, the account is banned immediately."

"What's the big deal?"

"Hunterino is known by Khalid. He knows that hunter belongs to you, Robert Barnes from England, currently living in Leiden. I simply never guessed they would actually find us in that black hole in the middle of nowhere. They must have guessed we'd use the auction house over there."

She hesitated before continuing. "That Jinn character got a visual of Hunterino. The question is, did he connect it, did he catch the name and will he tell Khalid about it?"

"What do you think?" Andy and Robert both asked simultaneously. They were back to deferring to Rebecca as the guru of WoW.

"I think he didn't connect it. The gold mafia typically uses only level one characters for their business. They lose accounts all the time because Blizzard pursues them actively. There's no use investing time in an account like that. They must be expendable. That Jinn fellow wasn't looking for medium level characters. So I think we're in the clear. I would say we got away with it."

"Let's get drunk," Andy suggested. "Just not here. I need some fresh air."

CHAPTER XXXIII

K halid's access to his account was restored to him shortly after completing the call. A friendly young man verified his identity, and after ensuring he was the rightful owner of the account, told him that all his possessions were going to be restored to him. It was going to take some time though, anywhere between several hours and several days.

He logged on once, just to make sure the account was his again. He found Argus lying dead on the wooden planks at the Blackwater auction house in Booty Bay. He was simply too frustrated to make the effort of resurrecting and walking his ghost all the way back from the cemetery to his corpse. What good was Drimm, or Argus, to him, when he was stripped of all of his superior gear?

Only an hour later, he decided that lying on his bed, smoking cigarettes, wasn't a fruitful way to pass the time either. He got up and logged on again. He would prepare himself for the moment his gear was restored to him. Besides, only two more levels and he'd be at the new pinnacle of level eighty-five. New epic gear would become available to him then, and he would soon be equipping himself with items vastly superior to what had been the ultimate summit at level eighty. Until then, there was a new operation to prepare for. He'd already missed this evening's training session. His guild would supply him with adequate stuff to participate. Those items would take him to level eighty-five, if his own things weren't restored by then.

He resurrected at the graveyard, accepting the penalty of the so-called resurrection sickness. It temporarily lowered a player's stats and a player incurred enormous damage to his gear. Well, at least that was one thing Argus didn't have to worry about. Immediately after coming back to life, he used his hearthstone to return to Ogrimmar.

Robert had no idea what time it was when he grudgingly emerged from a deep slumber. His mind was still fogged by the after effects of all the beer they had drunk. He wasn't much of a beer drinker to begin with, and his two drinking mates obviously had more training in beer drinking. As punishment for trying to keep up with them, he was experiencing the all too familiar headache. Rebecca tugged at his arm again. He sat up with a groan, shielding his eyes from the light of the single lamp. The movement made him feel even worse. Instant nausea threatened to overtake him and he quickly lay back. He wondered briefly how it was possible that they had made love before going to sleep.

"Come on, wake up!," she repeated urgently.

"What is it? What time is it?" He hardly recognized his own voice.

In answer, she tossed him the shirt he had been wearing the day before. He sat up again, this time more slowly. Their clothes were scattered all over the floor, and she was collecting them frantically.

"No time to explain. Just get dressed," she whispered. "Please?"

"Okay," he answered, shaking his head in an effort to dispel some of the fogginess. He put the shirt on and started to tug on his underpants. By the time he had his jeans on, she was fully dressed. He looked around for his socks.

"Just put on your shoes!"

"Rebecca, what's going on?"

She hushed him with a telltale finger to her lips. "We have to get out of here," she whispered. "We made a serious mistake. They might come here. I have this feeling. Please hurry!"

For the first time in his life, Robert actually *felt* Goosebumps form on his arms. It hurt. "The Hammer?" he asked disbelievingly.

With her lips in a tight line, she nodded.

"Where are we going?"

"Anywhere." She waited impatiently while he did the laces of his shoes. With one arm she was holding his coat out to him. With the other she held the door open. Now they were standing in the corridor together. It was cold. Out of habit, Robert locked the door behind him. The ancient house was shrouded in silence. It was dark as well. Most of the lamps in the hallways were broken, only a sorry few actually worked.

They were halfway down the stairs to the second floor when they heard a distinctive sound from below. The front door had just been opened.

They even felt the faint tug of draft caused by a small window set right in the turn of the stairway at eye level. It was slightly ajar. She squeezed his arm hard. They looked at each other in the darkness. Robert felt the last vestiges of drowsiness disappear. A boost of adrenaline had just kicked his senses to full alert.

"What now?" he mouthed.

She pointed downward. Tip toeing, they finished the last few steps. The last wooden step creaked when Robert removed his weight from it. They both froze at the sound that seemed like a loud crack in the dark silence. The second floor was even darker than the one above.

Suddenly, Robert remembered the emergency exit down the hall on the floor he lived on. There must be another one at this level, most likely at the same location right at the far end of the corridor. He took Rebecca by the sleeve of her coat and drew her with him down the hallway. She halted after some fifteen feet, where another stairway gave access to the lower part of the house. She bent slightly and looked down over the railing. He jerked her back with force as a bright narrow beam of light suddenly moved over the wall below. Another followed. At least two people with flashlights were ascending from ground level to the first floor.

At this, panic threatened to squeeze all the air out of his lungs. For a precious second, he was immobilized by fear. Then his survival instincts took over and he led Rebecca swiftly to the end of the hallway, where it widened a little. The small alcove was illuminated dimly by the green light of an emergency sign. It held a wide door with a cross handle that had to be pushed down.

He gripped it with both hands and applied just enough pressure to unlock it, careful to make as little noise as possible. Behind them, stairs creaked. Right after, they saw circles of concentrated light moving on the wall only a few yards away. Whoever was out there was on the same floor now. Immediately, they both pressed their bodies flat against the wall, trying to keep out of sight. Robert strained his left arm to keep the heavy door from swinging shut. That sound would give them away for sure. He had to stretch parallel to the wall and was barely able to apply enough pressure with his fingers. He silently said a prayer of thanks to the architect who created this small sanctuary at the far end of the hallway.

They waited for what seemed like an eternity for the lights to cross to the other end of the corridor, to the stairs that led up to Robert's floor. Just when he thought he couldn't keep up the pressure on the door any longer, darkness returned. The intruders had reached the next floor. How long would it take for them to open the locked door and discover they were gone?

Mercifully, the heavy emergency door didn't make a single sound when it swung open. They stepped out onto a small iron balcony.

Khalid watched as the man he always referred to in his mind as Pharad felt the mattress with a flat hand. His leader smiled.

"Warm," the man stated with satisfaction. "They must be close."

Khalid let the beam of his flashlight traverse the small space. A stack of papers on the desk lit up under the harsh light. He sheathed his knife and used his free hand to rummage through the papers on the desk. One of the first things he came across was the print of the overview screen of the Hammer of Grimstone that Robert and Rebecca had been using in their efforts to track them down. Without a word, he handed it to Pharad. The other examined it for a second and smiled with grim satisfaction. He nodded. Khalid scooped up all the papers on the desk and put them in the flat rucksack he was wearing.

They stepped out of the room again and stood silently in the corridor. Khalid concentrated briefly. As he had been trained to do, he had surveyed the building thoroughly. He rarely stayed in any place without scouting it for possible escape routes first. He pointed in the direction of the other end of the corridor. Pharad's gaze followed the motion and fixed on the green exit sign. They started moving again. Following his leader's example, he put his knife away and replaced it with a gun. It was equipped with a slightly unwieldy silencer. Pharad had already used his knife once tonight. Khalid hoped they would kill again, but this time he wanted the blood of the person who had betrayed him. He had been led by the nose like an amateur. His light beam momentarily danced on dull steel as anger flared up in his chest.

Before he opened the door, Pharad signaled with his left hand. They both extinguished their torches before stepping out into the night.

The fire escape was at the back of the house. Narrow metal stairs, with small landings at each of the floors, had been bolted to the dark wall. Robert's guess that it must end in the small backyard, partly visible from the window of his room, proved to be correct. They had descended silently and were now standing next to each other on the ground. They were surrounded by an incredible mess of derelict plastic garden furniture, rotting wooden planks, and a small mountain of stinking garbage bags. Two demolished bicycles were lying entangled on the ground, embracing each other in mechanical death. Against one wall stood a sofa. Robert shuddered at the thought of how much water it must have soaked up by now and what must be living inside it.

Some sparse light fell out of the grimy window of the kitchen door, the only access to the backyard. He tried the door. It was locked. He turned around and looked at the concrete wall again. It was too high to climb. Even the sodden sofa wouldn't allow them to climb over. They were trapped.

He suppressed the urge to hold Rebecca back when she took a few steps backward into the yard. Couldn't she see it was futile? There was no way out of this place. He sensed with clarity that despair was about to overtake him. He stood paralyzed for a few seconds. His heart was hammering irregularly in his chest. He even had trouble breathing. Was he going to die here? Would it be quick?

"Come on!" she whispered.

He tried to shake his fatalistic thoughts off, angry with himself. They should try anything to escape, not wait to be slaughtered.

Rebecca was climbing the fire escape again. Instead of going up to the first level, she halted somewhere in the middle. He saw her peering out into the darkness, and suddenly he understood. He tried to measure the distances from the ground. Could it be possible? Swiftly, he followed. It looked doable, but he knew how deceptive the dark could be.

They had just reached the tight landing at the first level, when they heard a loud metallic sound above them. Creaking, the fire escape door all the way to the top of the house was opened. Robert's mind processed the sound and came up with the conclusion that they had been lucky that the door on the second floor had opened so silently. Rebecca's fingers on his cheek brought him to his full senses again. She used her hand to turn his face toward her.

"Jump. We can do it!" she said softly and kissed him lightly on the lips. She edged her back against the railing to maximize her take off. She tensed, took a great step, and jumped.

It was probably a little over eight feet from where they were standing to the wall. Their position was only a little higher than the top, and for a heartbeat Robert feared she wasn't going to make it. But her timing was perfect. Her hands gripped the top of the wall, and she used her momentum to create an explosive upward motion. Her sneakers found just enough purchase on the concrete surface to help her to the top easily. She was astride the wall for a second, then she was over. He heard her feet hit the ground on the other side.

Unfortunately, Rebecca's escape had been far from silent. Above him, Robert heard dim voices cursing, followed by the sound of footsteps racing down the stairs. He took a deep breath and jumped as well.

He knew immediately that his jump wasn't perfect.

It wasn't. His balance was off, with his body leaning backward instead of forward. He hit the wall with a dull thud, and his left knee exploded in excruciating pain. One of his flailing hands still managed to grab the top of the wall, if only barely. His fingers dug into the cement with all the power of true desperation. He willed himself to block out the pain in his knee and to concentrate on the wall. With an extreme effort he squeezed his fingers, pulling himself upward on only one arm. He needed only a few inches!

He swung his other arm, knowing he would have only one chance. If he failed, he was dead.

Time seemed to stand still as his other hand found a firm hold on the wall. He felt something sharp, but he ignored the pain just like he was blanketing out the pain in his knee. Right before he heaved with two arms, he told himself that he had done this often before. He was no natural athlete, but his wiry body was young and strong.

He mustered all his strength and pulled. Upward he went, straining his muscles to the limit of their endurance, until his arms were finally under him, and he could lock his elbows. He sighed in relief. He resisted the temptation to rest in this position and pulled himself half onto the wall. He was resting on his stomach now, his legs still dangling on the wrong side. Another heave and a kick in the air, and he was lying alongside the wall.

Suddenly, lights were on him. He looked up against the glare and saw two dark silhouettes on the stairway, standing where he had been only moments ago. One was aiming a gun at him. At the same time, the violent sound of splintering wood came from the far side of the courtyard. A bright light came with it. Involuntarily, he looked over his shoulder in that direction. Someone else had entered the courtyard, and he realized there was a direct access to the streets after all. There had to be a gate or something in that far corner. A dazzling flash blinded him and, at the same time, the wall right under his hand exploded in countless tiny shards and fragments of concrete. Some of it hit his face, numbing the left side of it.

With an unreal sense of detachment, he realized someone had taken a *shot* at him, and missed somehow. The shot had come from the newest intruder, not from the men on the stairs. By unexpectedly entering the scene, and by missing his shot, his attacker had bought him a few extra seconds. Robert wasn't going to waste them.

He did the only thing he could think of, he rolled over.

He was over the wall only milliseconds before several more bullets hit the crumbling concrete where he'd been lying. One shot hit a tree nearby. Another ricocheted back into the dead bicycles with a terrible din. While he floated between heaven and earth, he actually heard one of the wheels spinning through the air. Then he hit the ground, chest first. All air exploded out of him.

He might have lost consciousness had it not been for two things. The first was his injured knee. Pain he had never even imagined before lanced up into his mind. He experienced it as visual, the color white, blooming behind his eyes like fireworks.

The second was Rebecca. She was waiting for him on the other side of the wall. When she saw him tumble down, she managed to catch one of his shoulders and, by throwing her own weight into his fall, she prevented his head from impacting with the ground too hard. It must have hurt her as well, but she scrambled to her feet swiftly and tried to pull him up.

The realization he wasn't dead granted Robert new strength. He pushed himself painfully to his feet. When he tried to put weight on his knee, he nearly went down again. He doubted if he'd ever be able to stand on it again. Not that it mattered, if they didn't manage to get out of here fast.

He looked around. They were in a very tight alleyway. It was four feet across at most. When Rebecca wanted to start to the left, he limped after her and held her back with effort.

"There's another one of them there," he whispered. "At a gate to the backyard."

She nodded her understanding. "Can you walk at all?"

"I must!" He grabbed her shoulder. "Can you support me a little?"

In answer, she started to walk in the other direction, setting a pace he could just keep up with. They came upon a sharp turn and followed it for another fifteen yards or so. Suddenly, they were on the square. Just as their feet touched the neat cobblestones, they heard the sound of running feet behind them.

It was the third man who was the first in pursuit. Even though the attack had been hastily planned and executed, they had studied a map of the area beforehand. The Pieterskerkhof was a strange place. Officially a square, it was actually a cobblestone road that wound around a massive medieval church. Not only were there several little streets and alleys leading off the square, there were also many dark spots and corners that were perfect hiding places.

Their pursuer was a stranger to Leiden. He might have studied the layout of the square beforehand, when he didn't see them immediately, he assumed they were behind the church. Worse, with so many possible exits, he didn't know where their most likely escape route lay. He turned left to circle the ancient church clockwise, while Rebecca and Robert were limping in the other direction, down the narrow street that led to Barrera on the corner of the silent Rapenburg. They reached the grand canal shortly.

Historic streetlights threw their yellow light across the motionless water. While they had been walking, Robert had come up with an idea. It was so outrageous that he thought it might actually work. He shared his thought with Rebecca, who at first dismissed it. When he shrugged and admitted it was probably craziness, she changed her mind.

"Let's do it," she said softly. "It's so insane that they'll never expect it, and we're dead if they catch us anyway."

He led her to the side of the nearest bridge and pointed it out to her. It was an incline in the steep canal wall, more like stairs, that enabled people to climb out of their boats onto the street above. She nodded.

Silently, they descended. Robert held his breath as he put one foot into the icy water. He hesitated. This was madness, it was nearly winter, and the temperature of the water couldn't be more than several degrees above zero. He had called this plan crazy, but suicidal was more on the mark.

"Come on!"

He let go and slid into the canal. At first he felt nothing, but then the cold wetness penetrated his clothing. Still, it wasn't as bad as he feared. With a soft splash, Rebecca was in as well. He heard her gasp as the water touched her skin.

Keeping to the wall of the quay, they silently moved sideways until they were under the bridge. Total darkness enveloped them. The Rapenburg was so deep that their feet didn't touch the bottom. Fortunately, they didn't have to keep treading water. Rebecca's groping hands accidentally found a rusting iron ring that stuck out of the slippery wall. They both gripped it. They didn't talk, instinctively sensing that they should preserve even the tiniest bit of energy. They just hung on for life.

Their pursuers arrived only a scant few minutes later. Robert and Rebecca held their breath as they actually came to stand right on top of their bridge. Even though they were speaking in a foreign language and their voices were down, it was quite clear that they weren't amused by their escape. One voice especially was nearly hysterical with anger. After some discussion they split up, evidently to cover different sides. Robert started breathing again, but the cold was getting to him. He began to gasp. His fingers were getting numb, and the effort of holding on to the ring was getting harder. It was obvious that Rebecca was experiencing the same. He wondered how long it would take before their pursuers gave up. The centre of Leiden was a maze of small streets.

The men hadn't been gone long when the sound of sirens suddenly rent the quiet night air. Blue strobes of light reflected on the still water of the Rapenburg. Two police cars raced at high speed over the narrow street on the other side of the canal. They turned sharply at their bridge, went over, and disappeared. Shortly after, an ambulance followed. Robert tried to determine where it stopped by the sound of the siren. Close by. Maybe even at his own house.

"Shall we go?" he asked. "I think it's safe now."

She nodded. "Yes, please!"

They started to swim. It was hard. Their bodies had been exposed to the water for quite some time, and their muscles were cramped from the cold. Finally, they reached the place where they had entered the canal. Only when he tried to pull himself out of the water, Robert felt how dead tired he was. Somehow he managed, and he even had some strength left to help Rebecca out of the water. Supporting each other, they stumbled up the few steps and fell onto the street. They both started to shiver uncontrollably.

Footsteps ran in their direction. Hands pushed him on his back, then lifted him. Was he on a bed? He didn't know and didn't care. He was dimly aware that someone was tugging at his clothing. What was that silver stuff they kept trying to wrap around him? Where was Rebecca? Was she all right?

A bright light shone in his face, bringing him back a little. A face appeared briefly before him. It seemed familiar. Who was it? Then he heard a voice. "It's him, thank God!"

Now he knew. The face belonged to Fitzgerald of the AIVD. Too late, as usual. Should he smile at that thought?

He passed out before he could make up his mind.

CHAPTER XXXIV

"It may sound funny, but jumping into the water was actually the best thing you could do," the physician announced. He stopped probing Robert's knee and shook his head. "Nothing is torn or broken. Your knee would have been twice as thick now if you hadn't gone for a swim."

Robert grimaced. Despite the injection for the pain, he still felt his knee pulsing. He was feeling dull and detached. It was as if the events of tonight still hadn't caught up with him yet. On some level he was aware of his surroundings and the doctor who kept talking to him, but it all felt as if he was looking at himself from a distance.

"You know, usually ice is applied to an injury like this as soon as possible, to minimize the swelling," the white-coated doctor continued. "Dipping your leg in cold water for such a long time was unorthodox, but certainly effective. Still, I'd counsel against it next time!"

"Don't worry, it won't happen again," Robert replied producing a tiny smile. He forced himself to concentrate. "When will I be able to walk again?"

"At a guess? Tomorrow it'll still be painful. The day after, a little better. Ten days from now, you won't be feeling it at all."

They were in a small room in the Academic Hospital of Leiden. On the floor was blue linoleum; the walls were freshly painted white. The doctor was on a low swivel chair, Robert was sitting on an examination bed. They hadn't been in the water long enough for actual hypothermia to set in, but it had been a close call. He had been told several times that another ten minutes or so, might have led to cold shock and then drowning.

His left hand was bandaged. Apparently, when he groped for the top of the wall, a piece of glass had embedded itself in the palm of his hand. Again, he had been fortunate, as no sinews or main blood vessels had been damaged. He also had many superficial scratches on one side of his face caused by fragments of concrete when the bullet hit the wall. All in all, he had been extremely lucky. Rebecca even more so. She had survived the ordeal without barely a scratch.

As soon as the doctor was finished with him, Robert fled the small examination room. He longed for some privacy to let his mind come to rest. Unfortunately, he limped right into Fitzgerald and Broerse. They were sitting on either side of Rebecca in the waiting area adjoining the examination room he just left. When he approached, Rebecca looked up at him with a wan smile. The thought of more talking appalled him. He was so fatigued that sleep and rest were the only things he really wanted. Or maybe he craved Rebecca's arms around him even more.

"I just want to go home," he said to no one in particular.

Fitzgerald stood and shook his head. "Impossible," he said. There was sympathy in his voice. "Not for a few days at least. Your place is a crime scene now."

He looked at Rebecca. She nodded. Suddenly, there were tears in her eyes. "They killed a girl," she said and started sobbing uncontrollably. She flew into his arms and squeezed his neck so hard she nearly choked him. He looked over her shoulder at the two men.

"Lisa Duchamps," Broerse confirmed. "Probably went to the bathroom at the wrong moment. Her throat was slit."

Robert felt the bottom drop out of his stomach. His painful knee buckled. He closed his eyes. He knew her, of course. A petite dark haired girl from France, in Leiden for a stint at the Chemistry faculty. She lived on the ground floor. Now she was dead. Because of him. Was there no end to this nightmare?

They took them to a nearby village called Wassenaar. Broerse drove, Rebecca and Robert were in the back of the car. She rested her head on his shoulder and, by her regular breathing, she seemed to be asleep. He stared out of the window with unseeing eyes.

The car turned into a long driveway and stopped in front of a large luxurious mansion. They got out and let themselves be led to a spacious bedroom. They didn't need to undress. Some kind of night dress had been issued to them at the hospital. Within minutes, they were asleep.

They slept the remainder of the day and the next night. When he finally woke, he felt remarkably fresh. He got out of bed and winced at the painful soreness of his knee. It got better after he stretched it several times. There were clothes on a chair next to the bed, jeans, a T-shirt, and a comfortable woolen jersey. They fit perfectly. He was just tying the laces of a pair of brand new sneakers with some effort, when he heard the sheets rustle. Rebecca was sitting up and looking at him.

He crossed over to the bed and sat next to her. Suddenly, he was at a loss for words. For some time, they just looked at each other. Finally, she smiled at him.

"You saved our lives," he whispered softly. Then he asked the question that had been haunting him all along. "What happened? How did they find out about us?"

A shadow crossed her eyes, making the dark brown go actual black. "Hunterino," she said solemnly.

"But I thought you said-'

"I know." She slumped back against the cushions. "We were stupid and greedy. Or maybe we just tried too hard to make it look like we were real account raiders. Remember how we sold all his items and stuff for a few coppers each to Hunterino? Think it through!"

"Yes, and-' He broke off as it suddenly dawned on him. "My God. The mail!"

She nodded. "Yes. It takes an hour for the monetary proceeds of any auction to reach the seller. During that time, the check is 'in the mail'. We didn't think of that."

"So when Khalid logged on again," he supplied, "he found a mailbox full of transfers from the auction house. Each one named Hunterino as the purchaser!"

"Exactly. Don't ask me how, but it came to me in my sleep. Somehow, I immediately sensed that they would want revenge. They're not used to losing. What we did to them, everything we did, must be an unbearable humiliation to them."

An hour later, they had wolfed down an enormous breakfast and drank so much coffee and orange juice that Robert felt he was about to burst. His body responded to the nourishment with a pleasant sense of fatigue. He stretched his legs under the table and looked across at Broerse and Fitzgerald. He knew this conversation was inevitable, important even, and he was ready for it.

To his surprise, it was Rebecca who kicked off. "Why couldn't we reach you? Why weren't you around when we were more or less arrested? Why didn't you tell those goons that we were the good guys, the only ones who had actually achieved something? It wasn't our fault that the arrests were a cock-up. It was thanks to us that they could even try in the first place!"

Fitzgerald merely inclined his head at her anger. "It may not mean much to you, but the case was taken over by the highest levels in our organization. That's why we were suddenly out of the loop."

"And now?"

"Now it has been decided that we are acting as your contact again."

Broerse took over from his colleague. "The consensus is that after the terrorists had evidently been found out, they must have abandoned WoW as their tool. They took the information that each of their virtual characters, avatars they're called I believe, had disappeared, as proof of that. The fact that the Hammer of Grimstone was disbanded only added to that conviction."

Robert and Rebecca both shook their heads. "Of course not," Robert said. "Those guys are addicted."

"That may be, but the current evaluation is that they abandoned WoW. It could be that our colleagues are pulling strings with Blizzard, but somehow I don't think so."

"How can they still hold to that position after what happened last night?"

Fitzgerald sighed. "Be realistic." He looked both of them sternly in the eye. "If what Rebecca told us at the hospital is true, now they're aware that their anonymity in World of Warcraft has been compromised. They'll keep their distance. They might try another game comparable to WoW or create all new accounts, but for now they're called off."

This was said with so much conviction that Robert was tempted to believe it.

Broerse opened his mouth as well. "You may be the experts on computer games, but we're the experts on terrorism after all. Trust me, when a communication channel is compromised, it's abandoned. Rule number one. Period."

"And what if they don't play by the rules?" Rebecca asked.

"In that case, we have you two to tell us." He reached beneath the table and came up with two laptop computers. On top were the familiar boxes of World of Warcraft software. "We'd like to ask you to monitor World of Warcraft for us, just in case they pop up again. The game is installed on both PCs. Will you do that?"

They exchanged a glance. Rebecca nodded. "We will," she said.

CHAPTER XXXV

They were alone in the villa, except for Nellie, a bald woman of about fifty years old who was in charge of running the household. Broerse and Fitzgerald had departed twenty minutes ago, with the assurance they could be there within an hour if necessary.

Rebecca was leaning against the wall of the study, looking out through the French windows at the spacious grounds. In the distance, two guards were patrolling a high iron fence. It was dark green, with mean spikes on top. Robert came to stand behind her and put his arms around her. He kissed her neck and let his hand trail down her spine. To his surprise, she shrugged him off.

"Let's get started," she said, looking at him meaningfully.

Robert didn't feel like playing WoW at all. He didn't understand her eagerness. "Do we have to start now?" he asked. "Can't we wait a bit?"

She winked at him, sending an obvious sign. "No, let's do it now."

He finally got the message. "All right," he gave in. They seated themselves across from each other at a conference table, the computers between them. All he could see of her was the top of her head. He logged on.

Gunslinger was in Ogrimmar. He still wasn't used to the new look and feel of the city after Cataclysm. His screen told him that Killermage was in the city as well. As expected, he received an invitation to form a Party with her. He heard Rebecca typing furiously on her keyboard. Right after she finished, he received the message in his chat log.

"After all that happened, I prefer to talk in private," she told him.

"What do you mean?" he responded.

"I guess this is what they call a 'safe house'. It's probably wired inside and out, and there must be cameras all over the place."

He hadn't considered that. Suppressing the urge to look around for hidden cameras, he hunched over his keyboard a little more, shielding it from possible prying eyes. He replied, "You're probably right. Do you think they're watching us?"

"Who knows. I have to ask you a personal question."

He hesitated. What was this all about? Involuntarily, he looked up and caught her watching him. He huddled behind the screen again and typed: "Sure, what do you want to know?"

"Do you want to back off or do you want to catch those guys?"

He took his time to think the question through. Their close brush with death had taught him that he didn't want to come near any of those terrorists again. The death of Lisa Duchamps, his housemate, had shaken him as well. He felt angry, terrified and furious at the same time.

"Of course I want them behind bars," he replied. "I don't want to pay for it with my own life, though. So shadowing in WoW is okay, but in real life I want to stay far away."

She typed: Good. Same here! Then she looked around the screens and smiled warmly at him. Then she typed some more.

When he looked back at his screen, he read: *Because they'll be coming after you!*

"It's a matter of ego," she explained that night. They were lying in bed in what could only be described as the master bedroom. Nellie had prepared them a traditional Dutch meal which didn't look attractive but tasted very well. It was called *andijviestampot*, cooked potatoes and a slightly bitter vegetable mash called *andijvie*. It was topped off with bacon and some greasy sausage. Robert claimed it was eaten in the UK as well, and was called endive, but Rebecca didn't believe him. Even his protest that his father was a restaurateur, didn't convince her.

At the end of the afternoon they reported back to Fitzgerald by phone. There wasn't much to tell. As expected, none of the previously known characters existed anymore. The guild *Sphyrnidae* didn't exist anymore either, at least not under that name. Fitzgerald had an interesting piece of information for them. He had looked up the meaning of the word *Sphyrnidae*. It turned out to be the scientific name of a shark variety commonly known as Hammerhead sharks.

"Predators with a hammer," Rebecca answered to that. "Unfortunately, I see little justice in a shark."

Their heads on the pillow were so close to each other that her hair tickled his forehead. Their whispering was so soft he had to concentrate to understand what she was saying.

"What those so-called professionals don't understand is that Muhammad al-Moutti hasn't been playing by the rules from the beginning. The man is a lunatic on a personal crusade to avenge the murder of his son, his wife, and his brother. He's here in Holland because it happened to be a squad of Dutch military forces who killed them. Had it been Canadians, he'd be on the other side of the Atlantic. This guy takes things personally. I think you can be sure he'll come after us."

Robert had to admit she certainly had a point. It was quite possible that the authorities were having no success because they were trying to predict Al Mouddi's behavior by applying 'normal' standards while this man and his team were on a mission of personal revenge.

"How do you think he's going to find us?" he whispered.

"I think he knows, or at least suspects." She was barely audible now. "He must have been trying hard to reconstruct what went wrong. He knows his guild has been compromised, infiltrated even. He must have been looking for coincidences, for things out of place. Now, who were there all the time, hovering right behind his shoulder?

Who were there, conveniently, to form up a party with them to ride into the dawn of Cataclysm together?"

"Gunslinger and Killermage," he said breathlessly.

"Correct. He might even remember your encounter with Drimm and him on the beaches of Stranglethorn Vale. If so, he must wonder at the speed with which that little helpless hunter leveled up to eighty."

"How are we ever going to find them?" he asked.

"I don't think we'll need to," she answered. "I think they'll find us this time."

Rebecca's assessment of the reaction of Muhammad al-Moutti was accurate. Almost forty-eight hours after the failed assassination attempt, Khalid still heard him raving about it. That worried Khalid. He preferred their leader to be cool and collected. Khalid had a lot to worry about these days. Their secret communication channel, their meeting place and training ground, had been exposed. He had always prided himself on their impregnable security. As far as he knew, they had been the first to use a MMORPG in this fashion. Their security had been breached, with almost catastrophic results. He didn't fool himself; he was fully aware of how close they had come to being arrested at their various hideouts.

And now this botched mission. It had been a gross violation of their established protocol. So far, every operation had gone exactly as planned because their preparation and training were always thorough and meticulous. Pharad wouldn't accept anything less than perfection. How could he ever have ordered a mission, born out of anger and frustration, with just a briefing of two hours and no preparation or training whatsoever? He admitted that he had been eager to participate. It had been his account that had been compromised after all, his riches that had been looted. He wanted to taste the blood of Robert Barnes and that skimpy girlfriend of his.

Khalid didn't underestimate the consequences of their recent setbacks. Their communication channel was no longer secure. Their training ground was compromised. The members of the Hammer narrowly escaped arrest. Above all, they failed to kill some twenty years old students, simple amateurs. It was in the eyes of his team members. It was in the way they walked, how they held themselves. Their confidence had been shaken badly. They had always been invincible, invisible even, most of the time. The realization that they were vulnerable after all was gnawing at morale. That didn't bode well for the upcoming mission. It was to be the crown on their work in the Netherlands. After completion, they would all disappear and enjoy some much deserved rest in Yemen or Pakistan.

While Pharad should have been directing his energy to bolstering the morale and confidence, he seemed preoccupied with those students. Instead of finalizing their attack plan, he was thinking of ways to get back at them. If not in real life, he wanted to humiliate them inside the virtual world. He was convinced they were freelancing, operating without supervision or consent of the police.

Khalid had gotten the assignment to watch for the appearance of Robert and Rebecca, his former neighbors. They had deduced that they must be the people behind the characters of Gunslinger and Killermage. Nearly every member of the Hammer of Righteous Justice recognized the names. The mage and the hunter had been seen in their vicinity a little too often; far too often, to be a coincidence. And, of course, they were the players who joined their group so conveniently right after the launch of Cataclysm. He had some grudging admiration for the way they had achieved all that.

This afternoon, Gunslinger and Killermage had been online briefly. They logged on and logged off together. They went nowhere; they just stayed in Ogrimmar. He tried to find them there, but they disappeared while he was still combing the area. One of the drawbacks of Cataclysm was that Ogrimmar had become a busy beehive. So far, the Englishman and his girlfriend proved to be as elusive in the virtual world as in real life.

Only this time, as Pharad had repeated several times, they were chasing them. The tables had been turned. He just hoped the man was right. The good news so far was that his gear and gold had finally been restored to him this afternoon. Good old Blizzard had delivered, his recent renaming and change back to the Horde faction notwith-standing. All his things had been sent to him by in-game mail.

What worried him most was the way in which Pharad kept look-ing at him. The fact that he, Khalid, was to blame was undeniable. Somehow, he had given himself away and allowed his secret account to be compromised. It was hard to swallow for a perfectionist as him-self. Were there going to be repercussions for him? He couldn't stop thinking. *Is it going to be my turn next time around to undertake a suicide mission?*

Sometimes, unexpected things turn the tide of events. Neither Rob-ert and Rebecca nor Muhammad al-Moutti had counted on Andy. Their friend, the loyal Andries van Eck van den Berghe, had been so furious at the vicious attack on his friends that he entered the virtual world all by himself. Afterward, he confessed he didn't even know exactly why he did it, just that he wanted to undertake some positive action, to have the feeling at least, that he was contributing some-thing. Anything. As far as he knew, they were still in the hospital, maybe even fighting for their lives.

He had played several times with Gunslinger, Robert's hunter, while they had been grinding through endless battlegrounds. Dur-ing some idle time, he halfheartedly tried to level up an Orc shaman, using an account he had opened for himself. Now, he had taken that pathetic little level nine Orc and gone in search of their enemies. Against all odds, and by pure chance, he had succeeded. Having un-covered one member of the terrorist group, he was able to identify others as well.

He couldn't reach them by phone, and the house on the Pieter-skerkhof appeared to be closed down for the foreseeable future. He could think of only one place where they might be reached: Azeroth. So he looked around for a mailbox and sent letters to both Magekiller and Gunslinger.

CHAPTER XXXVI

"Terokkar Forest?" Rebecca exclaimed in disbelief, forgetting about their self-imposed rule of silence.

They were both reading Andy's letter in astonishment. It was just that Rebecca's surprise was aimed at another subject. Robert was simply amazed by his friend's perseverance and spirit and more than a little proud of his achievement. When he finished the letter, he started again, rereading the message word for word. It was sent in installments, because there was a maximum to the length of a single letter.

Dear Robert and Rebecca,

I do hope this letter finds you soon, and in good health.

I have no idea of what exactly went down at your place, because nobody is telling me anything. I did speak to Michael, one of your housemates, and he told me they were being relocated because that French girl has been murdered. How terrible! I liked her. Rumor has it that you two were dragged out of the Rapenburg more dead than alive. A friend of mine, a med student who works at the hospital, won't tell me anything more than that the part of you being brought to the hospital in the middle of the night is true. Someone else said that Robert was seriously injured, but I don't know how trustworthy that info is. However, it's clear to me that the Hammer tried to kill you and nearly succeeded.
Good job, staying alive!

Today, I used my own account to enter WoW. You know I have this level nine shaman. I was in Ogrimmar when I saw something weird, a level eighty-two Tauren hunter who was all naked. That got my attention, because I was there when we stripped Argus. He was at a mailbox for a long time, and suddenly he was dressed. He was wearing exactly the same stuff as Drimm used to have!

His name is Esjnn. He belongs to a guild called Odin. Not subtle, don't you think? Like hammering me on the head, lol! I looked up the guild on the Armory and there are seven members. I'll send you all the names separately. Like we did before, I entered the names in my social log and waited. At around five thirty, each of them came online. They went to a place called Terokkar Forest. I couldn't follow them, of course. They stayed there for nearly two hours. After that, most of them logged off.

That's all for now. I'll try to keep an eye on them. I really hope to hear from you soon!

Andy

"What about Terokkar Forest?" he typed when he was ready.

"I'm trying to figure out what's there to do for them," she replied. "It's a totally uninteresting zone for a bunch of level eighty plus characters. So it must be connected to their next operation, don't you think?"

He thought about that briefly. So far, each time they witnessed the Hammer of Grimstone converge on a low level zone, it had proven to be a training ground. It had been that way in Ashenvale, Stranglethorn Vale and the Blood Furnace.

"I think so," he replied. "They must be operating out of Stonebreaker Hold, now that they're Horde again."

"Or Shattrath City. Don't forget that's the capital city over there, with all the facilities they could possibly want. And it's more anonymous, with Horde and Alliance mingling."

He shrugged. "One way or the other, we'll find out more in less than an hour."

"You're right. Arena training each day at 11:00 and 18:00 hours. Something must be going down at those times!"

"Do you think we should change the names of our characters as well?"

"Maybe later. I do think we should keep our heads down just now. We don't want to distract them from whatever they're planning to do. So we log off now. I'll switch to my Alliance rogue Magekiller, and you create a new level one Horde character for the occasion."

Robert created an Undead priest. He didn't even bother to move it from its starting position. He just opened the social tab and added the seven members of the guild of Odin as friends. Now he would be kept abreast of their comings and goings and their approximate location whenever they were online. At the moment, they were all listed as offline. Meanwhile, Rebecca transported her level eighty Alliance rogue, of which they could safely assume the Hammer had no knowledge, to Shattrath City. She positioned it at a strategic location in the doorway of the center hall. From there, she could keep an eye on the spot where players using portals appeared, as well as on the flight master outside. They sat back and waited.

It took twenty minutes for the first of them appear. It was a Blood Elf mage, presumably the one Robert had once followed through the endless stretches of Aszhara. He went by the name Marvin now.

He entered the world in the Undercity, but teleported to Shattrath City instantly. Robert came to stand behind Rebecca, and they both saw the level eighty-five wielder of the Arcane materialize at the designated spot. He cast a spell, and suddenly he was mounted on a golden dragon. He took off straight at Magekiller. Robert flinched. He soared past them and, once out of the building, started to climb swiftly.

Rebecca remained calm. She summoned her own flying mount, a blue and black feathery bird of impressive proportions, and took off as well. Magekiller followed the dwindling Blood Elf over the quarter called Lower City and past the adjoining city wall. They exited Shattrath and entered the zone of Terokkar Forest.

The flight took them in a southerly direction. They soared over tree tops for a while, until the forest ended abruptly. They entered the immense Bone Wastes, one of the most desolate places in World of Warcraft. Its surface was all ashes, a dark grey desert that stretched for as far as the eye could see. Robert knew that when on the ground, the occasional coaled remains of trees could be seen. Bones and skeletons were all over the place. Nothing grew in these wastes, still there was life. All of it was hostile. In the north, travelers had to be wary of huge winged scavengers around Carrion Hill, while cultists of the Shadow Council threatened nearly everywhere.

Marvin continued to the south until the ruins of Auchindoun appeared on the horizon. Robert blinked. During his short visits to this area, he'd completed some quests in the north of Terokkar Forest before setting off for adjoining Nagrand. His travels had never taken him this far south.

Auchindoun was so huge, it defied belief. From the air, it looked like a gigantic bowl, or a massive coliseum. Ahead of them, Marvin was descending. He landed on the ground, right in the middle of the flat surface on the bottom of the bowl. The structure was so high that, when Rebecca settled her bird on the outer ring, the Blood Elf mage was only a tiny figure down below. Robert's thoughts went back to a vacation in Spain with his family several years back. Their father had taken his sons to a soccer match of Real Madrid. He vividly remembered the awing impression the Estadio Santiago Bernabéu had made. Their tickets had been for places all the way up in the stands. Together with eighty thousand other people, he'd cheered for the matadors in white, who had been like tiny little puppets from where they were seated. That same sensation was with him now.

His thoughts were interrupted by a sound from his own computer. He hurried over.

"Three more Grimstones came online just now," he reported. "Esjnn is one of them."

"Where are they?"

"Two in Shattrath, one in Ogrimmar."

When he hit enter, two more came online, only a second apart. A minute later, the final member entered the virtual world.

"They're all in Shattrath or Terokkar now," he confirmed a little later. His eyes were glued to the screen, following their progress.

"One arrived here," Rebecca announced from her station. "Correction, two more. Esjnn is here and the guild leader too."

He walked around the conference table again and watched for himself. Four figures were now standing in the middle of the huge floor. Shortly after, the remaining three descended from the sky.

"Shouldn't we hide?" he whispered in her ear.

She shrugged, but put the rogue in stealth mode anyway. Down below, the little group dispersed. Four took wing and flew away in the four directions of the compass. One was heading their way.

At that moment, the door of the study opened, and Fitzgerald and Broerse entered the room. They looked up in surprise. With a flick of her wrist, Rebecca exited the program.

"How are you feeling?" Broerse asked by way of greeting. "Recuperating well?"

"Much better, thank you," Robert replied. Out of the corner of his eye, he saw Rebecca's screen light up with the standard desktop of Windows Vista. He stepped around the table to shake hands with the men. Rebecca wasn't far behind.

"Are you having any luck?" Fitzgerald asked.

Robert didn't dare to look over. He certainly understood her need for privacy, and he resented being spied upon as much as she did. He wondered if she really meant to hide their progress from them?

"We might be making progress, but we're not sure yet," Rebecca replied. In vague terms, she proceeded to describe how they had found a bunch of players who resembled the original Hammer of Grimstone. She concluded by saying they were investigating it.

"Well done." Broerse positively glimmered. "Keep up the good work, I would say!"

They chatted for some time, sharing a cup of coffee. The two men weren't forthcoming at all with information about the progress being made on their end. They did inquire about their wellbeing several times and asked if they needed anything, like more clothing.

Robert shared his worries about his upcoming exams and asked when he'd be allowed to attend classes again. They surprised him by saying they had taken care of that. Some special allowances were being made for him. He would be able to pass the exams of this term individually at some later moment.

"It has all been taken care of, my boy!" Fitzgerald assured him. The men rose and they said their goodbyes.

When they were gone, Robert looked at his watch and concluded that the Hammer's training session must be over by now. His computer screen confirmed this. The terrorists were offline; all of them, but Esjnn. He was in Ogrimmar.

"He's on the lookout for us," Rebecca whispered. Her certainty carried clearly in her soft voice. "Let's tweak his nose a little."

She sat down and launched Killermage. She appeared in front of the bank, next to the mailbox where they had retrieved Andy's letter earlier. She glanced at her watch and after a full minute had passed, she started to cast the teleport spell to Silvermoon City. A few seconds later, she was on another continent, in another city. She walked out of the building, mounted, and rode some distance away. She stopped when she was out of sight of the immediate vicinity of the place where all portals led to.

"Now let's see what he does," she said with satisfaction.

CHAPTER XXXVII

The sudden appearance of Killermage jerked Khalid to full alertness. Their session of this morning at Auchindoun had been good, but the intense concentration had left him a little tired. Immediately afterward, he had taken up his station at Ogrimmar. While hanging around the city, essentially doing nothing, his thoughts had started wandering down the all too familiar dark paths again. Now he was fully alert.

He clicked open his social tab. To his satisfaction, her location was listed as Ogrimmar. It wouldn't be easy to find her here, but certainly possible. His perfect vantage point had been chosen with that challenge in mind. He had only just begun to scan the crowds below him, when the listed whereabouts of Killermage suddenly changed from Ogrimmar to Silvermoon City. *Damn those mages and their ability to travel the world at will!*

He looked around and spotted another mage not far from him. He sent a message, offering ten gold for a portal to Silvermoon City. When he didn't get a reply after twenty seconds he approached another mage. This time he was more successful. They joined Party, and he waited impatiently for the other to start casting the spell. When nothing happened, he realized he had to pay first. He quickly traded the gold and was rewarded by a shimmering portal a few seconds later. He stepped through, and his computer loaded the new location. While he waited, he fired off a text message from his cell phone.

Killermage was off again. As soon as Khalid's hunter stepped out of the building all portals to Silvermoon led to, the location of his target changed to Undercity. He swore. As usual, the streets of

Silvermoon City were practically deserted. In any other city it was usually easy to find a mage willing to provide transportation in exchange for a few gold, but he doubted there was even a single mage of high enough level in this place.

He was loathe to use his hearthstone. It had a cooldown of thirty minutes, meaning he could use it only twice an hour. If he used it now, his only means of traveling far distances without aid was expended. But he had no choice. His hearthstone yanked him to Dalaran, where he sprinted to the little garden with the fountain that held the Horde portals to all other major cities. At least, it used to be that way. He stared in bewilderment at the walls, that had reverted to being just that; plain brick walls. Not even a single shimmering portal was to be seen. At first, he thought he was experiencing a bug or a glitch, which happened sometimes. He even clicked with his mouse on the spot where the portal to Undercity used to be. Nothing happened. He ran back into the streets.

"Where are the portals?" he asked of a level seventy-two Blood Elf paladin, the only player in sight.

"Didn't you know? They have been removed with Cataclysm."

It felt like a rebuke. Stung, he snarled with frustration. The worst of it was that he realized how unlikely it would be that he'd find a mage to create a portal for him. Dalaran had become a ghost city. Seeing no other option, he selected the worldwide trade channel. *Paying 200 gold for portal from Dalaran to Ogrimmar* he typed. The outrageous advertisement appeared in the screen of every single player who happened to be in any of the major cities, from Ogrimmar to Thunder Bluff. Within seconds he had several offers and no less than three mages instantly teleported to Dalaran to offer their services. He traded the insane amount of gold to the first of them to appear en finally stepped through a portal to Undercity.

He couldn't believe it. He had just reached the centre of the commercial district of the Undercity, ready to start his search for her, when Killermage hopped again. Now she was in Dalaran, the place he just left at such expense. What the hell was she doing? Fortunately, there was another mage at the Undercity bank who was willing to help him quickly. He judged he was less than a minute behind her when he, too, materialized in the capital of Northrend. He hesitated in Runeweaver Square. Where was she? Then he finally had a stroke of luck. Through one of the arched porches that gave access to the streets beyond the central square, he spotted someone riding by with a bright light blue nametag. He couldn't read it, but he didn't need to. The color said it all; it was someone marked as a Friend, and Killermage was the only one of those online. He smiled and mounted.

Khalid turned sharp left and exited the square through another porch, effectively cutting Killermage off. He emerged on the street only fifteen yards behind.

He felt a presence behind him. Without looking back, he knew who it was. He knew only one person who moved so silently, Muhammad al-Moutti. There was one more person staying at the double apartment in Haarlem, also a member of their group. He guessed Omar was in his usual spot, on the couch in front of the television. He didn't know where the other members were staying.

"It's Rebecca," he explained, pointing at the back of Killermage. "She's alone."

The other nodded. "Going to Krasus Landing."

True to this prediction, Killermage mounted the steps to the flight platform. She walked up to Aludane Whitecloud, the flight master. Apparently, she was going to use the taxi service. A second later, she was carried away on the back of a Wyvern, an amazing breed of animals resembling lions if you overlooked the bat wings and scorpion tail.

Khalid didn't need any instructions. Quickly, he summoned his own flying mount to take off after her. He knew that the time it took to summon his mount would put him far behind. He also knew that the wyverns of the flight masters followed fixed paths through the air, much like airliners. Those routes were typically designed to be panoramic rather than swift, weaving across the highlights of the different areas. All these patterns were known intimately by Khalid, so he would have little trouble overtaking her before she was too far away from the city.

Unexpectedly, Muhammad stopped him by gently taking the mouse out of his hand. He tapped the screen, pointing out another player who had just taken off in southerly direction. It was a level eighty Dwarf warrior.

"It's covered," he said. "That's one of Rachid's characters. He has several Alliance, too. Now log off and switch to that Alliance character I ordered you to maintain. Or did you convert them all back to Horde?"

It suddenly dawned on Khalid why that order had been given. If it had been up to him, he *would* have changed all of his three characters back to the Horde faction. Even though he usually only played with his hunter, for always Drimm in his mind, those other two were still dear to him. He had played them all the way up to level eighty, after all. Leaving one in the Alliance camp didn't feel right.

He nodded in confirmation. "Of course. My warlock. He's right here in Dalaran."

"Good. Get him out. Go on Teamspeak, regular channel."

Pharad turned on his heel and left the room, already talking into his phone. Khalid logged to his Human warlock, and soon he was invited to a Party. There were five of them, the regular set up for a standard instance.

These weren't main characters, but so-called Alts. As a consequence, they were all still at level eighty, three levels below the Undead mage they were pursuing. Their owners simply hadn't gotten around to leveling these characters up yet. Still, they were well equipped and together they'd be able to overwhelm Killermage.

Khalid always thought of a configuration of five players as a standard platoon. Dangerous bosses with millions of hitpoints could be brought down by a balanced group of five. Enormous damage could be endured by such a group, if they cooperated well and played it smartly. There were no players more experienced and dedicated than the members of the Hammer of Grimstone. Their parties had fought together countless times, in and out of the virtual world. Everybody knew his role instinctively. They were attuned to each other in ways unimaginable to ordinary players. He almost felt sorry for Killermage.

***

"He gave up!" Robert laughed, exhilarated. "He just couldn't take it anymore!"

They had received the message that Esjnn had logged off with satisfaction. Rebecca had been right again. Their enemies had finally figured out who they were. Their names were now known by the opposition. The determination with which Khalid had followed Rebecca's mage around the world had proven that beyond any doubt. They had seen his desperate plea for a portal out of Dalaran as well. There was certainly a chilling side to this. Before, they had been safe on Azeroth. They had spied on the Hammer of Grimstone from the shadows, protected by their anonymity. They had been just faces in the crowd. That was over now.

It felt good to do something in return. Of course, they both realized that sending a virtual character on a little goose chase wasn't much in the way of retaliation. Not when a twenty-year-old girl had been murdered in cold blood, and they had escaped the same fate by only a hair. To be alive at all, to be able to play a futile and petty joke on one of the men who had shot at him was victory in itself.

"He must have realized there was no way he could find me again, after I left Dalaran through the back door."

He stretched and yawned. "Do you think there's something like a wine cellar here?" he asked. "I could use a decent drink by now."

She looked up from her screen and hesitated. Killermage was still on the wyvern and she hated to log off while airborne. It was impossible to abort a taxi ride. She shrugged. What was she worrying about? None of their enemies were online and, even if they were, nobody knew where she was. It was a big world out there.

She pushed her chair backward and stood, leaving her screen unattended.

"I have to go to the bathroom," she said. "I'll ask Nellie about the wine. Do you prefer red or white?"

He waved at her. "I leave it entirely up to you, my dear. I'm sure you won't disappoint me!"

She came back nearly ten minutes later, cradling a bottle of wine. Robert recognized it as a Bordeaux from a distance. In her other hand she held two glasses. He smiled with genuine pleasure.

While he was busy with the cork screw, Rebecca threw an idle glance at her computer screen. Killermage had reached her destination some time ago and was now sitting down at the little sandy beach at River's Heart in the zone of Sholazar Basin. River's Heart was a lake in the middle of the zone, fed by the influx of water from two rivers that flowed through an immense tropical jungle. On the northern side of the lake was the destination she'd chosen at Krasus Landing, a tiny settlement with a flight path. It was remote, and an unlikely hiding place.

The cork plopped and Robert inhaled the rich aromas of the Bordeaux.

"Come on, give me some!" she begged.

He obliged and poured another glass for himself. They toasted. "To being alive!" Robert said.

"To being alive," she repeated. She looked for a place to put down her glass, which was difficult because of the computers. "Let's put this thing away."

She reached over and clicked twice, meaning to exit the game. Killermage was still with her bottom on the beach. A warning, signaling an invalid command, sounded softly. She frowned and looked up at the screen.

You can't do that while in combat

"The bastards!" she screamed at the top of her lungs. Without hesitation, she hit one of her hotkeys and immediately, Killermage was encased in a protective block of ice. An instant later, a barrage of fire and lightning rained down on her. A magic bolt, closely followed by a bullet, came streaking in from another angle. As if that wasn't enough, a plated figure rushed her out of nowhere and swung a vicious two handed sword at her head. His attack was joined by the fangs and teeth of a ferocious tiger, apparently belonging to some hunter.

Robert leaped to her side and watched with open mouth. He recognized the Ice Block around Killermage from experience. It was one of the most infuriating abilities in the game, because it made mages completely invulnerable to any damage. He also knew it lasted only ten seconds.

Rebecca appeared to be in a trance. He had never seen her like this before. Her fingers flew over the keyboard and her mouse clicked furiously. He noted some small changes to her screen. It appeared some of her buttons had changed. He guessed she had just optimized her interface for player versus player combat. It had taken her no more than two seconds. While doing this, she muttered under her breath, "Mage, warlock, hunter, warrior and shaman." She was hitting the Tab key in rapid succession now, cycling through her attackers, even those who weren't visible. She marked them as targets one to five. They were all Alliance, naturally; otherwise, they wouldn't have been able to attack Killermage.

He didn't dare to speak, afraid he might break her concentration. She started to talk softly, seemingly as much to herself as to him, without any excitement in her voice.

"Hunter is the most dangerous, then warlock. But warrior is first."

He saw her glance at the timer of the Ice Block. Its effect was nearly exhausted. Her fingers tensed over the keyboard, ready for action. Robert held his breath.

A Frost Nova exploded out of Killermage, freezing the warrior and the tiger in place. They would be immobilized for the duration of the spell, which didn't mean the warrior couldn't swing his weapon, though. She also activated her Ice Barrier, a glowing nimbus of ice particles that could absorb a fair amount of damage. Now Killermage used Blink, a spell that teleported her over a short distance, enough to be out of range of any damage the warrior's sword could have done. In player versus player combat, mobility is the key, and if the warrior had managed to Hamstring or stun her, the fight would have known an early and sad end right there on the beach. The Horde mage was moving.

Rebecca seemed to have a timer in her head that kept track of the casting time of each of their enemy's spells. She used Presence of Mind that allowed the instant release of a spell that would have required her to stand still while casting. Most mage spells, at least the really damaging ones, had relatively long casting times. She hit the hunter with a Frost Bolt that dealt over seven thousand damage, roughly a quarter of his available health. The bolt would slow his movement speed by fifty percent for a short duration.

"Always good to draw first blood," she said evenly. "And I can't have that hunter after me too soon."

Now she pressed the key to target the warlock. Robert knew first-hand how decisive their Fear ability could be. Once cast on an enemy, the player would lose control over his character. If Killermage came under its effect, she'd be running around aimlessly in mindless fear. Robert saw to his horror that the warlock was almost finished casting Fear on them. Rebecca hit Counterspell just in time, which effectively destroyed the spell. Even better, it prevented the warlock from casting any spell out of the Affliction category for some time.

"Let's get out of here," she said in that same disembodied voice. "Let's see if we can escape this trap."

First, she made use of an ability called Mirror Image. It projected three exact copies of herself next to her that mimicked her every move. They would keep for twenty seconds, offering multiple targets to the enemy, reducing the chance she would be hit.

Then she had Killermage running at full speed toward the rock wall that encompassed the northern side of the lake. Two of her copies exploded and died. She kept running toward the rocks that loomed close by now. There was an exit at the end of the beach where a steep and narrow path led upward to the plateau above. This was where she headed. Of course, the enemy knew this as well and had anticipated this.

She was hit from behind by a Concussive Shot from the hunter. The damage was absorbed by the Ice Barrier, but her speed was reduced significantly. At the same time, the enemy mage stepped into their path. He released a Frost Bolt, and now her movement speed was reduced even more. The damage also shattered the protective barrier. It ate roughly twenty percent of her maximum health. Rebecca was still unfazed.

"Might as well make use of the moment," she said calmly and targeted the mage. His cast bar showed that he was preparing another Frost Bolt. Killermage started casting a spell as well, and she released a split second sooner. The enemy was turned into a sheep.

"Always remember that the casting time of Polymorph is shorter than that of Frost Bolt, with the right gear," she told the sheep as she ran past.

She reached the top of the path and ran into the shaman. He had been standing on top of the cliff, and Robert understood he was the healer of the group. His task was to protect his fellows from a safe spot by casting spells that restored lost health.

Shamans are dangerous opponents for a mage. They have abilities to Silence wielders of magic, rendering him temporarily defenseless. Rebecca didn't even bother to engage him. She just activated Cold Snap, which finished all cool downs on her Frost spells and protected herself with a new Ice Barrier. Her Blink ability had also just become available again, its cooldown finished, and she used it to put distance between her and the shaman. The shaman tried to hit her with an Earth Shock, but the damage was absorbed by the new shield.

They encountered dense vegetation now. Rebecca went for it, even though Robert knew the jungle was teeming with cobras and crocodiles.

"LoS is the key now," Rebecca said.

For the first time, Robert dared to respond. "Los?"

"Line of Sight," she answered. "Always look for ways to break LoS when you're in danger. They can't hit you if they can't see you."

Killermage entered the rainforest and continued in a northerly direction for some time. Rebecca looked over at him briefly. "Is Gunslinger still in Ogrimmar?"

"Yes."

"Get him and put him on the zeppelin to Warsong Hold in Borean Tundra. Take the flightpath to Bor'Gorok Outpost at the border with Sholazar Basin. I'll be fleeing in that direction. It's the only way out."

He nodded, but flicked an eye at Killermage's status. Unfortunately, she was still flagged as in combat. A pity, because the moment she was out of combat, she'd be able to use her flying mount to get the hell out of there. The game prohibited players from using their mounts while in combat. She couldn't use her Teleport ability either, let alone her hearthstone.

She seemed to read his thought. "It's not going to be that easy. They're right behind me and they have me targeted as we speak. Don't forget they have a hunter with them. He'll be able to track me easily."

"Can you keep ahead of them?"

"I hope so. I'm just out of their attack range now. But you know how tricky that can be."

While they were talking, he was launching Gunslinger. "They won't see me coming," he realized. "They're all using Alliance characters now, so I can't be on their social tab."

She confirmed this with a slight nod. "That may be our only advantage. I won't be able to hold these guys off forever."

Luck was with him for a change. The zeppelin was just leaving the tower in Ogrimmar when he got there, and he was able to jump aboard at the last instant. He accepted Killermage's invitation to a Party as soon as his feet hit the wooden deck. For an instant he was distracted. Did he just hear the sound that accompanied the queue for battlegrounds? It couldn't be, and he put it out of his mind.

At Warsong Hold, he used the flight master for the next stage. The flight would take a short while, so he came back to watch what was happening to Rebecca.

She was heading in the direction of the lake again, now approaching it from the northwest, where the cliffs were even higher. Robert noticed that most of her cooldowns were reset by now, meaning she had her whole arsenal of abilities available again. It also meant she had been on the run for several minutes now.

"Now we're going to see how good they really are," she said. "I'm going to try to lose them. Let's see what happens."

Killermage was almost at the edge of the cliffs. Robert expected her to jump over and try to swim for it, but Rebecca had a more intricate and bold plan in mind. She turned around and faced her attackers. They were right on her heels, just out of range of guns and spells. Now that she was standing still, they closed the gap swiftly. Rebecca flexed her fingers, ready to pounce.

They stopped a short distance away. Maybe they were discussing what to do. Whatever they were about to decide upon, they weren't prepared for Rebecca's next move.

Killermage used Blink to jump *forward*, landing right in front of the group. The moment her feet hit the ground, she cast a Frost Nova, this time capturing all of them in blocks of ice that would prevent them from moving for some precious time. Next, she targeted the warlock and frustrated him by interrupting another Fear spell. She cast Mirror Image again, turned, and sprinted for the cliff. She was hit several times in the back but the damage was not lethal. Line of sight was broken the moment she went over the edge.

At the same time she pressed the button that activated Slow Fall, another unique mage ability. It reduced her falling speed, allowing her to maintain her forward running velocity while going down. Her pursuers, when breaking out of the effect of her Frost Nova and following her over the ledge, would plummet into the water at the base of the cliff and would have to swim across the entire lake. Swimming was a lot slower than running.

She hit the water a satisfying distance from the shore. Without looking back, she set out for the beach on the far south side of the lake. When she reached it, she used another Blink to hopefully disappear from sight in the dense underbrush. She pressed her trump button simultaneously: Invisibility.

Robert watched mesmerized how Killermage's vision of the world slowly faded to a shimmering and colorless outlook. It reminded him of looking into a badly illuminated aquarium. Once her disappearance was complete, Rebecca struck out in due westerly direction. She raced through the jungle while the short lived effect held. *Damn, why wouldn't that 'in combat' icon disappear?*

They were good. In fact, they were so good that they were lying in wait for her at the border crossing between Sholazar Basin and Borean Tundra. They knew she was unable to use her flying mount, because Shard, the hunter in their party, had managed to keep her flagged as in combat all the time. It had been a close call, but he succeeded, with considerable help from his tiger pet.

The rest of the group had disengaged at the lake and simply waited for their flying mounts to become available again. If only she had known that there was only one person pursuing her, she would have stood her ground. But she didn't, and kept on fleeing blindly toward the border.

The road took a turn and started to ascend, becoming rather steep soon after. There was an impenetrable mountain range between the two zones, and the road led through the only pass there was.

"I'm almost with you," Robert said. He was approaching the border from the other side, but conveniently on the back of his flying mount. "If crossing the border doesn't allow you to mount, let's try to reach Warsong Hold on foot. We'll be safe there, too many Horde guards for them to follow you inside."

She just nodded and kept on running.

Robert started to descend, noticing several characters below. He idly wondered what those people were doing there. He was so preoccupied with Rebecca's escape that he simply didn't grasp the situation until it was too late.

"Watch out!" he yelled, just as Killermage was hit by a Frost Bolt, a Chain Lightning Bolt, and a Curse of Agony, all at the same time. Instinctively, Rebecca refreshed her Ice Barrier and dispelled the curse, but she got no chance to hide under an Ice Block again. This time, the warrior's Charge stunned her, rendering her powerless. She used her Medallion of the Horde, escaping the effects of the stun, but her Blink accidentally brought her right in the middle of her enemies.

"Fuck you!" she screamed in powerless frustration. Robert realized her death was inevitable.

Gunslinger swooped down and landed behind the melee. Robert understood perfectly that he was going to get killed as well, but he was determined to send at least one of those bastards to the graveyard as well. He focused on the enemy warlock, a cloth wearer and thus most vulnerable to the bullets of a hunter like him, and opened fire. His pet lion charged immediately.

A hunter could inflict spectacular damage in a short time, especially against targets with little armor. By pure chance, all of his shots were critical hits, meaning they hit for almost double damage. He commenced with an Arcane Shot, followed by a Silencing Shot. The last rendered the Warlock defenseless, as he couldn't cast any spells for the duration of the silencing effect. By the time Gunslinger pumped his final Chimera Shot into the Warlock, two ordinary bullets had left the barrel of his gun as well. The warlock died without even realizing the damage had come from behind. He did warn his guild mates, however, and this provided the distraction Rebecca so desperately needed. She was almost dead, with only a tiny sliver of her health remaining, but as her attackers looked around to face this new threat, she was finally able to cast Ice Block and find temporary shelter.

Robert targeted the mage now. He'd be overwhelmed in seconds, but he also knew that he'd be able to hurt that mage seriously before he died himself. He used Readiness, resetting all his cooldowns, and opened fire again. This time, he started with his Multi Shot, simply because it would do damage to two others as well. Again, as if the Gods were on his side, he seemed to score only critical hits.

A sound. A new window in his screen. What was that all about? If he was ready to enter a battleground?

"Just do it!" Rebecca yelled at him. "Now!"

Suddenly, he understood. Rebecca had put them in the queue for the next battleground. Their slot had come up at the most fortunate moment imaginable. If Robert pressed *Accept* now, he'd be transported there instantly, no matter where he was, or what he was doing. It was brilliant. Nobel prize winning genius.

Smiling, he glanced at his own health bar and that of the mage. It was a judgment call. He disobeyed Rebecca's order and continued firing. Four people were attacking him now, but he was dressed in PvP gear and hunters are hard to kill. The enemy mage died just before he did. The main difference between them was that the mage fell down on a road somewhere in the mountains between Sholazar Basin and Borean Tundra, and that Gunslinger was whisked away just in time to be restored to full health in Warsong Gulch instantly.

Dazed, Khalid was staring at the corpse of his warlock. Crumbled next to him was the dead body of a mage. *Pharad's mage.*

Their enemies had just vanished into thin air. Alive. How on earth had they accomplished that?

He knew what was coming. The howling began loud, but soon became unbearable. His door was kicked open, and Pharad charged into the room. His face was a red mask of uncontrolled fury. He kicked the table and tore Khalid's computer out of the socket in the wall.

"You're all incompetent losers!" he screamed. "What the hell is going on? Do I have to do everything by myself?"

He kicked again, this time destroying an Ikea drawer. He looked at the pitiful remains of the piece of furniture and seemed to calm down a bit.

"We'll never speak of this again," he said. His sudden calmness was even scarier than his anger. "I don't care about your Robert and Rebecca anymore. Let them be. Let them gloat. We have other priorities."

Khalid nodded wordlessly.

"Good." Then, as if to emphasize his words, he tossed the computer away as if it were a piece of useless junk.

CHAPTER XXXVIII

If not for the serious expressions on their faces, it could have been a cozy social gathering, like a birthday. The six of them were in the living room of the villa in Wassenaar. Robert and Rebecca were sitting next to each other in one of the luxurious leather sofas. Broerse and Fitzgerald occupied the matching chairs, while the other two were seated on chairs that belonged to the set in the adjoining conservatory. A fire crackled in the hearth and a coffee table had been set in the middle. Drinks for everyone. There was even a crystal can filled with orange juice. Robert longed for a nice chilled Sancerre.

The woman was talking. She was in her early forties, pretty but businesslike with carefully blown blonde hair and meticulous make-up. She was a psychiatrist.

"We must consider that this was essentially a totally unproductive endeavor," she was saying. "Even if they had managed to kill you in that virtual world a hundred times over, it would have accomplished nothing. Not really."

Rebecca nodded in confirmation.

"Would you say that they invested much time and energy in capturing you?"

"Yes," she answered. "They had one, maybe more people on the lookout for us. We did the same to them before, and I can assure you that it's time consuming to monitor WoW all the time."

"And they were able to lay a pretty elaborate ambush in a short time," Robert added. "They must have had a team on standby all the time, just in case we showed up."

The woman looked meaningfully at the other men. "It's as I thought. Now let me ask another question. If being killed inside of World of Warcraft doesn't really mean anything, why did you put up such a fight? Why didn't you just let them kill you, and be done with it? Wouldn't that have been easier? Don't tell me you didn't suffer virtual death numerous times before!"

Robert sought Rebecca's eyes. She flexed her shoulders and answered for both of them. "Because this has become personal, you know. One of those monsters lived only a few yards away! All other players are ordinary people just like you and me. They may be a school kid behind a computer in Stockholm, a lawyer in Madrid, or a nurse in Auckland. And being killed by a computer-controlled monster is a nuisance, nothing more. These guys are terrorists. They blew up a train station and shot God knows how many other people. They invaded our home and killed someone we knew!"

Robert took over, surprised by the sudden clarity of his feelings. "I've never been so afraid in my life. I can't even describe it. I was certain I was going to die that night. When I was climbing that wall and a bullet missed me by a hair, I was expecting the lights to go out forever." He leaned forward, looking the psychiatrist straight in the eye. "They reduced me to a blubbering bag of fear. I wanted to surrender to them, do anything to please them, if they just let me live. They took something away from me that night, and I won't let that happen again."

"How does the victory in WoW make you feel?"

He hesitated. "Better," he said slowly. "By beating them there, we balanced the scales somewhat."

Now Fitzgerald entered the conversation. There was compassion in his eyes as he addressed Robert and Rebecca at the same time. "I understand how you feel. It's only natural. I can assure you that your escape that night was an incredible achievement. Two of the people killed by the Hammer of Righteous Justice were protected by professional bodyguards with guns. It didn't help them a bit. As far as we know, you two are the first to survive an attack by them. You showed courage and initiative. You outsmarted them. Be proud and thankful, instead of feeling lessened."

The blonde woman was nodding vigorously. "That's the whole point!" she said. "What you're feeling is nothing compared to the humiliation they must have felt. The only reason they've gone to such lengths to punish you, for that's what it is, is because you defeated them. You shattered their confidence. You provoked them into irrational behavior."

It remained silent in the room for some time. Rebecca took Robert's hand in her own and stroked it softly. He looked up and gave her a little smile. She squeezed in response.

"You've given me some important insights," the woman said finally. "I think most of this is good news for us."

At this, the other man spoke for the first time. He had an American accent. Robert had never seen him before, not even when they had been taken to the headquarters of the AIVD. "What's the good news?"

"Robert and Rebecca have seriously distracted them from their main goal, whatever that may be. The terrorists dedicated lots of time and resources to get back at them. By trying to kill them in Leiden, they took a terrible and unnecessary risk. By sticking to that computer game as their vehicle for communication and training, they took another risk. They went to great lengths to change their appearances, only to reveal themselves again to kill Rebecca virtually."

"Will they continue to use World of Warcraft?"

Anja shook her head. "In my opinion, no. They might return to it later or switch to a comparable game. For this moment, I think they'll avoid it. The pride of Muhammad al-Moutti has been wounded seriously. He'll be telling himself now that he doesn't need WoW after all, and that Robert and Rebecca aren't worth the attention of a lofty terrorist like himself."

Rebecca sighed. "So you think he'll leave us alone now?"

"Yes, but that's the end of the good news. The bad news is that they'll concentrate and focus on their next operation now."

The analysis of the psychiatrist proved to be right, as far as they could tell. Rebecca and Robert kept up their vigilance as watchers of the virtual world, but nothing out of the ordinary happened. They were playing, but their heart wasn't in it. They leveled their characters to eighty-five, but couldn't bring themselves to start collecting some of the new epic gear available now. They didn't even explore a single one of the new end game dungeons.

Two days later, Broerse came to tell them that Blizzard Entertainment had cooperated willingly with the authorities. They had handed over all available information pertaining to the accounts the various characters belonged to. Sadly, all the accounts had been closed just before. There seemed to be little to go on, because playtime was paid for with anonymous game cards, and of course, the identities were all fake. Still, a full investigation was going on, focusing on the location of the IP addresses that had been used to access the game servers. Even if that yielded something, it would probably only lead to more abandoned places.

Broerse had also come to take them home. He drove them to Leiden first, where Andy was waiting for them. They didn't say much. Their friend went up to the all too familiar room with them, where Robert and Rebecca quickly packed their bags. The air was stale, and the place felt cramped after their sojourn in the large villa. Still, he felt a pang of regret to be leaving. They embraced Andy with the usual promises to keep in touch. Only this time, Robert thought the promise would be kept.

As Broerse's car set off for the airport, Robert silently said goodbye to the house at the Pieterskerkhof. He was also looking forward to being in the warm safety of his family. It would take some time for his mother to calm down, though. His parents were frantic with worry, and he hadn't been able to reassure them on the phone yet.

It was near the end of the afternoon when Broerse dropped them off at the main terminal of Schiphol, the airport of Amsterdam. Robert found a trolley for their luggage, and they entered through the same hall where he had arrived when he picked up Rebecca only a couple of weeks ago.

Terminals One and Two were attached to either side of a big hall that served as the train station as well. It was a smart design, because it encouraged travelers to take the train to and from one of the busiest airports of Europe.

It was busy in the hall, but mostly with train travelers dressed in identical red and white shirts. Robert recognized them as supporters of AFC Ajax, one of the prominent soccer clubs of Holland. Apparently, there was a big match tonight.

They left the hall for the Departures terminal and had just joined a check-in queue, when something clicked in his mind. He turned to a man next to him, who was holding a magazine in the Dutch language, and asked him a question. The answer electrified him.

He grabbed Rebecca roughly by the arm, turning her around. She had been deep in thought, not paying attention to her surroundings, and her reaction was one of irritation and fright.

"What's wrong?" she asked.

"Do you still have the numbers of Broerse and Fitzgerald in your phone?" His own phone had still been in his pocket when they fled the terrorists in the night and subsequently been lost in the Rapenburg. The phonebook of his new one was still almost virginal. Rebecca's mobile had been returned to her by the AIVD.

"Yes," she answered hesitatingly. "Why?"

"Call them now," he said urgently, stepping out of the queue and drawing her with him. "I just figured out what their next target is. It's going to happen tonight!"

CHAPTER XXXIX

Once, they had been frustrated and angry because they weren't taken seriously. There had been a time when their discoveries and conclusions had been dismissed out of hand. No matter how well they had tried to argue their case, they had been brushed aside as some game-addicted kids who were mixing up their virtual world with the real one. That had changed dramatically.

Less than five minutes after the end of the call, they were approached by two officers of the Royal Marechaussee, the Dutch military police. They were escorted to a large, busy office, evidently the central command post of airport security. Soon after, they found themselves in a conference room. They were joined shortly after by Broerse, who hadn't even left the airport grounds when the call reached him.

A teleconference was set up with Fitzgerald and the same man they had seen in Wassenaar. They appeared on a big LCD screen on the wall, sitting next to each other in a room that looked much like the one they were in. Their voices came out of a hidden audio system. Again, the American didn't introduce himself.

Robert repeated what he'd already told briefly on the phone. He told about the guild message they had intercepted that announced Arena training twice a day. He explained that they had wondered about it, but that Arena fighting was simply another part of World of Warcraft and that they had dismissed it in the end.

At that point Rebecca took over. She told about their discovery that the Hammer had been coming back to Terokkar Forest, and how they had followed them to the abandoned ruins of Auchindoun. She described that it looked like a coliseum, much like a large stadium.

"When I saw those supporters of AFC Ajax, I suddenly remembered something," Robert continued. "I remembered that the guild message didn't say Arena training, but used the word ArenA instead. With a capital A both at the beginning and the end of the word. It caught my eye when I saw it the first time, but I put it down to a simple misspelling. I forgot about it until I saw a supporter with the name Amsterdam ArenA on his shirt today."

He could see that the men on the other side of the camera were believing him. He wasn't ready yet: "Then I asked a Dutchman what kind of match Ajax was playing tonight. The answer frightened me. They're playing a match in the Champions League against a club out of Tel Aviv, Israel. That's when I thought it's likely that whatever they're intending to do is going to happen tonight."

He was finished. His last words fell into an abyss of silence. When he looked sideways at Broerse, he was shocked to see naked fear in the man's eyes.

The American was the first to speak. "I do believe you're right," he said. "Please, spell out the name of that place in WoW for me. We must act immediately." He glanced at his watch. It was a little less than three hours to the start of the match. The majority of the spectators would start streaming toward the stadium in two hours. His next words were directed at Fitzgerald, who was sitting next to him. "Get me a map of that WoW place and the Amsterdam Arena."

The National Coordinator for Counterterrorism was responsible for overseeing and coordinating the activities of no less than twenty different agencies involved in this field. He was the first person to be apprised of the situation. Only minutes later, he had the Minister of Security and Justice on the phone. His Excellency walked straight out of a television studio, where he was about to go live with an interview for a news program. From his limousine he called the Prime Minister first and then his colleagues from Interior, Defense and Public Health.

Having reached consensus on the course of action, he ordered the protocols to be set in motion. He looked at his watch. Only one hundred and thirty minutes to the start of the match.

***

With only ninety minutes to go, Rebecca was going over the layout of the ruins of Auchindoun again with the secretary-General of some important department, two men of the AIVD, and someone in his early thirties of the NCC, the National Coordination Center in case of calamities. Unfortunately, the latter happened to be a dedicated WoW fanatic. His eyes were glittering as it dawned upon him little by little what they'd become involved in over the last months. He kept asking probing questions, trying to find out more, and Rebecca was having a hard time fending them off.

On the table were blueprints of the Amsterdam ArenA, from the underground parking lots to the stadium above. They were comparing them to many different prints of Auchindoun. They were looking for similarities that would point at what the terrorists might be after. At the moment, they were discussing some tunnel that led to an instance in Auchindoun, and that resembled a more or less corresponding tunnel in the ArenA.

Robert was sitting squarely in the window sill, with his hands wrapped around his knees. They were still somewhere at Schiphol Airport, where they had been transferred from one of the hearing rooms of the Dutch Royal Marechaussee to a meeting room in one of the hotels on the Schiphol complex.

While trying to block out as much of the conversations around him as possible, he tried to focus his thoughts on what plan the terrorists might have. He tried to approach the puzzle from the opposite side. What was their goal? At the train station they had detonated a bomb. A bomb aimed at killing as many people as possible and creating terror. They had succeeded then.

In Antwerp they had also used a bomb, but its function had been mainly to cause people to panic and run. Then they had entered the chaos and started shooting at the crowd. Three of the terrorists had been killed as well. They must have known in advance that they would never get out alive.

So what did all of this tell him? First off, that they wanted to kill. Also that they wanted to inspire as much terror as possible. They targeted tight and crowded places, where people couldn't easily get away. One bomb had gone off in a low tunnel, the other in a narrow street.

What would happen if a bomb went off in a packed soccer stadium? He thought of the mass panic that would break out. Maybe that would cause as many casualties as the bomb itself. Although the number killed by the bomb would depend on where it went off, how heavy it was, and whether the people at the other side of the stadium would feel threatened as well.

His thoughts broke off when the door opened and several men entered the office. They were talking loudly. One was Sjoerd Broerse. He was trying to placate an obviously agitated man, while trying to remain calm and even deferential.

They turned to the men who had been working on the plans of the stadium with Rebecca. One didn't need to know a single word of Dutch to understand what was being said. The disappointment in their voices and expressions was clear.

Broerse motioned for them to follow, and Rebecca and Robert went with the little group, trailing behind.

"That's the mayor of Amsterdam," Broerse whispered. He slowed his step a little, so he was walking with them now.

"Why is he so angry?"

"Because he wanted to call the entire event off."

"Why wasn't it cancelled then?"

"By cancelling, we would only force the terrorists to strike at another opportunity, when we're *not* forewarned." They both understood the dilemma.

Rebecca said, "So you're trying to catch the Hammer tonight?" It was a statement, not a question.

"Yes. They're going to leave the place either in chains or in coffins. Let's just hope that they don't take any casualties with them. If only we knew what they intend to do. We need a how, when, and where." The man looked at his watch. Robert did the same. There were seventy-one minutes to go. "Too bad you didn't see more of what they were doing at that stadium in World of Warcraft."

A few more steps down the hall, Broerse surprised them. "Are you coming?" he asked.

They looked at him in surprise. "To the ArenA, you mean?"

"Yes. I'm leaving in five minutes."

***

Khalid shuffled another few inches forward. There were still a lot of people between him and the checkpoint. Most were wearing thick winter garments in combination with at least one item with the bright Ajax colors and logo. He had equipped himself with an Ajax shawl and a red-white cap.

He judged it was going to take at least another ten minutes before it was his turn to be casually frisked for forbidden items. He had been here twice before, as part of their preparation. He knew the sloppy technique the stewards employed. He bet he could smuggle an Apache helicopter in, if he really wanted.

When it was his turn, he made a show of putting his crutches against the gate. He spread his arms, making it clear to the fat man in a fluorescent yellow tricot that he was ready to be searched. Unfortunately, his balance wasn't well, because of his broken leg with the heavy plaster cast. He swayed a little on his one good leg. The man understood his predicament and quickly patted his back a few times, just for show. Then he helped him back to his crutches and waved him on.

The feed of the security cameras was being streamed to a large truck parked in the extreme corner of the ArenA Boulevard, over at the train and metro station. With its satellite dishes and antennae, it looked like the kind of vehicle that television stations used at events. Inside, some twenty men and women were concentrating on screens that showed the live images of the cameras at the various entrances of the stadium.

"The main purpose of these cameras is to record who enters the stadium. Several cameras inside record what happens in the stadium for later use," the woman in charge said while she led them into the interior of the truck. "Every square inch of the stands is covered. In case of misbehavior, like vandalism, fighting, or even riots, the recordings are used by the police or the club to identify the guilty people."

She halted behind one of the screens. A middle aged man was watching it intently, not even acknowledging their presence. The screen showed a tiled area just beyond a series of metal swivel doors that admitted spectators one by one. The full color camera was mounted high on a wall, maybe even on the ceiling, and they were looking down on the heads of the people on the scene. Each visitor was searched by a security guard. Robert recognized the procedure. It was the same in England at concerts or big events. Most people underwent the procedure without complaint and incidents were rare.

On the camera, a minor incident was happening. A man of about thirty years of age was complaining about something while he was being searched. He made an angry gesture. After a short discussion, he allowed the search to be finished. When he stepped away, he tilted his head a little. The agent pressed a key and the screen froze for an instant, the man's face clearly recognizable. The small digital numbers on top of the screen froze as well. 20:16; only twenty-nine minutes to the start of the game.

"We're making stills of everything that's even remotely out of the ordinary," the woman explained. "Unfortunately, it's impossible to check the face of each of the fifty thousand visitors tonight. As it is, there are over six hundred images to see." She looked questioningly at them.

Broerse looked a little embarrassed. "We'd like you to look at those pictures," he told Rebecca and Robert. "You two know him. You have the best chance of identifying him, if he's here at all."

A photo printer was spewing out enlargements of the pictures they were to look at. They sat at a small table in the back of the truck. Rebecca divided the stack in two and they went to work.

***

Khalid lit another cigarette. The stadium was filling up now. He estimated that over eighty percent of the spectators had arrived. The steady stream of people coming down the aisle in search of their rows and seats had lessened considerably. The players had just left the pitch, where they had been doing their warming up.

His eyes scanned the other side of the stadium again. The distances were so great that it was almost impossible to recognize the faces of the people on the other side of the field. Of course, it helped if you knew what you were looking for. He had studied the stadium so extensively that he thought he could have pointed out the seats of his team members blindfolded. Two of the three were in their seats, waiting for it all to begin. Only Pharad's seat was empty. He checked the time. 20:31; only fourteen minutes until the match started.

***

It was Rebecca who hit gold. They weren't even halfway through the pictures when he was alerted by a sudden hissing sound from her.

"What have you found?" he asked.

"What do you think of this?" she answered, sliding a picture across the metal surface of the table.

He took the picture and saw immediately what she meant. It showed a man on crutches wearing a cap, which obscured his face somewhat. It could very well be Khalid, but he wasn't a hundred percent sure.

Rebecca waved her hand and, immediately, the commander came over. She listened to what Rebecca had to say and picked up the photo to take a look for herself. Then she walked over to the nearest computer terminal and gave the picture to the man behind it. She motioned for them to come as well.

The man squinted and read the tiny letters and numbers printed just below the picture. He fed them to his computer, and almost immediately they were looking at the video recording.

"It's him!" Rebecca and Robert yelled at the same time.

Broerse had materialized out of nowhere and was studying the footage as well. They watched together how Khalid got his crutches back and walked out of view. The screen showed that he'd entered the ArenA over forty minutes ago.

The technician grabbed a large piece of paper and looked something up. He fiddled with the keyboard, then they saw Khalid going up some stairs. It was easy to follow him on the camera, because people gave the man with the broken leg the room he needed. Another camera had him going into a restroom. A full five minutes passed before he came out again. He was no longer on crutches, and the plaster was gone.

"Gun," Broerse said. "Damn!"

***

The time was 20:41. The opening ceremony was drawing to its end. The two teams were lined up, listening to the familiar hymn of the Champions League.

Four minutes later, a lot of things happened at the same time. Ajax kicked off to the deafening roar of the crowd, eager for a good result of the home team.

A plain clothes police officer fished several pieces of hard white plastic out of a waste bin at the restrooms of section hundred twenty-four. The cast on Khalid's leg hadn't been made of plaster after all.

With fifteen people dedicated to the search who knew exactly what they were looking for, six more people entering the stadium on crutches had been identified. Two were female and one was an elderly man. Three were males in the right age range. The study of other footage in which they appeared was about to commence.

The most spectacular development was the swift way in which the perimeter of the stadium was sealed off. There had simply not been enough time to mobilize enough police to do the job, so the army had been brought in. Unbeknownst to the fifty thousand people inside the stadium, over a thousand soldiers were deployed within ten minutes. Most jumped out of green trucks that had been arriving for the last hour, but had been parked out of sight until now. Others disembarked from a swarm of transport helicopters that seemed to come out of nowhere. Nobody in the stadium heard the sound of rotors over the singing and the chanting.

At 20:58, just when the ArenA erupted in cheering at Ajax' first goal, the perimeter was declared safe. Two rings of roadblocks and barricades now encircled the brightly lit stadium. All exits on the nearby motorway had been blocked, and all train traffic had been diverted. By that time it had been determined that all of the three suspects were indeed with the terrorists. They had all followed the same routine, going to a restroom shortly after arriving at their section, and leaving it after some minutes without the crutches and the brace. Identical plastic casings had been retrieved from nearby waste bins.

The four terrorists were in range of no less than thirty-one cameras. Even their tiniest movement was observed in the truck and in a special studio inside the stadium. Extra police officers had been positioned in and around the sections where the terrorists were. In the conference room of the Board of AFC Ajax, the briefing of several SWAT teams had just begun. Meanwhile, snipers began looking for spots that provided the right angles.

CHAPTER XL

A t 21:01, Muhammad al-Moutti felt a buzz in his pocket, indicating an incoming text message. The team was using cheap mobile phones with prepaid cards tonight, the kind that could be bought for twenty Euros at any store. While he was reading it, he received another message. It held exactly the same information. Even though his face remained impassive, his adrenaline level tripled in the few seconds it took to fully digest the information. The area around the ArenA was crawling with military and police. Their getaway cars couldn't even get close to the stadium.

He stood from his seat and started to move sideways past the other people in his row, smiling and apologizing. Meanwhile his mind was racing, going through all the options open to him. He had to assume they were the reason for the massive turn out of the law. That also meant he had to assume that they knew who they were and that they might be watching him right now.

He reached the broad steps that led to the restrooms and also to the stall that sold drinks, sandwiches, and candy. A Steward in one of those bright yellow tricots stepped aside to let him pass. Still maintaining a relaxed posture, he joined a short row of people waiting to be served.

The reason they hadn't been apprehended yet was obvious to him. It wasn't easy to control a mass of people of the magnitude gathered here. If they acted too rashly, panic could easily break out. They would want to try to control circumstances as much as possible. They didn't know how heavily armed they were, and the authorities would want to avoid civilian casualties if possible. For the moment, he was safe. But time was running out.

The girl behind the counter smiled at him, and he ordered a Coke, paying with the requisite plastic card. He turned away and walked slowly in the direction of the toilets. He spotted two men trying too hard not to look at him.

It all came down to the question if he wanted to live or not. He could give the order now, and eight hand grenades would explode in the densely packed stands. It would be followed by the fire of compact machineguns. They had four clips of ammunition each. They would kill many, and the inevitable hysteria would kill even more. Their most conservative estimate was that two thousand people would be killed in the inevitable stampede that followed the explosions and gunfire, squashed to death by a hysterical mass.

They would certainly be killed in turn. Their escape plan was based on confusion and panic on the side of the police. If they were forewarned and prepared, he wouldn't get out alive. Going out in a blaze of glory might have its attraction to some people, but he wasn't one of them. He was prepared to die, but only if there really was no way out. His gut told him there was.

He made his decision. He would escape and live to fight another day. He would bring out his team as well, God willing; all but one, because he needed a diversion. There was no doubt as to who was responsible for this disaster. One had failed him miserably. One of their team had brought this down on the others. With a grim smile, he brought out his mobile and sent off three short text messages. All possible scenarios had been rehearsed, and this was just one of them. They would know what to do. Just as in WoW, mobility was the key. It was time to start moving.

***

Rebecca and Robert were standing hand in hand in the crisp night air. The ArenA loomed ahead, lights blazing, like a galactic battleship out of a science fiction movie. By the roar of the crowd, they could guess at what was happening between the chalk lines. Just now, a concert of angry whistling carried to them, no doubt in response to an adverse decision by the referee.

They had witnessed the events of the evening enfolding first hand. The gravity of the situation weighed heavily on him. People were going to die tonight, that much was certain. He shivered and leaned into Rebecca. In response, she squeezed his hand. Suddenly, they heard raised voices in the truck. Someone shouted.

"Something is happening," he said. *Dear God, please protect those innocent people from the beasts.* "Shall we go and see?"

She sighed. "I just hope this is the end of it."

They entered the truck again. Nobody challenged them, in fact nobody took any notice. His eyes immediately went to the upper-most row of monitors. He saw at once that something was amiss. On three of the cameras, the terrorist's seat was empty. Only Khalid was still in his place. He was looking at his mobile phone.

"My God, it's starting!" Rebecca said.

***

Khalid read the message for the fifth time. Again, his eyes searched out the spots where his friends had been sitting until a minute ago. What was going on? Where were they going? Why was his heart hammering in his chest like that? It seemed as if every nerve in his body was on edge. His instincts were trying to tell him something. Whatever it was, it wasn't good.

Until now, he hadn't considered this mission to be more dangerous than any of the others he had been part of. True, there was a certain risk in the fact that it was going down in such a public place, in the midst of so many people and police. But there was also something like safety in numbers. There was no better cover for their escape than fifty thousand panicked people who wanted to get out of a confined space. The police would be aware of the cause of the mass hysteria, but they would have no other option than to open up every single exit. Rule number one in crowd control in case of an accident was to let the mass disperse as soon as possible. The first focus would be on damage control, not on identifying the cause.

Their plan was based on *four* different sources of panic. That way, the confusion would be spread over the entire stadium. If there was only one hot spot, there was a serious risk that the area would be quarantined instead of opened up. He would never be able to get out.

His recent orders said the timing had been changed. The first grenade should now go off at 21:14, instead of in the last minute of the official playing time of the first half. That specific moment had been chosen because many people would already be on the move, going to the toilets and getting drinks. The aisles and galleries would be choked with people, adding to the confusion and making their getaway easier.

He looked at his watch. 21:12, he had only two minutes left. His fellows of the Hammer of Righteous Justice still weren't back in their seats. It dawned on him that they weren't returning either. He was going to be the only one. *What the hell was going on? Was their operation compromised?*

There was only one way to find out. For the first time since his recruitment, Khalid disobeyed an order. His seat was directly at the concrete steps, so it took no time at all to reach the exit of section hundred twenty-four. He walked quickly to the restrooms. Luck was with him, as there was no one else around. He reached into the waste bin where he had deposited his plastic brace earlier. It was gone.

Cold sweat suddenly broke out on his forehead. He could feel the vein in his left temple pulsing heavily with dull thuds. Suddenly, all the pieces of the puzzle fell in their right place. Yes, their operation had been compromised. Muhammad al-Moutti had given the order to abort. But they needed something to distract from their flight, and that something was to be him. He was being sacrificed!

He looked in the mirror and studied his face. Would this be the last time he saw his own reflection? He gently touched his cheek, then pinched it. Would that flesh be on a cold concrete floor in five minutes, in a puddle of his own blood and brains?

He looked at his watch. The time was 21:14. It was now or never. He made his decision.

***

The tension in the truck was so thick, that it was almost like a physical substance. Tight faces were staring at monitors that didn't show anything. All four terrorists had disappeared into a restroom, although Khalid had been minutes later than the rest. Now, there was nothing to look at but four doors. They were up to something, but what?

It would have been a perfect moment to strike at them, but the SWAT teams weren't in place yet. Broerse was muttering all kinds of ugly things about that.

Robert had been watching Khalid mostly. Because he had known the man for quite some time, he thought he could read him a little. There was no evidence to support this, of course, but his intuition told him that Khalid was under a great deal of stress. Since he had gotten up just now, he looked like a man in fear, not like a man about to sow fear. It was in the way he moved and in the way he held his head.

"They know their cover is blown," he said out loud.

The commander looked at him for a full second. Then she turned and started to talk into her tiny mouthpiece. She and her team were the eyes of the entire operation. It was her job to share each and every development and observation. Behind her back, on three of the four cameras, terrorists stepped into view again. Two had changed their appearance, a fact reported immediately. Only Khalid was still inside his hiding place.

***

21:14 had come and gone. The disobedience of Khalid was a surprise, but something to be tucked away in the back of his head for later contemplation. Now, survival was all that mattered. Mobility was the key. Muhammad al-Moutti had known that for almost as long as he lived. From the moment he stepped out of the restroom and into the gallery, he was in a fluid motion, like a dancer on stage.

There were four people outside. He shot the two men he had marked earlier within the space of five seconds. Tap-tap, two shots to the chest each, and they went down. Years of surviving by violence told him that to his right, near the stairs, was another threat. He turned and fired before the man between him and the stairs could even get his gun out. He glanced at the fourth man, who was dressed in a red and white Ajax training suit, gaping at him with open mouth, eyes bulging. He disregarded him, turned, and lifted his gun at the security camera on the ceiling. It shattered at the first shot. Behind him, the Ajax supporter finally bolted. Now he was alone. Not for long, because he heard many running footsteps approaching.

Eight police officers of the Special Arrest Team exploded into the gallery with their guns drawn. Their leader surveyed the scene. He saw three men down. He knew at a glance that they were dead. A Steward was down on his knees next to one of the fallen, cradling his head in his arms, a bewildered look in his eyes. There was a blood smear on his distinctive yellow tricot. He pointed a trembling finger in the direction of the stands, which erupted in a deafening cheer just at that moment.

The commander motioned for his men to follow him outside and ordered the Steward to leave the scene. The man scrambled clumsily to his feet and backed away.

Robert and Rebecca were watching alongside the crew in the truck. They saw the gun being aimed at the camera and the monitor go blank. There was a stunned silence in the truck. It had been like watching a movie, only this time the blood had been real.

On two of the other screens, the movie continued. Even though the cameras were covering areas over a hundred yards apart, the images showed more or less the same scene. It was like a perfectly choreographed play, the same events in both screens happening almost exactly simultaneously. It all unfolded so fast, they didn't even have time to avert their eyes at the horror of it.

A man walking casually away toward the stairs that led to the exit. A man doing his job. A man in the bright yellow outfit of a Steward. A man reaching the stairs. A man walking down. A man walking out of the view of the camera, but being picked up by another without a flaw.

A man reaching the landing below. A man unaware of other cameras that showed uniformed men with automatic weapons coming purposefully down a corridor. A man who turned a corner. A man who halted suddenly. A man who jumped to the side, rolled once and came up in a crouch. A man with a gun! A man was shooting! A man was hit! A man was thrown backward by multiple impacts. A man who slumped down, leaving bloody smears on a white wall. Two dead men who had their guns kicked away from them.

Khalid fingered the grenade, preparing himself. He had two explosive devices with him, one heavy grenade and one smoke bomb. The latter had been meant to add to the panic, by making it look like the first explosion was much more serious than it actually was. But he was about to use it for what it was originally designed, to provide cover. His gut told him that he didn't have much time left. It was a miracle that no one else had come to use the facilities by now.

He crouched next to the door with his back against the wall and threw the grenade around the corner of the doorway into the hallway beyond. There was an immediate reaction. People started yelling and screaming. It must be a lot busier in the hallway now. He counted to five and started moving.

Covering his face, he walked right through the smoke in the direction of the stairway that led to the exits. Halfway down, he met a team of some kind of paramilitary forces. They noted his police uniform and one actually smiled at him. He stepped aside to let them through.

He came to the corridor that led outside. The police were everywhere, but he also saw some soldiers. He set a quick and decisive pace, his face in a determined expression, trying to convey the impression he was under orders and going somewhere specific. Nobody took any notice of him. There were so many uniformed people around that he blended nicely into the background.

***

The Steward who had been so helpful emerged from the toilets at ground level shortly after he had been dismissed. Only now, he wasn't wearing his distinctive yellow anymore, but only the police uniform that had been underneath all the time. Without anyone challenging him, he left the stadium, and now he was moving away from it. He quickly sized up the situation. It was apparent that his police uniform wasn't going to get him out of here. The perimeter was guarded by soldiers only, and they were challenging anyone who wanted to get in or out.

He looked around and saw what he was looking for. Luck was still with him. Not far away, a single soldier was lounging against a vehicle.

***

Double doors led out of the building. Khalid stepped through without hesitation and turned right. He pictured the surroundings of the stadium in his mind. It was actually situated in the middle of large business park, but the nearest office buildings were quite a distance away. On the other side of the railway was an urban area. He decided he should be going there.

The open area around the stadium was crawling with uniforms, a mix of soldiers and police, but farther away it was all military. He even saw some green armored vehicles. He started walking in the direction of the train station, down the ArenA Boulevard. He forced himself to walk erect and keep his head up, to appear like he belonged. He met the eyes of a police officer going in the other direction, and he answered the man's nod. Ahead, he saw a large truck of a TV station. Two people were standing outside. Civilians.

Robert couldn't stand it anymore. He felt like vomiting, and the fresh air didn't lessen the feeling. Still, he was glad to be out of the truck. He also didn't want to look at those screens anymore.

"Will they catch them?" he asked of Rebecca.

"Khalid and his boss, Drimm and Pharad?," she asked. "Yes, they'll never get out of here."

He nodded. He just wanted it to be over. Ahead, a police officer was coming their way.

CHAPTER XLI

Khalid couldn't believe it. What were Robert and Rebecca doing here? But he knew it in his heart: they were the reason for this disaster. Since that Englishman had come into his life, things had started to fall apart. His stomach contracted at the thought of how he had been led to believe that he had been introducing him to World of Warcraft, while he was being led by the nose all the time.

He suppressed his anger and veered away from the truck, letting his feet carry him back toward the stadium. He couldn't risk an escape on this side, now that the only people who could recognize him were there. Involuntarily, his head had gone down with worry. He jerked his posture erect again only to find himself looking straight into the eyes of Muhammad al-Moutti.

The leader of the Hammer of Righteous Justice was in the uniform of a corporal of the Dutch Army. If he was surprised to see him, he didn't show it.

"Come with me," he ordered.

They walked away together, just two of many uniformed young men around. Khalid suddenly noticed that the buzz of the stadium had changed. The constant roaring and whistling had taken on a distinctively different quality. The stadium speaker was addressing the crowd at length.

"You disobeyed my order," Muhammad stated in an even tone.

Khalid didn't answer. He could think of nothing other than to just keep walking.

"What do you have to say?"

He shrugged. "Robert and Rebecca are here," he said, motioning in the direction of the television truck. "I nearly ran into them."

There was a gleam in Muhammad's eye. "They are not to blame," he answered. "You are. You're responsible for everything they found out about us."

They reached two large vans with the reflective striping of police vehicles parked back-to-back at an angle. The cars were deserted. For a second, he guessed Muhammad wanted to hijack one of them. But the man took him by the arm and drew him with sudden and violent force into the secluded space between the two vans. Khalid felt the cold touch of the nuzzle of a gun against the back of his head. Muhammad's lips touched his ear, almost like they were lovers. His whisper was far from a caress though.

"You know the price of failure. I gave you a chance to redeem yourself today, but you failed even at that."

Khalid wanted to protest, to swear that he was still loyal to the cause, that he wasn't to blame for what had happened, but that he would make amends anyway. Before he could utter a single word a bullet ripped right through his head, shattering his skull and taking away half of his face when it exited in a spray of blood and brain tissue. He body slumped to the ground, and what was left of his head came to rest in the middle of a growing pool of fluids.

"Goodbye Drimm," Pharad said. "Resurrection is on cooldown. Try the Spirit healer."

"Let's take a little walk," Rebecca suggested. "I can't stand the tension standing still like this."

He agreed by taking her hand. They walked with their heads down in the opposite direction of the stadium, toward the train station. There were many soldiers there, keeping watch with guns at the ready. They veered to the left, following the railway tracks. It was quieter here. They saw only one soldier, coming in their direction. When they were at the point of passing each other, Robert heard a mumbled greeting. He greeted back, still not looking up. But he felt

Rebecca's hand suddenly tense in his own. She took a sharp breath. He finally looked up, straight into the barrel of a handgun.

"Good evening Robert and Rebecca," Muhammad al-Moutti said. "Or should I call you Gunslinger and Killermage?"

Robert felt remarkably calm. It was as if he had always known it would come to this. He wasn't even surprised that his mind seemed at peace with the thought that he would die here, tonight.

"Pharad."

The eyes above the gun swiveled to Rebecca. She acknowledged him in her turn with a nod. Robert had no idea how she was feeling. Was she scared? Was she calm and resigned, like him?

"I must commend you on your achievement," Pharad said. "In WoW, it would have been worth a hundred Achievement Points. But this is no game. This is the real world."

They both didn't answer. There seemed to be no point.

"Are you scared to die?"

"Yes," Rebecca said, her voice trembling.

"Good. Because I want you to know that I bested you after all. You're good, very good, so good even that I didn't think it possible. I never thought I'd meet someone who was as good as I am."

He paused, looking around. They were still alone. "You infiltrated my guild and thwarted my plans. For that, you deserve to die. It should never have been possible. But the one responsible, the one who failed me, has already paid the price."

Pharad lowered his gun a little and laughed softly. He seemed to be thinking, contemplating something only he understood. Robert stole a glance at Rebecca, but she was staring at the terrorist, mesmerized by the moment.

"I'll let you live," the man suddenly announced. "Only to let you feel the bitter taste of defeat for the rest of your lives. Whenever you think of me, remember this moment. Remember that I could have killed you if I wanted to. Remember that you didn't win!"

With these words, he turned and sprinted away. He was fifty yards away before their paralysis was broken. They saw him weave between several vehicles, then he was gone.

EPILOGUE

The level one Worgen named Phloyd sat on the ground immediately after being born into the world. Gilneas was one of the new zones that had been added with Cataclysm, behind the Greymane Wall that had always been impregnable until now.

Being reborn out of a new untraceable account, as the member of a new race, in a world made anew, was fitting. Being born in a new zone, out of sync with the rest of the virtual world, was even better. To him, this city was populated and filled with characters he could interact with. To other players, the streets would appear deserted and he himself was invisible.

He would be reborn again, in other worlds, more realistic worlds, ever more violent worlds even. But for now, World of Warcraft would do.

Phloyd realized he had become nearly unglued recently. He knew he had acted irrationally and thereby, irresponsibly. For much of what had gone wrong, he had to blame himself as well.

He wouldn't make that same mistake again.

He contemplated the virtual world. He was proud of the fact that he had been the first to apply its endless possibilities to the goal of making the world a better place. He knew that most people wouldn't agree with him, but as long as his conviction and dedication were strong, he would be victorious.

He was convinced that computer games would play an increasingly important role to people like him. Already, he had been approached to share his experiences and give advice on how to set up an operation like he had. He had no problem with others adopting computer games in the same way. It would only make it harder for the opposition to pin down one specific organization.

The more realistic the virtual worlds would become, and the more facilities the gaming industry provided for in-game communication, the more useful and important this medium would become. Blizzard had recently introduced a feature that allowed players to interact across different games on their platform.

This was the future. He would be like the captain of a fighter plane, rehearsing his strikes on the flight simulator as often as he liked.

He decided against playing with this new character now. Its birth was enough for the moment.

Phloyd shimmered, became transparent for an instant, and disappeared.

END

ABOUT MASSIVELY MULTIPLAYER ONLINE ROLE PLAYING GAMES AND MORE

By the time you finished this book, much of the world of Azeroth as I described it has changed beyond recognition. Such is the fate of digital worlds. What is perceived as cutting edge, thrilling and fantastic today, will be obsolete in only a few years. Players need ever more taxing challenges and long for new horizons to explore. In that respect players and developers are the same. Technological developments will continue to present new possibilities to create ever more realistic environments and experiences.

World of Warcraft is the mother of all MMORPGs. It may not have been the first, but it certainly became the biggest thing out there. Don't forget that many other games present fantastic game play as well, though often with a different emphasis. People who play games like Everquest, Final Fantasy, Lord of the Rings Online, Age of Conan or any other MMORPG will recognized many aspects from their own virtual worlds in this book.

I started playing World of Warcraft early in 2007 and got hooked immediately. I struggled in what many people today call "Vanilla WoW" in a time when level 60 was the maximum and a hundred gold was still a fortune. I remember spending two weeks in the Barrens before my Undead mage was ready to move on.

Many of today's players don't realize that leveling has become a lot easier since those days. With the introduction of the Burning Crusade the amount of experience points required to progress to a higher level was decreased for the first time, while at the same time the experience rewards were increased. There certainly were no heirloom items granting experience bonus for killing monsters and completing quests.

I share many melancholy thoughts with countless other people when I reminiscence about the old days. The joy of spending hours and hours on getting that ultimate level 29 hunter twink just right! The burst of pride when I acquired my first mount at level 40. Today one can't imagine that many, if not most, players couldn't even afford the epic riding skill at level 60!

Is today better? Probably. I understand most decisions by the manufacturer. Even if I don't like them all, I accept the reality they are dealing with. The people at Blizzard Entertainment® achieved a major accomplishment by creating this world. They deserve even more respect for the way in which they manage to keep the game attractive and challenging after all those years.

How I made the virtual world suit my story

Hopefully, those of you who play WoW will agree that most of what I wrote is accurate. Or was accurate at some point. I wrote **MMOR-PG** between 2008 and 2010 and it often happened that the latest patch overtook me. At some point, I simply stopped bothering. I had a story to tell, I wasn't updating the Wowwiki!

Many observations and descriptions are based on interviews with other players. Everything I wrote about Cataclysm for instance, is based on what was shared with me by players who had access to the Beta of Cataclysm.

Gunslinger started on the Hellscream (EU) server but along the way I decided the story needed to be situated on a PvP server. So I created a new character for myself on Sylvanas. I thoroughly enjoyed this new dimension, especially since I decided to play on the other side of the fence this time. My Gnome mage started without a copper but served the Alliance well. I learned what I knew all along: those Allies aren't so bad. In fact, they resemble Horde players rather closely. For those of you who are interested, the mage I created specifically for the writing of this book is called Gkky. He lives on the Sylvanas (EU) server.

Of course, I took some shortcuts and simplified many things. I wrote this book with non-players in mind as well. All those people who never played a computer game in their lives should be able to comprehend and enjoy the story too. I tried to let the learning curve of Robert coincide with the introduction of non-gaming readers to the online world.

Keen readers (and players) will have found errors. I apologize for any errors and inaccuracies that were unintentional. Sometimes however, I deliberately made mistakes. Some people pointed out to me for example, that the warrior who rushes Killermage on the little beach at River's Heart should have used Shattering Throw to destroy her Iceblock. That's correct, but wouldn't that have ended the fight then and there? I hope you'll forgive me for ignoring that ability in favor of a nice fight, a desperate pursuit through Sholazar Basin and a heroic last stand in a deserted pass in the mountains.

How I made the real world suit my story

The house Robert and Khalid live in doesn't exist. It could have existed though, because there certainly are student houses that resemble it. I took great liberties with other locations as well. The Amsterdam ArenA for instance, is definitely not like I described it. I molded it to resemble the ruins of Auchindoun and to accommodate the climax I had in mind. The only reason I chose this stadium is because of its name and, of course, because it's situated conveniently in Amsterdam, close to Schiphol Airport.

I must stress that the Amsterdam ArenA is one of the safest stadiums in the world, complying with all safety regulations of the KNVB, UEFA and FIFA. AFC Ajax did compete in the UEFA

Champions League in the season 2010-2011, they just didn't play against Hapoel Tel Aviv. So I made that up as well.

About account theft and gold sellers

Everything I wrote about gold sellers is true, from their modus operandi to the scope of these operations. The University of Manchester published a thorough research report in 2008, which is a must-read for anyone interested in this topic. According to this report, the gold farming industry employed 400,000 people in Asia in 2007, with an estimated turnover of 1.6 billion USD. I shudder to think of the magnitude this industry must have reached today. Of course, this industry serves a multitude of different online games, not only World of Warcraft.

Blizzard Entertainment® is doing everything in its power to put a stop to these practices. But just like in the real world, the police is always one step behind the criminals. It must be said however, that Blizzard tightened the procedures to gain access to an account considerably. The way in which Robert, Rebecca and Andy hacked Khalid's account wouldn't work quite as easily today. This is one of the subjects in which I took some liberties with the current situation. It should be mentioned here that Blizzard Entertainment® offers a very affordable authenticator to their players which makes account theft virtually impossible. I was the victim of account theft myself once, and I encourage every player to take any precaution possible.

MMORPG and terrorism

The CIA report quoted in this book is real, as is the lecture by Professor Dwight Toavs. Some time before I finished writing this book Blizzard made an addition to its user agreement. Nowadays, all users have to check a box and give permission to Blizzard Entertainment to monitor their in-game conversation. We all know where this is coming from, don't we?

Still, I am convinced that criminals are using computer games for the purposes I described in this book. Why? Because if I were a criminal, that's what I would do. The facilities are just too perfect and convenient for someone seeking secrecy and anonymity. What is the use of monitoring in-game conversations for suspicious phrases and words when the very game itself is about killing and violence? To quote Krick: *"Enough moving around! Hold still while I blow them all up!"*

About counter-terrorism

I interviewed some people with ties to the Dutch counter-terrorism community. They all told me that what I described in my book wouldn't work in quite that way in reality. I don't doubt they're right.

Truth be told, I don't know much about counter-terrorism beyond what I managed to learn through reading and research. If I misrepresented regular procedures of the AIVD or any other agency, I apologize. What I tried to convey in my book is how the intelligence community is struggling with emerging social media, of which online computer games are probably the most challenging.

About me

If you want to know more about me, visit my website at **www.emilevanveen.com**. On my website you can share your feedback, contact me, or participate in the forum about **MMORPG**. I look forward to meeting you there!

If all else fails, just /poke Gkky when you bump into him!

CPSIA information can be obtained at www.ICGtesting.com
Printed in the USA
BVOW08s2256120116

432727BV00001B/12/P

9 781456 318086